An Insignificant Family

a novel by Da Ngan

translated by Rosemary Nguyen
adapted and with an introduction by Wayne Karlin

CURBSTONE PRESS

A LANNAN TRANSLATION SELECTION
WITH SPECIAL THANKS TO PATRICK LANNAN AND
THE LANNAN FOUNDATION BOARD OF DIRECTORS

FIRST EDITION, 2009

Cover design: Susan Shapiro
Cover artwork: Do Doan Son (1974-); "Mother and Child"; oil on canvas, 60cm x 90cm; ©Do Doan Son / lic. by Nguyen Art Gallery, Hanoi, Vietnam.

Printed on acid-free paper by Bookmobile

This book was published with the support of the Connecticut Commission on Culture and Tourism, the National Endowment for the Arts and donations from many individuals. We are very grateful for this support.

Connecticut Commission
on Culture & Tourism

Library of Congress Cataloging-in-Publication Data

Da Ngân.
[Gia dình bé mon. English]
An insignificant family : a novel / by Da Ngan ; translated by Rosemary Nguyen ; adapted and with an introduction by Wayne Karlin. -- 1st ed.
p. cm. -- (Voices from Vietnam ; #8)
ISBN 978-1-931896-48-1 (pbk. : alk. paper)
I. Nguyen, Rosemary. II. Title. III. Series.

PL4378.9.D275G5313 2009
895.9'2233--dc22

2009010069

CURBSTONE PRESS 321 Jackson Street Willimantic, CT 06226
phone: 860-423-5110 e-mail: info@curbstone.org
www.curbstone.org

INTRODUCTION

An Insignificant Family follows the life of Nguyen Thi My Tiep, a woman whose girlhood was spent as a guerilla fighter participating in a war for national liberation and an ideal society and whose adulthood became a struggle for personal liberation and individual love. Tiep's journey and the journey of her "insignificant family", coincide with her country's journey from the end of the Viet Nam-American war into the twenty-first century, from the headiness of liberation and reunification (at least for the winning side), to the disillusionment and deprivation caused by post-war policies that fostered corruption, inefficiency, and a continued enmity between losers and winners, and finally to the time of renovation—*doi moi*—, and beyond, as the country addressed and attempted to redress many of the mistakes of the past—sometimes successfully, sometimes not, and always with a host of new complications.

While Tiep's story occurs within and can represent these three epochs—liberation, deprivation, and renovation—Tiep herself is never merely symbolic: Da Ngan has created a fully-realized individual, the antithesis of the stereotype of the pure-minded revolutionary prevalent in war and post-war, pre-*doi moi*, Vietnamese literature, or the Confucian ideal of the submissive woman. The author makes us conscious of the struggle to be such as individual by making Tiep a writer, and thus someone—unlike the rest of her more conventional family—whose horizons and sense of choices have been opened and expanded by her exposure to literature:

> There was no doubt but that she and her loved ones lived in two different worlds. On their side there was no First Circle of Hell, no quietly flowing Don River, no *Lover*, not even *Les*

> *Miserables*...while her side was full of novels and notebooks, pen and ink, movement and desire... The women of her family, who knew only too well how to exploit their control, cared only for hierarchy and order, for the four traditional feminine attributes of industry, appearance, speech and behavior, and above all for peace and comfort. To them, the job of a cadre was to bring glory to the family by advancing one's position, and the job of a peasant was to be industrious and solicitously attend the family altar. Tiep's newspaper articles they could grasp, but this thing called literature that aged her night after night was deeply suspect...

Tiep, always a revolutionary and always a reader, refuses to see the world through either traditional or ideological prisms. During a time, for example, when people were forbidden to speak well of those Vietnamese who had been on the other side of the war, and in spite of her own fight against that side, she admires the integrity and strength of character of the wife and daughter of a former South Vietnamese colonel, homeless and desperately poor because of its connection with the losing side, more than the apparatchiks and hypocrites with whom she works. In this, as in many other ways, the novel reveals both social context—here the split in the country that remained after the war's end in 1975—and Tiep's strength of character.

Tiep's paternal and maternal families, Southerners, from the Mekong Delta region, are both traditionally Confucian and also traditionally revolutionary. After her father dies in a South Vietnamese government prison during the war, Tiep and her brothers all join what those on the other side of the war called the Viet Cong, the southern National Liberation Front guerillas fighting against the government and against the Americans; a struggle she also joins when she is only 16. When she first meets Tuyen, the man who will become her husband, he is also a combatant, and their relationship is intensified, and indeed—she later reflects—perhaps even created by the intensity of the war:

> Tiep hunkered deeper into the foxhole with this young man who might die with her in the shower of fragmentation bombs, penetration bombs, cluster bombs; whatever they were, in that impenetrable and tireless chorus of bullets, dollars and wealth that was trying to make mincemeat out of that river fork and their sheltering Combretum tree. Tiep's ears rang but her eyes shone with emotion because Tuyen had pulled her up by the hair and had pressed her down into this grave of a foxhole. She cackled, and then her cackle changed into whimpering, and then the whimpering gave way to sudden silence as she realized two hands were pressing her down, and the buttons of her blouse somehow had come undone, and there were her breasts hardening and trembling under two greedy hands in the water the color of dirty milk. How strange. This delightful feeling of being caressed while at the same time the torment below as her body lifted and sank rhythmically in water that stank of hell.... Urgency mixed with pain and she wanted to scream out her survival her exposure her ecstasy her complete abandonment.... So it was that the taking of her virginity had what should have been all the ingredients of a great love: gratitude, commitment, the intensity of life in the face of death....

Da Ngan here becomes one of the few modern Vietnamese writers to directly explore the sometimes thin line between death and eroticism that occurs during war, and by implication, the seductive blindness of war itself. The bold lover, full of courage on the battlefield, becomes the sycophantic, fanatical bureaucrat and indifferent father and husband in the years of peace after the victory, "absorbed, diligent, and utterly pitiful." The fervid idealism of self-sacrifice and closeness to death that made their first love-making so exciting does not survive the pressures of peace-time life, and Da Ngan uses Tiep's sex life as a gage of that disappointment:

> Afterwards—after that unforgettable day of enemy soldiers pouring out of helicopters and unexpected, electrifying kisses and young bodies partaking for the first time—afterwards she and Tuyen had found plenty of opportunities for further exploration. They shared shelters and boats, death and survival, and most of all a common need for physical intimacy when life and death were measured in hours and days. But after [their son] was born, their sex life had turned suddenly uninspired. Despairing of her husband's character and soul, and especially his dwindling reserves of basic humanity, Tiep resigned herself to Tuyen's approximations of lovemaking...
>
> ...

While many Vietnamese writers, from Nguyen Du, author of *The Tale of Kieu* and the 18th Century poet Ho Xuan Huong onwards have used sex to explore character and social mores (and vice versa), the direct descriptions of Tiep's sexuality are rare, at least in translated Vietnamese literature we've seen. Tiep's dissatisfaction with Tuyen and her search for a more idealized, emotionally fulfilling love, leads to one disastrous affair, an even more disastrous attempt at reconciliation with her husband, and finally a tumultuous twenty year saga, as Tiep and Dinh, the married Northern writer with whom she falls in love, deal with the complications of divorce, children, career, and re-marriage, as in the microcosm of this one "insignificant" family, one sees a reflection of the struggle of the country itself. While the tasks that faced Viet Nam after the devastation of the war were momentous, Tiep's sense of disappointment that the fighters who were so efficient at defeating the enemy, were inefficient at creating a viable society is pervasive and tragic. *An Insignificant Family* is filled with vivid descriptions of petty acts of corruption, hypocrisy and favoritism, and the severe poverty and endless queuing for scarce goods and food that followed the war:

> Tiep asked Dinh, "If you had to do a sociological thesis about Hanoi in this era, what image would best encapsulate your ideas?" Dinh licked his lips thoughtfully, a sign that he was about to launch into his familiar biting sarcasm. "Well of course a thesis has to have illustrations. Me, I would draw a zigzag row of broken bricks, worn-out hats, old baskets, blunted brooms, torn thongs, broken plastic containers, and ripped shirts... the sort of things that are usually used as stand-ins to keep people's place in queue. I think that if you arranged them in front of a very still background, they would start to take on a life of their own. They have their own fates, their earmarks, their aspirations, even their own souls... they wear the faces of people like me, or my little sister, my friends, and someday, my children. You've never laid eyes on such a bizarre queue, I'm guessing. Everything is so much easier in the South, eh?"

As Tiep struggles to be with the man she loves, and as she struggles to define love itself and what shape it should take in her life, Viet Nam struggles to define itself and the future it wants for itself, and as Tiep makes mistakes, learns, and is transformed, so is Viet Nam. Visiting the capital today, its streets lines with thriving shops, its restaurants and cafes filled with energetic people, and a sense of dynamism everywhere, one can no more envision the universal poverty and hunger of the seventies and early eighties than one can envision the bombs that fell on these same streets in the years of the war. There is still poverty and repression, and all the new problems that come with the tension between the modern and the traditional and the onset of globalization. But there has also been an almost miraculous transformation. The novel takes us to 2002, with Tiep and Dinh, and their country, still plagued by unresolved issues, still struggling with self-definitions, but epochs away from the war and the devastated years after it: "As for Hanoi itself, it was churning with underground currents a new age: barriers were being broken, enterprises launched, opinions voiced, chains thrown off, hope emerging..."

Wayne Karlin

List of Characters

Nguyen Thi My Tiep (a.k.a. Tiep): Former guerrilla, author, a cadre at the Writers' Union of the southern delta town of Dinh Bao.

Tuyen: Tiep's husband, former guerrilla, now a cadre working his way up the ladder at the Bureau of Information and Culture.

Thu Thi: Tiep and Tuyen's older child, a daughter.

Vinh Chuyen: Tiep and Tuyen's younger child, a son.

Aunt Rang: The younger sister of Tiep's father. A widow, she decided to remain single after her brother's death to focus on raising his children.

Truong: Tiep's older brother, an officer in the military.

Hoai: Tiep's older sister. A widow with one son, Hon, she lives at the family orchard and helps Aunt Rang.

Nghia: Tiep's next-eldest sister, unmarried.

Little My: Tiep's youngest sister, a widow.

Boss Poet: Tiep's boss at the Writers' Union and chief editor of the Writers' Union newspaper.

Hai Kham: Tuyen's boss, Director of the Bureau of Information and Culture.

Trung Vy: A famous journalist visiting from Saigon with whom Tiep has a brief affair.

Bien: Tiep's friend and co-worker. An ex-ARVN officer, he was sent to a re-education camp for some time before being tapped by Boss Poet to work as a translator for the Writers' Union.

Hieu Trinh: Tiep's friend and co-worker, also a writer.

An Khuong: Tiep's friend. She is sent by the Writers' Union to Hanoi to study linguistics.

Quy: Tiep's friend. A former guerrilla, he worked as a journalist until he quit to run a tangerine orchard.

Thuan: Tiep's friend, an officer in the military and amateur writer who occasionally contributes to the Writers' Union newspaper.

Uncle Tu Tho: Quy's father and Tiep's mentor during the war.

Auntie: An elderly Chinese woman who befriends Tiep at the bus station.

Nguyen Viet Dinh (a.k.a. Dinh): An author, originally from the central area of Nghe Tinh and living in Hanoi.

Cam (a.k.a. Crazy Bertha): Dinh's wife, a high-ranking cadre.

Hoang: Dinh and Cam's oldest child, a son.

Bao: Dinh and Cam's second child, a son.

Xuyen: Dinh and Cam's youngest child, a daughter.

Hoa: Dinh's younger sister.

Su: Hoa's husband, an ultra-orthodox communist.

Ky: Dinh's friend in Hanoi. Abandoned by his wife.

Phuc: Dinh's friend in Hanoi, a writer. Married to a second wife.

An Insignificant Family

PART ONE: LIBERATION

1
Diep Vang, Fall 1981

Last year Tiep, in disgrace, had not dared to attend her father's memorial. Her brother Truong had been absent for the eminently forgivable reason of a battle on the Cambodian border which required his attention; her absence, on the other hand, had been explained as "she doesn't dare show that sorry, adulterous face of hers." This observation was duly carried back by Nghia who communicated it to her younger sister with a face full of distress and sympathy. This year Truong was absent again for that same very proper and grand reason and Nghia was in the middle of her final exams, so that left Tiep as the sole person who could represent the three-member city faction of their family at her father's memorial. She had no choice but to slink home to face her family's reproach, not only because she had an obligation to her father's memory but also because several months before, Hoai had made the long trip up to the city and packed Tiep's children off to the countryside with her. "To fatten them up," Hoai had said, but Tiep suspected her real motive was to give her and her husband some time to, as it might be theatrically described by Tiep's literary friends, "ponder their personal tragedy."

Previously, she had managed to make the trip from Dinh Bao City to visit the family home in a little hamlet outside of Diep Vang two or three times a year, despite the fact that it was a journey of almost a full day: first, a bus trip from the city to the town of Diep Vang; then, if her sister Hoai could not pick her up, a ride on a small ferry for another two hours; and finally, if she was unable to hitch a ride on a passing boat at one of the ferry stops along the way, she would get off on the bank and make her way, walking and wading, past another six miles or so of rickety bamboo bridges before finally reaching her family's orchard. It wasn't so bad when she went home for her grandfather's memorial day, which fell during the second month of the lunar calendar when the skies were clear, but when the day of her father's annual memorial arrived in the seventh lunar month, Tiep and her children would always arrive covered in mud. Even so, once ensconced under the sweet-smelling mosquito netting of the bed in the middle of the house, surrounded by her mother, her aunt, and her sisters, Tiep always felt well compensated for her effort. The murmur of water hyacinth on the Cai River, the sound of someone's long oar strokes softly gliding by, the sighing of the nipa palms on the far bank of the river, the flutter of memories of canals and bamboo screens...all wove together in a melancholy but deeply comfortable tapestry.

As usual, after the memorial ceremony Hoai would ferry Tiep and the children to town. But now it was still the small hours of the morning, that clinging, dreamy time of day which was so intensely familiar to Tiep, and just like every other time, their mother had risen early now to start the kitchen fire and bail the water out of the skiff. Tiep could hear her bare feet pattering busily back and forth, as though she had sworn lifelong loyalty to a gait that was more a run than a walk. Tiep lay unmoving under the mosquito netting, listening. Her mother was almost sixty now; her footsteps were slower and occasionally stumbled on the uneven ground. Then there was the sweet fragrance of coconut wood burning in the stove, mingled with the rustle of bags, and Tiep knew her mother was preparing gifts for her to take home.

Hoai appeared from the inside room. Though she was barely over forty, she had been a widow for over a decade and so carried with her an air of absorbed misery and strain. Hoai set a lamp—it was the same storm lamp with a glass chimney that in her youth Tiep had scoured with a stiff brush every afternoon before dusk—on the cracked and scarred dining table, near the bed where Tiep and her children lay under the netting. If only everything were well between them, Hoai would have climbed under the mosquito net and Tiep would have scooted over to make room, and then they would have talked, and visited, and shared confidences and advice. Now, everything was different; Tiep was strained, unfathomable. So Hoai announced her presence by simply setting down the lamp and turning up the flame, as though giving a warning.

Young ladies take care, the moment you wake you must straighten your hair! That was one of the lessons in Hoai's personal primer, and when Tiep was small Hoai had taught it to all of her younger sisters. She considered it her mission, ordained by Aunt Rang, who relied on her like her right hand. Tiep had always loved to watch Hoai comb her own hair. First, she would comb the hair extensions that she called her "borrowed" hair until they glistened with coconut oil; then she would set them aside and begin waltzing the comb across her own pathetically sparse head of hair, and then finally swish a clip in a long arc from ear to ear. When she finally gathered everything up into a bun, her hands were always supple and solemn, skillfully tucking in every last strand, as though performing a morning ritual. This morning, however, her eyes never left the lamp, her face was long and sullen, and her hands moved through the motions of combing and gathering in a curt, overstated way, as though she was pouting. She cleared her throat.

"Are you up yet, young lady? Come on out then and tell your Aunt Rang and me how things have been going between you and your husband. The house has been so full of people these last few days what with the memorial. We wanted to hear about it but haven't had the chance!"

Tiep continued to lie still, looking at the shadow of her sister looming on the other side of the netting, at the knot of hair on the nape of her neck which seemed to appear and disappear as she moved back and forth, wiping the tabletop which no doubt still smelled of fish sauce. Thu Thi, who was lying on the inside, sat up and crawled across her brother to whisper in Tiep's ear, "Are you going out there, Mom? I thought you were going to get out of this!"

Tiep gestured for her daughter to return to her place, then threw both arms over her forehead as though she could bury her head like an ostrich. It had been drizzling continuously since the day before and now the splatter of raindrops in the corrugated metal gutter at the end of the walk was gradually thinning. Even that small sound was enough to weaken her nerve and make her want to surrender, to abandon every one of her dreams if only she could once again be united with her family. There was no doubt but that she and her loved ones lived in two different worlds. On their side there was no First Circle of Hell, no quietly flowing Don River, no *Lover*, not even *Les Miserables* or Robinson Crusoe, while her side was full of novels and notebooks, pen and ink, movement and desire. At times like this, Tiep felt that her work as a writer was truly odd, her ruminations truly frivolous, and the things that pained or inspired her truly in vain. The women of her family, who knew only too well how to exploit their control, cared only for hierarchy and order, for the four traditional feminine attributes of industry, appearance, speech, and behavior, and above all for peace and comfort. To them, her job as a cadre was to bring glory to the family by advancing her position, and their job as peasants was to be industrious and solicitously attend the family altar. Tiep's newspaper articles they could grasp, but this thing called literature that aged her night after night was deeply suspect; it was shapeless, it had no redeeming value, and in the final consideration, it was nothing, utterly unimportant.

Aunt Rang was her father's younger sister. She was Aunt Rang the Commander, Aunt Rang the Boundless, and right now she was no doubt long awake and striding down from the wing of the house which held the ancestral altar with an aluminum pail of betel nut on her arm. As always, she would look worn down and frail from her life of hardship. And as always, even in the hottest weather, she would be wearing an extra layer inside her nylon peasant pajamas of discolored white and have a red and white striped scarf wrapped around her neck in order to highlight that appearance of imposing frailty. Tiep knew that she would have to crawl out of the netting and resign herself to the attack. She pictured her aunt's sad, square face—her own face was but a copy of that face—and saw the powerful eyebrows knitting together on that rigid, luminous forehead.

Thu Thi lifted herself up to see if her mother had moved, then lay back again. Her legs shifted and stretched nervously.

"Where is Little My?" It was Aunt Rang, her voice grating through a mouthful of betel nut. "Tell your mother to come up here for a meeting; we are going to have a discussion to see how Tiep and her husband have been getting on with their reconciliation in the city while we've had the kids here for the summer. Come up here just a few minutes, older sister. Sit down, Hoai, my child. Older sister, why are you wrapping up so many things? Too much attention is just wasted on that disgraceful little tramp!"

Inside the netting, Tiep bolted upright, and then sagged. Aunt Rang's code of conduct, which she nurtured with the fanaticism of a religious leader, was unflinching honesty, boldness, and decency. But why, then, was she apoplectic simply because Tiep had informed Tuyen in all honesty that she had found someone else and wanted a divorce?

As usual, Tiep's mother had heard her sister-in-law's command, but didn't respond immediately. She felt little need to snap to attention when all of her children were already marching in lockstep to their aunt's commands. In her heart, however, she knew that her autocratic sister-in-law was right, and that Rang was only doing her best to set her daughter straight. So she called up from the kitchen, "Well, I just got back from the city a few days before Tiep arrived. They seemed to be talking to each other like normal."

Tiep suddenly wanted to laugh out loud, picturing the veins bulging on her mother's neck as the old woman tried to sweeten her voice. She was a pessimist who seldom spoke but had a ringing voice when she did, and the effort required to reply nicely to Rang always raised a myriad of veins on her neck. No doubt because of the constant undercurrent of animosity she felt toward her sister-in-law who, though brazen and thoroughly unfeminine, had been chosen by her husband to raise her children, as though she herself were no more than a rented womb.

"Did you see them sleeping together or separately, sister?" Aunt Rang asked. It was an embarrassing question, but not out of place in an atmosphere that more and more resembled a trial. The only thing missing was the defendant, who continued to procrastinate, refusing to crawl out and make her inevitable appearance in the dock.

"Well, their house has two beds, and I took the one out in the living room, so they were sleeping together in their room as usual. But whether they've reconciled or not, I don't know!"

Tiep straightened her collar and smoothed her hair. Again, that feeling of wanting to disappear, to dissolve, to sink into the earth. Anything would do, as long as she did not have to hear her loved ones discussing whether or not she had slept with that man Trung Vy yet, or whether she and Tuyen had made up yet or were still estranged.

Little My suddenly appeared from the inside room, where she had been sitting with her young daughter and Hoai's son, Hon, so that they would not get in the way of the interrogation of their seditious aunt. She hastily lifted the mosquito netting, thrust a comb into her sister's hand, and crawled in to shake the children. "Thu Thi! Get your brother up to get ready. It's almost dawn, and you still have to get dressed and eat!"

If Nghia was a life preserver, Little My dared only to slip Tiep a taste of cool water before she ran the gauntlet.

From the porch, where she was fetching a needle and nylon thread to mend the strap of Vinh Chuyen's plastic sandal, Hoai scolded, "Why are you waking them up so early? It seems you'd rather the grownups didn't have this discussion?"

Little My ran down to the kitchen. "Aunt Rang told you to go on up, Mother, so just go. It'll just get worse if you keep delaying!"

Tiep's mother mumbled something but still did not appear to sit with her sister-in-law. Tiep finally emerged from the mosquito net and dangled her legs over the edge of the bed, her posture one of defiance. She announced, "If Aunt Rang and Hoai keep beating me up about things that are done and over with, sooner or later I won't dare come home any more!"

Seizing her advantage, Hoai shrilled, "You see, Aunt Rang, she's the one in the wrong, but we make the tiniest mention of it and she's willing to blow off even her father's and grandfather's memorials from now on!"

Aunt Rang was clearing her throat repeatedly, the coughs ringing out like a policeman's whistle, as though without that sound her aura of invincibility would fade or she would disappear altogether. "I don't see it as being done and over with, my child," she said. "All right, so it's in the past, you've made your mistakes. But I still don't know if things are back to normal for you and your husband yet. I want to hear it from your mouth, what your mother said was too vague for me."

"Some people can't even find a husband, and here she's got a gentle man, as easygoing as a row downstream, and she's still looking at the grass on the other side!" Hoai bit off each word angrily in a sentence that Tiep had long since memorized, having heard it countless times since the story of her and Trung Vy had first erupted into the open.

Tiep sat, listless and miserable, swinging her gaze from the glass chimney of the storm lamp to her aunt and older sister and then back. She was trapped within a blockade of war widows; a widowed aunt, widowed mother, widowed sisters—even her younger sister was widowed!—they surrounded her like four walls of mirrors, and whenever she gazed into one she always felt compelled to forget her youth and desires in the face of the stern reminder that no misfortune could possibly compare to the misfortune of widowhood. She lowered her voice.

"I know I've disgraced our family, but for the past few months I've been feeling things out to see if I can make up with Tuyen. There."

Aunt Rang slammed her betel knife down into her pail. "You have to completely change your ways, there's no 'feeling' about it! Back when we were first telling you to stop, you wouldn't listen to a thing we said. Now, whether the firewood you've got is dry or rotten to the core, you have to try your utmost for the honor of the family!"

Hoai was struggling angrily with her thread. Her body was curled low, close to the lamp, and in the puddle of light the vein on her forehead was beginning to swell as it always did when she was preparing for battle. She said, "I ask of her only that she do it for the children, not for my or anyone else's honor. I don't need it!"

Tiep's mother called up from the kitchen, "Isn't it enough that this house has nothing but children who have lost their fathers? You want to split up so that your children suffer too? Heavens!"

Aunt Rang's voice again, sharp and scolding: "What good does it do to call on the heavens, sister? I asked you to come up here and join us in setting her straight but did you do that? And as for what Hoai said, it doesn't sit well with me either. No matter what, you've got to think about honor, children! Suppose your grandfather and father, even your aunt right here, suppose we didn't sacrifice for you; do you think you'd be what you are today?"

Hoai's voice: "My honor is my faithfulness to my husband. Your kind of honor is too lofty for me, if I had to uphold that as well, I wouldn't be able to bear it. As far as I can see, it only brings suffering and loss!"

It appeared that the conversation was veering off to

another issue even more vital than Tiep's marital problems. This time Aunt Rang threw the betel knife, hard, down onto the table. Then she stood, arms akimbo, fists planted firmly on her hips, her eyes blazing at Hoai.

"You just keep on with that disgruntled voice, young lady, and tell me how this family won't end up falling apart!"

Hoai began to sniffle. Tears were a standard dodge of hers, and the older she got the more easily they came to her. "I'm not disgruntled; I just don't like war! I don't like our family's miserable honor!"

Tiep stood up and passed by her sister to step out into the courtyard. The weather had been bound to clear up after several days of rain, and sure enough the air was now exquisitely pure. She was not happy that her interrogation had been downgraded to a lower priority once the commander and her deputy had started arguing about the value of the losses and sufferings that Aunt Rang called their sacrifices. Instead, Tiep felt an indescribable sadness to think that they were still having the same argument they had had when she was a child, and then a teen, and then continued to have after she had left to live at the guerrilla base and finally in the city. It proved that her loved ones knew only how to grow older but did not know how to change. Was it really selfish and unprincipled of her to simply recognize that she was not happy in her marriage, that she was still young, and that she had the right to make a new peacetime life for herself in the hopes of fulfillment?

She strolled all the way down to the dock. She still remembered clearly the late-night arguments of her youth. If it went according to script, any minute now Aunt Rang would let loose a dazzling, drawn-out howl, then Tiep would hear urgent footsteps chasing each other down to the pier, then Hoai would cry, and she and her sisters would cry, and her mother would cry as she helped her children restrain their aunt's arms and legs so that the old lady couldn't throw herself into the river in her fury.

Honor, in the opinion of her family, meant sacrifice, and the fact that she was struggling to be free of Tuyen meant that she did not have the virtue of sacrifice. Which was why she had to be pummeled again and again; she had threatened the strand that bound them together, a strand plaited from multiple sacrifices made by multiple people over the last half century, beginning before she was born when her father donated his silk-weaving factory during Gold Week[1] and became a model revolutionary overnight.

Tiep sat down on the edge of the dock and scooped water to wash her face. The house was completely silent, as though everyone was holding their breath. Perhaps Aunt Rang and her sister were concentrating on her rather than their argument. She heard Little My call Thu Thi out of the mosquito net: "Run after your mother and see what she's doing down there by the river!" Then the sticky sound of her daughter's bare feet on the wet earth.

"Aunt Little My thinks that you want to commit suicide, mother!" she said, and plopped down next to Tiep.

"Have you ever thought the same thing as Aunt Little My?"

The child shook her head, saying nothing. She looked as aged as an old woman in her suffering, caught in the hornets' nest of her parents' marriage and all its complications. Tiep put her arm around her daughter's thin shoulders and drew her close. She showed her the morning star which had risen over the far bank above the nipa palms, telling her that the weather was sure to be clear today and that it was a lucky sign for the three of them for their trip home to the city.

Tiep had never considered suicide over the past few years, even when public opinion had been at its most crushing. She believed in the sincerity of her ambitions and that her children would grow up and thrive in that sincerity, whether Tuyen was around to see it or not.

1. "Gold Week" was a movement organized by the Viet Minh government to solicit donations to be used for the resistance against the French.

2
Dinh Bao, Summer, 1979

The day when Tiep first decided to break her marriage vows had begun early for her. At seven o'clock she was already standing on a pretty little balcony at the Committee of Propaganda and Training, waiting for the weekly press conference to begin. The Committee was housed in a white two-story villa that had originally been the property of the Vietnamese-American Association. After 1975 it had been requisitioned for the use of some department or another in the military command; later it became the headquarters of this terribly important committee with a terribly important commander-in-chief named Hai Kham who had been imposed on them by the regional command.

It had been more than a year since Tiep had transferred away from this Committee to the work for the provincial Writers' Association and so completely abandoned her husband, Tuyen's, Master Plan for their lives. She was no longer on the road toward the Academy of Politics, then an Assistant Directorship, then onward and upward, carrying the burden of the provincial revolutionary mission together with her husband. But her new agency still fell within the orbit of Hai Kham's authority, so the general editor of the Literature Magazine, whom she affectionately called Boss Poet, often sent her to the regular press conferences at the Committee because, as he would say, "at the very least, you are a daughter-in-law of that august body."

Tiep liked to wait alone at this spot on the balcony, where the rustle of the coconut trees in the graveled courtyard below was not drowned out by the meeting-room racket of voices and laughter from the people who—as Boss Poet often had to remind her—were "our comrades from the trenches" and. more to the point, were the leaders of a province with a population almost the size of Mongolia's. She disliked them despite his reminders. Ever since Vinh Chuyen had learned to sit, to play by himself, and was no longer at risk of falling out of the hammock when napping, Tiep had begun the work of creating a small, private world for herself. It was no bigger than an egg, fragile and modest, but it had a life of its own, and it carried within itself her burgeoning career. Now Vinh Chuyen was three, she had escaped to an agency that gave her more freedom, and her name was beginning to attract notice in provincial literary circles. Her little egg flourished, but also estranged her from the provincial brass because they, as men and women of the political hierarchy, seemed perennially nonplussed by such a suspicious and eccentric assumption of individuality.

As always, behind her the Hau River was bestowing upon the town the breath of cool air that only it could do with such benevolence. The river did not run past the Committee headquarters, but its presence was felt everywhere as a kind of enduring spiritual backdrop to the town's activities. Tiep could make out the faint sound of the boats and knew they were following one another, like a march of ants, along the length of the river. The floods last year had been of historic proportions, and the refugees were still on the move, rowing or using large nipa palm fronds as sails, exchanging their jewelry, furniture, and even their altars for food while waiting for the fever of collectivization to pass; this, while the men at the heights of power heralded the decisive nature of the times, and Hai Kham was forever pressing Tuyen to give him ever more detailed weekly reports on the progress of the glorious revolution.

And as always also, when she turned her face to the meeting room, she couldn't help but see Tuyen in the upper corner of the room, sitting at the second-string desk immediately behind the spot reserved for Hai Kham. Tuyen's job was to do weekly rounds from one department to another, staffing to foodstuffs to payroll, collecting statistics that he could present as weekly progress in a report—complete with comparisons and remarks—for the mandatory Monday morning press conference. He was also struggling to learn speech-writing so that he could provide the men in leadership with the proper histrionics to deliver in their meetings and summations. And, in addition to that, he visited various facilities to speak on the party's version of "current events" and taught classes to low-level cadres on his beloved subject of the New Lifestyle and the New Man. Overall, his work had earned the favor and patronage of Hai Kham, which he took as a sign that he was on the right track.

It had been more than four years since the end of the war, when she and Tuyen had together begun their "workaday life"—as it was called at the time in literary circles—and often when her husband was away, Tiep would close her eyes to see what image of him appeared in her mind. It turned out that the first image was always that of Tuyen squatting—this was his preferred mode of settling himself, even when eating dinner—on a little jute stool at his desk in the living room, wearing nothing but a pair of boxer shorts, his long back stretched into an obsequious curve, his concave, rarely-exercised chest, and his hand clutching a pen and wrestling with the words that tangled themselves across the page in little curved loops. Or sometimes she saw him as he was now, before a press conference: his left hand balled into a fist pressed against his temple, his back blending with the table to create the shape of a sickle, and his right elbow poking out of his shirt sleeve like the rough, brown, pointy end of a loaf of French bread. He was absorbed, diligent, and utterly pitiful.

Hai Kham emerged from the Director's office and crossed the meeting room. He was of medium height but as lithe and distinguished as a panther in a room full of chickens. His eyes were all-embracing, full of potential favors. They drank in the sudden hush in the room with obvious enjoyment, like a teacher who knows that his students are straightening themselves up for him. As he moved through the room, he occasionally glanced over, with the look of a monarch examining a special subject, to where Tiep was standing. And on that day, on that memorable day, something special happened: the Committee Director threaded his way through the rows of chairs holding all those provincial bigwigs and headed straight for Tiep with a step as smooth as a glide and hands as soft as a noodle, neither hot nor cold nor betraying any body temperature or emotion whatsoever. The hand of power extended itself to her.

"How's it going, my young authoress?"

She had never heard a question so completely without meaning and yet so full of implication. It didn't matter how she answered, as the speaker wasn't interested in her response.

"I'm fine, Uncle[1] Hai."

"I've read your recent stuff, both here in the province as well as up north. You're publishing quite a bit, eh?"

"Thank you."

The line of inquiry was gradually taking a more concrete turn. Tiep flinched inwardly. No doubt an admonition was about to come.

"Remember, little one, that you are the daughter of a war martyr, a great war martyr no less! Followed in the footsteps of the great Le Lai[2] and sacrificed himself to save the provincial party secretary! Your father was quite famous back then. Write whatever you want, but don't forget to reflect the proper viewpoint in terms of politics and class. Just a reminder from a fellow author, eh?"

The display was more than generous; a public bestowal

1. In Vietnamese, family nomenclature is commonly used in larger society to indicate rank. Tiep calls Hai Kham "Uncle" as a sign of respect and recognition of her subordinate status.

2. One of Le Loi's general's who sacrificed himself to save Le Loi from the Minh armies. He created a diversion by attacking the Minh armies and claiming that he was Le Loi so the Chinese would capture him. He was executed, but in the confusion the real Le Loi escaped.

of favor that was more than she deserved and an admonition given in the spirit of collegiality. It was actually true that Hai Kham was an author; his poems were regularly published in the provincial newspaper and even appeared in solemn volumes—compiled and designed by Boss Poet himself—filled with helpful appeals to the people such as:

My friends!
Over a flowing river
Where the water sings
Don't a toilet build there
It's not a good thing
To do."[1]

Hai Kham moved on. That was when Tiep saw a strange man appear at the head of the wooden staircase. A mature man, slender, with a tan, movie-star face. He wore a short-sleeved shirt the color of a myna bird's egg and moved with a blithe, self-possessed stride, like a peacock who knows he is being admired. Tiep saw him gesture a greeting to Tuyen, then stop to shake hands with Hai Kham as though they were equals, then go on to wave at several of the other bigwigs. Then those unsettling black eyes, nestling under eyebrows so beautiful they looked as though they had been penciled on, turned toward Tiep. She felt them drill directly toward her. She felt as though they were following a path that destiny had laid out for them. In fact, all that really happened was the strange man had discovered Tiep's astonished and admiring gaze and so naturally stepped up with a jaunty cock of his head. But all Tiep could see was that, up close, his eyes were even more magnetic.

"And just who might this little miss be, eh?" he asked. A pleasant fragrance emanated from his body.

1. This poem is referring to the practice in the southern countryside of building outhouses on bamboo platforms over streams or ponds so that the waste drops into the water and is either carried away or consumed by fish.

Disconcerted, Tiep shook herself. "Where did you just fall down from? Heaven?"

A peal of overweeningly confident laughter. "Why yes, so I did..."

Tiep suddenly remembered. "Ah, you're the big shot journalist, aren't you? Trang Trung Vy, right? The one who makes people shake in their boots if you write about them and worry themselves sick if you don't."

An admiring, conspiratorial look. An introduction both expeditious and candid. Trung Vy leaned against the balcony rail next to her and they both gazed at the gravel courtyard below as though listening to something that had just happened, something scintillating, disturbing, and completely extraordinary.

Hai Kham may have been a suave panther, but this peacock of a man was every bit as suave. The peacock turned and squinted at Tiep.

"I don't believe you've told me where you came from?"

Tiep responded with a flirtatious gesture but did not answer.

He continued, "So, am I to assume you are a permanent member at these so-called press conferences?"

"Why do you say 'so-called'?"

"Oh, don't tell me you think this is a real press conference?"

"So you're allergic to useless meetings? But aren't you worried about getting on the bad side of the Director?"

"Every week it's the same: the rate of progress in tilling and planting; irrigation; enlistment numbers for the army; harvest yields...all taken from the reports of some paper-pushing bean-counter in each department. They should be talking about the real issues, and taking a real grilling from the press. About events that aren't being told, like the war at the border, the exodus of boat people, the flight of people leaving their land behind to escape the upheaval of collectivization, and so on."

"Those are matters of national importance. Do you think you can demand the right to discussion and official comments? Don't tell me that you would actually dare write about them?" Tiep's question betrayed more bitterness than sympathy.

Trung Vy became animated. "Even if we can't write about it, we have the right to know," he exclaimed.

"What's the point, if you can't put it in your pen?" Tiep gave a gesture of surrender, as if to say, end of story.

"But press conferences like this—it's like getting invited to dinner and when you get there all the food is cold!"

Tiep tossed her head. Her body swayed slightly. She gave him an impish glare. Never before had she met a person whose thoughts so perfectly matched her own. She felt suddenly liberated, happier than she'd been in a long time.

"You've only just popped your head in for a quick look, my friend. I may be only a 'little miss' but I've been putting up with it for a long time. I've become completely saturated with boredom!"

"So why haven't I seen you at the last few press conferences?"

Tiep was losing interest in the flirting, and so answered directly. "I just come when I have to stand in for my boss, the poet."

"Ah!" The man clapped his forehead. "Your boss is that bony little man with the pale face, thin lips, and a gift for gab, right?"

"Back in the old days, every time that bony little man read a poem or made a speech, even the ants would crawl out and enlist for battle."

"What about you, my dear? Do you write poetry or prose?"

Tiep suddenly felt shaky and uneasy. She said evenly:

"I'm the wife of that paper-pushing bean-counter over there who is the author of your menu of cold dishes."

The man looked surprised, and not a little sorry for her.

"Ah, I was talking about the press conference in general, not any one particular person. The man responsible for the sclerosis you see here, the banality and waste, is Hai Kham of course!"

The conference bell rang, pulling them away from each other and into the room. Tiep felt rather than saw the people staring at her, judging, dubious. She threaded her way to the bench in the far back corner of the room. She was well-acquainted with this corner, with its odor of spider webs and cockroach droppings that was always there because no one ever bothered to clean it. Now she could pull out that book that her friend Bien had found and lent her to kill time. Others were equally shameless: some, like the our-comrades-from-the-trenches women, pulled little mirrors out of their pockets and began to examine their heads for gray hairs to pluck; others, like the men at the tables in the front who were waiting for the opportunity to start blathering away about pigs and wages, pulled up their pants legs and scratched crustily at their bony shins. There were even those who, like herself, were improving themselves by taking in a book. As for Trung Vy with his movie-star looks, Hai Kham insisted he sit up front. After a moment's hesitation, he stepped up to reluctantly sit shoulder to shoulder with Tuyen, separated from him by only a narrow aisle.

Tiep often thought back to that curious morning, like a girl dreaming that her special day will come or a woman in a romance novel hearing the proverbial thunder when she falls in love. She tuned out the reports on staff and foodstuffs and salary, tuned out Tuyen's painful fawning, tuned out Hai Kham's solemn chieftain's face and his smoothly gesticulating wrist...ignoring it all, she laid her unfinished book on her lap and leaned back to enjoy to the fullest the sweet, unilateral sensation that welled up inside her towards Trung Vy who sat, as compelling as a peacock in full display, before her. I will love this man, she decided. I will nurture this secret, solitary love. I don't need to know where it will lead. I don't need anything, not a beachhead nor a berth nor any other kind of clear ending point. She justified herself. Tuyen hustled things along too fast, he used his position at the guerrilla base. He begged me and laid siege to my sense of compassion. So now it is time for him to pay the price for the marriage certificate he finagled out of me. I've never loved Tuyen. Somehow or other, my heart will know what love is.

3
Dinh Bao, Winter, 1979

"Father's home! Mommy, Father's home! He's back from the county and he managed to get a whole lot of stuff, Mommy!"

It was an afternoon shortly before the Lunar New Year. Tiep was standing in the kitchen, shoving a few handfuls of coal briquettes into the big stove before setting a pot of bran on to boil for the pigs when she heard the happy cries of the children cutting through the sonorous praise of our glorious achievements pouring from the speakers attached to the electrical pole out in the street. Then there was the sound of a car door slamming, and Tuyen's voice "Move back, move back don't get under my feet" and the heavy Thanh Hoa accent of Quan, the driver: "I see a little girl and a little boy who'd love to come around to the trunk and see what's on display!"

To run out or not? Tiep hesitated. Not. She couldn't. She lifted the kettle of hot water off the small stove and replaced it with a pan of grease. She was right in the middle of frying a fish, wasn't she?

Tiep had taken a fateful step during the few days Tuyen had been gone. Now, as a person with a strong sense of fairness and propriety, she felt that they were standing on two opposite sides of a yawning chasm, distant and awkward.

The driver entered the house first. He had mischievous eyes, a friendly, garrulous mouth, and hands that carried a string of dried snakehead fish and a package of dried shrimp.

"I must say, ma'am, you are one lucky woman. Mr. Tuyen worked hard to truck home so much stuff. All that's missing from that lot is a cloth for you to wash his feet!"

Tiep smiled politely and stepped up to relieve him of his load. She didn't resent his polished flattery. She even felt glad for his presence. It would help alleviate the tension she felt toward her husband.

"Let me get you some ice," she said, and crossed over to the refrigerator where Quan was standing. They had to flatten themselves against the wall to make way for Tuyen, who staggered into the house with a massive bag of bran on his shoulders. Red-faced and purple-eared from the effort, he looked at his wife and gave her a wide, easy smile. It made Tiep think of Vinh Chuyen. Inside, she cried out: they look so alike, it's as though the heavens are mocking me!

Seeing that his wife did not return his affection, Tuyen plopped the bag of bran onto the metal bed they had set up in the kitchen and went straight out to the back patio to check on the pigpen. He'd become only too familiar with his wife's erratic moods recently. Sometimes sudden fits of lashing out at nothing, other times singing pointless little songs to herself for hours on end.

Tiep struck up a conversation with the driver. "So how many districts did you visit, Quan?"

Quan was on a roll. "Oh, the gentlemen down there really did love Mr. Tuyen. Future Deputy Director of the Committee, you know!"

"Did you get any dried shrimp like Mr. Tuyen?"

"That's a special benefit reserved just for the bosses. The driver's happy just to get a whiff of it!"

"I'll divide this and give you half to take home to your

wife, okay?"

The driver waved her away hastily and winked. "I was just saying that; of course I got some. No matter what, I'm still the grand chauffeur, you know!"

Tuyen returned and looked straight at her. He was still breathing hard.

"I have to say, those guys out in the districts really know how to take care of someone. Let me stir up a pot of fresh bran and we'll give the pigs a meal they won't forget!"

She returned his gaze this time, and said shrilly, "You have to bring all the stuff in first so that Quan can put the car away and get home to his wife. It's almost dark, or have you forgotten?"

As she said it, her gut was telling her to scream even louder, find words that were even sharper. She couldn't stand how attentive Tuyen was to their two pigs. Her husband rarely played with the children. He'd never tossed Vinh Chuyen up in the air or carried him on his shoulders as men do who are proud of their sons. But he loved to take care of the pigs' every need; they brought him a more practical form of happiness.

Tuyen obeyed, bustling out to the car with Quan. A moment later, the two children staggered into the kitchen under a stalk of large bananas. They had no sooner deposited it on the kitchen floor before they were racing to get a knife and squabbling over who got the ripest fruit. Tiep snapped at Thu Thi to bring the straw broom and dustpan out to sweep up the bran left in Quan's car

While Tuyen stirred the pot of fresh bran and washed out the pigpen, Tiep sent the children off to take a bath. Thu Thi saw her mother's irritability and wondered why she wasn't happy about the new bran and new rice and dried fish and bananas and shallots. Unable to figure it out, she edged up to her mother and asked as though testing the waters: "This bag of bran must be about two hundred pounds, don't you think, Mommy? It'll keep the pigs for two weeks, won't it, Mommy?"

Tiep ruffled the little girl's hair, trying to share with her for a moment the joy that she knew her daughter was feeling with her whole heart and soul. When it came to pigs and bran, she thought, I could write a piece of reportage called "The Art of Acquiring Bran" as long and surely as sensational as back when Vu Trong Phung wrote "The Art of Acquiring a Western Husband." It was because Tuyen was always busy. He was busy at the office, busy when he got home, busy reading newspaper reports for Hai Kham's daily summary and busy writing speeches into the wee hours of the night. The two children were busy: they were busy eating, busy learning, busy growing up. But the family's two salaries were barely enough to stuff between one's teeth, and the money she made off their refrigerator's small freezer unit—waking up in the middle of the night to crawl over her husband, take out a batch of ice and put it in the styrofoam container, then start a new batch, every night until she was sure she would never know a normal night's sleep again—was only enough for one week's groceries. And so, to supplement their income, their family had sectioned off a pigpen in their house like everyone else, and now Tiep often smelled the odor of swine on her clothes just as she smelled it on everyone else.

She kept a notebook with the names, numbers, and addresses of the our-comrades-from-the-trenches folk who were now guarding the gates of access to commodities. She even noted the date every time she hit up one of them so that she wouldn't make the mistake of begging any one person too many times. It was too awkward, and she was too likely to be refused. Standing in line for the entire day was nothing to her, as long as there was bran to be had, even moldy bran would do. She knew that back in the office Hieu Trinh or someone else would cover for her on the timekeeping board. And not just her. Later on, Boss Poet decided the board was a joke and so put a summary end to its long history of service.

One time, she learned about a bran warehouse over twelve miles from the city. She pedaled over to the school and took Thu Thi out of class. It was unavoidable; although her bicycle had a lock, it could still be stolen while she was crawling around inside the warehouse scraping bran out of the corners. They had to stand in line all afternoon. Finally it was Tiep's turn to go inside and Thu Thi stayed outside, hungry and thirsty, to watch the bike. At dusk, Tiep piled everything onto a three-wheeled taxi, the full bag of bran, the bike, and the exhausted daughter, and they teetered home in a euphoria of lightheaded gratitude to the heavens and earth. No doubt the little girl hadn't forgotten that trek, and was now more thrilled by the bag of new bran than she was by her father's return after days of absence. Just as her father was more interested in the pigs than in her.

Tiep arranged the foodstuffs on the table and covered them with the bamboo screen. She could hear the children fighting over the comb in the upper room while Tuyen poured water over himself and hummed in the bathroom. He had the habit of knocking the aluminum scoop against the side of the water cistern, which caused the loose floor tiles to rattle. When they were first allotted this house, the kitchen and bathroom were filled with mountains of plastic bottles of all shapes and sizes. It turns out that the "foolhardy gang of border-jumpers" that had abandoned it for the government to confiscate were really no more than petty merchants who dealt in fish sauce. Tuyen gleefully set about disposing of the mountain of bottles through successive rounds of gifts to rural relatives who were only too glad to receive them in a time when plastic items were scarce. But that was where his efforts stopped. He didn't glue down those tiles in the bathroom so they wouldn't rock and clatter. Tiep was the only one who knew that he had never lifted a hand to pound a nail or patch the leaky roof in their home, all while having to listen to resounding praises about him: What a hard-working man! Dedicated! Steadfast! What a future he has! Perhaps it was her Aunt Rang's influence, but Tiep appraised people's worth based on their value in real-life situations. To her, a man who was unable to pound a nail wasn't really a man. People like him might succeed due to their family history or dedication to the current understanding of what it meant to be loyal, but they were not people who changed history or brought greatness to their era.

The suggestive aroma of Co Ba soap was drifting out of the bathroom now along with the cool smell of water. Tiep heard Tuyen scrubbing himself longer than usual. No doubt he was not only ridding himself of the last of the road dust but also preparing for an evening in bed. A fleeting image followed, and the trepidation that had been lurking in her mind all day suddenly leapt out to confront her. What to do? She stepped into the inner room, hastily changed out of her house clothes, then grabbed her daughter and instructed her, "Mommy has to go over to Miss Hieu Trinh's house this afternoon. You eat with Daddy, don't wait for me. Remember to break the fish into little pieces for your brother. Tuna doesn't have many bones anyway, and I made a really yummy tomato sauce for it!"

It was nearing the end of the year, but the town looked anything but festive. The authorities had included songs and poems in praise of the year's accomplishments in a steady diet of propaganda broadcast through the system of public-address speakers, and there were a few strings of blinking Christmas lights around the plaza of the Central Cathedral on Main Street put up by its parishioners. But the surest sign of the season was the northern wind that rustled over the town, bringing with it the fresh odor of the Hau River's waters which were full and clear now, not like the muddy, ochre-colored waters of the rainy season. The dry weather was also an incitement to the younger generation to pour out into the streets, like monkeys on bikes. It didn't take them long to transform that humble means of transport into racing vehicles, streaking past each other under the reddish glow of the low-voltage bathroom bulbs that had been pressed into service as street lights in this era of constant electricity shortages.

She had to wait until the children were asleep and then she would go home to talk with Tuyen. But finding a safe place to pass a few hours wasn't an easy proposition. Hieu Trinh was still living with her mother and younger siblings, and Tiep had misery written all over her face; if she went there she wouldn't be able to hide it, and in the end she'd spill all, she'd tell them how she'd taken the plunge with the journalist Trung Vy. What about An Khuong's place? No, her younger and more innocent friend would be surprised to see her showing up unexpectedly with no specific reason, and anyway her house had too many people in it. The relatives always edged in and out of the room when she was there to observe the "Viet Cong lady I heard somewhere writes controversial stuff and wouldn't you know she does look a bit off." Or maybe she should stop by to see Quy or Bien? But both of them had women who were predisposed to see her as a literature bitch who specialized in tempting other people's husbands. Boss Poet's house? Even worse! He lived alone in a very private apartment where he regularly received young women who were willing to brave any element for a little tête-à-tête with him; if she showed up there, the streetlight at the head of the alleyway would surely put her in the same category. Or her brother Truong, or Nghia? No, absolutely not, she had to have the conversation with Tuyen first before she could confide this sort of thing to her relatives. Telling the family too soon would only lead to being called up to the executioner's block that much earlier.

So Tiep rode around aimlessly, languidly. Once, she found herself passing the street where Trung Vy was staying in a guest house acquired by the province in the recent fever of seizures, requisitions, and expansion. She saw him emerge from the building. The youthful blue of his shirt glowed brightly under the privileged light of a place that never lacked electricity; his hand dangled an expensive cigarette; his gait was charmingly off-kilter. But the peacock didn't appear to see her as she pedaled slowly by in a puddle of darkness, because he was wholly absorbed by the plump young journalist who had just dismounted from her bike in front of the guest house. Tiep was curious but, fearing he would feel awkward if he saw her, and believing in the unconditional and pure nature of her own heart, she rode straight by.

From the day she had taken the plunge, from those moments trembling by the door while the guest house security detail grilled her and throughout everything that happened after—while it could hardly be called a smooth beginning—Tiep had felt every cell of her body surge with an awakening of sacrifice and commitment. She'd been sitting on the sofa and he on the narrow single bed in his room when he had told her that he was separated from his wife in Saigon. She had thought she would be able to resist her impulses, but instead her legs had obediently stood as though to step into a waltz with him. And then everything happened in a whirl and flurry and with great dispatch, hustled on by the numerous eyes they knew might be spying on them from the stairway or through the crack in the door. Then she turned her head and saw her peacock engrossed in wiping himself with a towel from the coat rack near the door, while she sat curled up and distressed at having been picked and peeled far too soon for a proper love affair. He switched the light back on and the harsh neon scrubbed the scene clean; the door was also flung open immediately to allay the suspicions of the guest house security. Danger over. Tiep took a deep breath of relief.

That very night, she wrote Trung Vy a novel-length letter full of ardent prose and unsolicited confidences. How she would be content with her fate if she thought he were happy at home; but once she had learned that he was also estranged from his family, she had no regrets for her boldness. In the letter, she promised she would worship him and sacrifice all for his work, she would bear him a son, she would serve him to bring him the happiness and fulfillment he craved, and so on and so forth...

In the end, Tiep didn't go to anyone's house. She found a stretch of grass by the Cypress River near her house and rested under a coral shower tree that was pregnant with cascades of silky buds ready to burst open right after Tet. The mangrove-wood warehouse nearby steamed with the odor of waterlogged bark. On the other side a small café jutted out into the river on stilts; this was the café where every morning Tiep would stop by to deposit a bag of ice and receive in return a few hundred dong in tin coins. The river's face was dark and melancholy, with only a few silent boats gliding by. All that was missing were the cypress trees and a few fireflies and the river would look exactly as it did back when it was first given its name.

She remembered the odor of grass and irrigation ditches of home. From the time Little Tiep had first learned clumsily how to work her blouse buttons or comb her hair, she had been drilled in Aunt Rang's lessons on propriety. Young ladies take care... the first thing you do in the morning is take a comb and untangle those rats' nests properly; if an adult calls or gives you a command you say yes sir yes ma'am properly; when you eat you sit straight and hold your chopsticks and bowl properly… A little older and it was don't be lazy—it's not proper; don't break a promise—it's not proper; don't lie—it's not proper…

But not lying meant telling the truth. So if she told Tuyen that she was in love with another man would she be proper or improper? That was obvious, no married woman who was having an affair could possibly be considered proper. Tiep suddenly realized that although Aunt Rang's primer, so thoroughly drilled into her by the diligent Hoai, taught that Honor was proper, in fact proper to them meant nothing more than saving face. And saving face meant flaunting the good while keeping the bad well hidden.

But Tiep could not possibly share a bed with Tuyen while at the same time giving herself to another man on the sly; that was clearly a minimum requirement for any self-respecting woman. And self-respect was, after all, proper. She had to preserve her self-respect first, she decided, and the honor would have to come from that.

Feeling as though she had found the solution to a particularly thorny equation, Tiep thrust herself resolutely to her feet. Much later, after Trung Vy had jumped ship back to Saigon in an attempt to save himself, and the scandal of the peacock and the well-fleshed young journalist became public, and Tiep felt that the bitter gossip about her own relationship with him had become more than she could bear, she would torture herself wondering why, when working her way through that equation, she hadn't taken into account the variable representing her children. Had she been too impatient, or too confident of her ability to shelter them, or simply too selfish and blind? At the time she knew only that life was long and twenty-eight was but the beginning, so there was no reason not to make a fresh start. She knew only that ever since that hasty night, she had felt as giddy as a schoolgirl. Day and night, at home or about, while wide awake or while drifting into sleep...

Hearing her mother's bicycle, Thu Thi opened the door and blurted out, "You said you were going to Miss Hieu Trinh's house to try on your new shirt, but she came here to bring it to you!"

She ran into the house to bring out the shirt as proof, but Tiep stopped her with a stern look. "You go down to the kitchen and put the dishes in the washtub to soak, then come back up here. I have something important I want to tell your father, and I want you to hear."

Something important. The announcement was designed to create an atmosphere her husband could not ignore. Tuyen was sitting on the wooden settee, his back bent low over the newspaper spread out on his thighs, a toothpick stuck in his mouth, and, as was his habit, one hand scrubbing dryly against his cheek, stretching the skin tight on the way down then bunching it into little rolls on the way up. He looked as if he had a toothache. At Tuyen's feet, Vinh Chuyen lay with all four limbs splayed out like an angel, watching a Bulgarian spy movie.

Tiep sat down on the second settee and gazed intently at her husband across the small mica coffee table left by the previous owner. His undershirt was not the culprit, she realized. Nor were the striped shorts he was wearing. It was the toothpick that made her crazy, the way he worked it back and forth in his mouth with his tongue. And his habit of bending himself almost double over his newspaper. She shuddered. If he should suddenly change his position to a squat she would likely not be able to control herself.

Thu Thi stole up from the kitchen, her still-wet hands gingerly lifting her pants legs and her face worried and furtive. She had the heightened sensitivity of a writer herself. When Tiep was irritable she would usually just ask brightly, "You're writing something, aren't you, mother?" But today her mother was different, like nothing she had seen before.

Tiep stood up decisively and turned down the volume on the television. Only then did Tuyen straighten his back and look at her, cocking his head as if to say, seems my erratic wife really does have something important to say. Then, to Tiep's surprise, he spoke first.

"Something up at the office? I told you, you should've stayed with the Committee and just done your writing on the side. But you had to transfer to the Writers' Union and lose your chance to study politics and become a core cadre, and not only that it has all those problematic people. Now you're hanging out with puppet officers fresh out of the re-education camps[1] no less, like that Bien guy and who knows who else. So, what, the cell leadership gave you a warning?"

Such a superior drawl coming from her husband would have, on any other day, set Tiep to bristling. She would have

1. "Puppet officers" The term for former enemy officers of the Army of the Republic of Vietnam (ARVN), which was seen as a "puppet" army of the Americans. Many former ARVN soldiers were put into forced labor "reeducation" camps after the war.

let fly a sharp retort designed to swing the balance of power back in her favor and send him shrinking back to his paper. But today Tiep wanted to keep their dialogue civil while Thu Thi was watching.

"Tuyen. I know that you get worried and frustrated by my writing, my temperament, the things I like, even my friends. It was the war that pushed us together, and now I don't see any point in prolonging a marriage that has no love. And... has it ever occurred to you that I might have found someone else?"

There. The leap had been taken. Tiep felt as though she were in an uncontrollable, headlong freefall. No, worse than that. She felt wounded by the explosion that her own words had set off. She felt the muffled patchwork of sound and emotion around her, saw Tuyen distort and freeze as though he were a character in a movie that had suddenly been paused, saw Thu Thi drop the fan she had been using to chase mosquitoes away from her brother and retreat to crouch defensively by the foot of the bed they kept in the living room.

But at least she had left behind that pile of rubble that was the eight years of monotony being married to Tuyen. There was no going back.

Apparently Tuyen had heard and absorbed her words. His hands pounded unconsciously against his knees and he gave a grim laugh.

"You've got to be joking."

Tiep had not anticipated such an arrogant response. She took a few gulps of air.

"I'm utterly serious. I'm only twenty-eight, and you're only thirty. We can both start over."

Tuyen leapt abruptly to his feet. He paced back and forth, the veins on his forearms bulging like blue tortuous snakes. She was used to this habit of his; when working on a speech for some important official he would stride about the house, then return to squat on his chair and write. But today the familiar movements seemed oddly threatening to her.

Then he clasped his hands behind his back. My God, she thought, he looks just like one of those men on the standing committee or secretariat that he so wants to be like. At this rate, any minute now he'll be pounding his fist on the table to show that he is in charge. She hadn't expected this of her normally passive husband.

But he didn't pound the table and he didn't look in charge. He continued to pace, mumbling, "You're just making it up, imagining things. I don't think you have anyone else. You wouldn't dare. And anyway I haven't done anything wrong, except give in to you so much people say I'm henpecked. Give an inch and you take a mile. So what kind of game are you playing now?"

Tiep assumed a grim smirk like her husband's. How dare he be disdainful of her, when he himself was so utterly clueless.

"You and I are like fire and water, Tuyen. Like cats and dogs. You'll be happier if you find someone else. And probably when the time comes you'll thank me because I set you free while still taking care of your children."

Tuyen came to an abrupt halt in front of his wife and threw his arms out aggressively. "I told you that getting involved in writing was the road to perdition. So who is it? Which goddamned poet or writer is it?"

Tiep recoiled against the back of the settee, shocked by her husband's crassness. It was pathetic. But it made Vinh Chuyen jump and start to cry, and for the first time she realized how rash and mistaken she had been. She had acted out of a desire for propriety, but the situation had now spiraled out of control. She couldn't give any kind of a meaningful answer to Tuyen in front of the children. Tiep said gently, "Thu Thi, let's take your brother into the bedroom, shall we?"

Tuyen charged at them, grabbing at the children. "Who do you think you are to be touching them? You haven't answered me yet; did you sleep with him? Right, when I came home this evening it was him you were off with, wasn't it, not trying on some shirt!"

Thu Thi threw her arms around her mother's legs. "Mommy, don't leave me and Vinh Chuyen, Mommy!" Vinh Chuyen hugged her knees and cried too. Tuyen grabbed their shoulders and shook them like a puppeteer working his puppets.

"Go ahead and cry, children, cry as loud as you can so that everyone can hear!"

Tiep thrust herself into his face. For a moment they stood like that, volatile and weirdly contorted. Then, emphasizing each word through gritted teeth, Tiep said, "I forbid you to treat the children like this. I forbid you to interrogate me like this in front of them. If you stay calm we can resolve this peacefully. If you play the dictator I will leave this house!"

"You'll leave this house and become a whore, that's what! I told you that hanging out with that blabbing poet would turn you rotten!"

Tiep looked at her husband for a long moment. The flame in her that he had never been able to stomp out was now slowly dying of its own accord. She knew that they had both violated the other's most sacred places, their personal articles of faith. Their differences were eternal and boundless.

When she herded the children into bed, Tuyen suddenly rushed after them and collapsed onto his knees by the bed. The gesture reminded her of their days at the guerrilla base when he had knelt before her in the same way to beg for just one nod of her head, just one nod, if not he would enlist in the infantry and leave his corpse on a battlefield somewhere...

She bent over and extracted her legs from his arms, fearful of a scuffle in front of the children. "Go on outside. When you're calm we'll continue the conversation."

Tuyen refused, reaching out and hugging her to him. He looked savage and pitiable, like a man about to breathe his last after being mortally wounded.

Much later, after she and Thu Thi had left that long, narrow house, Thu Thi one day confided to her mother that her essay in school had gotten a perfect score but the teacher had not read it aloud to the class as usual. Hearing this, Tiep knew her daughter had written something about their family. As she had guessed, the assignment was to "Write your feelings about your most memorable experience." Thu Thi told her she had written her impressions of the terrifying night when her mother had told her father she wanted a divorce. The teacher had cried as she graded it and couldn't read it to the class. Naturally Thu Thi couldn't read it to the class either.

That day, as she gazed at her daughter's chubby face and listened to her talking about her writing class and essay, Tiep felt the true extent of her vileness. She had been too insistent that everything had to be out in the open and too daunted by the thought of a night in bed with Tuyen. She hadn't known how to suppress her emotions like so many other women in similar circumstances, how to wait for the right time. It was a black mark on her conscience that did not fade over time.

4

The familiar red-and-white striped scarf wrapped around her neck to protect her from the uncertainties of the road. The pickle-colored khaki bag left over from the Nhu–Diem era. In one hand, the small purse plaited from nylon fibers that was a keepsake made by her brother in prison; in the other hand, a rattan basket containing betel nut. Just as Tiep had suspected, it didn't take long for Aunt Rang—Aunt Rang the Chief Justice, Aunt Rang the Dispenser of Life or Death over Tiep and her siblings—to appear in town. It was a natural law, like the wind that appears when the weather changes, or the thunder that follows lightning, or the vicious rain that follows the thunder, clawing at your face and sometimes even knocking you off your feet from the first flash in the sky.

Both Tiep and Tuyen were at home when Aunt Rang came. Her somber face amidst the clamor of the children when she stepped inside, along with the way she brushed Tiep's hand aside to stow her things herself on the outer bed then stride into the inner room with knitted brow, were all signs that it would be a long storm indeed.

"You're home from work early today, Tuyen?" In her best Aunt Rang the Terrible form, she pointedly ignored Tiep and only spoke when she met Tuyen near the back door.

Tuyen dropped the knife he was using to slice stalks of morning glory in his elation at seeing her.

"God, Aunt Rang! What did you take to get here? It's almost evening—did you stop off somewhere?"

Never before had Tiep seen her aunt acquiesce to a greeting so blatantly loaded with an agenda. Tuyen had often complained to her about Aunt Rang: she could split a single hair into quarters, he said, her demands were too rigid, she was nothing like the simple and unpretentious folk of his family. Even without fearing her as Tiep did, he found it hard to feel comfortable with her. As for Tiep, every time her aunt was present she worried that Tuyen would commit some indiscretion. He might be too cold to her, or worse yet, try to flatter her with shallow sycophancy. Neither attitude would escape her scrutiny and both would be considered a direct insult. With Aunt Rang, it was either perfect respect or nothing.

But as the culprit in today's drama, Tiep did not dare to greet her aunt with her usual affection. Instead, she stammered, "Did you come from Truong's house, Auntie?"

Her aunt gave her a quick glance—just enough to achieve the effect of formidable disappointment—before turning to continue her march into the back room, saying, "Got off at the bus station at noon. Took a three-wheeler straight to your brother's house. He insisted I stay for dinner but your old aunt here is too agitated."

Your aunt. It wasn't simply an expression of family kinship, but also of rank, and to Tiep and her sisters it was as natural to worship that rank as it was to worship their parents. Tiep loved her mother with the earthy, fleshly love of a mother and daughter, mixed with no little pity; but towards her father's youngest sister, this woman who had foresworn remarriage in order to take her brother's place in caring for their elderly parents and then had taken on the additional burden of his flock of children as well... Tiep loved Aunt Rang with a emotion so heartfelt it bordered on sacred. It was this love that always made her soften and give in to her aunt.

"What would you like for dinner, Auntie? I'll go to the market." Tiep followed closely on Aunt Rang's heels, feeling as though she owed her aunt a hug and kiss.

Aunt Rang cleared her throat with her familiar authoritative cough, then said, "I'm not in the mood for anything. All I want is for you two to get back to being cozy with each other. That would make even a bowl of plain fish sauce taste good."

Silence followed, the dramatic silence that follows after a king has spoken. Tiep knew that many more important words would follow, but first Aunt Rang had to perform many more such brief silences in order to thicken the atmosphere to the right consistency.

Aunt Rang went down to the kitchen, carrying her basket of betel nut with her. The children followed her like a long tail. She took up residence on the plywood platform in the kitchen, scooting back until she found the most imposing position, and—still not deigning to look at her felonious niece—crooked her index finger and said vaguely, "Which one of you is going to get me a glass of water?"

Tuyen was the fastest to respond. "Water, water for your grandmother, Thu Thi! Get your grandmother some water!"[1]

Thu Thi ran over to the water dispenser and returned with

1. "Grandmother" is a term of respect and endearment in this case.

a glass which she respectfully held out to her grandmother with both hands. Aunt Rang took a sip, and then spat into the condensed milk can that she always carried in her betel nut basket. She had been chewing betel since childhood, and rolled her own cigarettes to puff on during the lonely nights. Sometimes Tiep had woken at night to see her, chewing and smoking and widowed, looking as harsh and pugnacious as she did now. She wasn't yet sixty, and her teeth were still strong enough to chew the tough leaf without having to crush it first.

"Tiep, you go over to Nghia's for a bit. Take the children with you too. I want to hear what your husband has to say first. Go on, we can have dinner a little late. Whatever you've got is fine, don't make anything special."

"How's Mom and everyone? Hoai, Little My, and the kids?" Tiep still lingered, not wanting to be accused of not having asked after anyone. Aunt Rang looked at her now, her stately eyebrows raised high against the square of her face. "Fine, they're all fine! After hearing what's going on with you two no one dares to get sick anymore! Enough, take the kids and go!"

In fact, the first person that Tuyen had enlisted to help him was Tiep's brother Truong, and it was he who had initially interrogated her. As a firstborn son of a firstborn son, Truong held a special position in the family, and Tuyen had long ago reluctantly resigned himself to his brother-in-law's natural authority. Tiep knew, however, that this did not mean he wouldn't try to exploit Truong's power when necessary. Fortunately for Tuyen, Truong had just been transferred from an infantry division command in Cambodia to the Regional Military Command in their area, and so was present in both body and spirit when his younger brother-in-law showed up to beg for help.

That day, Truong had arrived at Tiep's house at noon, which was a rarity. He rode the old scooter that, like Tiep, he had bought with money from selling his wedding presents. She preferred to see him in regular office attire; he was a neat and careful man, a perfectionist by nature, but the military had severely limited his ability to express his personal aesthetics. Every time he arrived at family events in his civilian clothes he would all but gleam, and Tiep always felt closest to him then. He was the image of their father, just like the picture on the family altar; the same intelligent face, long eyebrows that reached almost to the temples, and warm, cheerful mouth.

But on that day, the day he came, he looked distant and stiff in his military dress with its very correct military cap. He went straight to the back of the house to check on his little sister's pigpen—his wife had also just jumped on the pig-raising bandwagon—then returned with an air of sorrowful exasperation.

"So? News is you intend to leave your husband? You got a case of the grass is always greener? Is it for real or are you just trying to be bohemian?"

Tiep sat down on the same wooden settee that had witnessed her talk with Tuyen and gave her brother a long look. His brusque approach betrayed how deeply the militarism had eaten into his soul, something that Aunt Rang often fretted about: "He's gotten too used to battles and killing and death and orders. His father was so much more flexible. Not only that, he doesn't know the rituals for worship and offerings, how will he take care of the family altar?" Truong had joined the guerrillas while still a minor, right after their father had died in prison. The move forever terminated his dream of becoming an architect, and kept their grandparents up many nights sighing and worrying over their promising grandson's future as a soldier. As for Tiep, she always thought her brother looked like a college student gone astray: forever bright, delicate, and imbued with a gentlemanly, delicate sophistication.

That was why the tone of his question caught her off guard. Tiep folded her legs beneath her on the settee, and tried to stay calm.

"If you keep on with that condemning tone of voice, I won't tell you a thing. Let's just say I am telling you for purposes of proper notification that I will leave Tuyen."

"Leaving him for someone else?"

Tiep squirmed. "I'll take my punishment. Living with Tuyen like this, it was bound to happen sooner or later."

Truong maintained his position standing by the door, but he turned his head to look at her now, as though he had never seen her before.

"And the children? You're willing to orphan them even when there's no war?"

"Why would they be orphaned?"

"Well, clearly they'll have a father but no mother!"

Tiep sprang to her feet. It was unimaginable that her brother, her own flesh and blood, would so cavalierly conclude that she was unfit to raise her children. Back when she was a child, Hoai used to say, if Tiep were spanked unjustly she would howl for however long it took for one of the grownups to finally give in and comfort her, an implicit recognition that she had been a victim of injury and oppression. As she got older, it was always Tiep who went charging headlong into any situation where she saw injustice. It was always Tiep who was considered to be most like Aunt Rang. Now, Tiep demanded justice for herself. She wanted recognition that her life with Tuyen was a waste, and that even Tuyen would be happier and more at peace with a person who better fit his agenda. Panting with rage, she confronted her brother: "You know only too well that Tuyen and I are like night and day. That I'm both the husband and the wife in this family, both mother and father. What, you think I'm just power-hungry? Honestly, if we were talking about anyone else...but with a person like Tuyen I have to be the one to raise the children—if not they wouldn't find their way back to me anyway. I'm not afraid of losing them, so don't you drag them into this to try to pressure me!"

"Who gives you the right to custody? If the family doesn't agree to it, the courts won't. Think about it carefully, Tiep. I'd advise you to watch out for people who are just passing through and looking for a way to kill time during their assignment here."

If only she were less impulsive, Tiep wouldn't have made the mistake she made now, and only much later would come to recognize. But this was back when Trung Vy had not yet absconded; he was still eager for her eighty-four-pound body whenever he had the chance, and she still believed she would be able to hold his interest with the sincerity of her love. So when she heard her brother disparage this man whom she held sacred, she leapt at him and all but screamed in his face, "Don't you jump to conclusions! You just watch and see how I do in my new life!"

Truong withdrew his judge's gaze as though holstering a weapon and stepped out of the house with a disgusted expression. Tiep felt she would burst with the injustice of it all. Her beloved brother, the man who had replaced their father in her life, had come to her today only to take the side of Saving Face and Condemnation, not to ask about or listen to her side of the story. She followed him outside, howling like a dog, "If you're going to judge me so unfairly, don't ever come near me again!"

The motorcycle's weak engine revved. Truong's face drained of blood.

"Prepare yourself, sister. Your unit, the Party, your family, his family, the neighbors, even your friends: you just be prepared to answer to them! Prepare yourself to answer to Aunt Rang too. If you're not careful you might end up tongue-tied. Got it?"

Her bicycle was too small to carry both children, so, in order to obey her aunt's command, Tiep grabbed their hands and led them out of the house on foot. She knew that it was not by chance that Aunt Rang had sent her to Nghia's house; no doubt the old woman was hoping she would be more open to advice and correction from her sister because of the closeness of their age. Tiep and Nghia were like shape and shadow to each other, as bound to each other as two fingers on the same hand. When Nghia cooked, Tiep washed up. When Nghia went fishing, Tiep held the basket. When Nghia rowed in the back of the boat, Tiep rowed in the front. When Nghia slept with their mother, Tiep slept with their aunt. They studied in the same classes after they left home, and accompanied each other to join the guerrillas of the National Liberation Front on the same day. Still later, Nghia worked at the print shop while Tiep worked for the newspaper. And now: "Nghia's doesn't even have a love to call her own, and there's Tiep with husband and kids in spades and still looking for more!" Indeed, the two sisters were like a comical illustration of the Creator's Law of Compensation: one measured, the other flighty; one contained and focused, the other flying off in ten different directions; one pinched, the other profuse; one a loner and the other happiest in crowds.

Actually, Nghia had been in love once, but that boy had been killed in the war along with millions of other youths who laid down their lives. After that, any unfortunate man that approached her either had armpits that were too smelly or a back that was too long, or if they weren't too squat they were too lanky. With such standards, Nghia had never trusted Tuyen as Hoai had, and had even expressed sorrow at the idea that her next-to-youngest sister should marry a man who by all rights should be better in every way. Tiep had been avoiding her sister for days, not wanting to confront those long, curled eyelashes that were so often stained with tears now for the misfortunes that would befall her niece and nephew if their parents broke up. As for Nghia, she hadn't visited Tiep's house since hearing the news from Truong. She did not want to get within range of the needy, grasping hands of this brother-in-law of whom she had never approved.

Tiep took the children to the stretch of grass under the

coral shower tree on the riverbank near their house. Once more she was reminded of the irrigation ditches and watery smell of the orchard back home. She thought of her mother and sisters. She knew that her story would send shock waves through the entire area. She would be made into something worse than a leper, so disgusting that oblivion was too good for her, and her loved ones would have to hang their heads every time they stepped out of the house. She imagined what her mother was doing at this moment. It was dusk; her mother would be down at the river's edge, squatting impassively for a long moment before finally scooping up a pail of water to pour over herself and the slabs of areca wood that served as a dock. Tiep knew that her mother would not methodically analyze her situation with alternating gentleness and severity the way Aunt Rang did; rather, she would simply say with that trembling, blurry voice of ever-present melancholy, "It's a woman's fate to suffer, child; just try to bear it a little longer and it'll all be over when you die!"

And then there was Hoai, forever caught between her mother and aunt, who would vacillate between advice and tears while still taking advantage of the opportunity to send a little attitude her sister's way. Tiep braced herself. She had no doubt that, as soon as Aunt Rang arrived back in the orchard, Hoai would hop on a ferry or take her skiff to speed up to the city and unleash her storm of tears on them. She would rage until the vein in her forehead bulged about why Tiep and her husband had not made the proper offerings or chosen an auspicious date for their move into this house which after all had belonged to border-hoppers—if their marriage weren't a victim of a curse set by those people then at least it had met with calamity because of Tiep and Tuyen's impiety—and then settle into a protracted drizzle of tears that penetrated to your very bones before finally giving out a mighty cry: "Some people can't find a husband at all, and you, what more do you want? He may not be compatible, but he's better than nothing!"

As for Little My... Tiep remembered the day, shortly after the conclusion of that violent April of that violent year of 1975, when Little My had herded Tiep and Hoai and their kids into the skiff for a celebratory jaunt to Diep Vang. They had spent years as evacuees there before the Paris accords, and now she wanted to bid a proper farewell to those miserable days of trying to cook with canal water stinking with human and pig excrement. That day, in that atmosphere of intense joy and sorrow, people looked at Little My with secret envy: her husband was a regimental-level military cadre, and everyone knew he'd make general someday. Then wouldn't she and their children have it made! But it was shortly after that trip that Hoai's son Hon shattered his leg when he stepped on an abandoned shell in their orchard, and Little My received the letter informing her that her husband had laid down his life. And so the family returned again to the all-too-familiar activities of funeral preparations and mourning. But this time, deep within, a new war was smoldering: a secret and painfully sensitive awareness that the cadres in the family would go to live in the city with its paved roads, private houses, electric lighting, television, and everything else one could wish for; while the widows would remain stuck in an orchard full of poisonous snakes and millipedes, bomb and artillery craters, and leftover mines which no one could clean out because no one knew where they lay. The entire orchard was like a great amorphous crater, widening its maw to swallow them up.

At dinner that evening, Tuyen delivered a steady stream of self-satisfied conversation, as though he thought his sudden regard for Aunt Rang would weaken Tiep's position. Never before had Tuyen been so effusive; never before had he so enjoyed the upper hand. This was clearly a competition to him, with winners and losers, and Tiep realized that her wishful thinking had led her to underestimate her husband. But the shrewd and haughty Aunt Rang understood her son-in-law only too well. She made an occasional sharp comment or told some irrelevant story that Tuyen couldn't follow, but most of the time she was silent, morosely concentrating on her chewing, aware that not only Tiep's standing with her husband, but also her own, had been severely compromised. Tuyen's tactics revealed a cunning that Tiep had not expected; realizing it now made her seethe, but the anger smoldered and sputtered instead of giving her strength.

After dinner, Aunt Rang gave the command that it was Tuyen's turn to take the children out so that she and Tiep could talk.

"I'm worried, Mom. Great-Aunt Rang is going to rake you over the coals!" Thu Thi whispered in her mother's ear before stepping outside.

Vinh Chuyen, on the other hand, was thrilled and clambered up onto the gas tank of their '67 Honda to wait. Thu Thi ran to fetch a thin cushion for him to sit on. Tiep quickly turned away into the house. Strange, she thought, her fear of Aunt Rang was still as whole and real as when she was a child. Even though she knew her mother detested it when her children were obsequious and submissive to their aunt, she couldn't help herself.

"Let's go in to the inside bed, Auntie. You'll have something to lean on there while you talk, so your back won't get too tired!"

Aunt Rang didn't say a word. She went stonily downstairs to fetch her basket of betel nut herself, then followed her niece into the back bedroom to the marital bed which Tiep had fashioned by joining the two narrow single beds they had brought up with them from Diep Vang to make a double bed that was reasonably comfortable if one ignored the seam running down the middle. Aunt Rang lay down and propped three pillows under her neck in a morose position that half faced her niece and half turned away. The only thing that was missing was a rolled cigarette dangling between her fingers.

It reminded Tiep of so many peaceful nights snuggled in bed with Aunt Rang, with her grandmother's bed pulled up next to theirs at a right angle, and Hoai, Nghia, and Little My in the row of beds against the opposite wall: a veritable army, made up entirely of women and children ever since the day her grandfather had gone to sleep and not woken up, shortly after the news of her father's death. Dangling a cigarette as fat as her finger, Aunt Rang would tell rambling stories to Tiep about how her paternal grandparents, tired of the constant flooding and storms of the Tien River, had left their ancient orchard in Cao Lanh near the Cambodian border to travel down to the Hau river and establish a new orchard. How her father had stepped forward and told the enemy that he was the man they were hunting in order to cover for the escape of the Secretary of the Provincial Party Committee, and how he had been acclaimed as a hero on the order of Le Lai ever since. And then there were the whys: why Tiep and her sisters should follow in their father's footsteps, why she and Tiep's mother were always at odds with each other, why she had foresworn remarriage after her husband's death in order to assume responsibility for her brother's family, and even why she had sent her only child, a daughter named Minh, away to the city to her paternal grandparents' house. Her stories were usually drawn out and disjointed, but also suffused with emotion and real sorrow. At midnight, when the little Tiep had finally drifted off, Aunt Rang would sit by herself to chew betel and think, or roll Tiep over to smother her in kisses and caresses, or rally Hoai out of bed to sit with her and chat the hours away like a mismatched pair of best friends. Tiep feared her aunt and so rarely slept deeply. She liked to listen to their conversations, feeling the words wrap her up in a protective blanket of sleeplessness, storytelling, and hard-won experience.

Later, when she left to join the guerrillas, Tiep missed her aunt no less than she missed her mother. When asked her ambitions, she would say: my aunt is almost illiterate, but I can only hope one day to be as sharp, aggressive, sophisticated, and expansive as she!

That was then; now, Tiep sat at her aunt's feet and

rested her back against the bedpost to brace herself for the onslaught.

"Well. Is there anything you want to tell me first?"

Tiep pressed a pillow hard in her lap, rolling the edges back and forth between her fingers. Should she talk about her writing? Her readers? Why did things that were normally so important to her become so meaningless when in the presence of her aunt and her family?

"What did Truong tell you, Auntie?"

"Why do you want to know?"

Tiep managed to stammer out: "Because... I want to know what's going on in Tuyen's mind, what he told Truong when he went there to ask for help. Tuyen may be dull and passive as a doormat, but that doesn't mean he won't stoop to tricks when he thinks it's necessary."

Aunt Rang popped up to a sitting position like a spring uncoiling. Her legs were perfectly folded, but her hands clenched furiously and her eyes blazed.

"Now it's Tuyen this, Tuyen that, eh? Back in the beginning, do you remember, back in the beginning when I saw you two together I didn't approve. But was I able to stop you? Like fire near straw you were. And the fire had burned too far, so if I'd kicked up a fuss it would've only hurt us because our family was the bride's side, and you'd have been nothing but damaged goods if he hadn't married you. In a world crawling with widows, here you are with a kid on each hip and suddenly you want a change of scenery? All right, so you're tired of him, you're unhappy, but why did you have to go and make it a big production, 'I have someone else, dear husband, got me a new man, see!' When you kill your reputation, you kill yourself and kill the good name of your entire family. Then later, if Tuyen decides he'd like to do you in, who'll dare to stop him? He's got a gun, you know. Remember that! No one would blame him if he shot you. And then he'd go to prison, and your children would be full-fledged orphans!"

Aunt Rang fell silent, like an actress who's been chewing

up the scenery before an audience and is suddenly overcome by her own eloquence. Her legs hadn't shifted out of their habitual lotus position, but her fingers were squeezing the tiny toes one after another, and she was gulping air like a fish about to suffocate. Then she started bowing and mumbling, and Tiep knew she was talking to Tiep's grandparents or to her father the hero who was sitting up on high or somewhere down in the underworld. Back when the family had received news of her father's death in the cells of Con Dao, and then again when their grandfather had passed away and left the family and every leaf and blade of grass in the orchard orphaned of any male presence, Aunt Rang had sat on the earthen floor of the porch and prostrated herself repeatedly exactly in the same manner. She had cried with the same labored keening as now. But she was a woman of no ordinary resources, and Tiep knew that even her tears were dangerous, calculated to induce trembling and submission in anyone who happened to be nearby.

Even so, Tiep burst into tears along with her aunt. She cried for the dearth of men for her loved ones and their orchard, and for her love for this immeasurable woman, and for her own lost youth. She prostrated herself as well, but did not right herself as her aunt did. Instead, she fell into her aunt's lap, her slender shoulders shaking as though in childbirth, her body trembling uncontrollably, jaws clenched as though locked and unable to form words.

She remembered a particular morning in Dong Dung during the war, one of those mornings that carry within it the seeds of death that could suddenly blossom anywhere, from bombs and artillery rained down from above, or from random bullets shot from enemy positions on either side, or from mines underfoot in fields that never got cleaned up because their creators were dead, sacrificed in the war, and no one knew where the explosives lay anymore. On one such morning, a young man and a young woman, the youngest in their unit, were trapped by a blockade of water hyacinth, that bully of the plant world that multiplies out of control wherever people aren't present, at a fork in the river in the middle of the free-fire zone near the Dong Dung guerrilla base. They heard the sound of airplanes taking off, and then almost immediately the howl of a pack of grim reapers ripping tightly across the sky, and then the bombs—fragmentation bombs, penetration bombs, cluster bombs, you name it—an entire orchestral composition whirling around them but the only problem was it wasn't playing Beethoven, and then the pillars of water shooting up on every side stood their small boat on end amidst a rain of shrapnel and mortally wounded vegetation as though they were in the eye of a storm. Tiep leaped and found herself in the water but she didn't know how to swim. How could she know how to swim—hers was a family of women and the river was so deep and fast that no one had learned except Aunt Rang, and one of her greatest fears during the war had been that she would have to ford a river and would either kill the soldier carrying her or would drown ignominiously, forever ineligible for the posthumous title of war martyr and all the benefits that went with it for her survivors...

From the rudder, Tuyen crawled over, stooped low under the sound of explosions, and grabbed her hair to pull her out of the water. "Grab an oar and let's go backward toward the bank. With any luck there'll be a foxhole!" he yelled. And indeed, they found a foxhole, as long as a grave, at the base of a combretum tree. It had no cover and was filled neck-deep with water, but it was a great stroke of luck at a moment when they would have considered even a fallen tree or a riverbank overhang to be a fortress safer than their mother's womb.

Tiep was nineteen, with five years' experience as a guerrilla fighter under her belt. She had experienced the sear of Agent Orange across her back like a snake across the desert. She had been targeted by an airplane on a scouting sortie that had left her boat in shreds. She had nearly suffocated in a hidden bomb shelter during the flood season, and had survived a strafing by a B52 that leveled every bit of plant life around her. But that morning seemed particularly desperate; the violence of the war had been escalating, and the complete lack of shelter to be had in the deep swift river was punctuated by the overabundance of artillery that pounded them. Death showed its fangs, and then retreated. Auntie, can you hear me? Mom? Hoai? Nghia? Tiep hunkered deeper into the foxhole with this young man who might die with her in the shower of fragmentation bombs, penetration bombs, cluster bombs; whatever they were, in that impenetrable and tireless chorus of bullets, dollars, and wealth that was trying to make mincemeat of that river fork and their sheltering combretum tree. Tiep's ears rang but her eyes shone with emotion because Tuyen had pulled her up by the hair and had pressed her down into this grave of a foxhole. She cackled, and then her cackle changed into whimpering, and then the whimpering gave way to sudden silence as she realized two hands were pressing her down, and the buttons of her blouse somehow had come undone, and there were her breasts hardening and trembling under two greedy hands in the water the color of dirty milk. How strange. This delightful feeling of being caressed while at the same time the torment below as her body lifted and sank rhythmically in water that stank of hell. How strange. It seemed he was panting something about how he had had his eye on her for a long time, ever since he first joined up, he'd marked her and dreamed of making her his wife...

The air around them suddenly fainted away into dead silence. Disaster had passed. Tiep bobbed up to the lip of the foxhole and pulled herself out to sit, breathing heavily, on the earth. The smell of pulverized plants and dirt mixed with the memory of the lips of the young man who had just explored her lower half in the foxhole and the smell of her own body as it stirred from the inside out for the first time. Urgency mixed with pain and she wanted to scream out her survival her exposure her ecstasy her complete abandonment. Then

Tuyen was beside her, helping her stand. "We have to go check the boat and then find someplace to hide. They were just softening up the area, it won't be long before the paratroopers come!" So it was that the taking of her virginity had what should have been all the ingredients of a great love: gratitude, commitment, the intensity of life in the face of death....

After they had cried quietly together for a long time, Aunt Rang stroked the hair of her once-promising niece and comforted her. "I know, I know. I know you aren't happy in your marriage. We all wanted you to be happy, you're the star of the entire clan. But to spill every last bean like that to your husband... you were being stupid, not proper. A truly shrewd woman is both proper and shrewd. You have to preserve your life first, because without that you can't raise your children, and after that preserve your name. Even though what's done is done, you need to think hard about this. Whatever it is you're going to do, make sure you do it right. If you're going to be picky about your man, make sure you pick one that's a gem. I'm warning you, if you make a mistake and have to come crawling back with double the dishonor, all that will be left is for you to do yourself in!"

5

Fall, 1981, Diep Vang

Despite being abandoned by her lover and excoriated by her family, Tiep felt optimistic as she and Thu Thi left the little dock and the whispers of the water hyacinth behind them, and walked back to the house hand in hand to prepare for their journey back to the city.

Hoai dropped Tiep and her children off at a small ferry. "To save you the extra baggage fees on the bus," she said, then gunned the little Kole Four outboard motor that was almost as moldy as she and headed her skiff over to the market pier to haggle over a few bare necessities for the women and children who waited for her in the family orchard. Tiep knew she would linger at the homes of relatives and a few old girlfriends from the old days until dusk, then leave just in time to make it home before dark. Hoai was fearless when it came to boats and water. She could maneuver the propeller of her outboard motor to grind through the patches of water hyacinth that choked the river, sending her skiff slicing across the surface as though her hands held reins and her boat were a horse running a steeplechase. Gawky and indefatigable, she worked all day like the stork and then all night like the heron; still, Tiep thought, if it hadn't been for the war, her sister would have preferred to simply stay at home and be a housewife. Even now, though her hands and feet were calloused and lumpy from laboring in their fields and orchard, she was always eager to immerse herself in cooking and entertaining whenever the opportunity presented itself. It was only because Aunt Rang had trained her and imposed authority on her that she had developed the fortitude to be the family's second-in-command.

Tiep lingered on the bow of the boat, watching until Hoai's ungainly, crow-pheasant figure had disappeared into a press of boats on the far side of the river. Once more, she felt the weight of her guilt, the pain she had caused her mother, her aunt, and her sister; but as soon as she bent down to creep into the cabin of the ferry her thoughts changed, teetering from one extreme to the other as they did so often these days. Suddenly, in her mind, the umbilical cord that connected her to her family became a tenacious noose, dragging her onward when she felt content and then cinching her back when she wanted to leap ahead.

Diep Vang was no longer the vibrant young provincial town that it had been back when Tiep used to sit in the boat with her mother or aunt or sister on their way to the market; it now looked more like a lonely and spurned old maid. In the old days, the previous government had imposed on Diep Vang the grandiose status of "gateway between the nerve center of Tactical Region Four and the U Minh area," but after reunification in 1975[1], the new people calling the shots had revoked its incorporation under the provincial government and returned it to county authority in accordance with the principle "every county a fortress."[2] Now, government offices and state-owned businesses filled the cavities once occupied by crowded, vibrant Chinese shops; drifting garbage replaced the bustling boats that had lined the banks by the market; and the storehouses and granaries which once jutted out into Xang Chu canal had now been turned into state-run coffee shops offering enticing scenery but less-than-enticing drinks. Even the noodle boats and sugarcane-juice carts that Tiep used to love had disappeared as though someone had spirited them away.

Xang Chu canal was the main artery connecting the frail Diep Vang with Dinh Bao, its more abundant and vital neighbor. Despite this, there had been a marked drop in the canal's motorized boat traffic over the past few years due to the deteriorating economy. Now, small skiffs and sampans, along with the occasional motorized barge, plied the canal, which was part of the government transportation network, carrying coal, firewood, rice, and U Minh bananas up to the city or farther. The early morning air was heavy with the smell of sugarcane from the state-owned sugar factory on the far side of the market, where a column of smoke and ash was drifting

1. On April 30th, 1975, the People's Army of Viet Nam, from the then North Viet Nam, took Saigon, the capital of the Republic of Vietnam, and ended the war. Tiep was a member of the National Front for the Liberation of Viet Nam, the Southern guerrillas fighting against the Americans and the South Vietnamese government sponsored by the U.S. Tactical region 4 and the U Minh are located in the Mekong Delta area.
2. According to this policy, authority devolved from the provincial to the local governments. However, the local governments largely lacked resources and oversight, and the policy failed.

upwards. The ferry pier itself lay a distance from the market. A gaggle of short-haul ferries—shabby canvas-roofed skiffs with license plates indicating joint government ownership—had brought the early-morning crowd to market and were now waiting, bobbing and empty, for return passengers. The grass and garbage that choked their propellers showed clearly how little their owners cared for their upkeep.

The long-haul Xang Chu canal ferry was a hulking, plywood-roofed structure, a kind of motorized house with enough space in the middle to hang a hammock to kill time. Long ago, Tiep had made several trips in this kind of ferry with Aunt Rang to transport their tangerines up to Saigon. There was more of a selection then; her aunt would choose the cheapest ferry that had the most space for their goods, to prevent bruising. On the trip, Tiep watched the passing scenery, then napped on the hard bench, then sat up to watch the scenery some more, then dozed some more, and still the canal stretched out in front of her with no city in sight. The Xang Chu canal was an impressive piece of work, built by the French at the turn of the century. She had heard somewhere that Monsieur Doumer, the French Governor-General, had set foot for the first time on the far side of the Hau river on the occasion of the official inauguration. And that the French plantation owner who had floated the idea of building the canal had received a massive land grant of six thousand acres for his ingenuity...

It was past nine o'clock now. Tiep guessed that Hoai had finished her shopping by now, while she and her children were still sitting as though tethered by the ankle to this single solitary long-haul ferry. She couldn't see the owners of the ferry, but could hear rustling sounds in the steering cabin, along with an occasional shriek of laughter from the wife as though she were being tickled. Every now and then the husband cracked open the door in the plywood partition to count heads. She had to admit that the number of waiting passengers was awfully small compared to the carrying capacity of the ferry.

Like a few mosquitoes hardly worth swatting.

An old man with his hair gathered up into a bun, black peasant's pajamas, and a reed basket clutched in his hands, complained to no one in particular: "It's the times, everything's backwards. These joint-venture transport people would rather stay put, sell their diesel on the black market, and save themselves the trouble!"

Two scrawny young men in white shirts—students, no doubt, who had chosen to take the ferry to the city in order to avoid the long lines at the bus station—gave each other a long look when they heard this. Sitting next to Tiep was a spry, resilient-looking woman of about seventy with the short pageboy haircut typical of Chinese women. She shook her head. "I've taken this ferry several times so I know that all they need is that cabin of theirs to carry on in. They don't need us!"

"So the ferry pier doesn't schedule the boats, ma'am?" Tiep asked, surprised. She hadn't taken this kind of ferry for years, not since she had tagged along with Aunt Rang.

The old woman answered briskly, "It was all right before, but its gotten worse the last few years. There's only one trip a day now, no schedule or hours at all!"

The old man with the bun looked fed up. He took out some tobacco and paper and began rolling a cigarette. "Don't get what our leaders think they're doing, but people everywhere don't want to work anymore. Just want to screw us over, bleed everyone dry!"

The old lady with the short hair gazed at Tiep with concern. "I like taking the ferry for the space, but the couple who own this boat are unreliable. How about you and me going up to the bus station? I have war martyr's priority papers; what about you? You look to be at least cadre[1] level; between the two of us we could buy four tickets. That would

1. Cadre level—an official of the Communist Party, a privileged position in postwar Vietnamese society. Tiep is cadre both because she is a veteran and because she is a writer who belongs to the province's official Writers' Union.

be more than enough for us, the two children, and that pile of stuff you have."

A few moments later, the old man with the bun jumped out onto the square of plywood that served as the pier, and the two students followed shortly after. It was several hundred yards from the ferry pier to the bus station, however, and there were no bicycles for hire that Tiep could use to walk her baggage up; apparently that means of transport, which was very popular in the cities, had not yet spread to this tiny town at the end of the world. After asking the short-haired old lady, whom she was now calling Auntie, to watch the children, it took her three trips up and down between the pier and the bus station to shift all of the bags and sacks that her mother had prepared for her.

The bus station was a squat, tin-roofed building that had already grown stuffy and hot under the intermittent but strident sunshine of the rainy season. The only items arranged on the pockmarked cement floor were a table selling refreshments, a ticket booth, and two lines of people patiently waiting amidst the ubiquitous odor of urine and garbage. There was a large fifty-two-seat bus idling nearby, its unevenly chugging engine inciting a mood of restless anxiety in the two lines. The station lay at the end of the provincial highway, and did not allow the three-wheeled taxis that ran to the neighboring markets; it was so small there was only space for the large state-owned and joint-venture buses that ran to the city. In spite of this, it had somehow managed to keep pace with its larger city cousins in terms of sheer disorder and stench.

There was no choice but to spread out the raincoat given to her by Nghia in a corner of the station for the children to sit on. After instructing them to keep a careful eye on their belongings, Tiep shouldered her way over to stand behind Auntie, who had appropriated a space for her by placing her purse on the ground behind her.

"My son works in the Military Zone," said the old woman.

"It's a difficult journey from where I live to his place, so I don't visit often. He said he's going to look for a house for me up there, so we can live near each other and save ourselves the trouble."

"If you're the widow of a martyr who served in the war against the French, your son must be at least a major or above. I'm sure you've got nothing to worry about!" Tiep said conversationally.

Compared to the "commoners'" line on the other side, the priority window line moved steadily as people were served quickly and went on their way. Tiep ran her eyes down the line of her "class comrades" and couldn't help but picture the contents of their bulky baggage: good, clean country rice, no doubt, and fresh pork, the kind that couldn't be gotten for love or money from the stale government distribution system. People visiting Diep Vang usually stocked up on these two commodities as they were the freshest and easiest to buy. They were also the commodities that were most coveted by the Market Regulation people, who liked to confiscate them because they were fresh and made a good meal.

Auntie nimbly stuffed Tiep's press card and travel permit in with her priority papers and pushed them through the slot in the kiosk window, confident that she understood this bus station better than Tiep. She bent down to talk to the ticket-seller inside. "Will you let me and my daughter each take on an extra ticket, ma'am? We have two small children and a lot of stuff, ma'am, see, they're squatting over there, ma'am!"

The ticket-seller's face looked as though it weighed a thousand pounds. She examined the items in her hand, then pushed her glasses up to peer through the netting of the booth and identify the two women before her who were holding their breath, awaiting her decision. She had the exaggerated mannerisms of one who knows she holds the power of life or death in her hands.

"You just decided to be mother and daughter, didn't you?"

Her voice dripped with a thick, rural Northern accent.[1] "Look here, in the travel permit it says your so-called daughter is on vacation and will return to one town, and your war martyr's papers say you are going to another town. See!"

Auntie turned to give Tiep a hopeless look. Tiep stepped up, grimacing like a pupil who has been caught red-handed in a lie. "I hope you can understand our situation, sister. This lady saw that I was traveling with two small children so she felt sorry for me. That and I have so much baggage."

"Suppose everyone at the priority window asked to buy two tickets like you? You think the common people over there should just have to walk?"

Auntie pushed Tiep out of the way, bent down, and barked, "Why don't you just go ask anyone here and see if they don't believe us? There's the two children over there, large as life, and there's her mountain of stuff! What more would anyone need to know? No doubt we're scalpers who'll whisk those tickets off to the black market, right? No doubt that's why there are several people who never spent a second in line but already are sitting in their primo front row seats on the bus out there! Eh?"

The ticket-seller gave an emphatic push which sent the papers sliding back to the two supplicants, then crooked her finger to signal that the next person should shove their way up to the window, saying, "Either the children sit on your laps, or you take the ferry. I'm almost out of tickets anyway!"

Auntie furiously collected the papers and allowed herself to be pushed out of the way, complaining "Doesn't she think she's God!" No one sympathized with her, however; they were too busy worrying about keeping their own places in line.

Tiep tried to console her. "Never mind, Auntie, you go ahead and get back in line so you can get your ticket first. I'll wait for the next bus or go back down to the ferry pier."

1. After the war, many northerners came south to take over positions from former Republic of Vietnam officials, etc., or to take advantage of economic opportunities. They were regarded by many southerners as carpet-baggers.

But the old lady flung up her hands. "Forget it! I don't want to go back and beg Her Holiness anymore anyway!"

A man's voice floated over from the "commoners'" line. "Be discreet, grandma!"

Auntie lowered her voice to talk to Tiep. "All of a sudden I feel so sorry for you, with the children and that huge pile of stuff. Surely sometime between now and the afternoon you'll be able to buy a ticket, don't you think?"

As though on cue, a large bus with state-owned license plates swung into view and silently rolled into the space just vacated by the other bus. The passengers poured off, sullen and exhausted after forty miles of roads and traffic. Tiep suddenly noticed a man among them who looked like no one else in this remote place. He was in his mid-forties, with audaciously long salt-and-pepper hair. He wore a threadbare, cream-colored shirt with a gathered waist; dark, unfashionably straight-legged pants of thin cotton; and flip-flops. This, together with the bamboo water pipe poking like the barrel of a gun out of his yellowing, fake-leather, broken-locked shoulder bag, indicated that this was clearly a person "made-in-somewhere-out-there," maybe even from Hanoi. Oblivious to the curious stares of the bus station denizens, the man stretched his shoulders with pleasure, tilted his head to look around with the avid interest of a small boy who's just arrived in his promised land, then strode deliberately toward the bus station. He stepped inside just as Thu Thi and Vinh Chuyen, who had decided to play hide-and-seek to pass the time, ran past and bumped into him. They gaped at his water pipe, as though they had just run into a man from another planet carrying a strange weapon. The man paused to ruffle their hair lightly and let Vinh Chuyen touch the water pipe.

"Looks strange, doesn't it?" he chuckled. "Your father never uses one of these, I bet! You could catch eels in this, you know. Probably the eels here are really big, eh? Are they as big as this pipe? You two are brother and sister, right? City kids on vacation in the country, right?"

Vinh Chuyen couldn't stop stroking the barrel of the water pipe. Thu Thi glanced over at her mother with a shy smile. The man followed her gaze until he found Tiep, and his open, round face smiled heartily. A moment passed, and Tiep knew she had made an impression on him. He bent down to Vinh Chuyen. "This is for touching only, hear? If you play with it, it will get angry and burp out some really stinky water. Wait here, and in a bit I'll put on a show for you, make it shoot tobacco."

The lady in the ticket office had just stood up and was leaving her booth carrying a ring of keys when the man blocked her way.

"May I ask you, madam comrade, why this bus station does not post the bus schedules and ticket prices?"

Tiep had seen enough to make some generalizations: here was an adventurer, a drifter, with a fastidious temperament, a Nghe Tinh accent overlaid with shades of Hanoi, and a deep yet slightly hard-edged voice.

The ticket-seller planted both fists on her hips and glared. "And just where did you come from, old man, that you think you can waltz in here and grill me?"

The "old man" laughed out loud. "No matter how far I run, I just can't escape that accent. And I thought that in this far-flung spot I'd only hear a sweet southern drawl!"

The ticket-seller fixed him with a stubborn stare. "You haven't answered me. Where did you come from?"

"I could have fallen down from the sky or crawled out of the earth for all it concerns you. I posed a question, to wit: it is now the year nineteen hundred and eighty-one. This bus station has been under new management for five or six years, but this waiting room is still nothing but an unfurnished, messy, disorganized box. It looks like a market stall. Why?"

"Forget it, I'm not going to waste my words. If you're a customer of my booth you can wait for me to eat my lunch. If you're one of the plain folk, I invite you to get in line over there."

The man put on a stern face. "This citizen has stood in lines his entire life, I fear them not! But I demand my right to see properly posted information so that I can know what's going on and whether or not I can make it back to the city by this evening."

The ticket-seller gave a wave of her hand. "We have a comment box, over there, knock yourself out. And there's only one bus from now until the evening, and that'd be the one you came in on. Now, see if you can't get in line!"

Satisfied, the woman strode off in the direction of the market. Her stumpy arms swung rhythmically, giving her the air of a general reviewing his troops.

Now that he had no opponent to engage, the man who had "stood in lines all his life" deflated like a balloon. His eyes cast around for a moment, then settled on Tiep as though looking for some sympathy. But like many others, Tiep and the old lady were shoving their way back to their baggage in a chain reaction of panic set off by the news that there would be only one bus until evening. Tiep yelled at her daughter, "Thu Thi, watch your brother and the stuff, I'm going to take a load down to the ferry for Auntie to watch there, then I'll be back for another load!"

The man approached her. "There's a ferry? Would you like me to give you a hand?"

Tiep looked at him, friendly enough, but guarded. "The ferry makes just one run a day; once it leaves it won't be back until tomorrow. If you want to make it back to the city by this evening, you'd better not dawdle here. You might miss your bus or worse yet might lose that hippie haircut of yours."

The man grabbed a handful of the hair from the nape of his neck and stuck out his tongue like a child. "You really don't need me to help you?"

Tiep shook her head sternly, then grabbed two bags and ran after her altruistic Auntie. When she returned for her second trip, she saw him coming towards her with both hands full of bags with Thu Thi and Vinh Chuyen behind him dragging the last bag. By the time she ran over and helped her children, he had tromped down, deposited the bags at the pier, and was heading back towards the market without a word and without waiting for her thanks, his square hands waving goodbye in a flirtatious and not unappealing manner.

6

Sixty-five pounds of freshly husked white rice in an old urea fertilizer bag, enough to replace a month's worth of the damp, clumped-up, broken-kerneled ration-book rice from the summer crop that the government was distributing. An entire stalk of still-green sugar bananas for Tiep to hang by the stove for the children to eat as they ripened, or if she ran low on grocery money she could split some, grate them up, and cook them with coconut juice to make the kind of soup that back at the guerrilla base had been considered her finest dish. Another bag contained an uncut twenty-pound jackfruit, one of the saffron-yellow ones that their orchard was famous for and that Tiep's mother used to set aside to ripen behind Aunt Rang's back so that Nghia, Tiep, and Little My could "eat to their heart's content" because she could not believe they might be content when Aunt Rang dictated what they ate. Sharing the bag with the jackfruit were several shucked dried coconuts for Tiep to make pudding with, or to simmer with pumpkin, or to eat with the stewed barley that she made when rice was scarce and that Thu Thi and Vinh Chuyen hated like bitter medicine. "When it comes to impoverishing the people, not even Heaven and its natural disasters can outdo these collectivization-pushing politicians!" That was how Hoai had put it, in the tone of voice that Tiep's husband, the propaganda czar, and her brother Truong called her "nothing is ever good enough" voice. Hoai had dared to scold Tuyen with that very sentence once, after she had spent an entire day piloting her skiff up the Xang Chu canal to bring provisions of rice, firewood, and produce from their garden to her three city siblings. She had then returned to the countryside with Tiep's children tucked one under her each arm "so that they won't have to eat the stewed barley of a cadre!"

Altogether, their expedition's gear that day included no less than three bags, a suitcase with their clothing, and two large bags stuffed to overflowing with gourami sauce, blackfish sauce, lemons, pennywort, bitterleaf, sweet leaf bush, and you name it. There was even half a duck braised in fresh coconut milk and a package of sticky rice mixed with mung beans which her mother had saved from the memorial feast so that Tiep and her children would have something to eat on the way home. Aunt Rang had tried to stop her mother from wrapping up so much, as a way of cracking the whip over Tiep's head, and Hoai had scowled and fussed when she saw it waiting in the skiff, wondering how her little sister would manage such a pile. But her mother, the sole creator of that mountain of stuff, had just clucked her tongue and said, "It won't be cumbersome when she is just sitting on a ferry, and when she gets to the city she can call a cyclo to carry it all home for her. Which is more, the fare for the cyclo or the money she'd have to put out to buy all this?"

Well, there was no way she could have known that on this ill-fated day her daughter would be laughing and crying at the same time over her labor of love.

The ferry-owner and his wife had left to grab a bite at the market after finishing their morning recreation in the steering cabin. When they returned, they found to their astonishment a group of passengers waiting as obstinately as though on a sit-down strike. The wife, a fiftyish woman with vividly pink skin and vividly shiny hair who looked as though she had stepped out of the old saying about red cheeks and buckets[1],

1. A rough translation: "Ah, the red-cheeked woman, she's so creamy you could bail her out with a bucket and her cunt would still be wet."

gave a shrill laugh that exposed her bright gold teeth. "Aren't you all droll though? Sitting there so neat and tidy, and you don't even know if we are going?"

The husband, who had the face and build of the legendary Lao Ai[1] in the story of Lu Buwei, stabbed at his teeth with a toothpick and cleared his throat. "Well, my friends, I suppose you've missed your bus, so we'll go ahead and lift anchor. But we'll charge you a lump charter price for the whole boat. Better to tell you that up front than to have hard feelings about it later, eh?"

Tiep slumped backwards against the wall of the boat, despairing and furious but not knowing who to rage at. If only she could have a good cry, or stand on the prow of the boat and fling curses. She did some mental math: there were only fifteen people in the boat, so if the charter price were divided up per head... why, she would have to pawn her watch and wedding earrings and even that might not be enough for the three of them!

With an exquisite aplomb fitting her wiry, resilient appearance, Auntie urged Tiep to her feet. "This time we'll take whatever we can get, okay? Let's go back to the station and get in line for that bus. If we can't score four tickets we'll get three, or at the very least two will do, anything will do! Go on now, I'll watch the children, and you take your time to shift your stuff. Don't overexert yourself, you'll end up with a bent back and that'll just be more misery for you and your family!"

As small and distressed as she was, moving a mountain of luggage three times up and down a hill over the space of half a day should have been too much for Tiep to bear; still, she felt that her labor was as light as a feather compared to the crushing mountain of uncertainty that awaited her in the bus station. Light was beginning to fade from the sky now.

1. The paramour of the Queen Dowager, mother of Shi Huangdi, China's first great emperor. He was rumored to have been exceptionally endowed but pretended to be a eunuch so that he could be a part of the harem. The emperor executed him when the pretense was found out.

While the children sat on the raincoat in the corner of the bus station and wrestled with the duck and sticky rice, Tiep and her newly adopted Auntie took turns keeping a place in line and straining until their eyes hurt to watch for the ticket-seller with her harsh accent and the crew of that final bus to return from wherever they'd disappeared to in the market. Around them, the opaque yellow glow of the caustic autumn sunlight was gradually fading to leaden gray as dark clouds drifted lethargically in from the direction of the ocean, warning of one of those rainstorms that come on as suddenly as Hoai's tears.

Auntie looked at the sky, then paced back and forth irritably. "I have a nephew who lives here. If we can't get out today we can always leave early tomorrow. I swear, I'll not give that bitch the pleasure of begging her, not even one word!"

"Then we have to split up," Tiep said decisively. "You get your priority ticket, but I'm determined to have at least two tickets; if not I will just lie down and die here!"

Having made up her mind, and since her travel permit granted her only one priority ticket, she ran over to the "commoners'" line on the other side. It was then that she noticed the man who had "stood in lines all his life" returning from the market. The eager, youthful air he had worn that morning was gone; he now looked dejected and distant, as though he had lost something and was absorbed in looking for it. He walked mutely towards the "commoners'" line and suddenly perked up when he saw the woman with all the baggage waiting there before him. Tiep gave him a smile—then burst into uncontrollable laughter when she saw that his shaggy head of hair was gone. The nape of his neck was as ragged and brushy as that of a little boy who couldn't sit still in the barber chair.

"Even in hell they wouldn't deal with long hair the way your Culture and Information people do here!" he explained, bitterly patting the back of his neck. "Oh well, at least I can take some small comfort in the fact that I get to stand in line behind a cute country girl like yourself."

Tiep turned toward him, managing to stifle her laughter at last. "So in your opinion, which circle of hell are we on?"

He forced a smile. "At least that of Solzhenitsyn, if not lower!"

"Surely someone as stalwart as yourself could have gotten away?"

The man's smile twisted in such a way that even Vu Trong Phung[1], if he were to return from the grave, would have a hard time describing it. "I was just walking along, and suddenly there was the sound of a whistle—a whistle, mind you, how's that for decorum?—and this team of three men with regulation red bands on their sleeves came rushing out from nowhere and grabbed me and demanded my papers like I was a wanted criminal. Then they pushed me up against a tree and with one slash of the scissors my poor hair was revolutionized as fast as Ah Q's queue[2]. There you have it. So what would you have me do, my little miss, stand still for them to straighten out the nape of my neck with a barber's shaver? Or make a run for it with a haircut like a crazy brat?"

Their eyes met, and suddenly each recognized in the other an unexpected commonality, a voice speaking of suffering and hopelessness...

And suspicion. Tiep turned away. She heard a long sigh behind her, felt his gaze on her back, weighing, searching, possibly longing. Before she had met the peacock who had passed through her life like a bolt of lightning and resurrected in her a virginal desire only to cause her to fall like a stupid, naïve bird; and for whom she had blurted out to Tuyen the righteousness of divorce, only to then fall to her knees and surrender before the vicious backlash from her family, public opinion, and the Party... back when she had not yet become

1. A famous humorous writer during the twenties and thirties. His novel *Dumb Luck* has been translated into English.
2. Referring to "The True Story of Ah Q," a long short story by the Chinese author Lu Xun. In it the character Ah Q hides his queue to pretend to be a revolutionary.

entangled in such terrible events, back then she had known what it was like to be moved by a voice, or a lock of hair, or a gaze. But she had cooled now to such transient opportunities. Towards this mischievous, unique, and no doubt amorous gentleman standing behind her, she felt curiosity and interest but also a healthy dose of apprehension, as though she were standing next to a line carrying high-voltage electricity.

A squall blew in with rain on its breath, and the sky darkened as though twilight had come. The wind flung dust, sand, and leaves into the air and ripped cast-off banana leaves that had been used to wrap sticky-rice cakes from the pile of garbage behind the station. The ticket-seller from the priority booth and the crew of the bus came pelting hunchbacked out of the market and ran over.

Tiep's line with its burned-black denizens shifted and straightened, then looked around in bewilderment, wondering where the ticket-seller was for their booth.

"'Don't worry, I've counted it out," the man said reassuringly from behind. "There's just enough seats on the bus for everyone. But why don't people here find a brick or something to line up for them so they can spread out a bit and take the weight off their feet?"

Tiep turned around to look at him in astonishment, as though he were telling stories from another planet.

"Up north, we have to line up everywhere for everything. Gotta get in line in the middle of the night no less. So we leave a broken brick, old hat, even a rag as a substitute for the person."

"You look like a cadre—why don't you have a travel permit so you can get a ticket more easily? The other line is faster."

He clucked his tongue teasingly. "Well, little miss, you don't look much like a farmer or trader yourself?"

A few isolated drops of rain fell. From the other line, Auntie interrupted by calling across to Tiep with the chiding voice of an actual mother, "Why aren't you covering up your stuff from the dust? Are you just going to stand there?"

The man said quickly, "Go ahead and take care of the children and your baggage, I'll keep your place with my bag!"

"Thank you."

"No problem. By the way, my name is Dinh."

Tiep hesitated, then nodded and ran to deal with her belongings.

As threatening as the sky looked, the rainstorm still did not come. When she had finished dealing with tickets for the priority customers, the stubby ticket-seller crossed to the other line and the business of buying and selling proceeded apace with silent urgency, without a word of pleading or interrogation, only the rumbling growl of the sky. The ticket-seller didn't even ask to see Tiep's papers; she just pushed two tickets at her, took her money and made change. Her face had lightened up considerably since that morning, no doubt cheered up with a good nap.

The man was holding ticket number fifty-two, the last seat on the bus. "What luck, I don't have to sit on a plastic stool in the aisle," he said merrily. "I'll take one of the kids on my lap to help you out."

It happened when she was pulling her children around to the back door of the bus to have a good view of the bus attendant as he arranged some of her baggage on the roof of the bus. Tiep heard a small pop, and then a warm stream of blood was pouring down her thighs to her ankles and slowly winding like a bright red snake across the sandy surface of the bus yard. She stood rooted to the spot, overcome with fright.

Vinh Chuyen was the first to see it. Perhaps because he was not as busy as his sister and so had more opportunity to notice that infernal snake. "Blood, blood," he cried out, and then Thu Thi saw it and was kneeling at her mother's feet, arms wrapped around her legs and screaming, "Mommy, what's wrong, Mommy?"

In the murky darkness, everything erupted into disorder

around her: the bus attendant was yelling something while ripping her baggage off the roof and throwing it down to the ground, the people sitting by the windows were poking their heads out, pointing and shouting hoarsely, the man in seat fifty-two was flying out and down, Auntie's voice from somewhere in the front of the bus was screaming hysterically "Save her, save her, save her!.."Tiep's knees shook wildly and she was frozen with fear, just as when once upon a time the B-52s had rained fire down on her. All she could think of was that she must be still and wait, although she couldn't remember who she might be waiting for. Then there was a feeling of gratitude that the bus had not yet left the station. Then a cyclo pulled by an old '67 Honda motorcycle was speeding over from the market, and the man from up north was lifting her and depositing her on the back bench, shouting, "Your number isn't up yet! It's a hemorrhage but there's a hospital nearby; you'll be okay!" Then her children were lifted in next to her, and her baggage. Then Auntie's voice again: "God above, she's all by herself, what'll she do, oh God!"

The cyclo-driver gunned the gas and shot around the perimeter of the market. Tiep turned to look back and saw the man start to run as though to follow her, then stop to stand helpless and baffled when he realized he couldn't catch up. After a moment's hesitation he turned to rush after the bus, which had started to slowly roll out of the station.

Afterwards, Dinh told her, he had wandered alone in Dinh Bao where the bus had deposited him, consumed with regret at how he could have left her that stormy evening. He had sensed her isolation and estrangement from her spirited yet sorrowful appearance. But after having his provocative head of hair whacked off by the "New Lifestyle" team from the Committee of Culture and Information, he no longer had the patience to stay on in such a remote backwater and his own lack of patience frightened him. Even though the old woman had pounded on the door and demanded the bus stop to let her off so she could run after Tiep, he still could not quell his unease.

And so it was that during the several days he spent in her city, he found the bridge over Cypress River through Thu Thi's childish description of it to him while he was helping them move their baggage. For several days he went there, hoping to see the child walking to school, then failing that, he walked the road that ran parallel to the river and scanned the clotheslines for the small turtleneck with a bright pomegranate-flower pattern that he remembered had made her seem so warm, vibrant, and memorable that day.

Finding no trace of her, he left Dinh Bao with the feeling that he had not been able to settle his debts. That he owed something to someone in a place that made him shudder every time he thought of that scene: being marched away like a criminal, the trunk of the peacock flower tree against his back, and then the sound of the scissors and shaver mixed with the raucous laughter of those damnably diligent cadres.

7

Diep Vang's municipal roads were abysmal. The floor of the cyclo was sodden with fresh blood, as though a faucet inside her had burst and could not be plugged. Tiep left her feet to steep in that gaudy red blood and groggily poked her head out of the cyclo's nylon canopy to see if she recognized anyone they passed. She had witnessed death during the war, had even been wounded in the calf by a grenade, but never had she seen such fresh blood in such quantity. It astonished her, the sheer wastefulness of it and the brilliance of its color as it poured out before her dull, frightened eyes. She thought about how slow the cyclo was, and then thought about the incompetence of the government-run medical system. She thought about her children and how they might remember this tragic evening as the night they lost their mother.

The hospital gate appeared like an old friend, with its riot of yellow peacock flowers growing up from the base of the wall. Tiep had birthed Thu Thi here. But now the cyclo driver was yelling angrily at the children to climb down. He was grumbling as he struggled with her bags and suitcases. He was shoving his stony face into hers and snapping out a cutthroat price. He was leaving her to go inside and lugging out a pail of water to wash off the bad luck that her body had left in his vehicle.

Each action was like one more drop in her inner cup of self-pity, which was already filled to overflowing. By the time the orderlies had placed her on a stretcher, she had only enough self-control left to stretch out her hands to the children so they wouldn't be left behind. But when their benevolent Auntie appeared and bent over them she allowed the pain to take over, closing her eyes and gritting her teeth. It was a long distance from the gate to the emergency room. Rain poured down on her face and mixed with her tears.

"Don't cry, I'm here now," Auntie was following her. "You're at the right place, the worst of it is over. Don't sob so much, you're frightening the children, poor things!"

Tiep grabbed the old woman's bony hand and laboriously croaked out an address in town. She told Thu Thi to go with Auntie, and with luck they'd find that Hoai was waiting out the storm there.

Auntie left Vinh Chuyen and the baggage in the hospital corridor for the nurses to look after and sped out of the gate with Thu Thi.

Birthing tables. Blood stench. Tools clinking. The sting of alcohol, shots, and commands: lower your bottom, relax your tummy, legs still, knees stiff... None of it was strange to her but it was loathsome nonetheless, simply because no woman ever really gets used to the miseries that are her worldly lot.

"You were pregnant, but I guess you didn't know it or else

you wouldn't have been lugging so much stuff, right?" The doctor asked reproachfully. "Probably you were just late with your period and hadn't realized it yet, eh? Well, you'll just have to grin and bear it now so I can clean you out. Wouldn't want any placenta left in there!"

"You'll have a lot of weakness after a uterine hemorrhage so be sure to rest and restrict your diet, hear?" The nurse's voice cut in. "You had two already, a nice boy-girl set, why didn't you get an IUD to save you the trouble of getting pregnant again?"

Tiep clenched her teeth. Her throat was parched. She felt as though she were running alone through a desert without a spring of water or blade of grass in sight. I had escaped, she wanted to tell them, but couldn't. I had extracted myself but then I had to prostrate myself and this is what my family wanted, this is the product of the nights I made up with my husband had to let him strut and crow over my arms, my legs, my thighs in that way he does when he's showing off his newfound creativity after a spell of fighting...

Then her hands grabbed at the stainless steel bars of the birthing table as the blows ripped into her like a hoe into dirt: prolonged, echoing, biting, mutilating. Her thighs shook violently. These people were ripping her in two, as one rips a frog in two before eating it. Her jaws clattered against each other. Cold, so cold, as if she had crawled deep inside the earth but then why were those hoes still boring into her, excavating her, pushing her down further and further, until she was standing on the final step of a stairway that led to hell...

The first time her birth control had failed, Tuyen had brought her to the provincial hospital early in the morning before his office opened, on the little '67 Honda motorcycle they had managed to buy with the proceeds of selling off the gold bracelet that was Tuyen's family's wedding gift to her. Tuyen's mother had shown it off to Aunt Rang before the two of them had together traveled to the guerrilla base to make the young couple's union official.

That day, Tuyen had dropped her off at the gate of the hospital as though it were just another other day, without a single gesture that might be considered appropriate to the occasion. Tiep had never been able to determine if her husband was a man with no conscience, or no humanity, or if he simply was no good at verbalizing and expressing his feelings. She only knew that, after a moment of hemming and hawing, he had turned and driven off slowly in the direction of his office: nothing but a long, gangly back under an army-green pith helmet, like some sort of generic class of being that carried the name of "cadre."

Having no experience with abortion clinics, she had brought only a pair of underwear, a sanitary napkin, a small amount of money for emergencies, and a scrupulously vague referral document—this was after all a sensitive matter—from the proper governmental authority. She was given a hospital skirt made of rough fabric the color of intestine porridge and stained with spots of dubious origin. Eyeing the frizzy drawstrings crimping out of the waist-seam, she stepped into a corner of the room to change. She removed her pants, bundled them into her bag, and stepped into the skirt.

Like everyone else, she had been given a razor upon admittance; now, she awkwardly rolled up her skirt, stepped out of her underpants, and tossed them on the bars of the bed. Then she set to work performing the crinkly and very comical task of shaving which must be performed in utter seriousness, even though one very much wished to laugh when one remembered the slogan "The Government And The People Work Together" that was so popular at the time; perhaps it was that very slogan that had inspired the medical department to have the patient put her own sanitary house in order rather than having the nurses do it on the operating table. Tiep noticed that some inattentive women had allowed that execrable shrubbery to fall loose around their feet; the ceiling fan had hustled it in all directions over the brick floor before whisking it out thc door. Where it was carried from there was anybody's guess.

Then there had been waiting, anxiety, holding the breath, and, in the end, crying out as each woman was called into a room to do the deed. Afterwards there was another room called the recovery room—which couldn't be said to be any cleaner—into which they were hustled, hunched over, hugging their bellies, barely able to stay on their feet in spite of the repeated reminders from the staff that "you made your bed, now you can lie in it."

Tiep had collapsed into the narrow iron bed and lay for hours, face down in the smell of old pillow and mat. She'd felt as though she had narrowly escaped an execution. She remembered when she had gone into labor the first time, and how she had she felt would die in that anonymous hospital room, but death kept playing coy, it did not come, and in the end it was Thu Thi that came rushing out to her, a miraculous rebirth that flooded over her, as though her life in all its fullness had not truly begun until that moment. In contrast, her first abortion trapped something murky and illicit inside her that would haunt her and darken her forever.

She had been thirsty. The thirst was made even worse when the relatives and husbands of the other women in the recovery room began to trickle in, bringing food and drink. She had heard the men's soft footsteps, murmurs of inquiry, even small intimate sounds between husband and wife. She'd heard it all as she lay with her arms thrown across her face, straining to listen for a visitor for herself. But when every one of her fellow-travelers had a loved one at their side she remained conspicuously alone, like a soiled woman with an illegitimate pregnancy. The nurse brought her a glass of water and a handful of pills. She felt the stares of the others in the room and knew they were thinking that she didn't look like the type who would sleep around and be abandoned. They began to tiptoe around the subject. "I guess your husband is gone on business and couldn't be here?" "Yes, he's gone on business." "My God, why risk it? Why didn't you wait for him to get back before you did it? All by yourself like this, if anything happened who would take care of you?"

She hadn't answered. She hadn't known what to say. She didn't know why Tuyen hadn't come; his office was not even a half a mile away from where she lay. Thu Thi could take care of herself with a little advance preparation—she could let herself into the house after school, lock the door behind her as she always did, and get herself some rice from the electronic rice cooker—and Vinh Chuyen was at preschool. Back when Tiep gave birth to Thu Thi, Tuyen was still working at the guerrilla base so her mother and Hoai had attended her. But now, what was keeping him? Maybe he was busy teaching the class they were giving the low-level level cadres these days: "The New Lifestyle and the New Man—What is It?"

That was the first time. After that came the second time and the third time. Each time Tiep climbed down from her husband's '67 Honda to single-handedly struggle through each stage of the process, to be hungry and thirsty afterwards, and, when evening came, to single-handedly buy her medications, drag herself out of the hospital gate, flag down a three-wheeled taxi, and go home to collapse on the bed like some kind of wilted palm frond. Tuyen had been in town each time; his office hadn't yet moved, and the provincial hospital lay along the same road he took for his daily commute. Perhaps it was because she was too resourceful and sharp, Tiep thought; Tuyen had gotten used to being the passive one and now didn't know how to conduct himself without specific instructions and reminders. Or maybe he felt like a fish out of water whenever he wasn't at the office, and his absolute dedication to his work as deputy manager of the Committee's Propaganda Office should be respected, even lauded? Back then, she excused her husband with such thoughts. She buried her reproach as soon as she was able to wobble off to the market and return to work.

She excused him, but what about Vinh Chuyen, how

could she forgive the events surrounding his birth? That question kept returning to her, again and again, as though Tuyen was a puzzle that she had not yet understood and so could not solve.

It happened shortly after April of 1975. Diep Vang was still the number two municipality in the province, Tuyen had left the guerrilla base to join the occupation team, and Tiep had reunited with him and their Committee after living at home for several years raising a small child and keeping her hand in with the local Party activities. Thu Thi was almost three when they finally enjoyed a belated honeymoon in the married soldiers' quarters of their erstwhile enemy. They had a small room that doubled as both sleeping and working quarters, with two beds and two desks arranged at right angles and an army of rats that rattled crazily across the corrugated aluminum roof. Every night, Tuyen would tap his wife's leg as a signal for her to crawl over to join him if Thu Thi was asleep. Then, on a wooden bed less than three feet wide, they would twine themselves around each other like two snakes inside the army-green mosquito netting that they had kept from the war; the shell was familiar but the physical sensations it encompassed were entirely new and strange.

Back when they were first married, Tiep had been surprised to find that her heart refused to be moved by her new situation. It stubbornly insisted that this was not her man; this was an exigency forced upon her by war and bombs, enemies and flooding, sinking boats and sheltering trees. This was a sharp pain in her hymen, a physical pain mixed with the pain of loss—loss of what she didn't know but she knew it was important—and the throbbing fear that she might be hit by shrapnel, or a bomb, or a stray bullet and die without a shred of clothing to cover her nakedness. Even when she became pregnant with Thu Thi, she felt that she had not yet tasted the full extent of what marital bliss should be. Her heart must be the kind with a lid, she told herself, and for some reason it was refusing to open up. That was why she did not feel the explosion of emotion she had always imagined she would.

But the emotion did not come in the three-foot-wide bed dressed with a cheap straw mat with Thu Thi occasionally waking with a howl on the other bed, startled by the sounds of cars and motorcycles and other such foreign noises of peacetime that she could not get used to. Still, Tiep clung to Tuyen on that narrow bed. Perhaps it had once belonged to a man or a couple who were now counted among the defeated, who had become history, people of the past, drifters somewhere out there in the wide world. It was possible, as their room was in what had been the family quarters for the army of the Republic of South Vietnam. But to Tiep, it was a bed of peace, of serenity. It was heaven at its most sacred. Tiep felt a constant sense of astonishment that they had all survived, she and Tuyen and Thu Thi. They had been reborn and were now living together under one roof with their future stretching out before them. It was over, really over. This war that they had thought would go on forever was utterly and completely finished. So what if this was it, this was all a whole and peaceful life looked like. Every night when they were interrupted by Thu Thi's cries, when she left Tuyen unfinished to crawl back to the bed with their little daughter, then crawl back again to her husband, Tiep felt that she had mastered her new life. The important thing, she told herself, was that every night she had the sensation of a new and free world dissolving within her. The existence of peace soaked into every cell and every pore of her being.

Vinh Chuyen began to take shape within her too. Tuyen said comfortingly, "The country is in the first stages of liberation. Our office will probably move up to Dinh Bao—that's the main city and this is just a town. We've got the whole world ahead of us now, just give me time to soldier on a little more and get a house allotted to us, and we can have more children."

Tiep found her husband's use of the words "soldier on" to be ironic. Hadn't she been soldiering on all this time, managing to keep one foot in her unit even with a small child under her arm? Three years of living at home, barely keeping her head above water between working the orchard with her mother and sisters and simultaneously taking on teaching jobs and playing gofer for the village guerrillas in order to maintain her party membership... Tuyen had no such challenges and even fewer enemies. Yet here he was telling her to wait even though they both knew a cadre couple was allowed to have up to two children. What was he waiting for, and how long would it take to get there?

Nonetheless she admitted that her husband had a point, if only because he didn't seem to like children. Given that, she wanted to have a little more time enjoying the relaxed atmosphere of peacetime before taking on another child.

"I have an aunt who practices medicine in Hoc Mon, in the Ba Diem district," Tuyen told her. "I've never met her personally but I've heard that she and my mother look just like two peas in a pod. Why don't you go up there and try talking to her, see how it goes?"

"You want me to go alone?"

"You can ask directions if you get lost, and anyway you're no stranger to Saigon. Hoc Mon is only a little way past Saigon. Nothing to it!"

"But if you've never even met her, who am I to...?"

Silence.

"Something important like this, how can you let me go by myself? It's a long way, I've never been there, and, what's more, your aunt is a total stranger to me!"

"Look, we're in the final stages of the takeover. I'm up to my ears in work, and anyway someone needs to stay here to look after Thu Thi. If we send her to your family they'll find out. And if Aunt Rang and Hoai get involved we might as well forget about it!"

So that was it. Tuyen had unilaterally planned for every contingency. He wanted the abortion to be done in secret and far away, in order to avoid the inevitable shocked question that would come from their family and co-workers: how could they bear to destroy this little drop of happiness that symbolized a new phase in their lives, in the life of the entire country?

Back then, the bus line that ran the Dinh Bao–Xa Cang route still maintained the lively air of a private enterprise full of hope as it entered the new era: clean coaches, skilled drivers, and smooth roads. Tiep had ridden this route many times in Aunt Rang's lap on trading trips that doubled as visits to bring care packages to her father before he was exiled to solitary confinement in a Con Dao cell and became a war martyr. It was true that she had never set foot on the far side of Saigon, but she was only twenty-three that year and overflowing with vigor and drive in everything she did and imagined and desired. She had complained to Tuyen about the distance because she did not think it right that she should go through this experience alone, but in fact she was not daunted in the least at the thought of traveling even farther than Ba Diem.

When she arrived at the eastern edge of Saigon, she was delighted to see scores of horse-drawn wagons, just as she had read about in the writing of Son Nam, Phi Van, and other authors. The entire area of Ba Diem felt familiar to her from reading about the execution of war martyr Nguyen Thi Minh Khai and watching over and over the televised play "The People On The Outskirts"– she remembered that it had been Tra On, an actress who was popular back when her grandfather was still alive, who had played the leading role. She flagged down a wagon and between the reed mat spread over the plywood floor of the cart and the clip-clop of the horses' hooves mixed with the fragrance of betel flowers, she decided that this was one of the most memorable trips of her life. Tuyen had always been reluctant to acknowledge this romantic streak in her. He felt it distracted her from the Master Plan he had laid out for them: from team deputy strive for team leader, then from office deputy strive for office chief, then take turns attending the National Academy of Politics, and then there would be an appointment to Assistant Director of a company or a department, and then onward and upward and so on and so forth...

Tuyen's aunt did look identical to his mother; it turned out they were twins, with the same high cheekbones and straight nose. His aunt also had the fair skin and plump figure of a woman who has never wanted for anything. Now the tables had been turned, and they—a wealthy city family running a private clinic—were suddenly being sought out by their guerrilla niece-in-law from the victorious side. They welcomed her with a mixture of hospitality and curiosity.

"I'd always heard the Viet Cong were decent folk. Do you mean to tell me the Viet Cong get abortions too?" she asked with sincere astonishment. "Sorry, dear, it's just that I'm used to thinking of anyone south of Saigon as a Viet Cong. But you only have one child—she's three, is she?—well, if she's three then it's just the right time to have another. Like your auntie here—and no doubt your mother-in-law too—I popped out one kid a year. That's natural family planning, just keep on giving birth and don't stop until the eggs run out. Well, you've gone through all the trouble to come here, so I'll give you a special kind of shot. If the fetus is weak it'll cause a miscarriage, but if the fetus is healthy it'll strengthen it. Okay?"

Tiep didn't know much about medicine, but she understood that she was being let down gently, even chided. How could any single medicine possibly have two such opposite effects?

Shortly after her return, she and Tuyen moved to Dinh Bao, the provincial capital, as part of the campaign to "change the skies and earth, rearrange the mountains and rivers."[1] Tuyen went to work for the provincial Committee of Propaganda and Training, and Tiep drifted into the Information Group

1. A campaign to take control of natural resources such as water and soil (changing the skies and the earth) as well as to redraw the administrative boundaries of the various provinces (rearranging the mountains and rivers).

of the Bureau of Information and Culture. Truong and Nghia also relocated to Dinh Bao under the title of "core cadre" thanks to their status as children of a glorious war martyr of the cells of Con Dao.

On the day Vinh Chuyen was born, Tiep took a shower and washed her hair as soon as she felt the pains start. She thought of the steep staircase leading down from the top floors of her Bureau, where small-fry cadres such as themselves had set up temporary homes while waiting for a call from the Bureau of Housing, and suddenly had an overwhelming longing for her mother and Hoai to be with her as they were for Thu Thi's birth. She knew that to a man who loved to "soldier on" as dearly as Tuyen did, wives and children were merely a distraction.

A woman in Tiep's office rustled up a driver and car to rush her to the provincial hospital. The same woman commandeered Tuyen's position at Tiep's side, saying, "That chump has the look of a real waffler. Let him stay at home and he can come to the hospital later!" It was still early, a translucent autumn morning, and the provincial hospital still retained the orderly appearance of the era before the invasion of the harsh northern accent, with nurses in white skirts, high-heeled shoes, and neat, fragrant little caps. There was no one besides Tiep in the waiting room, and after her co-worker left to "get Thu Thi ready so that wishy-washy jackass can come see you," Tiep was left standing alone beside a bag of clothes and a hospital-issue thermos. Alone, meaning she was heading out to sea with no life jacket or sail, and if she should exhaust her strength there would be nothing to do but put down the oars and resign herself to her fate.

The day she'd gone into labor with Thu Thi had also been a cool autumn day. Her mother had been beside her then, fanning her with a sheath of areca bark while noisily beseeching her grandparents and a host of other assorted ancestors to bring her girl and the baby through safe and sound. Hoai had been off at the market buying everything

Tiep needed with the meager money she earned selling rice and with which she supported the family, albeit barely, while they waited out the hard days of the evacuation. She had been surrounded by love.

Vinh Chuyen's day, on the other hand, came during peacetime, which meant that everyone was occupied: her mother was busy; Aunt Rang was busy with her orchard now thickly pocked with bomb craters; Hoai was busy with the disabled leg of her son Hon; even Little My was busy with her new and bitter status as a young widow. Tuyen was the only one who had no excuse to have gone AWOL.

In the end, she was all alone when the pain hit her from behind and the iron bars of the bed in the waiting room seemed to melt in her hands. She felt the child inside her twist and thrash desperately in its struggle to get out, to hurry up and become a person. Tiep felt as though every hair on her body was standing on end and every cell was turning into a blister. Her mother and Hoai called this stage of labor "moving the stomach", and indeed her stomach was moving now, and she was in an empty room, and Tuyen wasn't there, just as he'd never been there for her. Her water burst like a dam breaking. She curled up clutching her stomach and yelled for help. Nurses poured into the room from somewhere and hustled her into the birthing room. When she heard the baby's cry, Tiep knew that he would be a discriminating but weak child. Her name was written on the baby's thigh in Chinese ink for identification, and she was taken to a separate room. Such were the fastidious and luxurious procedures of that time.

It wasn't until after eleven o'clock in the morning, precisely the time of his office's lunch break, that Tuyen slunk in with Thu Thi tagging along behind. Much later, Thu Thi would tell Tiep that she remembered that day as though it were inked on her memory: there were these winding wooden stairways in the building. Daddy was looking for your room. He didn't know where he was going, and I was afraid of the strangers, afraid of the blood, afraid of everything, but Daddy didn't pick me up. I was just three and Daddy didn't carry me to relieve my fear or my tired legs. I saw you before he did, I saw you lying as still as a statue on the white bed, and I was so afraid something had happened to you. I didn't see my little brother and thought something had happened to him too...

As for Tiep, she would forever remember the towering French windows and faded whitewashed walls of the hospital, simply because she had stared at them for what felt like an eternity while waiting for someone to come. Her mother, or Aunt Rang, or Hoai, or Nghia; she yearned for someone to take care of her. If Tuyen was on the list at all, he was somewhere near the bottom. But he did appear finally, reluctant and unhurried, like a clump of water hyacinth that could only move with the tide, a wide, round face with two tiny ears. If in the days of old Russia Anna had suddenly noticed that Karenin had overlarge ears, Tiep now saw that her husband's ears were as small as those of a mouse. According to physiognomy, small ears predict a difficult career path even if the person is willing to sacrifice their most important and intimate relationships to succeed. It was a very real possibility that Tuyen would do exactly that, Tiep decided, given his smooth, vapid, and sycophantic personality.

"A boy. Name's Vinh Chuyen. Nine o'clock in the morning, remember that. You have to remember it to get the birth certificate right this time. Not like Thu Thi's birth certificate, where you gave the wrong birthdate just because we had to wait until after 1975 to get an official birth certificate. The birthdate of your firstborn child and you couldn't remember it. Honestly I don't understand you at all!"

Tiep kept her conversation with her husband to the bare minimum, all delivered from behind an arm thrown across her forehead so as to avoid seeing his face.

"I went to work this morning to get everything in order so that I could get permission to take the rest of the day off. Who knew you'd have the baby so quickly?" Tuyen's voice was barely audible.

Tiep wanted to throw up her arms in a gesture of disgust. Once again it was work and struggle, it was status and the Academy, it was those damn classes teaching The New Lifestyle and the New Man. She wanted to break things. She wanted a war. Right here, right now. But Thu Thi's breath was caressing her. The child was kneeling on the bed and leaning over her to peer into her mother's face. Her anxious posture, so full of unfortunate premonitions in a child a mere three years old, forced Tiep to calm down. I'll try to control myself, she thought. I won't let myself get sick postpartum. I have to be strong and clever in order to raise my children. I'll be as fearless and aggressive as Aunt Rang and will be as admired and respected as she is. I'll write down everything and become a writer like Uncle Tu Tho said I would. If only he hadn't died my life would be different. I know he's up there and he'll help me follow the path that we both hoped for...

8

Spring, 1982

Tiep's boss the Poet was an erratic person, as all poets are. Had he not been stuck with the position of Chairman of the local Writers' Union, he would no doubt be one of those charismatic and complicated men who wear their hearts on their sleeves.

"How's your health these days, Tiep?"

It was an ordinary day at the office. The coffee table was littered with the usual assortment of cigarette butts and soggy tea leaves that were a standard fixture in the reception rooms of the writers' unions. Boss Poet invited Tiep to sit down for a chat. Tiep settled all the way back in the rattan chair and tried to mold her face into a smile.

"Well, you're a bureaucrat, go ahead and do your own review!"

Boss Poet smiled too. But his face was pensive and betrayed a secret emotion that Tiep guessed had less to do with sympathy for her and more to do with his own inner world.

"How are things between you and Tuyen then? Patchable or permanently torn?"

Tiep looked out the window, focusing on the swaying of the orange bougainvillea that covered the old villa.

"What happened in Diep Vang that day went beyond the limits of what I can stand. As for Tuyen, if his heart is torn at all, each one of those fresh bloody pieces is reserved exclusively for the Committee and Hai Kham!"

Boss Poet leaned toward her with an expression of conspiratorial sympathy. "Well, you know yourself best, Tiep."

Images from that autumn afternoon flashed through her mind. The fat drops of rain slicing diagonally across the bus station littered with sticky-rice cake wrappers and flies. The strange man's long back and pungent odor of tobacco. The brittle, bone-dry voice of her elderly benefactress. And finally, Hoai's anxious face when she came to her at the hospital. Thu Thi had been more quick-witted than Tiep could have imagined that day. Rather than grabbing a three-wheeled taxi to rush off to the address Tiep had given her, she had pulled Auntie out to run the length of the market grounds and had found Hoai absorbed in fiddling with her rain-soaked outboard motor. Hoai came at a dead run and, when Tiep was brought out of the emergency room, was there to bend over her with that congenital expression of gloom mixed with regret and calculation; perhaps she guessed that the loss of a pregnancy meant her little sister's chances for marital reconciliation were equally lost. After getting Tiep settled in the recovery room, Hoai and Thu Thi wasted no time in finding a hospital phone to borrow for a call to the city. Back then they had no phone in their home—only after several more years of concerted "soldiering on" would Tuyen make it to such a privileged level—and so they had to get in touch with him through his office. It wasn't until the next morning that Tuyen finally responded with a message: "In three days, I'll come get you and the kids in the office car. Don't worry, I asked the opinion of a doctor at the Health Department of the Party Provincial Committee. As long as it's treated in time, hemorrhage due to a miscarriage is no problem at all!"

Boss Poet changed the subject. "What was that short story you just got published in Hanoi?"

Tiep gazed straight into the fair-skinned, likeable face of her boss and returned question for question. "Don't tell me you are so busy these days you don't have the time to read your favorite girl's stories?"

His face assumed the smile that was expected of him, but his body swayed and his eyes protruded slightly as though puffing up with the intensity of his unfocused, weary gaze. He was a man of prodigious energy, more than he could spend on poetry alone, and so was constantly stirring up work for himself elsewhere; publishing a newspaper, organizing writers' retreats and conferences, sending his writers off on fact-finding trips to inspire their work, and—this was his most difficult duty—contriving schemes to relieve the Writers' Union of having to crawl and beg for its budget. Through his connections with some our-comrades-from-the-trenches officials in Transportation, he had been able to acquire an old ferry and—thanks to a government loan also finagled from various acquaintances—had transformed it into a floating restaurant as a joint venture with the state-owned Tourism Company, thereby securing a well-stocked but thoroughly unofficial kitty for the Writers' Union. The first project he financed with his business proceeds was to publish a book of poetry by Hai Kham and a few other powerful provincial officials. If his life were made into a tragic play, thought Tiep, no doubt one of the acts would be titled "Hai Kham," and in it we would see Boss Poet, eyes squeezed tightly shut, lauding poems about flowing water and toilets for no other reason than that their authors could protect his secret venture with the Tourism Company and held the power of life and death over the newspaper that Boss Poet considered essential to the future development of the arts and literature in the province. A man of great confidence in his own abilities, Boss Poet had tiny pale fists that he liked to pound on tables like an overly dramatic actor doing Napoleon, but Tiep often imagined she heard the cold clank of chains when he passed; on one side, the criticisms he endured from his fellow writers, on the other, the imperiousness of the people to whom he had to shamelessly pander. More than once, Tiep had come upon her boss sitting alone, dispirited, eyes glistening with tears that she knew weren't part of the act. That was why, in spite of the local censure he was prone to, Tiep never wavered in her sympathy and support of her boss. Even so, she was always aware of the need to maintain a decorous distance.

Boss Poet quickly reeled in his weariness and made his voice as official as possible.

"Well, your story was well received up there in the North. I've gotten several calls asking about the author. So have you guessed yet why I asked you in for a chat this morning? In order to commend you, to encourage you, to remind you to keep building up your body of work. And to travel. You need to get back to traveling. You're a firebrand. Don't trap yourself in an organized junket, make it just yourself and the whole wide country before you. Go back to your roots. It'll help you take your mind off things."

Go she would. But not because Boss Poet was patting her on the back and encouraging her. It was the response from Hanoi. Like a rainstorm on a patch of barren ground, she suddenly felt that she wanted nothing more than to be curled up under a hedge of bamboo or the corner of a field somewhere with a pad of paper in her lap.

Ever since she had sent off that story, Tiep had been

pottering around the house like a victim of dementia. The story told of a particularly difficult moment in the life of a tiny and long-suffering woman, and how a chance encounter with a man had given her a taste of unexpected emotion that went beyond normal fellow-feeling, and how this bittersweet brush with a heartfelt connection had suddenly made her life a little less hopeless and given her the peace of mind to go on. She'd had a hunch that it would be published quickly and had been waiting anxiously as though expecting some auspicious sign, some as-yet-unknowable reply. She still read and wrote halfheartedly while waiting, but felt as though she were squeezing the words out of herself like juice out of a sugarcane, only to see them coagulate in the stifling atmosphere of her house. In the middle of the night, after her rendezvous with the ice in their freezer—she no longer had to crawl over Tuyen when she got up—she would turn on the light in the kitchen, place the pad of yellowish recycled onionskin paper on the table, and sit there, her mind dense and smoldering like a chunk of long-lasting peat from U Minh forest. Eventually Tuyen would get up from the cot in the outer room and she'd hear the metallic crash of the aluminum door to the bathroom followed by the gurgle of his urine, and her head would spin as though he had punched her.

They were usually able to avoid each other at lunchtime; Tuyen would find someplace else to eat, either in the communal kitchen at his office or at some committee conference. So Tiep waited until dinner. She kept her silence in order to maintain mealtime harmony while the children were eating. When everyone stood to clear the dishes, she spoke up.

"Tomorrow I'm going to Dong Dung on a fact-finding trip for a few days. You'll have to come home at lunchtime to take care of the children's lunch and see to the pigs."

Tuyen was squatting on his chair. He was wearing nothing but boxer shorts and his pasty white knees reached up almost to his chin. He gave a snort.

"You're going off to philander, not some damn fact-finding trip!"

Reflexively, Tiep roared back, "I forbid you to insult my work!"

"If you're not philandering then why is it one chump after another?" Tuyen continued bitterly.

"And exactly who would these 'chumps' be?"

"That poet boss of yours, for starters, then that journalist who turned heel and ran. And pretty soon you'll be flashing around another one no doubt!"

Tiep suddenly remembered the day she learned she had been assigned to the "core cadre" track, and how she had gone crying to the director of the Committee of Culture and Information, begging to be transferred. The director had telephoned Tuyen to discuss it, and that night Tuyen gave her the third degree, "What was with the crocodile tears when you asked to be transferred to the Writers' Union? People will think you and that poet are an item, and that's why you want to be transferred so badly!" He acted as though his wife's transfer to the Writer's Union was tantamount to her flying the coop. He must have continued nurturing this suspicion because, shortly after the scandal erupted around the journalist, Tiep came across her husband's '67 Honda parked at the foot of the staircase leading up to the Writers' Union. A short while later, she saw Tuyen step out of Boss Poet's office.

Now, she made a gesture of futility. "If you didn't believe him, what was the point of asking him for help?"

Tuyen stammered, at a loss for words, then fell silent.

"So deep down you think I'm just a loose woman sleeping around for kicks. Well, I know my own conscience, and that's all I need. You've never understood me anyway!"

Tuyen was on the verge of exploding. "I of all people don't understand you? I know you down to every last pubic hair, you think I don't know your character? God, you think you have a conscience now?"

Tiep glanced over and saw Thu Thi watching. She was

eight years old now, able to grasp some of what her father was saying, and soon she would be disgusted by both of them. Tiep stood as though mortally wounded in battle, suddenly realizing that this war was far more destructive than the war that had robbed her and Tuyen of their youth.

In a drained voice, she said, "If you continue on with that kind of vulgar language in front of the children, I swear I will take them and leave this house immediately!"

Tuyen stood to leave the table, deliberately turning his back on his wife before he spoke. "It only makes sense that you should leave. This house was issued to me, after all. A cadre of your rank doesn't rate a thing!"

Tiep gave up. She had lost, utterly. Once a man had started working out the details like that, there was nothing left but calculation and hate. Tuyen had transformed his position from subordinate to master, and now, like all the other high-handed young Turks around her, he had the whole world ahead of him.

She thought of the first two years of Vinh Chuyen's life, two long years of navigating the dizzyingly steep staircase from their tiny studio that doubled as an office down to the Committee's public faucets. She remembered the relief they had felt when the Bureau of Housing finally called them up to assign them their house. It was the first in a row of houses that lay one row removed from the river, and although its entrance was through a cramped alleyway, it was better than nothing. When they took possession, Tiep had made her way down the long narrow length of the house, soberly taking in the cheap cheesecloth mosquito netting left higgledy-piggledy on the bed in the kitchen—no doubt the former owners had been drawn into the border-hopping fever for economic rather than political reasons—and taking time to indulge her tendency for commiseration that Tuyen so often derided. Suddenly there was a loud crash of something breaking from the upper story. It turned out Tuyen had swept the large ceramic incense-burner off the family altar, and had even toppled the picture of the Buddha. Naturally the house of the province's future leading cadre could not have a trace of religiosity. But when she saw what he'd done, Tiep blurted out, "Couldn't you be a little gentler? Before removing the altar, we should at least light a stick of incense and pay our respects to the ancestors of this house's owner. And this picture here, you should have set it aside and I'd have taken it home for Aunt Rang or Mom. Once a Buddha has been installed on an altar you can't just take it down without the proper rituals!" Tuyen stared at his wife, taken aback by her words which so reeked of "the opiate of the masses". Then, without a word, he turned and strode down the long hallway to the back courtyard and began enthusiastically expounding about how this would be the ideal spot for a pigpen...

Now, Tuyen had retreated to the upstairs. Thu Thi hugged her mother's legs tightly. "Mommy, let's find another place to live! I'm scared that Daddy will hit you someday. And he's got a gun stored in the wardrobe too!"

Tiep sat down and embraced her daughter, promising her that she would return home as quickly as possible and make arrangements.

It was more than twenty-five miles from the city to the town of Quay Bridge, but Tiep chose to travel by three-wheeled taxi, preferring to knock knees and jounce along with the other passengers than to wait in line and buy a ticket for the bus. The town stretched along either side of the highway, with a market that spilled out of the market grounds and was encroaching up to the foot of the bridge. It was thick with the odor of fish from the fish-raising ponds, writhing clumps of water snakes in wire baskets, and bunches of moorhens, crakes, and rails tied together in squirming bunches and laid out on the pavement to tempt the wealthy occupants of passing cars. Tiep made her way to a ferry pier, a short distance from the Quay Bridge. Years ago, from deep within the recesses of the network of canals and tributaries, a much younger Tiep had longed to catch a glimpse of this very bridge. The bridge was the market, and the day she set foot on the bridge would be the day peace had returned to the country. To her the bridge symbolized opportunities for college and an education, but even more than that it symbolized survival.

The ferry that ran the Quay Bridge–Dong Dung route was a large skiff with a makeshift canopy of stitched urea fertilizer bags stretched over a frame of bent metal bars, and plates that identified it as yet one more joint government enterprise. The April river water was silver and heavy with the scent of water hyacinth crushed by passing boats, intermingled with smoke from the burning of the surrounding fields. Unlike the parched fields and nipa palms of Tiep's home in Diep Vang, this area was crowded and bustling, thanks to the French-built system of canals and irrigation ditches. The scent of water lay over everything, even the people. Tiep bent over to slip past the small, two-person plank benches that were arranged crosswise in the belly of the skiff. She saw her friend Quy, and stopped. Then she sat down on the bench in front of him, even though the space beside him was empty.

"Where are you going all alone, Quy?"

As slender as a girl, Quy cocked his head and looked at her with a smile playing on his lips.

"I could ask you the same."

Tiep struggled to maintain her usual air of self-confidence. They must have reached his ears as well, all those stories about the journalist who jumped ship, and Tiep demanding a divorce from Tuyen, and the unsuccessful pregnancy which revealed that she had tried to reconcile with Tuyen. After all it had been the prevailing scandal in the province's political circles for some time now. Tiep ran her eyes over the interior of the ferry to see if she recognized anyone else on board.

"Let's see, you're off to write an article for the special April Thirtieth commemoration issue, right?"

Quy gazed at her, this friend that she had never thought of as merely a friend. His sensitive eyes were melancholy.

"I've quit journalism. I bought a cheap piece of land in the countryside, and I'm going to be a farmer."

Never before had they sat together so privately and so close. Their knees were almost touching now.

Tiep said evenly, "I knew that a fellow like you would end up farming or in seclusion sooner or later. But I want to hear from your own lips why you decided to quit."

Quy looked at her silently, for a very long time. It was the gaze that a man reserves for a woman whom he has once held in his heart.

"The editors whittled my articles down to nothing. No commentary, no opinion allowed. They're afraid of the whistle in Hai Kham's mouth, or maybe afraid of losing their jobs. Whatever, it seemed that going back to my grandparents' profession of farming would give me more peace of mind."

They both sighed, then, and turned their faces outward to the canal. They were thinking of Uncle Tu Tho, Quy's father and Tiep's extraordinary autumn-spring friendship, the man who had predicted her future career as a writer. He was Tiep's immediate superior, and they had been inseparable during her five years at the guerrilla base. They had shared with each other every mile of the canals they traveled, every clear moon and starry night, and every song and poem broadcast on the Japanese radio, as small as a child's exercise book, that they carefully placed on the floorboards of their rowboat. They had cheated death many times. They were father and daughter, teacher and pupil, best friends, and loving confidants.

While alive, Uncle Tu Tho had always quietly hoped that Tiep and Quy would someday become a couple and fulfill his dreams for them by together sharing the profession he loved. But because of his position as chief of Tiep's unit, Quy had to be assigned elsewhere and ended up managing a mobile library for the Committee. It wasn't until after Seventy-Five that Quy was able to sign up as a journalist, as a posthumous fulfillment of his father's wishes for him. As for the other wish, before his death in an enemy raid, Uncle Tu Tho had learned that Tuyen, the only single man in their entire subunit, had robbed him of his intended daughter-in-law while his son was too far away to prevent it. It's been more than ten years now, thought Tiep. Ever since that day, they had maintained between them a regretful acceptance of their destiny; what was out of reach would forever be out of reach, and what was impossible would forever be impossible. Even so, they each watched and waited for the other in silence, reading each other's works and occasionally exchanging a few minimally necessary words in the hallways of their meetings and seminars.

"If Uncle Tu Tho was still alive to see the mess and degradation of today, what would he think, Quy?" Tiep asked.

Quy smiled softly. "I suppose he'd cheerfully resign himself to catching stinkbugs in my little tangerine grove!"

"So where are you heading to in Dong Dung today?"

"I'm going back to get permission from the local authorities to move my father's grave to our family home, so that it's easier for me to take care of him."

Another long, mournful silence ensued. If only I could turn my face to the sky and let out a howl, Tiep thought, how good it would feel right now! She had been ten years old when her own father had died in the cells of Con Dao. Her mother had cried, and Aunt Rang had cried, and Hoai had cried, and she had imitated them but in fact had no personal memory of her father because he had left the family for the itinerant life of a guerrilla before her birth. When she joined the guerrillas at fourteen she realized that if Aunt Rang could play the role of "husband" to her mother back at home, then Uncle Tu Tho could be her spiritual father in the true sense of the word. He sheltered her under a dome built of patriotic idealism and predictions for her future and the future of their nation that she believed with all her heart. She was nineteen years old when he died and orphaned her a second time. At the time she had felt that she would never find her way toward the goal of becoming a writer that he had predicted for her. The loss of two fathers in one lifetime left her utterly dispirited.

Several days after Uncle Tu Tho's death, his wife, a woman he loved passionately, found her way from the union office where she worked to Tiep's door. She informed Tiep that her husband had wished to take with him into death the daily letters he had written her, in order to avoid any outsider finding them and tracing them back to their relationship. Although he was a man of integrity, he did have enemies and could not allow his image to be twisted once he was no longer around to defend himself. It was a reasonable request, but Tiep still cried as she gathered up his belongings: the black peasant's pajamas he had asked her to hang out to dry for him before he left for the meeting where he had died; the nylon hammock he liked to leave at the hut at the base; the tiny lamp fashioned out of a bottle for reading and working under the mosquito net at night; and the letters that read like essays which he had written to her whenever he was far away, letters which always started with the words "My darling child" in the careful, calligraphic script of a Western-educated scholar. She sacrificed them to the deadly undertow of public opinion, to the barefoot masses who had never heard that this world can have relationships like Jean Valjean and his Cosette, and to Uncle Tu Tho's wife feared as all women did the scourge of public rumor. The woman invited Tiep to accompany her to burn the letters and send them off to Uncle Tu Tho, but Tiep had refused. She did not feel stoic enough to be able to bear those indifferent flames.

Tiep steered the conversation back to Uncle Tu Tho's grave. "You're going to bring Uncle Tu Tho home on April 30th? I'd like to be there. Let me know so that I can be there, okay?"

Their hands brushed, then Quy wordlessly and gently took her hand in his. There was so much that they could not say at this moment: not only their feelings for a good man who had returned to the earth and taken his goodness away from them forever, or their feelings for their husbands and wives, writings and newspapers, but also much bigger and more important emotions. It was as though their mutual feeling of being orphaned on a long road had brought them together on this boat trip today.

Tiep suddenly picked up her things. "Well. You go ahead and take the Quay Bridge Canal route. I've decided to take the land route to Can Canal and then head over to Dong Dung from there. I'd prefer to spend some time around the Can Canal area; it holds more memories for me."

Quy neither questioned her nor asked her to stay. Not only did he have Uncle Tu Tho's feminine face, he had also inherited his father's penchant for delicate and well-timed silence.

9

Dinh came back into her life a few hours later. From the town of Quay Bridge, Tiep took a three-wheeled taxi back to the Cay Gon intersection. There she got off and caught a transport—an old cargo truck fitted with benches in the hauling bed that bounced so hard the passengers had to hang on to the metal frame for dear life—to Can Canal. This was the same provincial highway that connected the city with Tiep's home district, and Can Canal was an unincorporated clump of population that lay right in the middle. When they joined up with the guerrillas in Dong Dung, Tiep and Nghia had made a life-and-death nighttime dash across this highway, assisted by some scouts for whom life and death was as familiar as their daily bowl of rice. Later on, when the war effort in the southwest was teetering on the brink of disaster, Can Canal was the gate through which the female cadres retreated in the face of the enemy's encroaching "pacification."

It was around noon when Tiep hopped off the truck. The highway stretched lazily across sunken rural fields. There were no sidewalks; people walked in the road, impervious to the honks of the traffic. The shops on either side were filled to the brim with fishing nets and conical-shaped varnished leaf hats. There were more hat-sellers than Tiep had seen in any other rural town; the entire street glittered in the sun.

The market was almost over for the day. Tiep walked over to the area reserved for the local peasants to sell their wares. All that was left was garbage and a few people squatting on the ground with baskets of wilted greens and dead crabs, some strings of sticky-rice cakes wrapped in coconut leaves and covered with flies, and mung-bean cakes leaking sugary juice into the April sunshine. Tiep didn't know what she was looking for here, but what she found was the muddy, crabby smell of the women who had once risked police arrest and enemy outposts to escort her and many other female cadres between regions. As Boss Poet liked to say, when traveling like this, one mined the mother lode that existed within oneself.

Tiep took a small boat up to the mouth of the Cay Gao Canal. After it dropped her off, it turned right to disappear into the depths of the canals where, on clear days so many years ago, she would stand up in the middle of her rowboat and crane her neck to see Quay Bridge in the distance. There used to be a small dam across the mouth of this canal, built by the local militias and guerrillas to retain fish and water for the supporters of the revolution in Dong Dung. She and Uncle Tu Tho had spent many nights laboriously dragging their boat over the dam in perfect unspoken harmony. Later on, a large garrison was built on the spit at the mouth of the canal to house a battalion of ARVN soldiers, there for the pacification effort, and it became the gateway through which Tiep had to pass, disguised as a peasant, every time she moved between regions. The soldiers bristled with beards and moustaches and trenches and ditches, and were quick to shove their submachine guns into the ribs of the women and girls who passed, but everyone knew they wouldn't dare to actually squeeze the trigger or drag a girl into a trench with them. From behind their snarls of barbed wire they were completely dependent on these women and girls to bring them their daily supply of vegetables and fish as well as delicacies such as snakes and turtles, and in return they generally let the people live in peace.

Now, a makeshift bridge made of bundled lengths of bamboo stretched across the mouth of the canal rather than a dam. There was a small medical clinic with leaf walls and a corrugated aluminum roof, and a few rowboats were tied up at the dock. A group of peasant women were sitting in the shade of a calabura tree and listening to a uniformed nurse give a talk; probably about the joys of family planning, Tiep guessed, judging from the peals of laughter. The spit was thick with dense stands of sugar banana trees surrounded everywhere by the exuberant green of torpedo grass. Dong Dung was a pocket of particularly rich alluvial soil, and the abundant vegetation that in the old days had helped to shelter the revolutionaries was now creating problems for the postwar reconstruction.

Suddenly Tiep heard her name being called from under a woven-leaf canopy strung up nearby that served as an open-air tea shop. It was Quy. He looked as though he had been waiting for her for some time. He rose from the tiny child-sized table, stooped low until he had cleared the canopy, then stepped to the side and motioned for Tiep to see the man he had been sitting with inside the tea shop.

"A few minutes after you got off the ferry, this man named Dinh got on and started asking the owner if she'd seen a youngish woman, small and nimble, hair cut short to here, who was headed to Dong Dung. I couldn't help myself, so I asked, and it turns out he really was looking for you. God, woman, what have you done that a fellow from Hanoi is down here looking for you?"

Quy was fairly bubbling with chummy, unrestrained chatter. It was like he was a different person than the man she'd met that morning.

Tiep's curiosity was unbearable. She stooped to step under the low canopy of the tea shop and almost couldn't believe her eyes. Eight months had passed since that stormy afternoon in Diep Vang, and the man's hair had grown out to once again cover the nape of his neck. He held the same yellowing, broken-locked fake-leather bag, although it was now even worse for the wear; his cream-colored shirt had faded to the color of pig-intestine porridge; his straight-legged trousers sported a rip in one knee; his bamboo water-pipe was flaking; and his cheeks had sunk in, giving him an ascetic appearance. The man named Dinh remained seated at the tiny table, his elbows resting on his knees, gazing at her with silent mischief as though drinking in every last drop of the stunned expression on the face of this woman he'd thought he'd lost. Tiep plopped down in the chair vacated by Quy, feeling thrilled and flustered at the same time.

"I never imagined...I couldn't have imagined we'd meet up again. Much less in a backwater like this!"

The man's square fingers didn't move from their resting place under his nose, but he couldn't hide the delight in his eyes.

"Well, young lady, are you impressed with my tracking skills? Just like Heaven itself was showing me the way!"

Tiep didn't dare look into those magnetic brown eyes for long. She turned away to look out at the spit and saw Quy standing on the bank, slump-shouldered, preparing to step down into a waiting sampan. Tiep excused herself and ran out to him. By the time she got there, Quy was standing on the nose of the sampan. He was back to his normal reserved self.

"I've hitched a ride to Kinh Dung. Be careful, Tiep. Don't make another mistake, okay?"

If there were an award for the world's plainest and

most heart-rending farewell, this would be it, thought Tiep. Reluctantly, anxiously, she turned back to the man in the tea shop whom she could no longer think of as a stranger.

The tea shop owner, a tall, lanky woman with a perpetual stoop from her life of exile under the low-leafed canopy, brought them two green coconuts with two muddy yellow straws made of recycled plastic. Under the striped scarf wrapped turban-like around her head, her curious, childlike eyes never wavered from these two customers who were so foreign to her reedy little spit.

The man began to speak, apprehensively now.

"I found you through your most recent short story. I called your Writers' Union and spoke to the chairman. Turns out he's the poet that I wrote a congratulatory letter to a long time ago, when several of his poems were broadcast over the radio on the "Works from the Front Lines of the Fatherland" segment. After unification, the fellow passed through Hanoi on his way to the Soviet Union and I heard he'd looked for me but we missed each other. Like we were playing tag. I don't know why, but after that, um, hair-raising experience last year when I was here, I wanted to do another trip down here, spend more time. You don't owe me anything, Tiep, it's not like you wrote in your story. It's I who owe you. It was despicable for me to leave you and your children in that situation that day. I was so angry about the injustice of what happened to my hair. My life hasn't been a walk in the park but never have I been so egregiously insulted as that day, never. But afterwards when my anger wore off I realized that my behavior was bad—no, it was atrocious. How could I have abandoned you all alone there with two children and a mountain of stuff like that? It's unforgivable!"

The man's long, garrulous confession piqued Tiep's curiosity even more. She gave a small smile. Inside her, a flame had been lit and she knew the glow enhanced her attractiveness.

"You haven't told me your name yet," she said.

Now that the atmosphere had been established as friendly, even tantalizing, the man gestured to Tiep to drink her coconut juice.

"I'm Dinh, Nguyen Viet Dinh. I've been a writer since you were a girl in primary school, I'd guess. After spending a night at the Writers' Union and several hours with your friend Quy on the ferry, I know more about you than you'd think!"

Tiep tried to look stern but couldn't help the fact that her heart was thumping wildly. Dinh went on.

"I signed a contract with a publisher in the north to do a collection of essays about the deepest and more remote regions of the southwest. I told your friend Quy that I was looking for you to ask you to contribute. Say, isn't he the son of the Uncle Tu something-or-other whom you wrote about in one of your short stories?"

Tiep was silent, truly on her guard now in the face of his overfriendly questioning that left her so little wiggle room. She understood only too well that he had not tracked her down just to ask her to contribute to some collection.

"Enough, let's dispense with the formalities. If I agree to contribute, what is your plan?"

First, it was his hand strategically positioned in the middle of the table where Tiep could easily take it in hers should she choose. Then a gleeful glance when the proprietress left to run out to the bridge on an errand. Then a toppled coconut, its clear juice gurgling out onto the dirt floor, and suddenly Dinh had stepped around to her side of the table and was hugging her, his entire body bursting with pent-up emotion.

"I've found you at last. I couldn't even eat or sleep properly until I'd found you!"

Tiep went rigid. His familiarity frightened more than pleased her. A well of emotion was rising inside her that made her want to cry.

"I'm fine, everything turned out okay!" she protested.

It seemed that something in her was colluding with him against her will. She felt as though her entire body was being filled with energy, a warm agitation that animated her and made her want to take action. Dinh turned her around, both hands planted on her shoulders, and said, "How are the children? I still remember your daughter like it was yesterday, she looked just like a cute little copy of you." Then without waiting for an answer, he released her to pay for their drinks, blithely bent down to finish off her coconut juice, and then just as blithely threw an arm around her shoulders and set off briskly towards the spit. Tiep didn't pull away; she felt light-headed, as though she were being led toward some strange, exciting place. There was an equally strange feeling flaring up in her that she had no name for.

"Where are we going?" she asked, and suddenly wanted to burst into laughter because she remembered Tuyen's words, "You're going off to philander; pretty soon you'll be flashing around another one, no doubt!"

Dinh planted his fists on his hips and squinted out at the canal. The water glared yellow in the noon sun, broken up only by the deep green and purple of the patches of water hyacinth that floated down from the direction of Quay Bridge.

"We'll wander wherever we want. We'll be completely carefree!"

"And where will we sleep? Where will we eat?" Tiep tried to imagine herself setting off like a devil-may-care adventuress.

"Well, where are those boats going? The ones carrying palm fronds and sugarcane?"

"Where can't they go, you mean!"

Dinh could barely contain himself. He looked more like an impetuous youth than a middle-aged man. "So we'll flag them down and hitch a ride! We'll float up the canal and down the canal, straightwise and crosswise, whatever! It's all fact-gathering, right?"

Tiep decided she needed to take matters in hand. She flagged down a ferry that was making its afternoon run out of Quay Bridge.

"Okay, you follow me. I'll be your guide. I'll take you to

where I started out as a guerrilla and we'll finish up at the graveyard where Uncle Tu Tho, Quy's father, is buried."

In high spirits, they found a spot with several empty benches in the middle of the ferry. It was the second run, well past noon, and the few passengers aboard looked more interested in sleep than anything else. The ferry moved at a sweet clip along with the current; this canal was a backbone of the waterway system and was less plagued by water hyacinth than the branches Tiep had traveled in the morning. The wild coriander, water pepper, and floating primrose had been cleared away on both sides of the canal, leaving a wide expanse of water almost three times the size she remembered from the old days. Dinh's eager, youthful manner, along with the trees, the cozy houses, the miles of canal as they slipped past one intersection after another through Dong Dung's intricate web of waterways—it all made Tiep feel as though she were a young girl again, in a dream, leading a strange youth backwards through time, through her personal past and the country's history, in search of something forgotten and left behind so long ago. She told stories. She told Dinh about the peasant family who had agreed to take her in when she had joined up. Back then her unit was still living amongst the people, and at fourteen years old Tiep found herself babysitting and cooking and laundering for a family in exchange for cold, awkward meals. Her longing for her family was nothing compared to her craving for a taste of the purple-ripe sugarcane in their garden, or anything else tasty for that matter. So she and Muoi—an older girl who was on the same team but lived at another house in accordance with the dispersal order—snuck away from their families to buy sticky-rice cakes wrapped in coconut leaves from a family nearby who made cakes for their living. The cakes had no filling but were piping hot and fresh out of the pot. They saved Tiep from her cravings and very likely saved her from the ignoble fate of deserting the cause. She talked and talked, completely lost in her stories, lost in every moment of her life as a guerrilla. Of course she did not leave out Uncle Tu Tho, her sister Nghia, or even Tuyen. When the ferry's engine suddenly died and it drifted to a nearby dock, Tiep realized that they were at the end of the line, much farther than she had intended to go.

"S'okay, no problem!" Dinh assured her with great enthusiasm, and took the lead in flagging down a small boat that was carrying sugarcane back up the canal. So it turned out that, without intending to, they were carrying out Dinh's plan of floating up and down, straightwise and crosswise. Tiep felt that her companion had an intense and irresistible power; he made her want to move, to discover, to wander together to the ends of the earth and seas. And she also felt, with painful clarity, that the gap between herself and Tuyen had widened even more, until her husband was all but lost in the distance. Her old berth was gone, and she had no idea what her new berth would look like.

PART TWO: SPOONS WITH HOLES

11

Dinh Bao, Fall 1982

It was still raining. Nothing but wind and drizzle, as though the entire earth were sluggishly sinking into river water the color of sweet milk coffee. Though it was the peak of the rainy season in that far-flung edge of the delta, such thoroughly dismal weather was unusual and could only mean there was a typhoon raging somewhere off to the north. Tiep sensed this without needing to hear it on the news; like all people of the southwest delta, her instinct for the weather was like a gift that she hadn't asked for but could not refuse. She cracked open the door and peered out, trying to gauge how wet she'd get if she went out bareheaded. The round light bulb that served as a streetlight at the head of the alley—though it was barely strong enough to light a toilet—was swinging laboriously. The public address speaker attached to the electric pole was choking and sputtering as though inhaling water. Along the small river in front, the eucalyptus trees were keeling over, struggling to right themselves and failing. And in the gloom of the far bank, the star apple trees in someone's orchard were swaying in an eerie, passionate ballet.

"You're going out in this rain, Mom?" Thu Thi, nine years old now, was sitting on the small metal bed in the living room. She lifted her face as she spoke and her lips, shaped like the curve of a water chestnut, were edged with strain and concern. Beside her, her six-year-old brother thrust both arms out the window to soak in the rainwater. Water poured down and off his elbows. When his mother and sister were not looking, he scooped up handfuls of water to lick with his tongue, and then turned to smile at them with his broad, easy grin.

Tiep slipped her arms into the raincoat that had been a present from her older sister, Nghia. It was tailor-made and stylishly long, with a thick rubber lining, white daisies dotting the outside, and fuzzy fabric-wrapped buttons. Tiep had loved it from the day her sister presented it to her, not only because it represented the special care that Nghia lavished on her but also because it was made of sturdy fabric and so would survive that era when even a trifle like a spool of thread couldn't be had until the government distributed it. Tiep had slipped into the coat immediately, then turned with delight in front of the wardrobe mirror in her sister's twenty-square-foot room, squealing, "I'll bet when it comes time to leave this to Thu Thi, it'll still be in good shape."

"There's a piece of paper in your coat pocket—be careful or it'll get all wet, Mom!" Thu Thi spoke again, as though probing why her mother was still determined to go.

Tiep tied the strings of her rain hat, tailor-made in the shape of a lotus flower, and tugged the collar of her raincoat higher. "The important thing is that you watch the house and take care of your brother like a good girl, understand?"

The child's mouth tightened and she nodded. She would lock the windows tightly, padlock the door from the inside and wear the key around her neck. She would turn on the TV and sit fanning her brother to chase away the mosquitoes. She would turn on the light and run down to the kitchen to grab a piece of firewood and swat the snouts of their two pigs when they started thumping against the wall of their pen as was their habit. She was not worried for herself or her brother; she was used to her mother being gone on working trips, or for meetings, or staying out late with friends. But this time she had a premonition that something terrible was happening to her mother, and that it involved her as well. She worried, but knowing her mother's temperament said nothing more; only her face filled with resignation and complicity.

Tiep slowly walked the bicycle out, hesitating a little at the threshold. Actually the storm was a good thing, she told herself by way of encouragement. No one she knew would realize that the woman hurrying by in the raincoat and lotus-shaped hat was The Infamous Mrs. Tiep. It was only fifteen minutes from the house to the provincial post office, so her timing was good. She didn't want to show her face there for long. She heard her daughter bolt the door behind her, heard murmurs of the older sister enticing her little brother with roast potato, roast potato, I'll run down to the kitchen and pull some roast potatoes out of the ashes. Then the sound of their Soviet-brand TV and the Khmer language program that came on before the local news.

The rain forced her to wipe her face as she pedaled. The coconut palm at the rise of the bridge over Cypress River was swaying like a drunkard; this was the place, Dinh told her, where he had stood morning and night for several days in a row to see if she or Thu Thi would miraculously materialize. Main Street, which ran from the foot of the bridge to the provincial administrative center, looked long and watery between the rows of cassia trees that dated back to the French Colonial period. A few cyclos pedaled toward her, their ancient canvas canopies flapping and their drivers so swathed in plastic that only their laboring skeletal legs could be seen. The entire city of Dinh Bao was floating in a thin sheen of rainwater. Still, it had never been swallowed up by the Hau river as the neighboring towns periodically were, and the city had been proud of this advantageous position ever since the Emperor Duc Tong had lost himself in poetry and so lost the country to the French. The first time he'd set eyes on the Hau River, Dinh told her, he'd cried out, "Truly a river deserving of the shed blood of our forebears!" Then he had gone on to compare her to an ear of corn, one of those rich, virtuous, and indescribably sincere ears of corn for which this side of the river was famous...

Tiep pedaled on, lost in her thoughts, feeling the distance between herself and her family stretching out ever larger, and the iron cage that was the Party looming ever more clearly, more convoluted, more preposterous, and more terrifying.

The provincial post office was a large building with a

domed, tiled roof and classic yellow wash. Though it was one of the city's few still-intact French buildings, its new managers had managed to run it down considerably in the short time they'd had it. Tiep locked her bike carefully inside the perimeter wall, ran up the front steps to take off her raincoat, then, deciding her hands should be free, ran out again to drape it over her bike. A few other newly arrived customers were stowing their umbrellas on the verandah with deliberate care, showing off their status as the urban elite by that valued possession, the Japanese umbrella. No doubt they were waiting to claim packages of goods sent to them from places called, in the political circles in which Tiep moved, the "Lands of Butter and Bitterness." Tiep moved past them, past wooden benches that looked as if they belonged in a train station, and granite counters dotted with filthy lumps of glue. She ran her eyes surreptitiously over the waiting room to see if she recognized anyone. She knew that anyone who'd made it to the cadre class generally wouldn't need to come to the post office on such a stormy night, but it never hurt to be careful.

While looking for a suitable place to wait, Tiep happened upon her reflection in a smeared, blotchy wall mirror left over from the previous era. She saw: a short pageboy cut plastered wetly to her head, accentuating the harsh angles of her square face; an undernourished complexion made even paler by her wine-colored blouse; and black, Western-style pants, fashionably flared at the ankles but soaked through with rain, making them sag on her bony hips. Thirty years old and only eighty-four pounds, she thought, there's practically nothing to me. Her husband Tuyen had always wanted her to gain weight. As for Trung Vy, the man she had loved at first sight, he had stared wordlessly at her jutting pelvic bones after stripping her bare like stripping the skin off a frog. And Dinh, Dinh had clasped her to him and whispered, "Back when I was young and foolish, I used to think that the important thing was the gift of beauty, and that a woman's personality could always be changed!" It was enough for her to understand that Dinh's wife had been a beautiful woman, possibly very beautiful, certainly more so than herself.

Tiep's Zaria watch, made in the Workers' Paradise of the Soviet Union, suddenly went on strike from too much rainwater. Like a criminal waiting to be called in to give a confession, Tiep peered up at the ancient pendulum clock mounted on the wall of the post office. Her hand clutched the appointment slip, rolled up tight like a goldenrod-yellow cigarette, and still dry, thanks to the pocket flaps on Nghia's raincoat. The day the envelope had arrived by post, small and square like a pocket, it happened that only she and her friend Hieu Trinh were in the office. It was yet one more stroke of luck that she and Dinh could string together with the others and exclaim, it's because we are true and sincere that the heavens have deigned to help us. The envelope was not sealed like the envelopes that came containing her royalty notices and so had escaped the scrutiny of the cadres in the mail room. Tiep had stood by her desk, her eyes glued to the slip of paper. Were it not for the fact that she had a lover thousands of miles away, she would never even have known that the post office's various services included scheduled long-distance phone calls at the central branch. Her expression of trembling surprise was enough to expose the nature of the paper to Hieu Trinh, who winked, smiled, and said, "Another love affair? Aren't you gun shy yet? Eh?"

A tiny old man advanced slowly to where a black phone sat on the counter. The postmistress, a middle-aged woman with pock-marked skin, frizzy hair that trailed down her shoulders like corn silk, and a nose that seemed oddly squashed onto her face, grudgingly glanced at the small yellow appointment slip.

"Who made this appointment with you?" She spoke with the rapid-fire, grating accent of a northerner.

The old man grimaced. "My kid did. As old as I am, who would be making appointments with me but my kids?"

"You're lucky your children live in Nha Trang. If it was any farther, what with this weather, we wouldn't be able to guarantee a connection, understand?"

"So does that mean the call will go through, comrade?"

"Don't 'comrade' me, it's aggravating! This miserable storm!"

She turned to look at the clock and told him to wait. Finally, the phone gave a long ring; things were looking good for the old man's appointment. Tiep focused her attention in that direction and suddenly realized that the customers had to conduct their long distance calls right in front of the postmistress, as though under surveillance. It seemed that the person on the Nha Trang end of the call was the old man's daughter-in-law, and she was needing money. Tiep thought of the human wave that was leaving the country by boat and could imagine what was happening from the old man's flustered, miserable expression. What an appalling prospect. She too would have to stand shivering in that exact spot to talk with her lover, in the middle of the waiting room, within full view of the postmistress's scrutiny, all the while wearing the guilty face of a condemned criminal! Well, she was done with being afraid, she had made up her mind, and now her only concern was that the weather not play nasty with her and Dinh.

A woman of about Tiep's age stepped into the room, dripping like a rat fresh out of the river. She spoke with a Hue accent. The postmistress looked at her unpleasantly.

"Here's a queer one! Hue, hell! Why do you need to call there in this storm?"

"Please help me, ma'am, this is the private telephone number at my brother's house."

"Oh, a real big shot, is he? If he's so important, why doesn't he call you rather than have you drag yourself out in the rain to come here?"

"Do you think I have a telephone for him to call me? Ma'am, my mother is there, and she's very ill, I just need to know what's going on so I can make arrangements!"

"So why don't you just live there with your mother then? What's the point of moving so far away?"

The woman looked as though she were about to cry. "Ma'am, please help me! Whatever the fee is, I'll pay!"

"Oh, you're a fine one!" The postmistress made a few perfunctory pokes at the buttons of the phone. "I suppose you think that whatever you give me for helping you is going into my pocket?"

"This is really important, ma'am. My brother said he'd find a way to notify us when the time came but I'm afraid I'll be too late. You know that to get from here to Hue we have to go to Saigon and wait in line for several days to get tickets for the train. It takes forever!"

The postmistress glared at her. "Didn't you hear me? If you keep on begging, I'll call in security! Go over to the telegraph office and send a telegram and be done with it. What a nuisance!"

The woman turned away, her lips as pale as death. "Nothing but carpetbaggers coming here and taking the best jobs, and they don't even know how to do the work!"

Tiep eased over to her side. "Why not ask to use the telephone at your office, so you don't have to come here and put up with this?"

"We've already taken leave from our jobs. We were in the middle of packing to go when I got a premonition that something happened. I never imagined that all I'd get would be the stench of shrimp paste in my face!"

Tiep plucked up her courage and worked her way over to face the postmistress, as tense as a criminal without an alibi. Luckily—luck, again!—the woman had pulled an ear of corn from under the counter, that same famous Hau River corn which Dinh liked to praise so fulsomely. The woman glanced at Tiep's appointment slip, turned to look at the clock, and then sighed, her mouth crunching away, "You're the recipient of the call, all you can do is wait. But don't get your hopes up with this weather!"

Tiep stared fixedly at the old black phone with its round white dial, shiny with human sweat. At precisely nine o'clock, the ringer convulsed to life with a strident sound, like the bell signaling an execution. The postmistress hastily swallowed the mouthful she had been chewing.

"Hello, hello... Yes... the customer waiting here is My Tiep, Le Thi My Tiep... Yes, I can hear you clearly, strange how clear it is actually... Where is the customer on your end, say hello... come on say hello, will you... what a nuisance!"

Tiep felt suddenly as though everything around her had been pushed aside, or rather as though she were resurfacing in the middle of an oasis, her body bobbing gently, lethargic, in sweet isolation. Propping her elbows on the counter, she forgot about everything, forgot about nature and its storm, forgot about the iron cage and its gossip, forgot about the postmistress and the kernels crunching between her teeth. Dinh's voice was lonely at first, but then surged, boyish, cheerful, trembling, as though he, too, had finally found escape. He spoke of longing, distance, letters, faith, and God; he spoke of the storm and how he was on a fact-finding trip outside of Hanoi and the pretty little postmistress was patching him through on an emergency microwave line normally reserved for government officials. Then on to how he missed her like crazy, and pleas for her to be patient along with reassurances of the truth of their love. Tiep was utterly unaware of her surroundings now; her body rocked as though Dinh were standing in front of her and, as it always happened, a thread of emotion unraveled from her heels until it reached her heart, where it exploded to spill into her entire body. If it hadn't been for the crumbs of corn clinging to the edges of postmistress's sour lips, she would have no doubt forgotten where and when she was; all was submerged to the desire for these moments to go on and on, forever.

Suddenly the line went dead. Horrified, grieving, impotent, Tiep stared at the receiver for much too long, then replaced it in its cradle and stepped outside. She didn't care what the postmistress was thinking. She knew only that she and Dinh had said what needed to be said, and that she was filled with a sensation of gentle relief and comfort.

12
Fall 1983

Without a word of explanation, much less an apology for the delay, the airline staff finally waved the group of passengers who'd been cooling their heels in the concourse onto the airplane. Dinh often said that the culture of the State monopoly in business had eaten its way into popular culture and destroyed people's sense of shame, and now even children no longer knew to say "sorry" and "thank you". At this rate, he predicted, the Vietnamese people would be reduced to expressing themselves entirely through insolence and curses.

Carrying a cheap, badly-made-in-Saigon satchel and an equally new black purse slung over her shoulder, along with the bag of gifts that An Khuong's mother had asked her to deliver to her daughter in Hanoi, Tiep hurriedly followed the others to scramble aboard the Vietnam Airlines shuttle. An ancient Soviet-made TU-model airplane was idling on the derelict runway of the once-proud Tan Son Nhat airport. Aunt Rang had brought Tiep here on one of their trips to bring oranges to the Saigon market, and had let her stand up in the horse-cart and peek over the fence "to get yourself an eyeful." She'd been ten years old that year. Her first glimpse of the airport coincided with the year Dinh fathered his first child, a firstborn son of a firstborn son upon whom the entire family doted. She'd gotten into the habit of comparing milestones in her own life with Dinh's, to see what he was doing back when he was still a stranger to her, what stage of life he had been passing through, and how completely at odds their ages were. When Dinh married she had been but eight years old; if they'd been neighbors, no doubt the child Tiep would have run, shrieking and laughing and possibly even half-naked, after the newlyweds to try to touch the bride's gown. When Dinh fathered his second child, she hadn't yet left to join the guerrillas or had a menstrual period. And Dinh's third child came along when Tiep hadn't yet lost Uncle Tu Tho and of course hadn't yet known Tuyen and the flooded foxhole under the combretum tree. As for what Dinh had been doing in Seventy-Five, she didn't dare think about it. She had no desire to conjure up images of the lovemaking that he and his wife, like every other couple, had no doubt enjoyed during those first heady days of victory.

The TU breathed out a cloud of cold mist. With just a little more huffing and puffing, it could pass for an old steam-powered train engine.

Boss Poet had never come right out and said he supported Tiep's affair with Dinh, but he often went out of his way to mention her lover or give her the latest news from Hanoi. This time, his expression had been openly sympathetic as he told her, "I'm giving you time off to take a trip up to Hanoi, just for the experience. Waiting to go until the Young Writers' conference is just too long. Go now, and take an airplane; you can experience that too. Your traveling orders only allow you the price of a train ticket, but I'll tell the Union to give you a little extra money from our business kitty. Go on, you'll be killing two birds with one stone. Remember to observe and remember everything, you hear!"

It wasn't only because of their personal relationship, or because he thought her talent equaled his, that Boss Poet made these sorts of arrangements for her. He had a myriad different ways of encouraging each of his charges, in part to redeem himself for his shameless promotion of the poetry of Hai Kham and other members of the Standing Committee.

But, Tiep had to admit, her boss had really put his head on the chopping block when he rescued her from drawn-out warfare with Tuyen by allowing her and the children to move into the Writers' Union offices. "So you both can concentrate on greater things!" he had said.

Dusk was falling outside, and Hanoi appeared below the wings of the airplane like a tiny, humble, electricity-starved mock-up of a real city. The post-harvest-moon Red River was low and lazy, but from the window of the airplane it still exerted that inimitable power of rivers to call up old memories. The old Gia Lam military airport, still functioning as the city's main airport, was ruled by torpedo grass—she just couldn't get away from torpedo grass—and poignantly modest for a capital city. A bus of considerably suspicious hygiene carried the Vietnam Airlines passengers slowly across Long Bien Bridge and past the Archeology Museum, then the Opera House, then down Trang Tien Street, then through a maze of silent and melancholy streets lit only by the dim reddish glow of 120-watt bulbs. A murmur of disappointed whispers arose on the bus as the passengers, most of whom were southern cadres like herself on their first trip to Hanoi, took in the sights. One passenger pointed to a crush of people like a market-day crowd on a stretch of sidewalk littered with ice-cream sticks. An imposing gentleman decked out in military regalia complete with captain's bars stepped out of the crowd and began to walk away. He was sucking rhythmically at the ice cream bars he held in each hand, first this one and then the other, like a clown performing a routine.

The darkness became the lake, however. Tiep disagreed with her fellow passengers on this. To her, the long history surrounding Ho Guom lake shimmered brilliantly through the inky-black water etched with arching tree shadows. Surely this was the true Hanoi, the eternal Hanoi of Dinh's tireless stories, the Hanoi that he had fallen in love with on his first trip here after graduating from the Nghe Tinh Region Four Military High School when he and a friend had taken turns teetering on each other's shoulders to catch a glimpse of Uncle Ho and General Giap at rallies. He had been entranced by the sweet, graceful flutter of ao dai tunics worn by the "most elegant girls in the country." Later, he had made Hanoi his home, sunk his second roots here, together with thirty to forty percent of his compatriots from Nghe Tinh who migrated to Hanoi with their pickled jackfruit and round cakes of peanut candy to escape the harsher living conditions in the central provinces. Naturally boys met girls and fell in love, and then children followed, and then Hanoi, the soul of Vietnamese tradition and character, had gradually devolved into the Hanoi which according to Dinh "has completed to all intents and purposes the process of discombobulation, just as the gentlemen in the Forestry Service have completed for all intents and purposes the process of deforestation!"

Hanoi had been sacred to Tiep even before she met Dinh, a reverence created in her by the countless stories she had heard broadcast over her little Toshiba radio at the guerrilla base. More recently, it had became synonymous with romantic longing as the place that kept her lover. From afar, she had always felt that it held some sort of supernatural power; but now that she had actually stepped into its environs she felt nervous, wondering what it held in store for her. If she and Dinh were to meet again with the same sweetness as the year before, would Hanoi be lenient or capricious, would it hunt them down or give them cover? All she saw around her now were the trees, and they were as grave and secretive as old village elders. She suddenly felt very small and alone, like a small fish that has boldly found its way back to its source waters but now doesn't know what to do.

Did Dinh have a premonition of how close she was? If it weren't for the difficult period of silence they had been going through recently, no doubt he would have been at her side already.

The bus arrived at the station. To Tiep's delight, her friend An Khuong appeared below Tiep's window, her painfully straight hair parted precisely in the middle, her eyes sunken and austere, and her teeth protruding slightly through solemn lips. But her voice was as refined and melodious as ever.

"So what do you think, Tiep, aren't I quite the devoted friend? I left as soon as I got the message to pick you up here and have been cooling my heels ever since afternoon. Your plane took off late, eh?"

Tiep launched herself off the bus into the weightless embrace of her tiny friend, whose head barely reached her shoulders. If it were possible to compress a person into a small bar like a piece of chalk, An Khuong would be such a person. Their friendship had begun with a rather unusual acquaintance; Tiep had been pedaling around looking for a place to buy piglets for her home pigpen and happened to see a piece of plywood with a scrawl advertising the very thing she sought, incongruously propped up against an upholstered easy chair in front of the imposing iron gate of a villa overflowing with bougainvillea and an air of erstwhile abundance. Inside the square courtyard, which had no doubt seen more than its share of lavish cocktail parties, an elegant-looking young girl wearing cotton pajamas was standing surrounded by piglets. Tiep couldn't say which had surprised her more, the family's beautiful piglets or their aristocratic daughter. Their business transaction that day had been swift, but they met again later at a writers' workshop arranged by the resourceful Boss Poet. They'd all but run to each other, laughing, immediate best friends. Though one had grown up barefoot in the country while the other was being chauffeured in the city, one was a guerrilla and the other was the star pupil in the Foreign Languages Department of the University, they sensed in each other a mutual lament for the bitterness of the postwar period. It was easy for them to commiserate with each other.

Under the ascetic light of the streetlamp, they pushed each other away to have a good look.

"You look sadder, Tiep, but it gives you an air of experience.

You must have a lot of admirers!"

"How about you, Khuong? Between studying hard and the harsh weather up here, you'll have wasted away before you can get your degree if you're not careful!"

Khuong grimaced and blinked a few times, quickly. "No kidding. I'm living in the dormitory here. Sometimes it gets so cold we have to scrounge for waste paper to burn just to get some heat. The entire university is a jungle. Every time one of us girls wants to take a shower or use the toilet, I swear twenty of us have to stand guard on either side. It seems like half of our time goes to taking care of eating and, um, sanitary needs. But oh well, I'm halfway through it now. Say, what did my mother send?"

Like a starving person, completely bereft of any trace of villas and bougainvillea and chauffeurs and silks, An Khuong pounced on the bag that Tiep held out to her. She opened it right there on the sidewalk and began to paw through the items.

"Medicines, Chinese sausage, ham, bath soap... oh God, this will be the end of me. Isn't there any toothpaste? After we get home can you remember to give me a little of your toothpaste?"

"What, don't people in Hanoi brush their teeth?" Tiep asked, astonished that things could be so bad. She felt a sudden wash of self-pity that she was too broke to buy anything for her friend. Her salary wasn't enough to live on, and of the subsidy goods that were distributed only the cigarettes could be bartered in the open air markets for a few extra goods. For any other need, she had been relying on Nghia's charity for quite a while. Before leaving, she had unscrewed an old toothpaste tube and squeezed into it a small amount of the cheap, powdery toothpaste from their family tube which had to be left behind for Hieu Trinh and the children to use. She hadn't imagined that An Khuong would need toothpaste even more than medicine, meat, and soap.

"No problem!" said An Khuong with a laugh that was just

a little too loud. "It's okay, I'll gargle with salt water. Good for the teeth. Salt's rationed here too, and we have to hoard every grain. But don't worry about me, Tiep, I have to have this master's degree. Hanoites live for education, you know. They say we southerners have been spoiled by our warm weather and overabundant harvests, so we're better at eating than studying."

Tiep laughed too, to cover her concern. "Well, everyone has a mouth, right? So what if we southerners like to eat, it means we don't have to talk so much. Northerners talk so much they can't get a bite in edgewise!"

An Khuong clapped Tiep on the back, suddenly as jolly as an emcee on a stage. "What about that Dinh of yours, is he an eater or a talker? Here, have a look—over there, in the darkest spot under the shadow of that tree!"

The toothpaste had been a shock, but this second shock turned her world upside down. It was Dinh. How could this be? Was he psychic, or was there really some mysterious, tenacious power bringing them together? Tiep felt herself go limp as though suddenly drained of strength. All her weapons of self-defense—anger, suspicion, interrogation—disappeared at the first glimpse of her loving adversary, leaving her passive and ready to run up the white flag.

She and Dinh had not had any contact for six months. Five months nineteen days, to be precise. A message from Hanoi had made its way to Boss Poet's ears; Dinh had resigned himself to waiting for her in their next life. But their current life was longer than Tiep cared to wait. She'd immediately written a letter to inform him that she had moved out of the house. That she intended to get somewhere, and so she was starting by putting one foot ahead of the other. And that he should forget about her. She was afraid of the lethargy that comes with age, afraid of complications, and, in all honesty, she did not believe that a man could leave a woman when the woman did not agree. Dinh's letter of response was succinct: "I believe in our love. I also believe that if you marry someone else, sooner or later you'll end up committing adultery with yours truly!" He had been silent ever since, a stubborn, proud, and reproachful silence that was quintessentially Dinh. Occasionally Tiep saw glimpses of herself in his newest stories, in prose that was sorrowful, trembling, and yet still extraordinarily romantic, also quintessentially Dinh.

She suffered dizzying bouts of longing for him. They came on at lunchtime, or dinnertime, or nighttime, fits of desire that struck her from above like bolts of electricity. They wrenched and swayed her, and she knew this was the sort of telepathic connection she'd heard people talk about. In spite of this, she hadn't arranged to meet Dinh in Hanoi. She was aware of a gulf between them, a hopeless vacuum that exceeded even separation imposed by war and political boundaries. She had planned to stay with An Khuong, and talk things over with a few of his friends, and only then submit herself to the "historic meeting" that was bound to take place at the last minute.

But now everything would happen according to Dinh's designs; if he wanted her, she knew she would not be able to wriggle free. And while Hanoi was far from her provincial Pharisees who were so eager to throw stones, there was a real risk of knives and scissors and even acid thrown in her face by a jealous wife, Dinh's Hanoi or no. If he was not frightened for her then she would have to be frightened for herself. She was the mother of two small children who needed her to stay alive.

An Khuong's gentle voice took on a businesslike tone. "I'd just gotten your letter when Dinh happened to stop by. As though the heavens themselves had tipped him off. Well, I had to let him see the letter. And then when I came to the bus station today I found him already waiting."

The man whom "the heavens themselves had tipped off," Tiep's man, was standing under the arch of black trees that lined the sidewalks of Ho Guom Lake, his arms folded in front of his chest, sanguine and impudent, enjoying his juvenile game of hide-and-seek. In the end, followed by An Khuong's conspiratorial laughter, it was Tiep who went to him.

She saw that he looked older and more decrepit than ever, as though he really had just emerged from one of the circles of hell: his overgrown head of hair glowed silver, his cheekbones jutted sharply, and his body was so thin it looked as though it had been stretched on a rack. He took one long step and spread his arms winningly to gather her in. Knowing he would try to kiss her regardless of An Khuong's presence—or anyone else's presence for that matter—Tiep lowered her face to avoid his lips. His body seemed suffused with heat, radiating fervor and yearning.

"All this bulky luggage, and on top of that the plane was late! What a pain!" Tiep cried quickly.

Dinh rocked backward. "It's aggravating all right," he said. "They're a monopoly so they don't have to respect anyone. We knew it was just because your plane was late, but An Khuong and I couldn't help but worry. Well, who's up for a bowl of noodles? Eh, An Khuong? To celebrate your friend Tiep getting here all in one piece, still in the original packaging, and best of all without any young men on her tail who might put me out to pasture?"

An Khuong giggled. When Dinh bent down to unlock the chain that secured his little Mobylette moped to Khuong's bike on the sidewalk, she leaned close to whisper, "Looks like you won't be staying with me at the school tonight. Dinh is ready to eat you up alive!" She giggled again in that exquisitely pure and comforting voice, and then her cheeks flushed red because virgins weren't supposed to be talking about people being eaten up alive. She was the type of person who would willingly forgo food and even the natural pleasures of youth for the more austere glories of education and degrees, just as her parents were willing to trade the fragrance of their once-spotless villa for the stink of pig manure. But unlike Hieu Trinh, when An Khuong saw how Tiep and Dinh quivered when near each other, she quivered along with them as though infected by their electricity. It proved that her heart wasn't entirely filled with pedantic lectures.

As for Tiep, the earthy desires that she thought had been successfully boxed up and put away now came bursting out like an animal escaping its cage. She couldn't shake off her awareness of Dinh's odor, right there next to her, barely a handbreadth away.

Without asking, he lifted Tiep's luggage up and began arranging it on the handlebars of his moped. An Khuong stepped in. "Let Tiep ride with me. It's safer."

Dinh hesitated. "But she's going to end up on my bike sooner or later!" he argued.

An Khuong put on a serious expression. "We'll cross that bridge when we come to it. I'm worried about getting caught, and then there'll be a big jealous brawl right in the middle of the street. As long as I am here I will do what it takes to protect Tiep. Tell me the address of the noodle shop; then you go on ahead with the luggage."

Unwillingly, Dinh obeyed. "All right, I'll take the luggage. But as for the person, she's only on loan to you until it's completely dark. Best to be safe!"

Tiep looked out at the stream of bicycles in the street. Suddenly she cried out.

"The north is supposed to be a paradise—don't tell me bicycles in paradise have to carry a license plate!"

Dinh gave an ironic laugh. "You've been led on by those poets who drive Volgas and get rich off their private shops on Ton Dan street! Yes, even the bicycles are licensed here—can you imagine how tightly people are controlled?"

"Don't you be making excuses about how your hands are tied and that's why you've left Tiep hanging," An Khuong interrupted. "If you're not careful you'll lose her faster than a bike left unlocked by Ho Guom Lake!"

Dinh argued back without taking a breath. "I haven't been making excuses. My oldest is studying in Eastern Europe and my second is preparing for his college entrance exams.

Anything happens to upset things for them and my mother will bury me alive. Okay, so I've procrastinated and made compromises, but I haven't surrendered. And anyway, your friend Tiep here hasn't finished her business either!"

Tiep absently followed the two bikes to the other side of the street. She was thinking of the day she had moved out of her house. On that very ordinary day, about one year after her trip to Dong Dung, she had clutched the paper that Tuyen had signed giving "my permission for my wife to leave the house" (required of her by Boss Poet), and while Tuyen was at work, quietly called two motorcycle-wagons to the house to transport her belongings to her office. It was a pathetically small pile of household essentials; clothing for her and the children, a bookcase, and a few pans and washtubs. The most valuable item was the refrigerator which she needed to earn money for Thu Thi and then later on for Vinh Chuyen, for she knew Tuyen would eventually go to the Academy and busy himself with matters of great significance. She left him almost everything; the television, the moped, the rice cooker... she had even agreed to leave him Vinh Chuyen in the short run so Tuyen wouldn't feel so alone. But on that day, unable to bear the thought of how lost Vinh Chuyen would feel coming home from school every day to a locked house, she ended up taking her son with her to the new place. All through the afternoon, Thu Thi and Vinh Chuyen huddled together on a bed that had been her office's guest bed, in a room no bigger than the kitchen of their old house, holding their breath every time they heard the doorbell ring on the lower floor and the solitary old artist who holed up in a makeshift room tucked under the stairway shuffle out to open the door. Finally they heard footsteps on the stairs, and Tuyen appeared. All four of them were utterly silent, as though acting out parts in a play which was now reaching its climax. Having been prepared in advance by his mother, Vinh Chuyen climbed down off the bed and stoically held out his hand for his father to lead him away. As he disappeared into the staircase, Tiep felt as though the tiny slapping sounds of his sandals were trampling through her belly. She wanted to throw herself out the window after him. Instead, she and Thu Thi clung to each other, sobbing silently, grief-stricken as the reality of separation and parting sank in. It was only the first of many such tearful sessions that would come.

At least she had Thu Thi; were it not for her, Tiep would not have been able to let Vinh Chuyen go at all. Still, Thu Thi was Thu Thi and Vinh Chuyen was Vinh Chuyen, and they were not interchangeable in her heart. Maternal love may be all-encompassing, but it is also divided into compartments, one for each child, and when one of those compartments becomes suddenly empty it cannot be filled by anyone or anything else other than the gravemound of the child lost.

After a time, Vinh Chuyen drifted back to live with them, saying "Daddy takes me along when he goes to drink with his friends, and I have to stay up so late, and the mosquitoes are terrible." So Thu Thi took up a shift at the house, until "Daddy's got some woman from his office that comes over and whispers to him a lot, so I figured I'd come back to you and let him have his new girlfriend!" After some more time, Tuyen transferred to the Academy of Politics, his first official step into the machinery of government and provincial leadership. But whenever she brought up divorce, he was abrupt: "I don't see that it's necessary!"

At least she had tried. She hadn't waited for her children to go to university. When she had left that house with her children in tow, Dinh was nowhere to be seen and in fact had even wanted to put her off until their next life. Despite his distance, she had taken a step forward for herself and for her own future. How could Dinh say that she hadn't finished her business, when he hadn't even taken the first step?

The issue had been brought up too soon, thanks to An Khuong's impatient and indiscreet mouth. They felt strained, awkward. Dinh put on a jolly face in an attempt to break the tension. Gesturing at his moped, he asked, "What do you two think, does my little "Green Fish" here do anything to improve my image?"

An Khuong laughed shrilly. "Isn't that the one your wife calls your 'pile of junk'?"

At the mention of his wife, Dinh shut up. He gave a pensive wave of his hand to signal that the two women should go first.

As she pedaled, An Khuong warned Tiep, "You two need to be careful. These northern women are vicious. If they catch you there won't be any escape hatch!"

"Has Dinh ever had you over to his house?"

An Khuong turned almost all the way around, causing her handlebars to wobble and hook onto the handlebars of another bicycle. The man riding it lurched away from them, trailing vile curses as he went.

"Just you wait, you'll see how ruthless they are. They all live such cramped, miserable, deprived lives, no one is happy here! You want to know about Dinh's house? All I know is the general area where he lives. As audacious as he may be, he still wouldn't dare invite me to his home!"

"Why is that?"

"Didn't you hear about the time she collared him on the street and they had to call the police? It wasn't that long ago. He had a woman on the back of his brand new little Green Fish. I'm sure the girl was just a friend who was hitching a ride. Well, his wife happened to pass by and see them, and the fight turned the entire block upside down. To be honest with you, I don't know how you two are going to pull this off. I don't want to get involved, but I feel for you and him so much."

"I'm enough to scare you off men completely, eh?" Tiep asked. Anything to get away from the subject of Dinh and his wife.

An Khuong sighed. "I'm thirty, you know. Younger men want nothing to do with me and older men are saddled with wives and kids. In the lingo of the Northerners, I'm stale goods!"

"I'm sure your mother is worried sick about you," said Tiep frankly. "I've got a daughter, so I understand how a mother feels."

"My mother doesn't worry about my miserable marital prospects so much as she does that I'm not making enough progress."

"Good God! As hard as you work, it's not enough progress?"

"It's just because she's thinking about my younger siblings. They need me to have a good position in the hierarchy so I can pull them up after me. Don't forget that our family was part of the bourgeoisie, and many of our relatives supported the puppet government!"

To comfort her, Tiep said, "If your misery is a ten, you can bet your mother's misery is up to eleven. Tears are no different than any other water, it all runs downhill..."

"So? What about you and Dinh; how is your family reacting?"

Tiep gave a rueful laugh. "Just an embargo for now. They've stepped up the punishment a bit since the journalist. My second offense, you know; I've got a criminal record and all. But Aunt Rang is still watching and waiting. Probably waiting to see if I mend my ways when Tuyen gets back from the Academy."

"So you're left hanging by Tuyen, and Dinh's left hanging by his wife. I overheard some of Dinh's friends saying that she'd laid down the law for him: 'No matter who the slut is, I'll hang you out to dry until you're too old to care!'"

The state-run noodle shop occupied the choicest location in an area of housing blocks, tall buildings painted a uniform yellow and bristling with decidedly non-uniform iron cages built onto the sides as makeshift balconies. A group of women were cursing each other at a public faucet that was set into the sidewalk nearby. Dinh found a spot where An Khuong could shove her bicycle into the tangle of bikes parked under the trees. All three stepped cautiously into the shop, scanning this way and that as a "security check." An Khuong laughed softly.

"I feel like a spy!"

Dinh gave a sigh of relief. There was no one in the shop he recognized. "My sarcasm has infected An Khuong, don't you think, Tiep?"

Tiep forced a smile. Her conversation with An Khuong had left her feeling vulnerable. She felt like a barefaced criminal, about to be caught red-handed and beaten up for the crime of husband-snatching.

The pho noodle shop was obviously a well-known eatery; mixed with the ubiquitous odor of charcoal and meat was the sweaty smell of a crowd. But it was a restaurant like nothing Tiep had ever seen before. Rows of people jostled each other into something that approximated a line, jamming shoulder to shoulder and nose to back, waving tickets like traders in the stock market. The tables were filthy and the floor littered with napkins and bones. The waitresses wore promising white uniforms with the initials S.R.E.—short for State Run Enterprise—printed neatly in blue, but all hope died when it came to their faces, which wore expressions distinctly lacking in courtesy. Over it all hung the smell of the so-called pho soup, completely different from the Saigon variety she had smelled on one of her trips with Aunt Rang. Her hometown had something they called pho, but there it meant pork broth with egg noodles, basil, sweet Chinese sauce, and an egg cracked on top, whereas the Hanoi variety was simply beef broth with beef. Could the separation at the 17th parallel really have created so many differences?

While An Khuong ran to help Dinh carry the bowls, Tiep found a table and sat down apprehensively. She was beginning to wonder if she had been foolish to agree to a trip to Hanoi. The uneasiness she had felt on the airplane grew stronger, like a sour lemon seed in her mouth. But retreat was not possible at this point.

Dinh finally managed to acquire two bowls of noodles, and An Khuong followed him with a bowl for herself. The bowls were lopsided and shapeless, made in the neighboring village of Hai Duong. As for the spoons, they were the oddest thing Tiep had ever seen. In each one, at precisely the spot that by all rights should have been absolutely inviolate so that the spoon might properly and satisfactorily fulfill its function, a small round hole had been carefully punched. Tiep gingerly lifted a spoonful of broth out of her bowl and watched it run out through the hole. She did it again, like a little girl engrossed in a new game. An Khuong was used to the spoons, but laughed along with Tiep. Dinh's face settled into the pained expression that signaled he was about to hold forth with an opinion.

"It's how they discourage theft, Tiep. Only a master thief could think up such a peerless method of theft prevention!"

"What, people here will even steal old spoons like these?" cried Tiep.

Dinh shrugged his shoulders dramatically. An Khuong's face fell, solemn and sorrowful. No one spoke. In the suddenly sober atmosphere, all three discarded their spoons and concentrated on eating with their chopsticks. Afterwards, they would agree with each other that it was the worst noodle soup they'd ever had.

13

After An Khuong had left for her university in Cau Giay district, the time came for Dinh's "pile of junk" Green Fish to step up and take over. Dinh stopped in a puddle of darkness under a crape myrtle tree near the noodle shop so they could tie up Tiep's bags.

"I have to run an errand downtown; then we'll go straight to my friend's place. Hanoi is wonderful this time of year."

Tiep had a different suggestion. "You've got cyclos here, just like back home. Why don't I take a cyclo and go on ahead, straight to your friend's place. It'll be safer that way."

Dinh bent down to adjust her bag, which he had tied securely to his front basket so that she could sit comfortably on the back. He said in an offhand way, "It's a good thing that my wife doesn't have any friends. She's got no reason to go out, so we don't have to worry about her rattling around the streets at this hour."

"But if you go home late tonight, how will you explain it?" Tiep pressed. She felt she had to pin him down, if not she wouldn't be able to bear the fear in the pit of her stomach.

"What, do you actually think I'd leave you somewhere tonight and go back home?" Dinh said forcefully and not a little indignant. He hopped onto the moped and kicked hard at the pedals to start the motor. It gave a gurgling cough, as dainty and mannered as a French woman, then reluctantly shot off down the street. Tiep ran full-tilt to follow him, but he was gone. Utterly at a loss as to why he would leave her behind, she began to pace back and forth under the canopy of leaves, trying to think of what she had done. Several pedestrians stared at her as they passed. They clearly recognized her as a southerner; her hair, clothing, purse, and shoes gave it away. Although the people of both regions shared the common misery of daily lines, southerners had a little more breathing room and so tended to be better-groomed.

After a moment, Dinh returned with an apologetic smile.

"I thought you'd gotten on. Up here we're used to hopping on when the bike starts moving. After I'd gone a ways without hearing you say anything, I turned around and realized I'd lost you!"

If it hadn't been for the recent long months of silence and the awkwardness of their reunion, no doubt the incident would have ended in laughter. As it was, Tiep reproached him. "Your bike would have to feel much lighter without me on the back. It's just because you are so worried about being seen, you didn't notice and look what happened!"

Dinh waited for Tiep to seat herself, then guided her hand to his hips.

"You don't know how demented my wife is; she's like Bertha in Jane Eyre. I can't anticipate everything, it's just too hard. In a few days I'll find a way for you to meet my mother and sister; you'll understand me better after that. Mom just came up from Vinh, you know. She heard that my wife and I were having more problems than usual and hopped on the train right away."

Tiep removed her hand from Dinh's hip in case they were seen, but all of her senses were tingling acutely. They were riding through the kind of autumn evening she'd only heard about it in poems and radio broadcasts; she was aware of the smooth, cool air on her cheek and the tantalizing smell of the man's back in front of her. She smiled sadly.

"So, are you taking me to our next life? I recall a message from you saying we'd meet up there."

"C'mon, I've been missing you like a madman, Tiep! But I'm forty-nine this year. You know the old saying that forty-nine to fifty-three are the riskiest years. My mother worries and won't let me take long trips..."

The moped circled Ho Guom lake, then turned up Hang Dao street to meander through the Old Quarter. Malabar almond trees on either side threw a low dark canopy over the streets, ideal for illicit lovers. Dinh stopped in front of a watch repair shop, told Tiep to watch the bike and her bags, and hastily stepped inside. After a long careful look up and down the street, he pulled a few packs of watch batteries from his pants pockets—they were the kind made in Japan, the ones that look like little buttons—and gave them to the elderly shopkeeper. The transaction proceeded expeditiously and in complete silence, without a word of bargaining or argument.

Dinh stepped out and thrust a wad of money into Tiep's purse.

"For you, to use when we're together. Wherever we go, or wherever we eat, you pay. That way people won't think we're a couple." Dinh gave a wry smile, and gestured to Tiep to stroll beside him as he walked the bike. "Some friends and I make a little on the side by selling batteries and electronic watches we hustle from Russia. I can't write these days. I miss you too much and the atmosphere at home is suffocating me. Without someplace to go where I can breathe a little, I can't even finish an essay. After getting back from Dong Dung, it took me forever before I could deliver the travelogue that the publishing house gave me an advance on. Not only that, I've been busy making rice wine and raising a couple of pigs at home to get the money for my son's college prep. Luckily he passed the exam. He didn't make it into the Polytechnic University like his older brother, but he passed. Talk about a relief!"

This is not the voice of grinding hardship and despair, Tiep thought. This is the voice of concern and struggle, writhing like some very fragile, anonymous plant that is crushed under a rock but worms its way out to proudly lift its leaves to the sun. If only she were free to walk forever at his side, to let go and depend entirely on those resourceful arms...

Dinh steered Tiep towards the sidewalk, where a tiny, delicate old lady with a black velvet scarf wrapped around her head sat behind a coarse table selling tea.

"Time for you to experience Hanoi tea in a real Hanoi sidewalk café!" said Dinh. He parked the moped within view, locked it carefully, then pulled Tiep over to sit close to him on a tiny bench that was as patched and decrepit as Hanoi itself. The sudden physical contact, disconcerting but satisfying, dissolved like so many soap bubbles every last word of reproach and suspicion within her. She felt her body stir and something like an electric shock shoot up from her heels; her heart softened with a pleasant feeling of release.

"When I heard your Boss Poet say that both children are living with you now, I was so glad!" Dinh said by way of small talk.

A mouthful of extraordinarily strong tea slid down Tiep's throat, bitter at first but gradually mellowing to a sweet aftertaste. She sipped in silence. She hadn't imagined that they'd be sitting together, this close, this soon.

"The kids will be fine with Hieu Trinh, no worries there. How long will you stay in Hanoi?"

"At first I thought I'd stay for my entire vacation, but now that we are together like this I'm not sure it's safe!"

Dinh looked as though he had just swallowed a bone. "I've got a plan. We'll go somewhere outside of Hanoi for a few days."

Tiep spoke softly, head down, so the old lady would not hear. "You want us to sneak around in secret? This is Hanoi, this is the north, it's not Dong Dung! And anyway our relationship is past the flirting stage like when we were in Dong Dung."

There it was again; the burn of resentment in her chest. She slumped and stared into the old lady's tiny oil lamp, the size of a duck's egg, and wondered why it was that she always wanted things to be proper, aboveboard, legitimate. And she remembered Tuyen and his long gloomy face when he appeared at her door to tell her that for the sake of convenience Vinh Chuyen would be transferred to a school closer to her for the next couple of years, and his flat refrain of "I don't see that it's necessary" when she suggested they divorce before he leave for the Academy in Thu Duc. Then she imagined Dinh's Crazy Bertha with wild hair. She'd heard that his wife was very beautiful. Beautiful and crazy, what a combination. Much more frightening than plain and sane.

Dinh was stammering. "This is the best time of year, when Hanoi is at its coolest and greenest. The more the northeastern wind blows in, the more I miss you."

Tiep shook her head miserably. "Let me meet with your

mother and sister first. I feel like I'm seeing you through a screen, through these words of yours that may or may not be true. I don't have the peace of mind to be able to enjoy myself. I'm not comfortable with our relationship. I don't have the confidence or the clarity to act. I don't feel like myself at all, I don't..."

Knowing that Tiep might burst into tears and decide to spend the night at An Truong's university, Dinh shifted to the bench perpendicular to Tiep's and borrowed the old lady's water pipe. Tiep studied him while he soberly prepared the pipe. He was wearing the same atrocious clothing he'd worn for the past two years, although the cream color of his shirt had now faded beyond the color of pig-intestine porridge and was additionally adorned with a hole the size of a lemon on the chest, and his dark, straight-legged pants sported rips in both knees that allowed two identical patches of skin to peek through, as though Dinh were concerned with the symmetry of his privation. Back in Dong Dung, while reclining comfortably on the nose of a long-haul sugarcane boat, she'd asked him about his wife. Dinh had responded with only a long sigh and silence, but she had been able to observe the state of their relationship through his clothes: the black thread used to resew buttons onto the cream-colored shirt; the seam sloppily mended with brown thread on the threadbare collar; the white thread clumped in little knots around the hems of his dark pants, which looked as if they had been let out; and the tear on one knee which had been patched with paper and glue like a poor peasant costume in a stage routine... all these details told her that his clothing had not seen the touch of a woman's hand. It was something that, despite her feminist bent, Tiep simply could not understand.

Dinh was drunk on the strong pipe tobacco now. He panted listlessly for a few moments, then pulled Tiep to her feet to continue their stroll. "To wait until all the inquisitive, prying eyes at my friend's place have gone to sleep," he said. As they walked, Dinh's eyes scoured the goods of the black-market sidewalk merchants. They sat behind large flat baskets, with or without a duck's-egg lamp, full of western medications, cigarettes, and countless other miscellany. Tiep knew that the entire army of baskets and lamps could be spirited away in a flash into the adjacent alleyways at the first sign of a member of the Security Police or Market Regulation.

Dinh handed the handlebars of the moped to Tiep and sprinted over to a basket containing medications that lay in the darkest shadow. She saw him ask for something, and then buyer and seller consummated their transaction with the skill and speed of a magic act—all that was missing was a dramatic soundtrack—and he ran back to her and stuffed whatever it was into her purse.

"I know you might not have prepared. If you're not at a safe place in your cycle, remember to take one of these pills every day. I don't want us to make a mistake that would make your life more miserable."

Tiep felt her heart soften. His resourcefulness and efficient foresight under such miserable conditions both surprised and aroused her. "You seem to know it all, eh? Where to sell, where to buy, even what medicine to buy?"

Dinh mounted the seat of the moped and shrugged. "Here in the north, you can't survive if you don't have the wits!"

The moped putted off towards what Dinh told her was the Vong Junction. In the dark of night, Hanoi's apartment blocks all looked the same: monotonous, haphazardly assembled conglomerations of floors rising out of the earth, dotted with unsightly, untidy caged balconies and strung together with clotheslines that completely ignored any concern of aesthetics or propriety. The farther they moved into the complex where Dinh's friend lived, the more Tiep became aware of the odors of burning charcoal, of rats and cockroaches, of mold and mildew, and of course the ubiquitous stench of public toilets that were evidently very short of water.

Dinh stopped the moped in a shadow.

"If you need to use the facilities, you'd better do it here.

My friend's place doesn't have a bathroom."

"I'll wait until I get my clothes out of my luggage, then I'll come down here to change."

"That would be risky. We're slipping in silently and will leave early tomorrow morning. If my friend's neighbors see us it would mean trouble." Seeing her hesitate, he added, "It's not that they'll think we're spies or some kind of troublemaker. But having someone stay at your place without giving proper notice to the authorities is a golden opportunity for some disgruntled neighbor to denounce you."

Then he shoved a box of matches into her hand and pointed her in the direction of the toilet.

The bathroom consisted of several stalls housed in a small, low-roofed building nestled against the fence at the end of a block of apartments. It was not a primitive doorless honey bucket like the execrable dormitory toilets An Khuong had described, but the shingles looked as though they might fall on her head at any time, the mortar joining the floor tiles was ulcerated and peeling, and the woven bamboo screens that served as doors to the stalls were rotting at the bottom. Tiep lit a match and peered into a stall. The toilet was made of unenamaled, pockmarked cement topped with two rough green ceramic footrests on which to squat. The stench was spectacular, like a wall that prevented her from entering. But to urinate in the shower stall was, well... in the end Tiep chose the shower stall. She had to guarantee herself a minimum level of personal sanitation after a long day on the road, in case she would not able to change her underwear any time soon. She had to use up several matches, looking all around during each brief flare to get the lay of the land. Dinh had once told her that he hadn't believed it first when he heard that southerners had lighters that burned long and steady on lighter fluid.

After discharging all the liquid she had accumulated over the day, and thanking her good fortune that her kidneys and bladder were still youthful and healthy, she lit yet another match to look for water to wash up. There was a rectangular cistern between the shower stall and the toilet stall, and she found a scoop of roughly hammered aluminum lying on the shower side. But as she picked up the scoop, she suddenly noticed a petite, yellowish lump of stool meandering languorously across the surface of the water. Tiep flung the scoop away and scrambled out of the bathroom as fast as she could, responding to Dinh's surprised look by mumbling something about too many rats. No doubt someone in the toilet stall had been unable to reach the aluminum scoop on the other side and so had rinsed out their child's chamber pot by plunging the entire thing into the basin, allowing that ill-mannered little piece of shit to escape. Tiep felt she couldn't tell Dinh, that telling him would only add to his mortification. Or perhaps it was because they didn't have the easy familiarity that husbands and wives share, and so were still selective in what they told each other.

Dinh told Tiep to carry her satchel so he could push the moped silently through the first floor of the building, which looked as though it had once been a meeting-hall or factory floor but was now a labyrinth of compartments created by woven bamboo partitions.

"This fellow didn't leave his wife; his wife left him," Dinh whispered as they walked. "Just because he was so poor. But the really awful thing is that she dumped their kid on him, a pale-faced little girl who is always as hungry as a bacterium."

They arrived at a bamboo-walled cubicle in the center of the labyrinth and, leaving the Green Fish blocking the door together with the homeowner's bicycle, stepped inside.

There was a bed immediately in front of them which took up half the space in the room, while the other half was occupied by a frame woven of thin bamboo strips and covered with a mat to make a temporary bed. A tiny slice of kitchen lay in the back. A single round light bulb shed its mournful light on the homeowner and his daughter who, because there was no place to stand or move around, remained seated on the bed as they greeted their guests. The man, who was wearing a pair of ancient striped pajamas so threadbare they were all but transparent, enthusiastically reached up to grasp Tiep's hand and welcome her to Hanoi, while the girl—who contrary to Dinh's description was not only pale but also jaundiced—politely folded her arms in front her chest and chirped, "Hello, Uncle. Hello, Aunt." Tiep sat down on the edge of the bed and pulled the child close to fuss over her a bit, troubled that she hadn't brought a present. The man, who had now been introduced to her as Ky, noticed and said to his daughter, "Auntie didn't know Uncle Dinh was going to bring her here. And our door is sealed for the night now, so you should go to sleep early so that they can rest too."

"Tomorrow morning I'll treat you and your daddy to a bowl of pho noodles," promised Dinh. "How's that sound?"

The little girl lifted her nose and gleefully sniffed like a puppy. "Don't forget, Uncle! I can eat two bowls. And a couple of balut eggs too!"

Tiep heard the child swallow a lump of saliva. Her father, who had the face and carriage of a born pessimist, looked chagrined but joked, "Go to sleep like a good girl and you can have five bowls of pho with five eggs!"

A cotton curtain that was riddled with holes was drawn between the bed and the bamboo frame. Ky stood up to arrange the mosquito net for his daughter, then pulled the light bulb over near the kitchen. Then he and Dinh sat down on the bamboo frame with a flaking white enamel tea tray between them. They murmured conversationally for a while, ranging from the Party apparatus to rumors leaked out from the "Imperial Court" of the government and picked up in the coffee shops and streets of Hanoi, to the latest satirical poems and political jokes being passed around. Tiep laughed so hard she couldn't stop, and occasionally had to be reminded by Ky that she was surrounded by only bamboo screens rather than walls.

Finally, the moment Dinh had been waiting for arrived.

Ky placed an old enameled iron chamber pot with a handle in the kitchen, saying "Go ahead if you need it. Don't try to go out to the toilet, it's just asking for trouble." Then he withdrew onto the bed and pulled the curtain closed as tightly as possible, and lay quietly.

Tiep opened her satchel and took out her pajamas. She turned to step into the kitchen but Dinh reached up to turn out the light, then pulled her to him in the darkness.

"You'll just take it off anyway, why not wait and put it on later... Come lie down with me!"

An opening kiss, as drawn out as their hundreds of days of separation. Languorous gestures gently removing one piece of clothing after another, like actors in a film played back in slow motion. Dinh stretched her out on the bamboo frame and began the long journey from her lips downward.

"I've never had the chance to see your entire body," he whispered. "Every night, I reward myself by thinking about you. Can you stand it, spending the night with me in a place like this?"

Tiep didn't answer. Instead, she wove her fingers into Dinh's hair as he drifted slowly down to her belly. But his efforts to make up for their surroundings did not arouse her as fully as she had imagined. For some reason, her thoughts kept drifting back to the image of that yellowish lump of stool floating in the cistern. Then the hole-riddled curtain and the bamboo screens on all sides. Then the thought of their host who lay, holding his breath, on the bed beside them with his pale, malnourished, motherless little girl. Why is it, she wondered, that Dinh's body and scent was so much more alluring when covered in sweat-stained clothes than in its primal state? He felt strange and foreign to her; was it a product of her mood, or their circumstances, or just because her requirements were too rigid? That afternoon in Dong Dung, that golden April afternoon suffused with the smoke of burning fields as they sat by a solitary haystack after their first too-eager kiss, she had whispered imploringly in his ear: "It's lasting happiness I want. I'm not just playing around. I won't accept anything that doesn't have a future!" Dinh had breathed back: "If I weren't looking for the same thing, I wouldn't have gone to the trouble to come all the way down here. In Hanoi, I can have it anytime I want. But you and I, we are destined to be together!" So she had stretched herself out, like now, a passive spectator more than a participant. She saw herself and Tuyen once again in the drowned foxhole on that deadly, funereal morning. Afterwards—after that unforgettable day of enemy soldiers pouring out of helicopters and unexpected, electrifying kisses and young bodies partaking for the first time—afterwards she and Tuyen had found plenty of opportunities for further exploration. They shared shelters and boats, death and survival, and most of all a common need for physical intimacy when life and death were measured in hours and days. But after Vinh Chuyen was born, their sex life had turned suddenly uninspired. Despairing of her husband's character and soul, and especially his dwindling reserves of basic humanity, Tiep resigned herself to Tuyen's approximations of lovemaking. She even came to terms with Tuyen's habit of removing only the bottom half of her clothing, a habit he hadn't changed since their war days when they both had a reasonable fear of dying naked. Tuyen had no need to admire and caress her body, nor did he feel it cumbersome when her shirt isolated her skin from his. He had never seen her completely nude. And so it went; always that feeling of weariness every time he brought her to climax, fleeting but crushing, as though her emotions were being poured out only so that someone else could immediately reclaim that which she had just discovered. She understood that this was the feeling of lovelessness between herself and Tuyen; her love-starved heart was sabotaging even the pleasures of the flesh. Then came Trung Vy, and love had struck her like a bolt of lightning. Her unilateral love for him had been sweet but brought her nothing but late-night dreams and butterflies in the stomach when they happened to run into each other at a meeting or on the street. She had hurled herself at him like a moth at a flame, but hadn't imagined that their coupling would happen so soon, and so like an acquisition, in that forbidding Guest House. She felt nothing, outside of surprise that it had all been so spare and that only he got to wipe himself while she lay draped over the side of the bed, paralyzed with embarrassment. But the lightning strike had penetrated deep, so she had continued on, offering herself up with blind devotion and sacrifice like a subject before her king. Only to be flattened when she learned that there were other moths, and they outweighed by far her meager eighty-four pounds... Even so, when Tuyen complained to Hai Kham and the other gentlemen of the Standing Committee, Trung Vy had vehemently denied everything. "How could you be so stupid?" he scolded her. "Why did you tell him about me? Don't you understand this place, these times we are living in?!" Tiep argued back valiantly. "I understand myself. I understand our times. That's why I told him—I have to be honest, to be proper. We made our bed, we should have the courage to lie in it!" But Trung Vy wrote her off as a naïve girl and in the end did not stay to endure the consequences with her.

And now here she was with Dinh, still unable to give herself over to him and to pleasure. That damnable need for legitimacy was still haunting her, rendering her miserable and awkward with a tryst in such a makeshift place.

Dinh, on the other hand, was full to the brim and quickly spent himself. He lay on top of her, unmoving, enjoying the release after an evening full of tension. With the altruistic spirit of a women who knows her man has abstained in preparation for this moment, Tiep lay still and let him relax. She held him like a vulnerable child, and suddenly love welled up in her. He's like an expert swimmer taking on a vast stormy ocean, she thought; he thinks he can survive but doesn't know the limits of his own strength. Suddenly she felt that it was she who owed Dinh, not the other way around as he had told her. Perhaps the debt was from their previous lives.

Whispered stories followed, mixed with primal flesh. For the first time, Tiep felt her hands close mischievously around that singular member of the male anatomy, teasing, tugging, tantalizing. She'd never done this with Tuyen, never felt the desire for it. Now she abandoned herself to drift over Dinh's body, scrutinizing it as he had scrutinized every last inch of hers. She felt bold and powerful. The rhythm of their flesh was fervent and sweet. She abandoned her defensive posture and threw herself into the position of aggressor. The second time was the polar opposite of the first. Tiep was aflame from heel to head; her body flowed and skimmed, to where she didn't know. She didn't know if this was legitimate or illegitimate, debauchery or virtue. She only knew that she was being truly herself, as she had always imagined herself, deeply and completely fulfilled.

The third time came in the wee hours of the morning, the buttery odor of their bodies mingling and tormenting them through fitful sleep. Once again she felt herself floating; somehow even more consummate and exhaustive than before, it was heaven and hell, nakedness and divinity, like nothing she'd ever felt before. Dinh breathed into her mouth:

"It's never been like this for me either!"

14

It was the morning rush hour, and Hanoi's citizenry looked like a swarm of tiny stoic ants on bicycles, some domestically made, others Chinese, and still others more prestigious brands that had been toted home from Eastern Europe. In spite of the slight gradations of class, they were still all bicycles, all with or without a license plate, and all uniformly leaden and depressing. Tiep was surprised by the aggressive, acquisitive energy of the women as they bustled along the road, while the men seemed to disappear like turtles into their shells under the ubiquitous army-green pith helmets which protected them from the elements and could even be used as stools in a pinch.

Back when Tiep lived on the guerrilla base, the cadres who returned from study in the North in their shirts of Ha Dong silk apparently considered the destitution of the rear lines to be a state secret, while the newspapers never ceased lauding "our heavenly North Vietnam" as described in To Huu's famous poem. After the peace, Hai Kham had sent Tuyen on a trip to the North for a month; his opinion upon his return was "Hanoi is small with lots of bicycles, but the surrounding agricultural communes are huge, large-scale operations. That's the right model for the future of us in the south!" Nonetheless Tiep had begun to have doubts about her ideal image of North Vietnam, especially when she was standing in line at the bus station, or chopping pork until her hands blistered to divide up rations for the others in her office, or thrusting her hands into a bag of ration rice to see if it was very moldy or only slightly moldy this month. Then one day in Dong Dung it had suddenly become crystal clear to her and she almost fell over laughing when Dinh had goggled at her, exclaiming, "Don't tell me you're using a ballpoint pen? You hedonist, where did you get the money to be able to write your stories by ballpoint? Where I'm from, ballpoints can only be had from people who've brought them back from Eastern Europe, and only then at cutthroat prices. If you can't afford it, you're stuck with a fountain pen!"

They had been pedaling around Hanoi for several days now, taking in the sights. While sitting by West Lake enjoying its famous shrimp cakes—in spite of its fame, there was no serving staff so it had taken them three runs back and forth to the kitchen to get all their food and condiments to their table—Tiep asked Dinh, "If you had to do a sociological thesis about Hanoi in this era, what image would best encapsulate your ideas?" Dinh licked his lips thoughtfully, a sign that he was about to launch into his familiar biting sarcasm. "Well, of course, a thesis has to have illustrations. Me, I would draw a zigzag row of broken bricks, worn-out hats, old baskets, blunted brooms, torn thongs, broken plastic containers, and ripped shirts... the sort of things that are usually used as stand-ins to keep people's place in a queue. I think that if you arranged them in front of a very still background, they would start to take on a life of their own. They have their own fates, their earmarks, their aspirations, even their own souls... they wear the faces of people like me, or my little sister, my friends, and someday, my children. You've never laid eyes on such a bizarre queue, I'm guessing. Everything is so much easier in the south, eh?"

They had not gone away on a long trip as Dinh had planned. With the exception of his unexplained absence from home on Tiep's first night, they had acquiesced to Dinh's mother and followed a protocol to ensure Tiep's safety: every day Dinh left home like a responsible husband going to work, and every day he and Tiep explored Hanoi, immersing themselves in the names and places that, according to him, she needed to discover in order to understand "Hanoi the longsuffering, Hanoi the silent, Hanoi the proud." They took the buses, thick with an atmosphere of bad-mannered shoving and squeezing, until her guide suffered a blow to his streetwise credibility when it was his sunglasses that were stolen while the horde of people along with them were left untouched; after that they defected to the electric streetcar, which had to be the most indolent means of transportation on the planet and so was considerably less crowded. They spent lunches on stone benches, sometimes on Nung Hill and other times in Thu Le Park, making do with bread so hard that, if thrown right, could kill a dog. It was at these times that their longing for each other would overcome them, torment them, and Dinh would look all around before pressing himself close and hurriedly planting several numb, secretive kisses on her lips.

A condensed image of Hanoi was beginning to form in Tiep's heart, like a souvenir lovingly displayed in a glass cabinet. But this morning Dinh was engaged elsewhere and she was on her own on An Khuong's mini bicycle. Without Dinh by her side, Hanoi looked bare and hard to swallow, not so much for its postwar hardship but rather for its self-indulgent dilapidation. Tiep pedaled past Cau Giay street to Lang Street with its stately African mahogany trees and their strangely austere burls. She came to So Intersection, where long ago the Cham army had been surrounded and destroyed. Then on a little farther to the university campus with its burnt-brick walls, where at age twenty Dinh had ended his university career with a single line of words stamped over an official seal: "Reactionary element sympathetic to the Nhan Van literary movement.[1]" He had left with the peace of mind that he would never be promoted or appointed to a position in the bureaucracy, that he would spend his life as nothing more than a torn rag holding a place in line, and so, free of the fear of being soured by official privilege, he would be able to maintain some sliver of independence in his writing.

Tiep's meandering inner monologue about Dinh was suddenly interrupted by a handful of sand thrown from a streetcar onto her head.

"Bastard!"—the voice of a man alongside who had gotten some of the sand.

"Goddamn their bloody bitch of a mother!"—a female victim chimed in.

Tiep stopped her bike, as astonished as she was angry. There was no doubt but that the sand had been intended for her. They knew she was a visitor; her bright turtleneck with the pomegranate-flower pattern—the same one she had worn in Diep Vang—and her relaxed manner gave her away. A distinguished-looking gentleman noticed her furiously brushing away the sand and stopped his promenade along

1. A movement of Northern authors who demanded freedom and democracy. It was tolerated for about three years and stamped out by the communist government in 1958.

the sidewalk to intone, "Those brats have to spend their days making trouble because they've got nothing else to do, miss. If they didn't throw sand, they'd just end up destroying something else!"

Tiep forced a smile to thank him for the explanation, and determined to pay more attention to the map Dinh had drawn for her. Chua Boc and Khuong Thuong, Trung Tu and Kim Lien—a spider's web of names jostling each other on the page, just as everything jostled everything else in this place.

The apartment block glowed a harsh yellow against the green rows of mahogany trees. Tiep struggled to push the bicycle up the switchbacks of each flight of steps, but just couldn't get the hang of it the way Dinh did. And there was that smell again, a musty, rotting sigh from every corner that spoke specifically of human squalor and not just the constant high humidity. The hallway was crisscrossed with laundry lines hung with homemade women's underwear and coarse grubby towels made by the state-owned enterprises. Then there were the charcoal stoves outside each doorway and the iron cages in which a few herbs were planted...all of it evidence that the "ruralization" of Hanoi had been carried out with impressive efficiency.

Tiep found the door with the antirust paint and the twig-thin welded iron bars at the head of the staircase. She snaked her hand through the bars to open the latch, then walked down a corridor until she saw Dinh's head poke out from a greenish door ahead of her. Furtively and swiftly, he pulled her and the bike into the apartment as though he'd been doing this all his life. Then, after the door had been securely locked behind them, he spread his arms out in a charming gesture and kissed as hungrily and as hurriedly as always.

While he was stowing the bike and putting away her hat and purse, Tiep took a quick look around the apartment. It was laid out with the kitchen in the front; at least it wasn't one of those apartments which, according to Dinh's description, "greet the guest with the stench from the toilet, as though we aren't even as clean as cats and have no need to hide our shit. They just slap out a design and to hell with how the masses live. After all, they have their beautiful tall houses and their shops down on Ton Dan street..." He looked like a porcupine when he got rolling with this type of story, all bristling and sharp, but in the end people only laughed at him because after all a porcupine is a relatively harmless creature who puts on a show of defensive bluster but rarely attacks.

Then Tiep heard his breath in her ear and felt his yearning and anxiety. He was steering her by the shoulders into the living room.

"Mom, Tiep's here! Mom?"

The scent of medicinal herbs drifted out from the inner room, and a moment later an old lady in her seventies appeared along with it. She was tiny and delicate, with a brown scarf thrown over a head of hair that was not yet entirely white. But her face was cheerful and open, as bright as mountain air and as pure as a high spring. Tiep thought suddenly of Aunt Rang. Her intuition told her that here was Dinh's counterpart to her own Aunt Rang, and she wished with all her heart that one day these two formidable women would sit down with each other, side by side. Surely she and Dinh could imagine no greater happiness that that.

Dinh's mother took Tiep's hand in hers and greeted her warmly. "You're quite the navigator, eh, finding your way here all by yourself? Sit down, child. Hoa's gone to the market. She said she was going to barbecue some pork for you so we can have bun cha noodles!"

Dinh pulled Tiep down to sit next to him on the wooden settee set next to a coffee table and wheedled, "Can I have some when I get back, Mom?"

His mother looked at him sternly, but her voice was cheerful. "You know we need to be discreet, for Tiep's sake! It's better you go."

Dinh stood up reluctantly, and Tiep sensed that the conversation she had been waiting for was about to begin, without any prompting from her. "Well, I'm off collect the money and the bottles for the rice wine," he said. "But really, it's all very fine to offer, but do you really think it's a good idea for Tiep to have lunch here?"

The old women drew herself to her full height behind his back and said pointedly, "I'll tell them I invited her. And if anyone wishes to make an issue of it, I'll take care of them!"

Tiep felt as though she were watching Aunt Rang; it was the same fearlessness and combative control, the same rule of iron, the complete package. Dinh stopped on his way to the door, undecided.

"I'm not afraid that Cam will cause a scene but I do worry about Hoa's lout of a husband. You know how belligerent he is, always with the slogans, 'down with the intellectuals, the bourgeoisie, and the landowners' and 'destroy them down to the very roots'. He could cause trouble!"

His mother raised her voice, "You think he dares to go up against me? If I hadn't made Hoa marry him, they never would have... When I think about it now I regret what I did to your little sister. If only she hadn't listened to me, she probably would've met someone better..."

Tiep was listening closely: here was a woman who lived for her children, who had high expectations for their future, and to whom their worth was the most important thing in her life.

Tiep stood up behind the old lady. The fragrance of betel washed over her, sacred and eminently trustworthy. Here she was, a part of Dinh's family now, but she knew she faced cold winds from all directions. There was still her family... every time she thought of the umbilical cord that stretched between them she felt as though she were at the top of a high tree, longing to be on the ground, but afraid to jump... How would they treat Dinh? With acceptance or frigidity, or would they just carp at him the way people carped at the postmistress of the provincial post office and the ticket-seller at the Diep Vang bus station? He was, after all, a northerner, like all the other northerners who had rushed to the south as soon as they could to grab at the golden opportunities. Did Dinh think of her as golden opportunity? As the favored son of a shrewd and authoritative woman who ruled her family with an iron hand, he'd spent his life strutting around doing as he pleased within the relative freedom he'd created for himself. According to him, his wife's family adored him as well. Would he be able to stand the loss of position he would feel in her family, a family whose foundation was built on traditional concepts of simple purity, quiet fulfillment of family duties, and a culture of rigid hierarchy?

Dinh walked into the kitchen and returned with a pair of scissors. He set to work removing the license plate on his Unity brand bicycle. "I've had enough of this thing! It's time to put an end to its miserable role in our history," he muttered with furious finality.

"Why didn't you ride the moped to save yourself the pedaling?" asked his mother.

"I knew I was stopping by here today so I rode the bicycle; it's easier to get up the stairs. Not to mention that the price of black-market gas for the Green Fish is through the roof!"

"Well, bring the moped here some day, will you? I need you to take me to buy some herbs to take back to Vinh."

Dinh looked at her imploringly. "Tiep's here, why rush back home? You've got to stay awhile so Tiep can come by and visit at least a few times!"

Both the old woman and Tiep were silent. His cajoling was sweet, but out of place considering the situation. His mother picked up the tin license plate that Dinh had just tossed away by the shoerack and engrossed herself in examining this souvenir of her beloved son's life journey.

"Aren't you going to keep it, son?"

Dinh clucked his tongue. "The sooner I get rid of it, the better I'll feel. What would I keep it for? More clutter in the house?"

With the license plate in her hand, the old woman opened

the door for Dinh to push his bicycle out. Tiep stuck her head out to say goodbye. Dinh's shirt today was as old and faded as all his shirts, but longer and baggier than usual. She noticed he had pulled the tails down to cover several ample patches on the rear of his gray pants. Add to that the army-green pith helmet perched on his unruly head of hair, and he looked remarkably like the wandering locksmiths that Tiep had seen on the streets the past few days. Dinh looked back at her, shrugged, then stuck his tongue out as though trying to compensate for his ragged appearance. She could see his pride squirming inside him behind the cheerful wink.

His mother reminded Tiep to bolt the door, then returned to the living room. After a moment's hesitation:

"Do you see, dear? He's devoted to the point of completely neglecting himself, but that wife of his is still not satisfied. And their professions are as incompatible as can be. Back before she got her university degree she still respected her husband, but now that she's sitting in the chair of organizing cadre for the city council, her husband might as well be an old worn-out hat. It's a hard one to figure out, child!"

They sat down again on the settee. Seeing her opening, Tiep quickly asked, "Can you tell me what's really going on in their marriage, Mother?"

She felt as though her heart would stop. This was the answer she'd been waiting for, from the most important eyewitness. But the old woman was brooding over the betel leaf in her hands—Aunt Rang all over again—then sent her sharp knife flashing over a pretty little areca nut. Tiep waited patiently and watched her. She felt a little in awe at being in the flesh-and-blood presence of the woman whom Dinh had described to her so many times, in Dong Dung, in his sporadic letters, even over the last few days. She'd never met anyone who worshipped his mother as he did; his mother was young and pure, yet old and wise, she was the epitome of thrift and good judgment. Her status as a saint had been enhanced after she'd suffered a year in prison on false charges during the period of land reform, and he'd all but elevated her to godhood when she took in his children during the evacuation of Hanoi. She was everything to him, a mother and a best friend, the sky and the earth, love and admiration. Perhaps this was why there was so little room in his heart for his Crazy Bertha city council member; how could any woman possibly compare to the woman he already had?

Tiep gently repeated her question. "Mother, if Dinh and his wife were to break up, how much of the fault would be mine?"

The old woman stood and walked into the kitchen to spit out the betel juice, then silently disappeared into the back room to look for something. Once again Tiep waited patiently. Once again she was a defendant at the bar, hoping against hope for clemency. Dinh's mother, like Aunt Rang, knew how to milk the proclamation of important decisions for all they were worth. Like Aunt Rang, she knew that she was the flagship, the slipknot that would unravel any issue to be decided. Dinh and Tiep had no need for Providence; they laid their supplications, with all their hopes and fears, at the feet of these two women.

But even if Dinh's mother offered her the hand of acceptance, thought Tiep, what would Aunt Rang do? Put on a show, no doubt. She'd play with Dinh like a cat tormenting a mouse. Because he was the provocateur, and she and her family the victims, the damaged parties. Once more, Tiep imagined the scene of these two formidable matriarchs meeting, even though the possibility of that seemed as unlikely as rapprochement between Vietnam and America.

Dinh's mother returned, carrying an old newspaper in one hand to wrap up Dinh's license plate and two sticks of some sort of medicinal root in the other.

"I'm going to keep the license plate for him, in case they make him put it back on," she said. Then, "You know, he keeps a framed photo of us at his house. He's only nine months old in the picture, and I'm holding him." Then a sigh. "Here's two sticks of ginseng. You're nothing but skin and bones, child. Take these back with you and when you start feeling tired just bite off a piece and suck on it for strength. The children too. Privation can lead to low blood pressure. When they faint, you can grind up some ginseng and soak it, then give them the juice to drink. Can you remember all that?" She thrust the gift into Tiep hands, then turned her attention to her betel basket just as Aunt Rang would do, and lowered her voice. "I really should have gone back home already, but Dinh begged me to stay to meet you. When I stay here with Hoa I can't stand her husband Su, and if I stay with Dinh I can't stand his Cam. I can't stand Hanoi either, I like being out in the country. Poor Dinh has to travel such a long way to see me, he might as well be just throwing all his money out on the road. Many times I've wished that he had a different girl, so that I could live with him. But who might this girl be, and how to make it happen?" She paused thoughtfully. "If his misery is a one, mine is a ten. But if anything happened to hurt the grandchildren, I wouldn't be able to bear it!"

Tiep held her breath as she listened, devouring each word. She was also beginning to digest the realization that Dinh's procrastination in leaving his wife was primarily due to deference to his beloved mother's fears. She gave a long, inward sigh and wished she could burst into tears. She thought of Tuyen's grandparents, who had raised him from a child and encouraged him to join the guerrillas. Tiep had loved them and cared for them, even more than Tuyen's parents had. They threatened suicide when they heard that she and Tuyen might separate. Then there was Tuyen's father, a tiny man who had been relegated to the role of servant to his wife, a woman of arched eyebrows and high, authoritative cheekbones. This small, silent man had rushed to his son's side when he heard the news, only to say, "Fine then, just poison the children first to get rid of them, and then you can do whatever you want!"

Dinh's mother continued. "This year I'm older than

Dinh's father was when he died. If there is one thing that I regret in my life, it's that I allowed Dinh to choose that Cam woman. If only he'd met someone else, his career would be so much farther along by now. His wife keeps pushing him down, child! You're not at fault, the fault rests entirely on him and Cam. How he is, how she is, and how they are together. She's so proud and arrogant, and he's the type who wants to be put on a pedestal and mollycoddled. He stopped by my house on his way back from Dong Dung and told me all about you, you know. The way he is, he can't keep anything inside even if you tell him to. Well, you go ahead and take care of things on your end first, you hear?"

There was a call at the door, a heavy Nghe An accent. Dinh's mother stood up and reassured Tiep. "It's just Hoa, back from the market. She'll tell you more, child."

Tiep followed the old woman to the door, flustered because she didn't know how to address Dinh's sister. Hoa was younger than Dinh, but a full twelve years older than Tiep. Should she address her as Older Sister because of their age difference, or Younger Sister because of her relationship to Dinh? But then a woman of about her sister Hoai's age burst through the door, chubby and more expansive than she could have imagined, a plastic Soviet-made basket in one hand and her other hand reaching out to squeeze Tiep's shoulder while she bubbled, "This is Older Sister Tiep? Heavens, you can't imagine how Dinh talks about you all day! Gives me a headache but I couldn't wait to meet you. How are the children doing while you're here, Sis?"

It was a question that didn't require an answer, for Hoa had already bustled into the kitchen to busy herself with lunch preparations. Tiep was left behind, stunned at the ease of their introduction. She couldn't help but compare Dinh's sister to her own Hoai; both were obviously and endlessly passionate about family and entertaining, the kind of people that Dinh defined as "if a thief broke into the house, they'd be sure to inquire to see if they had any relatives or home village in common before raising the alarm." Tiep realized that Hoa's generosity was born of a fierce loyalty to the clan, of putting the interests and happiness of her people above all, and of course the "people" in question here was Dinh; the warmth of her reception was due to Dinh, the eldest boy and an eldest son of an eldest son, the star of their clan.

Now Hoa was taking her purchases out of the basket and arranging them into various tubs and strainers, keeping up a rapid-fire chatter as she did.

"Been in line since the break of dawn until now and all I could get was this miserable piece of stringy old meat. Only the greens were any good today. Why don't you come along with me out to the public faucet so we can chat? Oh, but wait a sec, you should see this first! Get a look at what Dinh looked like when he was young, along with the whole family..."

Dinh's mother had returned to the living room with a pile of medicinal herbs and roots and was absorbed in the work with which she had managed to support her family after their fields were confiscated in the land reform. Hoa pulled Tiep into the inner room and took a framed black-and-white photo, about the size of a paperback book, off the wall and innocently told her it was a picture of the family taken after Dinh's wedding in Vinh twenty-four years ago. Tiep took the photo and stepped out into the living room, as though to see it in better light. In fact she wanted to be alone with this artifact that she could not possibly take in without mixed feelings, in spite of Hoa's simplistic intentions. She was grateful that Dinh's mother had not bustled around showing off this picture and that. The old woman truly was as discreet and wise as Dinh imagined her to be.

In the picture, Dinh was standing close to his new bride, a woman with fresh, flower-petal lips, as lovely as a dream and as dreamy as the full moon. He was wearing a smile that Tiep realized he had only worn once in his life, a virginal, rapt expression that he would never be able to give to her and she would never own. How could she; she had been only eight years old when the picture was taken, living in the roil of the southern rebellion, completely unaware of what it meant to grow up and know love, literature, happiness, and misery. How could she have known that in a place a thousand miles away, a man and woman were giggling together and "doing it over and over that first night" as he had confessed to her. Likewise, how could that man know that twenty years later he would betray the wife he had done "over and over" by desiring a honeymoon with another woman?

As Tiep passed the photo back to Hoa, she couldn't help but blurt out, "He looks so pleased with himself!"

"You said it," Hoa said, as oblivious as ever. More than oblivious; the woman was as thoughtless as a child. "Back then Cam was only eighteen, and the belle of all of Vinh. Who could possibly have thought life would hand them such a difficult row to hoe, eh, Sis?"

Hoa bustled on ahead, carrying the tubs and strainers of meat and greens. Tiep followed reluctantly. She felt superfluous now, as though everything that needed to be understood had been absorbed, through intuition and instinct. Now there was no point in turning her curiosity into self-sacrifice; if Dinh's Crazy Bertha suddenly appeared, or Hoa's belligerent husband Su returned home, there was no telling what might become of their bun cha noodle lunch.

But Hoa kept on, balancing her stack of foodstuffs as she crossed the road. She led Tiep into the Kim Lien complex, telling her that this was the mother of all of Hanoi's residential blocks. There was a public faucet under a canopy of arching mahogany branches, and in the distance Tiep could see a market, a collection of government-run shops that had an impressive air of authority but a distinct lack of sanitation and actual goods to sell.

Few people were using the faucet at this noon hour. There was a woman doing her laundry in two heavy, dirty-looking aluminum tubs, and a pale-skinned older man standing over a huge Soviet-made basin and enthusiastically pouring scoops of water over his half-naked body, the pertinent parts barely covered by a pair of thin boxer shorts. He was staring unabashedly at the bras and underwear floating in the woman's tub of water.

"You old goat!" shrilled the woman in a heavily accented Thanh Hoa voice. "Coming out to bathe at exactly this hour every day, sticking your hands down your pants to scrub it right out in the open where everyone can see! Disgusting!"

The disgusting old man responded with a vulgar grin. "So why do you come out to do your laundry every day at exactly this time, hm?"

"You know I'll be here, why don't you take your water home to bathe? Let your wife and kids watch!"

"My wife's at work. I like coming out here where I can look around while I bathe—where's the harm in that?"

"Asshole!"

Tiep stood, transfixed, expecting them to come to blows any second. But instead the atmosphere eased, as though the two were used to trading harsh words and equally used to withdrawing at exactly the right moment. Hoa was chattering to her about how at least they had running water here, no doubt it was miserable staying at the university with her friend, and did Tiep want to take the opportunity to wash her hair. If so she'd be happy to run up to the house to grab some soap and a towel? Tiep shook her head and sat down to begin snapping the stalks off the greens.

She thought of Tuyen's family again, but this time it was the image of his younger sister that floated into her mind. She was second-born, like Dinh's sister Hoa, and risked escape from the country in the hopes of rescuing her nine younger siblings. In the end she miscalculated and was arrested. Tuyen had refused to go to court on the day she was brought up on charges of treason, partly because he was angry and partly because he didn't dare show his sinless face in court. Tiep had gone instead. She feared nothing, and she wanted to see his sister one last time to slip her what few meager coins they could spare. In her heart, Tiep admired her sacrifice. If anyone could make her think twice about their separation, it was most assuredly not him; but rather the image of Tuyen's frail grandparents, his despairing father, and his sister, completely destroyed after serving her term in prison.

"Did mother tell you her idea, Sis?" asked Hoa, her voice serious for the first time.

"She only mentioned the situation between Dinh and Cam, and encouraged me to resolve things on my side. But my husband Tuyen will be away studying in Saigon for several more years."

"Mother said she'll talk to Cam, get her to agree to an informal arrangement. She's worried about people talking so doesn't want anything official done in the court. We're friends with the in-laws, you know. I even used to be Cam's friend. Complicated, huh! The main thing mother thinks about is the children. It'd be great if you could meet them, they're smart, good-looking kids. They've all got their father's genes, especially the boy who's studying in Poland right now. Mother's afraid that if Dinh makes a mess of the situation the boy won't want to come home. And if that happens, she'll be taking a razor to both of them, Dinh and Cam alike. She'll shave them bald!"

A wave of self-pity swept over Tiep, and she felt like crying. "But what about my children? They've suffered enough with their father and mother going separate ways. Now you want them to put up with the shame of having a mother who's either a slut or a mistress? I have my honor, for myself and for my children, for my whole family. Do you understand? The way things are these days, if it isn't official it doesn't count for squat. Dinh and I would still be outcasts, targets of vilification and rumor. How could I bear it?"

"Well exactly! I told mother that arrangements like that are old-fashioned. If you're not official, how could you start a new life together? And anyway Cam wouldn't let you alone to enjoy life, much less to write your books! You know, if my husband could put together a sentence—just one sentence—the way Dinh does, I'd worship the ground he walks on!"

At precisely that moment, Tiep noticed a pair of feet in clear plastic sandals standing near them. She looked up, and though she'd never met him before she knew without a doubt that this was Su, the man that Dinh's mother had pressured Hoa into marrying. He was small and pale, with short arms, a low forehead and a slightly pointed chin. Clearly a man of modest resources in every aspect except for his fanaticism, with which he was no doubt richly endowed.

"So this is the Ms. Tiep, eh?" His accent was from south-central provinces, and grated on her ears.

Tiep stood up, determined to be polite. "You're Older Brother Su? Pleased to meet you!"

Hoa stayed where she was, her hands hesitant and still in the tub of water and greens. "Older brother? Go ahead and call him younger brother, Sis, it sounds better!"

"Are you crazy, Hoa? She can't be any older than my youngest sister."

"This clod doesn't know the first thing about manners!" Hoa said to Tiep.

"Come on, Hoa, inviting this Ms. Tiep for lunch... do you really think it's consistent with moral principles?"

"I will not discuss moral principles with you!"

"Fine, then I will not sit down to eat with people who are immoral!"

"Oh really? It was mother who invited Older Sister Tiep to lunch. Are you implying that mother is immoral?"

Tiep glanced around. By a stroke of good fortune, the others had left by now. Equally fortunate was the appearance of Dinh's mother, quick as a flash and seething with anger.

"Whatever you're up to, boy, come into the house and have it out with me. What are you doing making a scene here, eh?"

Dinh's brother-in-law didn't stand a chance. He slunk away, resigned to the fate of lifelong gratitude for having been able to marry this woman's daughter. Tiep looked around again, lost, like a child looking for help but not knowing what to ask. If Aunt Rang should see this, she thought. If my mother, Hoai, or Nghia should see this, or my kids should see this, they'd all cluster around and put up a wail that would shake the sky. They'd cry for me, but they'd also be crying for themselves, because I've shamed them all. Su won't be the first to throw stones...

Dinh's mother was talking urgently. "Forget it! You two hurry up with the food while I go back to watch the apartment. It was lucky that I happened to be on the balcony and saw him, if not he would have picked a fight for sure."

Dinh's sister was back to her oblivious self. "No worries. That idiot won't be coming home for lunch!"

Tiep hesitated, then blurted out her fears as soon as Dinh's mother had left.

"Is there any chance Su might go and see Cam?"

"Oh, yeah," Hoa looked nonplussed. "Why didn't I think of that? Oh well. You wait here. I'll go up and tell mother and then be back with your bike and purse. I'll come see you at the university another day, and we'll go to a restaurant to have a real meal of bun cha noodles. Just wait, I'll be right down, okay?"

It was at that moment that Tiep decided she had to find a way to meet the Other Woman, Dinh's Crazy Bertha. Even if it meant marching straight into the lair of the tigress, she would find a way to talk to her, to make her own judgments and decisions. She alone.

15
Winter 1983

That morning, Boss Poet knocked on the door of Tiep's room, with a shoulder sagging under the weight of a faded green khaki bag—his "mobile office"—and an expression as if he had just returned from the doctor's with a terminal diagnosis. He slid wearily into the jute chair beside Tiep's desk and looked around the room that had once been her office. A narrow bed had been set up in one corner for the children, and the door to the inner office now led to Hieu Trinh's territory, where the children were sometimes "evacuated" if their mother was entertaining a guest into the wee hours.

"You've done a good job with the room, Tiep. I haven't been up to see it since you moved in. Gotta keep things squeaky clean with each other, in case rumors start flying around. It's hard to keep your spirits up to write when that happens, eh?" He smiled, revealing a missing tooth in the corner of his mouth. His eyes glistened wetly and his voice forced itself into a brittle, choked laugh.

"What's the matter?" asked Tiep.

"Are the kids all at school? No, no, I don't want any tea or cigarettes, Tiep. Let's go out on the balcony for a chat."

Her boss paced back and forth on the balcony, a large space as wide as half the width of the house. Tiep knew he loved this precious space. He'd bought several stone benches and placed them on the balcony for the moon-gazing parties he liked to organize. The melon vines and herbs that Tiep and the children had planted amidst the thick tangles of yellow chrysanthemums seemed to please him. He plopped down on a stone bench.

"This house has tremendous meaning to our organization, Tiep," he said thoughtfully. "Back during the takeover, the son of the colonel who owned the house was so undone by the injustice that he hanged himself, did you know that? From the ceiling fan in the room that Hieu Trinh is living in now. Did you know that?"

Tiep sat down on a second bench and listened carefully. She knew the story but hadn't mentioned it to the children. They were far too young for stories of victors and vanquished, takeovers and re-education camps, hangings and tiny boats launching out to sea in desperation.

Boss Poet pulled his feet up to sit cross-legged on the bench. His hands absent-mindedly rubbed his delicate arms.

"I feel sorry for the fate they suffered. I feel for that young soul who didn't understand that times come and go, and for this fine cultured house. When it fell into our hands, it was just perfect. Even had a place to sit and gaze at the moon. For the past ten years I've been doing all I can to make it a lively meeting place for all the artists and writers of our province. I've felt touched many times because you are one of the few people who recognize my labors. Isn't that right, Tiep?"

There was definitely something wrong, Tiep knew.

"What's happened? Just tell me, you'll feel better!" she urged.

The poet smiled painfully. "No matter what happens, you have to write more than ever. Get as many stories in print as you can, so you can be admitted to the Central Writer's Union. Of the three of you girls, An Khuong is too pedantic, but her English is good so she can be a translator. Hieu Trinh is as closed up as an overgrown snail; she can't hold a candle to you. You're the only one I have hopes for."

"Is membership in the Central Writers' Union so important?" Tiep asked. She was more worried about what was going on with her boss than how to make Hanoi notice her.

Boss Poet turned and looked at her, his face haggard in the early morning sun. "Huh! You have to be a member of the Central Union to have standing out here in the provinces. Say what you will, but people will give you more respect. And fewer restrictions!"

Tiep was studying him. "I'm sure that you did not come here this early in the morning today to talk about my admission to the Central Union."

He was silent. Finally, haltingly, his sentimental eyes so wet they looked swollen, he said, "I'm telling you this so that you can figure your own way out. I have my own troubles, as you know only too well. It's sink or swim for both of us. We'll be lucky to save ourselves, much less throw a life preserver to each other!"

Tiep thought of the girl with the impossibly curled eyelashes and a sincere, moist beauty, a fan of Boss Poet, who used to attend the Club events on the first floor. But then the girl's appearances had became fewer and farther between, and Hieu Trinh whispered, in that inimitably critical voice of hers, "It seems that the sweet thing is expecting, so she was sent home to forget about literature and try to scrape by, raising pigs while our boss here is about to be demoted!"

Tiep comforted him gently. "I've heard about your trouble. God, that's what's expected of a poet, after all. It'd be stranger if you didn't. But they're saying you might be replaced. Don't tell me Hai Kham can't give you a hand? After all, you did publish all those collections of his poems."

Boss Poet laughed bitterly. "It's no more than a bribe, like so many other bribes that he gets from so many other people, you know? When something needs to be done they do it. It's their positions that are important; my position is nothing more than a favor they once granted and can strip away at any time to give to someone else."

Tiep smiled sadly. "Well, our type may have scandalous reputations, but we've got our limits. We may be depraved, but certainly no more depraved than they!"

At this Boss Poet guffawed out loud, a great bubbling laugh that still managed to sound choked.

"Are you generalizing, or coming up with a defense for yourself? Because, my dear girl, what in the world were you doing in Hanoi that letters of denunciation should flutter down here like butterflies? I'm a snail that can't even carry my own shell. How am I going to save you?"

Tiep pressed herself against the back of the chair, like a condemned prisoner who has suddenly heard the clank of the key in the lock before being marched out.

Well, she thought, so be it. At least before facing the firing squad, she had lived those intoxicating moments with Dinh, not only in Ky's woven-bamboo labyrinth, or the afternoons spent exploring Hanoi's alleyways, or in the creaky loft in Dinh's friend's house on Son Tay street. In spite of his mother's fears, they had pressed the Green Fish into service to tour the areas outside the city as well—here the Duong River dike made famous in Hoang Cam's poems, there the arching canopy of a longan tree that reminded her of Quang Dung's poem "Son Tay Eyes"; on one unseasonably cold day, they had even risked a trip to Do Son beach where Tiep had rented an old-fashioned one-piece swimming suit from the Union Guesthouse and, after swimming, had wriggled in delight under the scoops of fresh water that Dinh poured over her body in the ramshackle bath house with no door but the terrycloth towel they had hung over the doorframe... If it was their fate to be tried in a Party court, and condemned, even sent to a re-education camp for violating the Marriage and Family Law, Tiep and Dinh would consider themselves courageous martyrs for their creed, the creed of Love, at whose altar they had willingly laid down their lives.

Boss Poet was opening his bag and pulling out a wad of official-looking envelopes. He started to hand them to Tiep, then changed his mind and returned them to the bag. "Forget it, what's the point of having you read them? Just bring you down even more. They're from a woman who says she is Dinh's wife. One sent to the Writers' Union addressed to me, one sent to Tuyen, four sent to other important addresses, all full of strident denunciation. They ended up on Hai Kham's desk and from there got served on yours truly so I can prepare myself for a review of my personnel management skills. Turns out this Cam woman is quite good at using power and the Party to get what she wants!"

Tiep's fingers twitched nervously; she squeezed them and wondered at the chill that had seized her body. If she was this cold now, how would she feel when she stepped up into the defendant's dock? Surely she hadn't lost the bravado and passion that Dinh had nurtured in her with his optimism and impudence? When Boss Poet spoke again, he avoided looking at her. They were more than just colleagues now, she realized. They were stuck in the same boat without the proverbial paddle, and he had no desire to pry into her pain.

"Do you know what Dinh's wife recommended in the letter she sent to the Writers' Union? She didn't ask that you be ordered to leave her husband alone. No, she's asking that we garnish your pay and send her installments to pay her back for the money you used out of the royalties Dinh got for some travelogue he wrote. Because you used up the money she needed to buy food for her and the kids, she says..."

Tiep snorted. Suddenly she no longer felt that she was standing on the execution grounds; instead, she felt as though she had scaled a mountain and from the heights she was able to see everything more clearly. The journey up the mountain had been hard but it had not been a waste of her strength and effort. She had not thrown away her life. From here, her future looked expansive, full, and worth every breath she took, while everything behind her was crystal clear and worth the challenge. With an ironic smile, she said, "Don't you think a woman who's only jealous of her husband's money deserves to lose him?"

Boss Poet laughed, and his eyes sparkled with affection. "True! But if that's your only defense, don't think you can make it past the gentlemen of the Standing Committee."

Tiep sprang out of her chair and began to pace like a caged animal while he continued.

"They're coming down to conduct a disciplinary hearing.

They'll expect you to write a self-criticism. It's up to you whether you accept or deny guilt. I believe in your intelligence and sincerity; you'll figure out what to do."

"All four of the Standing Committee members are coming down here just because of a few letters? My God, are they that bored?"

"My dear, it's a golden opportunity for them. By punishing you, they're admonishing me as well. Two birds with one stone, terribly convenient! And anyway, who told you to up and leave a future member of the Standing Committee? Not to mention the fact that your writing is, well, problematic."

"What does my writing have to do with the fact that I left Tuyen for Dinh?" she fretted.

"So it turns out my little girl is quite the naïve one, eh? How dare you write stories and become famous, or more to the point become more famous than Hai Kham? Unacceptable!" His voice turned grim again. "Look, I know all about the love affairs each one of those men is hiding in his past, back during the war. That's why I advise you never to let them see you cry. Men like them, who dust off their morality just long enough to use it to stone a woman—even God couldn't save their souls!"

Boss Poet left, and Tiep was alone on the stone bench. She was glad that Thu Thi and Vinh Chuyen hadn't been there to hear. Although she had a fairly clear picture of the woman now, Tiep still felt as though she were being stalked by an enemy who would always have yet another blow hidden up her sleeve. If only Cam had written to her directly. Tiep could have mined the words and emotions expressed between the lines to know if she should advance or retreat. She might have allowed herself to slip from Dinh's fingers, as silently and smoothly as a little fish. But now, she would never know what was truly driving the other woman. Wasn't that, after all, the timeless desire and also the timeless gulf between any two women who loved the same man?

She had seen her, Dinh's Crazy Bertha, before the woman had discovered her purloined "food kitty" and had sat down to write those letters. That day, after taking her leave of Hoa at the public faucet, Tiep had eaten lunch with Dinh's friend, the one on Son Tay street who acted as their "living mailbox." Later, when the strong noon sun had mellowed to gentle afternoon heat, she visited the art museum on her own and then sat out the Hanoi afternoon rush hour at the Tran Vu shrine in the Tran Quoc temple. Next she wandered around the Nui Nung park, listening to the mournful northeast wind and understanding just how badly Dinh had missed her because of this wind. Only after it had been dark for some time did she push her bike through a gap in the wall and leave the park. Many others were heading home too, but still she wondered nervously if maybe it was too early for what she intended to do. So she pedaled out to the Hang Co train station to confirm her reservation home. She killed yet more time by dawdling to see just how bad the lines were in this station. She didn't see any broken bricks or ragged hats reserving people's spaces as at the government shops.

Finally she stole her way to that particular row of flats in that particular apartment block. She saw walls of sloppily joined concrete slabs; frail, lopsided electrical poles strung together with jury-rigged wires that sagged like laundry lines on a construction site; streaks of moss licking along the path of the black-stained pipes carrying waste down from the upper stories; and a public cistern, lidless, in the middle of a small square courtyard that served the four rows of flats which faced onto it. Tiep found an old woman selling tea from the recesses of a niche under the staircase facing the row of flats in which Dinh's second-story apartment was located. She easily recognized it: a corner apartment with a caged-in balcony sporting several hydrangea trees that Dinh had so often boasted about. On the day his eldest son passed his exam to qualify for overseas study, the trees had blossomed with exactly twenty flowers. It all felt so familiar to her: the block of flats, the courtyard, the minutiae of inadequacy and privation, the hydrangeas and the shadows... familiar and melancholy but also suffused with a powerful sense of stalking hostility.

The old woman was about the same age as Dinh's mother, but more sturdily built. She wore a brown shirt with a large black patch on one shoulder, a brown scarf wrapped around her head in traditional peasant style, and faded black silk pants. In front of her was arranged a row of sad little glass jars displaying her wares: peanut brittle, candy-covered peanuts, gum, and loose tobacco, along with punks and a water pipe. She had taken good care of the hollow under the staircase so it was clean and dry, although not entirely free of the miasma of depression surrounding it. Tiep parked her bike where she could keep an eye on it and settled herself onto one of the tiny stools that gave her a good view up to Dinh's balcony. If he looked down he'd see nothing but a puddle of darkness. She was safe as long as he did not come down to the tea-seller for a toke on her water pipe.

The old woman had the eyes of a shrewd judge of people. Right away she asked, "Where are you from, young lady?"

"I'm from Saigon," Tiep responded politely, unable to think of a better lie.

"So are you looking for someone you know, or are you meeting someone here?"

"Why would you think I am meeting someone?"

The old woman cleared her throat and offered Tiep a tiny teacup with a chipped handle filled with dark tea. "Well, I just check out people's faces and get a picture. Is the tea here too strong for you?"

Gratefully, Tiep asked her to pour the tea into a glass and dilute it with hot water. Having had time now to consider her story, she said, "I'm from a publishing house in the south. I'm meeting a girlfriend here and then we are going to the house of a writer in this block. We have some business with him."

The old woman nodded knowingly, then jerked her chin

in the direction of the balcony with the hydrangea trees. "Ah, that Viet Dinh fellow, no doubt? Why didn't he ask you to meet him at his office? So you wouldn't have to find his house and all the trouble that goes with it?"

"Do many writers live in this area, Auntie?" Tiep asked.

The old woman winked at Tiep with friendly reproach. "You think writers are like mushrooms that every block should have several? We've got only the fellow there on the second floor. Ever since I left the countryside with my son to come here—and that was back when there wasn't a single balcony-cage on the block, mind you—I've known this area like the back of my hand. But you didn't answer me. Don't you think it would be better to conduct your business with him somewhere else?"

Tiep was beginning to realize that this old woman could be interesting. "Why do you say that, ma'am?" she asked innocently.

At that moment, a middle-aged lady turned into the alley from the main street and stopped by the tea stand to buy a few packages of peanut brittle. Tiep's breath stopped; she couldn't take her eyes off the woman, who despite her age had a very pretty face. Tiep always thought of Dinh's wife whenever she saw an older woman who had managed to maintain her looks. Unfortunately, the twenty-four-year-old photograph she had seen at Dinh's sister's house was no help. What if this is Dinh's wife, Tiep thought, and the old woman introduces me as someone who's come to "conduct some business" with Dinh? What will I do? The elegant woman returned Tiep's stare. Tiep heard the old woman blurt out, "This young lady is from the south. She's waiting for her friend to meet her and they have some business with the writer, something about publishing!"

Tiep's breath returned in a sigh of relief. So it wasn't Dinh's wife. The lady's lips parted in the slightest of smiles, and as she turned away she said to no one in particular, "Must be quite a tiger, to venture into the lair of a lion!"

The old woman waited until the lady had disappeared into the housing block before expanding on that comment. "You see, it's just that not too long ago—it was around lunchtime, not in the evening like now—there was this other young woman from some publishing house or another, some place far away like Haiphong or Hue or something, who also showed up here looking for their house. She asked me to watch her bicycle for her. A few minutes later he came running down to buy some candy for a guest, that's how I knew she was visiting him. I guess they must've really been enjoying their conversation and weren't watching the time, because the next thing you knew his wife came home and found her husband with a female guest and the dinner not cooked as usual. She shut the door and lit into them, smashing and breaking things inside. The main thing was that the guest was a girl. Didn't matter what she was there for. I swear she could've been bringing the husband royalty money and that woman wouldn't care, any female guest is unacceptable to her. It was lunchtime as I said, so no one was around and I could hear everything from here. Then the door opened and the girl shot out as if she ware being chased by the legions of hell. She stopped for a breath here and let me in on what happened, that's how I know. Poor things. Every tree has its flower and every family has its circumstances, I guess. That woman figures that with her looks and social position, she's entitled to break things and scream if anyone crosses her in the slightest way. Some days the husband closes the door so that the neighbors don't have to hear, and she throws the door open again and stands right there on the balcony while chewing him out. Poor thing! I know a writer doesn't make much money, but he's the only writer our little neighborhood has."

Tiep had been hoping for scraps of information; instead she had hit the mother lode, a veritable jumble of information. She kept on playing her role. "So, I should just wait until my friend comes and then take off, you think? Of course we'll have some tea and candy here first, to help you out."

The old woman was on a roll now. "Poor thing! The husband is busy all day with his rice mash and pigs, and then clacking away at the typewriter all night. It's because he does everything for them, his wife and kids I mean, that's why she's gone as bad as she has. A few months ago he bought a little moped to save himself some sweat on his wine runs. I always see him up there on the balcony clanking around trying to fix it. He's the type of fellow who's always finding himself something to do, you know. The rice wine is bootleg, and the pigs aren't supposed to be there on the second floor, but folks around here feel sorry for him so we don't say anything. It's the times, too. Everyone's hungry, everyone's got something going on the side, so we've got to watch out for each other."

Up there in the iron cage with the hydrangea trees, a small round light bulb suddenly lit up and a brown door opened. Tiep caught a glimpse of Dinh, shirtless and clad only in a pair of boxer shorts, wheeling his ancient moped out to perform some sort of maintenance on this troublesome locust he'd purchased with his bootlegging money. A young girl followed him, looking down at the tea-seller. No doubt he'd told her to run down and buy something for him. Tiep prepared herself for a unilateral audience with Dinh's daughter. Naturally enough, she was curious and thrilled at the opportunity to gaze anonymously at his child. The little girl with the chubby face and pageboy haircut disappeared down a hallway, then moments later appeared in full view at Tiep's level.

The old woman continued with her commentary. "That's her, their youngest child. If you want to send a message into the writer you can tell the girl."

Hastily, Tiep said, "Please don't say anything to her, ma'am! I'll just wait for my friend and then we'll leave. It's bad enough that I came here. If I send in a message asking him to come out and meet me at the tea stall, I'll have no escape if his wife comes out!"

The girl was standing before her now, and Tiep felt that

the effort and courage she had expended to come and sit at the tea stall were now well repaid. The child's almost perfectly round face and flawless skin were no doubt from her mother, but her eyes betrayed an unpretentious and sentimental spirit that was clearly her father's. Tiep felt as though she knew her. She desperately wanted this girl to love her, not to hate her as most stepdaughters do their stepmothers.

"May I have a packet of Tien Lang and a handful of punks?" the girl asked the tea-seller. Her eyes fastened on Tiep with a curiosity that seemed almost prescient. Finally she could no longer restrain herself and asked, "Are you from the south, ma'am?"

Tiep smiled and imitated the child's accent, saying, "Aren't you clever!" The girl grinned and a dimple appeared on her cheek. Tiep remembered Dinh telling her that when the girl was around four, she had fallen into the cistern. He'd seen it happen from the balcony but had waited a few moments, to teach her a lesson she'd remember, before running down to pull her out. "The scar she got has made her even more beautiful than her mother!" he had bragged to her.

"Is your mother at home, Xuyen?" the old woman asked, no doubt feeling out the situation for her customer, the "girl from the publishing house."

"Yes, she is," said the child, her eyes never leaving Tiep, not even to blink, only because Tiep was staring at her without a blink. Then Dinh gave a shout from the balcony and the girl whisked herself away. Fortunately, just as Tiep had guessed, the dark shadow of the staircase combined with the weak light of the old woman's oil lamp hid her from his view. He had no idea she was sitting there, watching him bustling around half-naked.

As her apprehension and unease faded, Tiep found that she was enjoying this game of spy. And it was at that moment that a sturdy female figure appeared in the doorway. She was wearing a pair of black pants and a print blouse, the standard home wear of any woman who has to rely on the government-run shops for her wardrobe. The clothing made her look quite ordinary, although she did have a short, permed hairdo that was more stylish than Tiep had seen in Hanoi. When she spoke, her voice carried the same heavy Nghe An accent as Dinh's sister's.

"Disgusting, smoking all day long! And what are you doing down at the tea shop so long, Xuyen?" (It was a double-barbed arrow, Tiep noticed: one for the husband and his tobacco habit, the other for the daughter who hadn't returned with the detestable tobacco fast enough.) "Where is your brother Bao?"

Tiep recalled that Dinh had described his wife as the type of woman who would willingly go hungry so her children could eat but rarely hugged or kissed them as he did. Giving in once again to her habit of drawing comparisons, Tiep realized that in this way Dinh's wife was very similar to her own mother.

Xuyen had arrived at the balcony now. Her mother gave her a push from behind that almost sent her sprawling into the wall. "I asked you, where is your brother Bao?!"

"He's gone to his friend's."

"Fine, you go pick up the pig shit then. Who could possibly put up with that stench!"

"Leave it and I'll do it, what does a little girl know..."

That was Dinh's voice, which rang out even louder than his wife's. The old woman gave Tiep a meaningful glance, as if to say, see, it's starting. Sure enough, the woman stepped entirely out into the light of the balcony, hands on her hips. There was a loud crash as her foot kicked something, no doubt Dinh's toolbox. "As for you, get rid of this damned pile of junk! I'm sick of you clattering around every night trying to fix it. It gives me a headache!"

Tiep did not hear any reply from Dinh. She knew that he could use silence as a weapon.

His refusal to engage enraged his wife. "Did you hear me? Only your little literature and poetry sluts would want to plant their asses on such a pile of shit!"

Dinh sprang to his feet, hurling something into his tool box. His arms were splayed out threateningly. "Xuyen, if you don't drag your mother into the house right now I swear I will damage her as badly as my junky little bike, you hear?" Then there was the sound of the girl insisting and the mother wailing, then the sound of a door slamming, and Dinh returned to park himself obstinately in front of his "pile of shit."

Tiep stood up silently, barely remembering to buy several packages of peanut brittle from the old woman to give to An Khuong. She knew now that if she had not come into Dinh's life he would have surely found someone else. Still, why did it have to be her? There was no understanding the mysteries of fate, the strange twists and turns imposed on humans by the will of heaven. She thought of how Dinh liked to brag to his friends, "The person who has most perfectly achieved the unification of the north and south is none other than moi!" His friends would interrupt to tease him. "Back during the war, when everyone else went off to fight in the jungles of the south, you stayed at home huddling behind your kids and university-student wife. Now that the feast is all prepared, you jump in and help yourself!" It always got a rise out of him, and he'd start justifying himself. "Well, I thought it would be good for her to get a proper degree, open up her eyes a little. Who knew she'd turn on me like that?"

It took about a year, but in the end, regardless of reasons manifest or mysterious, they came: the gentlemen and gentlewomen of her jury, all seething with righteous indignation, a typhoon no longer just predicted but blowing full force before which one could only sit and wait to see how far up the scale it went. A row of cars arrived, each one discharging a dignitary with an important black briefcase, a leaden stride, and a girth that was quickly widening beyond the dimensions of a "comrade from the trenches." While waiting for her hearing to begin, Tiep stood on the balcony and gazed down, watching Boss Poet as he smiled and nodded and pumped the hand of each, all while his face, neck, and even arms flushed bright red with the strain and embarrassment.

Tiep let herself into the first floor conference room and took the chair at the end of the large conference table. She noticed that the number of chairs at the table exactly matched the number of participants, an attention to detail usually displayed only at international summits. Hai Kham sat at the other end, opposite the "defendant," in the position reserved for the master of ceremonies. Beside him was the Head of the Examination Committee, a woman who had been famous throughout the guerrilla base for her overweening concern for the health of the Secretary of the Provincial Party Committee, expressed in repeated nighttime visits to "see how he is doing." No one was surprised when, only scant months after the death of his peasant wife in some unexplained accident, she became the Secretary's transitional partner until the prescribed period of mourning was finished and they could be married. From then on, the couple led each other up the ladder into ever more powerful positions until the Secretary unexpectedly passed away, leaving behind a wife of formidable power and talent along with his unfinished revolutionary mission.

Then there was the Head of the Organizing Committee, another official that Tiep knew only too well. Uncle Tu Tho's wife had mentioned this man specifically to Tiep when she came to collect her husband's letters. Later on, the man became infamous for a scandal involving a pretty secretary and a secret bunker. The secretary ended up leaving the guerrillas under heavy condemnation, her aspirations ruined, even though by rights he should have been held more responsible, given his presumably higher level of "revolutionary enlightenment."

Next to him was the Director of the Bureau of Culture and Information. Tiep wasn't sure why he had been invited, as he was not a member of the Standing Committee. Perhaps it was because he had been her boss once, after Uncle Tu

Tho's death, and they figured he could play the role of "good cop" in her education. Granted, he had the appearance of virtue—at least there were no fraternization incidents inked into his record—but she knew his penchant back during their guerrilla days to "mingle with the masses" rather than setting up his own tent as Uncle Tu Tho had done. There was one place he particularly liked to mingle, that being the house of a middle-aged woman with a giggly voice as though her armpits were being perpetually tickled and a pushover husband who was rumored to be impotent. Later, this man was sent to study at the Political Institute in Hanoi and when he returned he had acquired a plump, gooey-eyed "tail" whom he duly entrusted to Tiep's little Information Team. One difficult and tearstained day, the "tail" began to thrash when she realized that her paramour would never dare leave his wife, no matter how rustic and unsophisticated she was, simply because it would affect his position. As was only natural, the "tail" agonized about her sorrow to her co-workers, Tiep included, before taking the next train back to the north.

The final member of the panel, the Secretary of the Party Civil Service, was a northern-trained cadre, a paragon of revolutionary virtue, and Tuyen's distant relative. Tiep had no doubt that he would be the primary "assassin" in their little drama. This was a man who had once pulled a gun on his own son-in-law simply because when he returned from the north after the Liberation he found that his daughter's marriage was a done deal but his new son-in-law was nothing more than a barber, a petty, thoroughly insignificant occupation that was certainly not worthy of the daughter of an officially trained cadre such as himself.

In the final analysis, it seemed that only Hai Kham had the right to throw the first stone. His record was spotless, even during his days as a guerrilla, so he could dissect Tiep without shame. Only thing was, Tiep had noticed that he never allowed his wife, a former domestic servant, to accompany him in his car. Any time there was an important meeting, he was always seen with the Madame Deputy Chairman of the Committee of Society and Arts, arriving with her, sitting with her, and leaning over to whisper in her ear.

So there it was, her illustrious jury of comrades, some with their skeletons publicly outed and others with skeletons firmly tucked away, all participating in this game of crushing another person under the sheer weight of their collective positions. Some came out of duty, others had no doubt been forced into the game by Hai Kham, and others—Tuyen's relative, for example—participated out of congenital animosity. Tiep faced them defiantly and braced herself. Boss Poet opened the hearing with a statement of their purpose and an introduction of the participants and his own role as keeper of the minutes. He looked about as natural as a pond frog in the middle of rapids, and every bit as miserable. As for Tiep, her eyes were watering, her ears ringing, and a pressure was building in her chest that she felt might explode. She was astonished at the effort and diligence they were putting into a simple case of one writer falling in love with another. They were men, but they had forgotten what it was to be a man, forgotten that she was a woman and without women they would not know what it feels like to have one's world turned upside down. Boss Poet was done with the preliminaries now, and Hai Kham started to speak, his fingers like noodles drumming gently on the pile of letters that Boss Poet had just passed to him to add a desired amount of gravitas as he eased into his lecture.

Tiep sprang to her feet and asked for the floor. She knew that Boss Poet and her old boss, the Bureau Director, couldn't stand this bizarre spectacle any more than she. Hai Kham silenced her with a signal that said it was not her turn to speak, that she didn't have the right to speak, and in fact there was nothing she could possibly say at the moment. But she did not obey. Her legs were shaking as though her knees had dissolved but they resolutely refused to bend, they were determined to help her maintain an upright posture of self-defense. So she spoke. She spoke of the absurdity of such a group thrashing; of the letters of a woman who knew only the punitive exercise of power and resentment over money but betrayed not a drop of suffering or loss as might be expected; of this waste of the people's money which could have been spent on electricity or water or even cigarettes and tea rather than this useless display of power; about the character of the people who were sitting in judgment of her and the lies she would be forced to recite in order to make it through this ridiculous game of lies. Boss Poet went from encouraging her with his eyes to slowly losing all color in his face, while the comrades' expression went from displeased to gaping. Only Hai Kham retained his composure, his back ramrod straight, placid fingers thoughtfully placed just under his nose, and an inscrutable expression of satisfaction as though he had just solved some very difficult equation in his chieftain's brain.

Tiep stopped talking. She did not sit down. Hai Kham signaled to Tuyen's relative, who immediately handed him a sheet of cheap onionskin paper folded into quarters, no envelope. Hai Kham unfolded the paper with excruciating deliberation in the tense atmosphere.

"All right then. Let's go ahead and say that these letters from our esteemed comrade, Mr. Dinh's wife, are not sufficient proof of a sexual relationship. But has any one of us ever had their relatives submit a petition to the Provincial Committee asking the Party to completely dissolve all family ties with us? I dare say not... never has anyone in this province, nay, in our entire nation, never in our times has a person been so utterly rejected by their family. Never! We'll adjourn now. Here, Tiep, this petition for dissolution is yours. The Party will deal with you by other means. We all understand how difficult it is to reform oneself, but don't think the Party will hesitate to deal with impudence!"

They left with their leaden stride, in their expensive cars powered by expensive petrol and paid for with the taxes of the masses for whom they always so loudly proclaimed their concern. Boss Poet saw them out in accordance with his duties as an obedient peon. Tiep remained where she sat, her eyes glued to that thin, yellowing sheet of onionskin paper. She saw immediately that the text was typewritten, and littered with words familiar to her from the speeches Tuyen used to bring home for her to edit. Her Aunt Rang was illiterate... no doubt they had read Dinh's wife's letter to Aunt Rang, and Aunt Rang had allowed Tuyen to orchestrate and write the petition. And no doubt behind Tuyen was his fanatic relative who thought nothing of pulling a gun on his own daughter's husband.

Boss Poet returned and gave a ringing laugh. "You could face down Death itself, couldn't you, Tiep!"

Tiep pushed the letter toward her beloved if somewhat eccentric boss. Like a balloon popping inside her, her anger deflated abruptly and she hurled herself up the stairs to plunge spread-eagled onto her bed. She couldn't cry. Her entire body felt stupid and numb, as though she had just been lifted down from the gallows only to find that the court had slapped her with an additional charge. A charge which caused her more suffering and mortification than any other. Let them say she had committed debauchery, or adultery, or husband-theft, or usurped another woman's happiness... but to be marched up to execution by her own Aunt Rang, to be cut off from her clan, this she could not bear. Bereft of family, no Vietnamese could possibly be at peace.

PART THREE: RENOVATION

16

1985 - 1987

There was an old, empty myrtle-wood desk in her room on which Tiep worked. Not wanting to wake the children, or disturb Hieu Trinh in the inner room or the old artist below, she would use a checked peasant scarf from her guerrilla days to cushion the typewriter and mute the sound. She spread clean newspaper over the top of the old green filing cabinet requisitioned by her agency and placed a small incense holder there as an altar to the "martyred" son of the colonel who had once owned the house and was now in some faraway re-education camp. On the day of the full moon, when she reminded Thu Thi to light some incense for him, the child often added a few yellow chrysanthemum blossoms picked from the balcony. On the full moon of the seventh lunar month, a particularly propitious date, Tiep herself would arrange on the altar as many offerings as their chronically meager finances would allow. She believed that the youthful ghost occasionally returned from the other side to visit his old home, and hoped that he would favor her children with a little supernatural assistance in their lonely and difficult lives. She knew their little room was not sufficient for a family, but she was grateful for it. Like a shop's sturdy awning in a thunderstorm, she and her children could shelter there until the rain and winds had passed. Surely the wind would pass, she thought, and in the words of the immortal Scarlett O'Hara, tomorrow would be another day.[1]

She devoted herself to writing, and realized more than ever that literature was to her more a religion than an occupation. She daydreamed, drifting back to the pleasant afternoons

1. *Gone With the Wind*, with its setting in the Civil War and its themes of loss and survival, was very popular in Viet Nam in these years, and indeed throughout the war as well.

when, as a child, she would settle herself on the silky tip of a coconut palm spread out over a woven-bamboo platform and hum along with the sound of mynah birds twittering about a stalk of ripe bananas, or doves cooing in the stand of bamboo that lined the garden, or listen to the fish splashing in the nearby canal. Childish moments of heaven amidst the threatening atmosphere of wartime... perhaps it was because the grim face of death was never far off, and could appear at any time, that such moments became for her a powerful spiritual tonic. She remembered the lessons in Literature and History that so absorbed her in the little country school with its dirt floor and palm roof. When she shut her eyes, she could still smell the inky fragrance of her schoolbooks, and feel her heart thrill under the expectant, affectionate gaze that her teacher reserved for this child who had such an unusual sensitivity for words and writing. Her essays were almost always chosen to be read aloud to the class, and it was these moments of revelation that Tiep felt guided her soul. It gave her life meaning to know that she could write words which connected people to one another and help them understand each other.

Her teen years descended in a fury of fighting and bullets and bombs and loss. She was stripped of her father, her family's orchard, her school. The knowledge she had gained from her classes and textbooks was abstract at best while the baggage of experience she carried was heavy and distressing. As a teenager, sitting in a bomb shelter listening to explosions overhead or huddling with her family while the gun barrels of the ARVN soldiers poked around them, scouring their house for the enemy, Tiep thought only of how such feelings of fear and sorrow must be preserved. She felt her memories swell to bursting, not with pretty moments that could be used to adorn and enrich her future but with experiences that cried out to be written down, lines of a story that would no doubt be very sad. Was this the mission of literature, she wondered, to successfully describe people's sorrows?

As the war grew less and less forgiving of the civilians trapped between the endless fusillades of bullets from either side, Aunt Rang decided to move their house out from the village and onto the open fields to prove to those nosy ARVN airplanes that their family had nothing to hide. As for Nghia and Tiep, since there was no school to attend any longer, they were ordered to go join the local guerrillas. "There's bombs and bullets everywhere, so we might as well have them follow in their father's footsteps. At least this way we don't have to worry about them betraying family principles by marrying some puppet official or soldier!" Aunt Rang proclaimed with her characteristic succinctness.

Barely a teenager, Tiep became a "Viet Cong cadre-soldier" as they were called by the enemy helicopters that made regular fly-bys, issuing calls over scratchy loudspeakers for the guerrillas to abandon their posts. Her life in the Dong Dung guerrilla base was like nothing even her overactive imagination could have dreamed up. Water and reeds, mosquitoes and leeches, traveling by skiff instead of foot, hiding submerged in canals and ponds to escape the prying eyes of the lightweight, long-tailed helicopters that the guerrillas called "flying dippers." She sensed Death following her, and felt a profound regret that the thoughts smoldering inside her, the experiences she carefully filed away in her mind at the end of each day she survived, would never have the chance to be unrolled, re-lived, and shared in fulfillment of the mission Uncle Tu Tho had predicted for her future.

In the sparse assortment of books she managed to scrounge out of Quy's so-called library, Tiep found respite from her loneliness. She grasped at the tenuous thread connecting her Cosette to Uncle Tu Tho's Jean Valjean, and found that the war and destruction all around her was unable to bury her under hatred and despair. Night after night she lay on a woven-reed bed in her tent, her little oil lamp carefully sheathed in a circular tin shade so that the light did not escape to make her a target for an enemy scout plane, and read over and over again

Dostoyevsky's *Crime and Punishment.* She felt as though she had met her life's guide in that book. It contained something very different from the ideals Aunt Rang had instilled in her, something that was far away and unreachable, and yet for that very reason it yet exerted a power over her not unlike a religion. Compared to Dostoyevsky's creed, the war seemed finite and fleeting. Why was she even involved, she wondered. Was it the brave pursuit of her patriotic ideals, or simply the self-protective instinct of a girl pushed into a corner by fate?

The war did not allow her much time for such thoughts, however. A night did not go by that she was not awakened, if not by a stealthy bombing raid then by mortar attacks pounding at them from the ARVN bases surrounding Dong Dung, or by an order to paddle the skiff out for another mission, or by a command rousting them out of sleep to move the entire camp to a spot that hadn't yet been discovered. And the days... the days were chopped up into little pieces of fear, fear of an enemy raid, fear of strafing from above, fear that she would no longer count among the living at the end of the day. All she could be sure of was that she was still alive at any given moment, no more.

Still, Tiep quietly nursed her growing literary sensibilities by keeping a journal under Uncle Tu Tho's gentle tutelage. Bent double at night inside the cocoon of her mosquito net, she wrote about her experiences after a day playing cat and mouse with the war, or her feelings after reading a particularly memorable passage or book. When Uncle Tu Tho died, leaving her bereft of any father figure, she realized for the first time how completely different her destiny was from that of the others in her unit and how utterly alone she was. She also realized with profound certainty that her only escape was to write, if not now then sometime in the future.

Tiep had never been able to enjoy herself playing cards like Tuyen or the men of Uncle Tu Tho's age who were lucky enough to still be alive. She did not feel happy at the base parties where the other youths joined each other in raucous singing. She was the eccentric girl who preferred to be apart, who was given to aimless wandering, her face always troubled and her arms always hugging the base's little transistor radio to listen in secret to the Trinh Cong Son[1] songs played over the enemy stations. It all looked very unstable and romantic to the others. At self-criticism meetings, again and again she was labeled as antisocial, a dreamer, and too quick to tears, chronic characteristics that would have been understandable in an old lady but were out of place in a woman of barely twenty. Her marriage to Tuyen was like a pair of brackets that framed her fate and told her to go ahead and be like the others. It was her own personal war encased in the larger war, the inexorable march of one thing leading to another, cause and effect from which there was no escape unless one happened to end, in which case the other surely couldn't survive...

She had written drafts of her experiences many times, reshaping them with sighs and solitude and brooding, until finally Vinh Chuyen was old enough to allow her some time to herself. She remembered the day: it was a quiet and ordinary afternoon about two years after the end of the war. Filled with images of suffocating, spiteful postwar society and an ambitious, blindly ideological husband, she sat down at her desk while Vinh Chuyen lay in the hammock behind her. The first pages of a short story unfolded before her, filled with the relentless sound of artillery and the taste and smell of mud that somehow had grown sharper in her mind the more time passed. Sensations crowded into her consciousness and poured out onto the page, yet it was not Dostoyevski that appeared but rather her own pensive and gentle Uncle Tu Tho. She wrote about those painful days and about a man and a woman's sacred connection. How they were like father

1. Trinh Cong Son, Vietnam's most famous songwriter, is often compared to Bob Dylan. His firm antiwar stance alienated him from both sides during the war. Refusing to flee the country after 1975 like most of his peers, he suffered persecution by the communist government. However his songs, which are romantic, lyrical, and suffused with love for Vietnam, were so popular that he was eventually rehabilitated and allowed to live and write in relative freedom. He died in 2001.

and daughter, best friends, lovers and saviors to each other. She called on her readers to be tolerant and generous to one another, even when surrounded by death and bombs. She felt that she was truly herself in that moment, penetrating and pure, and doing exactly what she was meant to do. She never forgot the exquisite isolation of that afternoon; it remained with her as a milestone on her path to fulfill the bruising, bitter, and eminently worthwhile fate that had been decreed for her.

Every author is an island, and every literary classic is laden with its creator's sorrow. This understanding pervaded her now, more starkly than ever before, every time she sat down at her desk in a place where Tuyen was no longer nearby and Dinh was unreachably far away.

She found comfort wherever she could. Their tiny room had a benevolent window through which plum branches waved, dropping fragile white petals all over the desk and filling the room with perfume as though to secretly comfort her while she worked through the lonely, tranquil nights. Occasionally a cough would float up from the old artist below, who was another source of comfort. Tiep sometimes believed he had been sent to her by O. Henry himself as a sort of spirit-gift to her children, even though the plum tree outside the window bars had never lost its last leaf. The old man would stand at the bottom of the staircase and bellow, "Are you kids asleep yet? If not, I have something for you!"—and they would return with several pieces of fruit or a chunk of dried fish, presents given to the old man by one of his children who had stopped by to see if their father was still alive. He specialized in painting the large portraits of political figures that were needed to decorate the province's conference halls, and so Boss Poet brought him to live at the Writers' Union after his wife, fed up with his inks and paints, had kicked him out. From him, Tiep learned that if one considers oneself a victor despite all evidence to the contrary, one can be content with whatever piece of earth and sky, however tiny, happens to make up one's world.

Sometimes, if Tiep lost track of the date, the full moon would sneak up on her unexpectedly. It would appear as though rising out of the distant Hau river, at first hesitating shyly behind the plum leaves but then bursting out full and round, as dewy and pure as it had been back when Tiep had not yet known how much suffering the world can hold. At these times, Tiep and her children would excitedly call each other to come and press themselves against the window bars to watch the moon slowly lift itself into the sky. Hieu Trinh would come running out too—back then, of course, they were still close friends—and if An Khuong and Ba Bien happened to drop by then, there was no question but that a mat would be spread out on the balcony for a moon-watching party. Imagine if only Dinh could be there...

But Dinh was far away, hopelessly far away, both geographically and logistically now that Boss Poet was no longer offering his clandestine support. Traveling back and forth between north and south was impossible without a travel permit, not to mention their chronically empty purses and the difficulty of registering for temporary residence at their destination. Yet although Tiep's loneliness felt as heavy as a mountain, it was as high and pure as a mountain too. It was at night that she felt this purity the most; she could forget Aunt Rang's excommunication, and the averted eyes of her old friends from the guerrilla base when they ran into her in the market. She could even forget Hai Kham and the "embargo" he had imposed on her when he realized outright punishment was impossible. She would not admit a sexual affair had happened, and anyway Dinh had finally separated from his wife and moved his office. So the provincial "assassins" decided to strike at the inherently human fear of being forgotten or abandoned by society, and bury Tiep in obscurity by banning this scabies-ridden black sheep from all meetings. She was not allowed to darken the door of any conference or study session on the latest Party decree or appear in the provincial mass media. Her salary was frozen as well.

All that happened was that an austere, almost monastic calm enveloped Tiep. It worried Thu Thi, who felt that their tiny room and her mother's ascetic face might go on forever. "Mom, Dad got someone right after he got back from the Academy, Aunt Tam or whatever her name is, so why won't he sign the papers to give you a divorce? I'm tired of living like this. Are you and Daddy Dinh ever going get married?"

Thu Thi was a great comfort to Tiep. With her inimitable understanding of people's needs, the child would cook Tiep's favorite foods or find other, more unique ways of encouraging her. "Are you in the mood for a massage, Mom?" she would ask. "We'll try to scrimp a little more on grocery money, it should only take a few meals and we'll have enough for me to run over to the bus station and call a masseuse over for you. What do you think?" Tiep loved such solicitude when she was tired. She loved how it felt when someone leaned into the pressure points on her weary shoulders, or to lie spread-eagled to feel the points along her ribs squeezed to life. After a few minutes of such sweet, bruising treatment, her body felt as though trapdoors had been opened everywhere and everything was circulating, harmonious, elated. In spite of this, she only agreed to let Thu Thi bring home a masseuse when she was sick.

Sometimes, when Tiep started feeling that literature was a useless and impossible pursuit, she would leave her desk to play with the children or teach them how to cook a new dish. At these times, rather than being happy, Thu Thi would press her concerned little face against Tiep's and say, "You have writer's block, don't you, Mom?" To her, when her mother was irritable it meant that something was nearing completion, something that would be printed in a newspaper or made into a book and then eventually make its way back to their kitchen to support her and her little brother. It also meant that her mother was not withering away as her enemies had hoped, but rather soldiering on, on her own two feet, toward her goal of recognition for her writing and legitimacy for her relationship with Daddy Dinh.

From a certain spot at the window, Tiep could see down to the base of the wall surrounding the villa. It was a good place to stand and unwind, but she often saw things that were anything but relaxing. There was a lean-to made of palm leaves, as small as a termite mound, propped against the wall. What it looked like inside was anyone's guess, as its low roof made it impossible to see inside and no one had ever been invited in. She had heard that when the villa was appropriated—unimaginable, to be asked to leave your own house like that—the colonel was marched off to work out his repentance in the north while his wife and daughter drifted aimlessly around the wall of their erstwhile estate. Finally a kindly neighbor allowed them to set up the lean-to in the back courtyard while they waited for the times to change. Tiep knew the woman; she would nod in greeting to her just as she did to others she met when she passed through the gate of the villa that was now serving double duty as her office and homestead.

If Tiep happened to see the colonel's daughter while standing at the window, she would linger awhile to watch. The pink blouse the girl usually wore made her skin look smooth and fair, remarkably so considering her life of exposure and suffering. She would sit on a tiny stool in front of the lean-to, with its squashed door so low one had to bend over double to get inside, and lay out her manicuring implements. Her customers were the women who plied their trade behind the streetlamps and in the bushes of the bus station across the street. The girl didn't care; she concentrated entirely on her work, her dainty fingers flitting over coarse hands which could never match her own. Sometimes Tiep heard people talk about the girl's fearlessness, how she made regular trips up north, a female alone, to visit her father and bring him supplies bought with her manicuring money. The girl didn't know that Tiep was lighting incense for her brother, just as Tiep didn't know what the girl dreamt about in her little lean-to or planned for as she filed the nails of women who, if things hadn't fallen apart, wouldn't have been allowed to so much as touch the hem of her clothes. Sometimes the ant eats the fish and other times the fish eats the ant, as the old saying goes. Was the girl an ant or a fish in this miserable game of sleight of hand?

One morning, when Tiep was standing by the window bars looking down at the lean-to, the colonel's wife ran out into the courtyard from the row of houses behind. Her face was turned upwards, and when she saw Tiep she called out, "Miss! Your son is in a knife fight in the alley back there!"

Tiep hurled herself down the stairs, wondering as she did how the Colonel's wife knew she would be standing there by the window, and why their first exchange of words should have come so late and under such terrible circumstances. There was a noisy huddle of women below, pointing excitedly at the house of the woman who ran the neighborhood credit pool. It was a terrifying scene: the woman's massive son was starting the swing to bring a length of wood as wide as his forearm down on Vinh Chuyen's head, while Vinh Chuyen grasped Tiep's yellow-handled knife imported from Thailand and was launching himself at his opponent's side. In another second, it would have been a bloodbath. Tiep breathed a prayer of thanks to fate and the Buddha and this woman from the enemy side who had found her by the window just in time. Her son protested that his knife would have been faster than his opponent's stick, and that he could protect himself, but she knew that he wouldn't have been able to stab anyone with a shattered skull. She forced her son to apologize to the moneylender, to salvage her dignity as a cadre before the curious crowd in the alleyway, then marched him home.

From then on, Tiep and the colonel's wife exchanged friendly words whenever they ran into each other at the gate, with its cascades of orange bougainvillea that the woman herself had planted years before. Tiep continued to be haunted by a question, however: why was it the colonel's wife, and not one of the "revolutionary" peasant women who lived in the alleyway, who had run to find her? The question remained with her, even after the answer left town when the colonel was finally released and resettled with his family to America.

The window continued its faithful service after the leaf lean-to disappeared and left an exposed cement foundation the size of a double-wide mat. Some nights Tiep could hear the despairing rages and sobs of the colonel's daughter's erstwhile customers when a john refused to pay. Other nights when the moon was bright, scenes of their lives played out in full view, in clinches and thrashing on the lean-to's foundation. Tiep knew that when she was gone, Thu Thi used her desk to study and might very well look down. But what could she do? It was impossible to find a sanitary spot to raise a child anywhere in this world.

Thu Thi was eleven and just finishing primary school when they first moved into Tiep's office. She still wore her hair in pigtails but had two little nubbins starting to grow underneath her blouse. Tiep thought they looked funny, but she noticed that her daughter became a different person after passing that milestone of womanhood. She told Tiep, "If only you had enough money to buy me one of those mini bicycles, next year when I start sixth grade I could try to ride to school myself so you wouldn't have to come all the way out and get me." Money had never been important to Tiep, but at that moment money became the best way to express her conscience, the conscience of a mother who felt a constant, silent guilt knowing that her shattered life had burdened her children with lifelong consequences. Tiep did some math in her head, then replied, "Fine, you take over caring for the refrigerator and delivering the ice every day, and I'll swallow my pride and try to make friends with the moneylender in the back. If you deposit your earnings into the credit pool every day, with the interest you'll be able to save enough money for a bicycle. But I'm going to die of worry once you start riding. If anything happened to you, I'd drown myself in the river!" Though she was still a child, Thu Thi's thought processes were as philosophical as an old lady's. She replied, "We haven't done harm to anyone, so why should we worry about harm coming to us?"

But their old Toshiba refrigerator—which Tuyen had originally bought used from his "assassin" relative after the man returned from the north and went on a shopping spree as all the returnees did to upgrade their possessions—decided suddenly to retire permanently from its historic career soon after Thu Thi started making wobbly practice runs on Tiep's tall bicycle. She didn't complain. Instead, she cajoled her mother, "From now on you concentrate on your writing and I'll take care of the shopping. The market is close and I can walk. I promise I'll cross the road at the red light. I'll go to the market in the late afternoon when they'll sell the food for less, and that way I'll be able to save some money to put into the credit pool and earn interest until I can buy my bike." Tiep agreed, and from then on Thu Thi went to the market every day.

One day Thu Thi came home saying, "Mom, I was standing there buying some water spinach at the pig-feed stand, and I ran into Uncle Truong's wife. She was buying water spinach at that stall too! But she didn't ask how we were doing." Another day, Thu Thi came home from school and had barely put down her bookbag before she blurted out, "I just saw Aunt Hoai go by our house! She was sitting in a three-wheeled taxi and coming from the bus station. I guess she's going to Uncle Truong's house, I saw her carrying a bag of rice. She had bananas with her too, and a lot of other things, Mom!" Hearing this, Tiep once again swore inwardly that she would work harder to forget them all, every last family care and entanglement, in order to concentrate on her writing, raising her children, and waiting for Dinh. Only when their love was officially recognized could their reputation be restored and her children regain face. Only then would she reclaim her clan, and then she would have everything.

Over the years, they found ways to survive. Thu Thi came home from the market with an armful of pomelo peelings. The adult-sized conical hat perched on her head made her look like a mushroom as she spread them out on the balcony to dry. "The lady who sells pomelos said you can use these to smoke away mosquitoes, Mom." she explained. "I'll dry them and we can save them for when you are working late at night." She also collected used coconut shells from the refreshment stands at the bus station and spent evenings splitting them to use for the cooking fire. They ate pig-grade greens and slightly spoiled fish from the late-afternoon market. Or they used the pressure cooker given to them by Dinh to stew pork bones or the head or leg or neck or wing of some unfortunate animal until it was soft enough to eat. Even in the midst of their poverty, they maintained their pride: whenever a guest came or a colleague visited from Saigon, or an old guerrilla acquaintance from one of Tiep's trips to Cambodia was in town for a few days, thorny though the situation was, Tiep would give Thu Thi the signal to keep the guests occupied while she slipped out to the market to sell off another few pieces of the clothing that Nghia had smuggled to them in defiance of Aunt Rang's embargo.

But then there was the day Thu Thi bought five Thai ducklings and ran home panting with joy. "They said Thai ducks don't need a pond, Mom, I can raise them on the balcony. In three or four months I'll sell them and together with the money invested in the credit pool it should be enough to buy my bicycle, right?" After that, every day Thu Thi and Vinh Chuyen lugged baskets and tubs across the street to scoop tiny tender watermeal plants out of the ponds in the graveyard behind the bus station, then lugged them back to feed the ducks. The ducks grew as fat as gourds while Thu Thi saw her dream of a mini bicycle grow ever closer. But one morning when she opened the door onto the balcony, she was greeted by the sight of two looming black lumps, lying as motionless as two piles of coal. She brushed away her tears and went to school—even in mourning for her precious ducks, she still had to go to school—while Tiep rushed out to buy lemon grass and ginger to marinate the victims so they could eat them gradually. When she returned, she found that the remaining three ducks had followed their sisters to the other side, leaving behind their fat bodies and leaving Tiep wondering how much more lemon grass and ginger she'd have to buy.

They had been poor and Thu Thi hadn't cried; they'd gone hungry and Thu Thi hadn't cried; but when a child with a full belly cries the way Thu Thi cried that afternoon any self-respecting mother couldn't help but question whether she was fit to be a mother. Tiep clasped her daughter to her as they sat on the stone bench next to the bodies of her beloved Thai ducks. She felt the single-minded intensity of an arrow shot out of a bow. "I swear to you," she said, "That I will only love one man. I swear that we will be officially married, so that you don't have to live with this shame. I swear to you that I will make people recognize me, so that you can hold your head high and fulfill your potential. I swear to you that I will make them assign us a house so that we can escape this makeshift existence. I only need you to keep on with what you are doing—being smart and good and pulling your brother up after you. And then you will see how I live or die by my promise to you!"

But how to get her a bike? Tiep thought of the one door that was still open to her. Though the opening was barely a crack, it was still a door, and that was her sister Nghia. Over the past few years, although she had accepted with uneasy gratitude the gifts Nghia had slipped to her, she had never asked Nghia for a thing. But now... Tiep wanted to rush to her house immediately, but hesitated at the thought that she might run into Aunt Rang there.

Before Tiep could make up her mind, her benefactress

unexpectedly appeared. The cries of the two children echoed up the stairway from the gate.

"Mom! Mom! Aunt Nghia has come to visit!"

Then Thu Thi's voice: "She hasn't brought us anything, but that's good because we don't need anything. Right, Mom?"

Nghia had always relied on An Khuong or Hieu Trinh's help when she wanted to send blankets or clothing to Tiep's family; this was the first time she had set foot herself into Tiep's room. She looked healthily plump, no doubt because she had quit her job at the printer's and switched to tailoring for a government-run factory. She had always loved sewing. Now she stood before them, her eyes glistening with emotion as she took in the sight of her little sister and the children. Nghia took after their mother in both appearance and personality, and so never sobbed loudly the way the others did. Even when they received news of her father's death in the prisons of Con Dao, or when they left home to join the war, she maintained a style of crying that befitted a stern older sister: beautiful eyes open wide, rapidly blinking, an occasional dab at them with the snow-white handkerchief she always carried.

Tiep and her sister sat down opposite each other at her desk. Thu Thi and Vinh Chuyen huddled in the corner to witness the end of the thousand-day separation launched by an onionskin letter from Aunt Rang. After a long awkward silence, Nghia finally spoke.

"Hoai had to take Hon to the hospital to have his leg amputated, and now Mother's fallen ill. It's not serious, but she hasn't slept for several months. It just came on suddenly and now she can't sleep at all. Get yourself ready to come with me to visit her, will you, dear? The kids can come too. Do they have anything decent to wear?"

17
Early 1989

In the end, what had to happen, did. Boss Poet was dismissed for his womanizing and a new chairman appointed to the Writers' Union, a morally upright journalist with no literary leanings whatsoever. He'd been Tiep's boss when she used to work for the Information office. The Literature Magazine, deprived of its subterranean flow of nourishment from the floating restaurant with its colorful strings of Christmas lights, began to atrophy. The Writers' Union now had to survive on a dribble of funds from the official budget, and even that could only be gotten if the office girls remembered to prepare in advance a few bolts of cloth and an envelope or two before going up to the Treasury Office to grease the wheels of the funds disbursement paperwork. Tiep, however, felt more at peace than ever. Her new boss knew her well, and gave her freedom to think and to publish wherever she wanted, even travel wherever she wanted without a permit, as long as she didn't do something rash like try to take to a boat and leave the country.

With the royalties earned from several recently published stories and a generous prize she'd been awarded in Saigon, Tiep purchased a "hard bench" train ticket. It cost almost an entire month's worth of her cadre-level salary. This was the class often traveled by sun-browned peasants and low-wage workers; it would be heavy with the thick smell of misery and before even leaving the station the odor of urine would be palpable throughout the car. The sanitation teams were notorious for shirking their duties, passing off the toilet cleaning for the next shift who then passed it on to the next. But Tiep knew that, just as living creatures did not have the right to choose the family or country they were born into, it was equally natural that she should not have the right to choose a better seat on the train in this era of state subsidies. So she got in line, she held her breath to avoid the unwashed stench of the jostling crowd, she stiffened and shoved against the man behind who pressed against her with something unmistakably hard in his pants, she went without eating and drinking and peeing so that she could slowly squeeze her way to the front of the line and nervously kowtow to the inveterately disapproving ticket-seller. In the end, she held in her hand a ticket for a seat at the end of the car, where Vietnam Railway's famous outhouse stench would be the strongest.

Her benchmate was a young soldier with a long face and even longer body. From his faded, sweat-stained jacket, Tiep guessed he was a low-ranking officer on leave from the southwest border.

"This trip is only sixty hours, not bad, eh, Big Sis? It used to be seventy hours, three long days and three long nights. Your first time on the train, is it? Did you bring a hammock? No, well I did, so I'll use the hammock and you can have the entire bench to yourself!"

Tiep welcomed his friendly familiarity and accepted him as her new "younger brother." They stowed their luggage on the luggage rack and carefully tied it down.

"Here, you can have this piece of parachute rope." he offered. "I'll be getting off at Thanh Hoa, so it'll be easier if our stuff is tied separately".

"No need, I have my own rope. A friend gave me "thirty-six indispensable train tips" before I left. I forgot all the rest, but at least I remembered the rope. As for the hammock, you men are always faster with that sort of thing so I'll just make way for you. I'm happy enough to have the bench to myself."

The author of the "thirty-six indispensable train tips" was of course Dinh, a loyal passenger on the Hanoi–Vinh line for scores of years now. In the old days, he took the train to evacuate his children to their grandparents; more recently, now that his mother was as old and ripe as a banana about to drop off the tree, he had to ride the miserable rails to fulfill his duties as his mother's eldest son.

Before the train had passed through the suburb of Dong Nai, the "hammock-ization" of all overhead space was complete. Most of the inhabitants of the car were either long-haul traders or northerners returning home for a visit, both segments of the population which tended to have above-average resourcefulness and speed. The strong, smoky odor of the toiling masses reminded Tiep of a livestock transport.

The conductor, an unpleasant man who had checked each passenger onto the train at the door and then rechecked each ticket with a flashlight, now began to wander slowly along the car, studying the crowd, then back again to study them some more. He had a fleshy face with a nose that seemed to be slipping slowly down onto full lips and a plethora of pimples. Tiep had heard it said that the train staff and the traders were in cahoots with each other. She believed it, seeing how well-fed the man looked. Clearly, in this world, the clever survived and the long-suffering lost out. Then there was Dinh, her Dinh, who had lectured her, "When I have to take the train I always buy a bench car, not a sleeper car. If I want to lie down I've got the hammock, and I'm able to save one third on the price of a ticket. Think about it, is there any other activity in the world where renouncing your right to lie down earns you money? All right, so really I'm lying down when I didn't pay for it, but you know why I do it? I keep my spending down to the bare minimum because it saves me from having to sell myself as a hired pen or join in the dog-eat-dog fracas of trying to score an official position!"

The conductor discovered Tiep when she had to make a trip to the toilet. He stood, legs splayed suggestively, in the door of the staff compartment and looked at her as if he wanted to swallow her whole.

"If you want to lie down, I'll give you my room here. Go ahead, take a look. A real bed, a pillow, even blankets!"

"And what are you asking for it?" Tiep shot back. She was as thrifty as Dinh, but she couldn't deny the fact that she desperately wanted a private place to lie down, to forget about the long trip ahead with a good book. Not to mention the luxury of being able to change her clothes; two days and three nights was a long time.

The conductor's meaty lips puckered flirtatiously. "Just go ahead and move your luggage in, sweetie, the price ain't much!"

Tiep half-walked and half-ran back to her seat. Why had he chosen her? Was it because she was clean and pleasant to the eyes, or did she appear vulnerable, an easy mark? Or did she just have the words "I have needed a man my whole life" emblazoned on her forehead?

She was relieved to see the soldier from Thanh Hoa lying respectably in his hammock. The buzz of getting-to-know-you conversation around the car had wearily wound down to be lost in the labored chugging of iron wheels on iron tracks. Tiep lay down on the bench with her head facing out onto the aisle. She had just started to doze off when she felt the back suspended above her in the hammock brush across and back over her breasts, exploring, provocative. She sat bolt upright, all thoughts of sleep forgotten, and squeezed herself against the aisle to avoid that swinging body. A few moments later, the conductor appeared and clattered down the aisle with his flashlight. Without a word, he plunked down close and made an exploratory grope. His body exuded the dense odor of a male animal at night. Stoically, Tiep gathered herself over to the wall side, putting the hammock and the young soldier's back between herself and him. Then she gently slipped off one shoe and held it aloft, read to strike silently and efficiently if he should come at her again. He must have realized that this dish was not as easy to swallow as he had thought, and his feverish breathing began to slow down. He stayed for a few more minutes to save face—as though they had been having a pleasant conversation—then surreptiously stood up and returned to his compartment. Only after a very long time did Tiep dare to lie down again, and this time she oriented her head toward the wall. But this only meant that the swinging back now brushed against an even more dangerous part of her body. She gave up and hauled herself upright again. She must have woken up the soldier; he twisted his head around to look down at her.

"Did I bother you, Sis? Toss and turn or something so you couldn't sleep?"

"No, it's just because the bench is too hard and too short. And the train is so jerky it's hard to lie down."

"Would you like to take the hammock? I don't mind sleeping on the bench."

"No, no!" she said hastily. She didn't even want to think about what part of his body she'd be rubbing if she climbed into the hammock. "I'm not used to sleeping in a hammock. I'll just spread some newspaper out on the floor like those ladies over there."

Sleeping on newspaper spread out between the legs of a bench would probably never make it onto Dinh's list of "thirty-six indispensable train tips." Nonetheless, she made the best of it, fashioning a pillow for herself out of her handbag and her copy of *Sleepless*, a novel by a Russian author that was wildly popular at the time. She tried to close her eyes, but her body was bumped about worse than it had been on the bench, and the train's stench was even more terrifying down low. She curled up into a fetal position, feeling like an animal trussed up and thrown on the floor of a truck for the trip to the butcher. It had to be the longest night of her life. She hadn't imagined that her long-distance love affair would force her into an intimate relationship with a train car. She'd always hated trains.

She missed her children. Why wasn't she missing Dinh right now? she wondered. After all, she only had left her children a little over ten hours ago, and before she left they'd had plenty of time to prepare. Thu Thi was fifteen now, and Vinh Chuyen was old enough to ride to school on the mini bicycle Nghia had given to his sister as a gift when she entered seventh grade. If they needed anything, they could get help from the old artist who was O. Henry's gift to her from across the Pacific. Tiep knew she had to make this trip, but somehow it was different from the fact-finding trips she took, sometimes financed by herself and sometimes by a particularly insistent friend. This time she lingered with her children for a long time, unwilling to get on the bus to Saigon. Thu Thi was insistent. "You two have been separated forever; you need this trip. See if it helps you get over your depression."

It was true, for the past several months she'd been having headaches that incapacitated her. Everything seemed tedious, even the sunset. She needed regular shots of vitamin B to function.

Vinh Chuyen, as always, followed his older sister's lead. Ever since his father had married Ms. Tam-or-whatever-her-name-was, he seemed to have resigned himself to their situation. He would turn up their tiny radio when one of her favorite songs came on—"Hey, Mom, 'Missing You From Afar' is on!"—and would tease her occasionally, his broad mouth turned up into a hesitant smile. He was even grown up enough to know that he should keep the atmosphere light when they saw her off. "Mom, tell Daddy Dinh to come live with us soon. He promised me he'd finish teaching me how to swim and all my friends are already swimming like fish!" Neither Tiep nor Dinh knew when that would happen, or where or how. If it ever happened at all.

Tiep couldn't sleep. People trickled past her on their way to and from the toilet, and she was afraid she would trip someone if she stretched out her legs but her body ached from staying curled up. She couldn't get her children out of her mind. If only she and Hieu Trinh hadn't had that falling-out, the children would be better taken care of. And for such a ridiculous reason too. But every action has a reason behind it, and if the person's reasoning is bad, their actions will always follow.

She had met Hieu Trinh at the province's first writers' workshop, back when Boss Poet was still basking in the glow of being a "poet from the trenches" and they were still considered the region's most promising female writers, as eager and innocent as students stepping into the new age. They couldn't have been more different; Tiep arrived complete with a set of kids, while Hieu Trinh was over twenty-five and had never felt a man's hand on hers. She had the charming, fluttering eyelids of a child of privilege—white, virginal skin; a high ascetic forehead; and proper, almost fastidious, shirt-collars. She was as soft-spoken and sanctimonious as Tiep was quick-tongued and loud. In accordance with the law of the attraction of opposites, they took to each other immediately. It took only a word from Tiep to Boss Poet—you know my friend wants to write professionally—does she now?—and Hieu Trinh was transferred from the Municipal Youth Union to the Writers' Union. Together with An Khuong, they were the Gang of Three, the three stove-bricks that held up the kettle of women's literature in the province. But An Khuong was younger, still living at home, and worked for a different agency. So it was Hieu Trinh who became Tiep's confidante, the one to whom she divulged all: why she had so passively allowed herself to be taken into the bed of the Saigon journalist, and how she felt when she made up with Tuyen and ended up with a pregnancy she couldn't bring to term. Hieu Trinh had even been her and Dinh's "living mailbox," the same role played by Dinh's friend on Son Tay street in Hanoi. Occasionally Hieu Trinh, with the deeply flushed face of what was perhaps mankind's oldest living virgin, would hand her an envelope that had clearly been opened, protesting, "Oh God! I thought it was for me, but when I opened it up and saw it was to 'My Darling Lover', I thought I'd die of embarrassment!" Tiep was never sure if her embarrassment stemmed from having opened her friend's letter by mistake, or from the word "lover" and other associated images of desire and longing that invariably could be found in Dinh's effusive letters.

Several years before, Dinh had come for a visit on an invitation to ghostwrite a book. "Okay, so I'm prostituting my pen on a book no one will ever read," he told her. "It's a compromise, but an acceptable one considering all the compromises one has to make to survive these times. The main thing is, they are paying for a round-trip train ticket, I'm not out a penny. So why not? What do you think, dear?"

Tiep didn't often give Dinh the green light for a visit. She knew he didn't have the money to rent a hotel room, and even if he had, they didn't have a marriage license to flash at the receptionist as proof of their right to share a room. Nor did she know anyone in her small town who would consent to house Dinh for her. Even if she could find someone like Dinh's friends Ky with his small yellow child or Phuc on Son Tay street with the cramped loft, she didn't feel right lying to her children so she could sneak away to be with him. Nevertheless, she agreed to let him come this time, reasoning that somewhere in the "thirty-six indispensable tips" for lovers they'd find a way. So after several days at a state farm out in the far west, "sacrificing myself to the role of a true-blue hack," Dinh hurried down to be with her.

One day, while Dinh was teaching Vinh Chuyen to swim in the river, Hieu Trinh emerged from her room to sit in one of Tiep's two rattan chairs. Tiep usually stopped writing when she did this and sat down in the other chair for a chat, mostly because it was impossible to concentrate on one's writing when someone was sitting there staring at one's back. Hieu Trinh looked particularly tense that morning. Her eyelids fluttered, her lips pursed, signs of some inner struggle. It was some time before she finally managed to blurt out, "I think you are just really... slimy! Slimy from head to toe!"

Tiep goggled at her. Then she understood. Perhaps it was just Hieu Trinh's sanctimonious nature, but more likely it was because the children had been "evacuated" to the inner room for the past few nights and the nighttime goings-on in the outer room had disturbed her virginal sleep. She said gently,

"Well, what did you think that two people who are in love and write letters saying 'I miss you, I want you' actually do when they get together? Just gaze into each other's eyes and then talk politics?"

"But you should at least have some self-respect, and character!"

Tiep felt as though the words had slapped her, one, two, across the face. She sprang to her feet.

"And just what do you think character is? Have I hidden anything from you? Have I lied to my children? Have I shown a lack of character in how I treat them or my friends? Would you be more impressed with my character if we'd snuck out to do it in the bushes or on some little hillock somewhere? And how, according to you, shall we show self-respect? By waiting until sometime during the day when you and the children are out, then quickly closing the door and upsy-daisy on the bed for a fast one, always fearful that someone might interrupt? Dinh and I have endured through how many years, with our friends' full knowledge and support, and now you say we don't have character? Who are you speaking for, our agency or the family registration security office?"

Hieu Trinh stood up before Tiep could finish. She grabbed her purse, looking as though she were about to cry.

"No matter what you say, I still think the two of you are slimy!"

Slimy. Why that word, instead of something more companionable like, say, risky or unwise? Why slimy, when it was Tiep who, in their late-night conversations, had satisfied her friend's curiosity about every last intimate detail of her boudoir sensations, who had acted as a living primer on sex for this overage virgin? Was such a reaction rational, or the natural resistance of an old maid, or simply the strangling jealousy of a heart gone dark?

Tiep would have been willing to make up with her friend, if only she hadn't gone crying to the new Chairman of the Writers' Union. Hieu Trinh had left immediately to move back in with her mother, even before Dinh had returned to Hanoi, and then gone on to have a cryfest in the Chairman's office, the general gist of which was, "I hate to say it, but our old poet boss was the type who would tolerate anything. If I'd exposed them, both he and Tiep would've been out a long time ago!"

Fortunately, the new boss was an uncomplicated man who valued internal unity above all. "Exposed them?" he responded innocently. "Why, what have they done that needs to be exposed?"

At which Hieu Trinh had to brush away her tears and rearrange herself into a semblance of her everyday solemnity. "Well, I'm not just talking about her using her position to go off philandering. It's the things she says. Say what you will, if I went around spouting off the way she does, I'd be branded a reactionary!"

"Really, what has she said that's reactionary?"

Hieu Trinh's made a chopping gesture with her hand—and no doubt fluttered her eyelids—while saying with a clenched voice, "Well... it's just that dissatisfied tone she has!"

The new boss sighed loudly. "Oh well, writers only have their mouths as weapons, you know. I'm only interested in what they actually put down on paper. If all they are doing is talking, they can swear, spit, or blaspheme, and who cares?"

Tiep lost a good friend that day...

This damnable floor, it's intolerable, Tiep thought. She crawled to her feet and returned to the bench, glumly taking in the landscape of bodies tossing and turning, unconsciously jostling each other in the dim light of the car's two light bulbs. Our country is so long, north and south so far away from each other. Split by a wound that is still a painful bruised scar. Where are the golden forests and silver oceans the songs talk about? All I see is a country that is cramped and way too bumpy.

She sat there, swaying with the train in the hellish light,

surrounded by piles of living flesh packed all over the floor, and continued her reminiscing.

She remembered a morning just before the Lunar New Year the year before. Every winter, as soon as the northeastern winds began to blow in over the tops of the coconut trees and the markets filled up with corkwood flower and linh fish from Dong Thap Muoi, Tiep would feel herself go limp inside, like a guitar string that could no longer bring itself to vibrate. One more New Year past meant the children were one year closer to leaving her, and she was one year closer to her weary and belated fortieth birthday. It meant one more year that Dinh had spent living at his office in some cubbyhole no better than a cell, cold in the winter and hot in the summer. It also meant that Tiep had to hustle to buy as much as she could before the prices went up so her children could have a few Tet cakes and a kettleful of meat stew over the holidays. Ever since the tragic death of the Thai ducklings, Tiep and Thu Thi had given up their forays into entrepreneurship and animal husbandry, so affording a celebration like everyone else's was getting harder every year.

On that particular morning just days before Tet, Tiep had scored some subprime pork and was preparing to make a Chinese stew when the old artist hollered, "Where's Tiep? There's a letter for you here! Hurry up!" It was a summons: Ms. Le Thi My Tiep is requested to appear for the resolution of her divorce with ... on ... in the afternoon of ... two days hence. We earnestly await your presence on time at ... (signed). It hadn't been entirely unexpected. Several weeks earlier, Vinh Chuyen had stopped by his father's house and when he came home he reported breathlessly, "Aunt Tam is living at Dad's now, and they're buying everything they need to celebrate Tet together!" Tiep immediately dashed off a note to Tuyen: "You still owe me a court date, Tuyen, so both you and I can make our other relationships official. I daresay you see it is necessary now, unlike when you went to the Academy?"

The afternoon of the hearing was one of those oh-so-melancholy and unsettling days one often experiences at the waning of the year. Their final parting was like every other farewell when the players are saying goodbye to a time, to a piece of their life, and to a person who in theory should remain a friend but in reality never would.

Tiep rode her bicycle to the municipal courthouse. It was deserted. No one staffing the gate, the long yellow hallway hollow and empty. She parked her bike outside the gate and calmly stepped inside. Tuyen must have waiting for her; his head craned around the corner of a doorway and when he saw her he hurried over, mumbling, "When we go before the judge, we'll just tell him we're incompatible, okay? Neither of us need mention anything else—it'll just complicate things!"

Tiep smiled to herself. She had suggested this to Tuyen many times but he'd always shot down the idea, opposed it, distorted it, misconstrued it, all so he could leave her hanging these five long years. This sudden chagrined conversion was no doubt due to the fact that his record and his conscience now carried two blemishes, one involving a young lady in his agency which had ended when she requested a transfer, and the other with a fellow student at the Academy who Tiep had heard was quite a dragon lady. Now he was apparently done sowing his wild oats and wanted to settle down with this Miss Tam who, in Thu Thi's somewhat malicious assessment, was "young enough, but plasters on the makeup like plastering a wall." Tiep still occasionally had to endure people telling her how kind, or admirable, or what a paragon of virtue Tuyen was. She said nothing, only smiled ironically and wondered for the thousandth time why the divorce of two people who were as different as fire and water should be anyone's business but their own.

The hearing, such as it was, was held in the judge's office. Tiep saw no nameplate on the desk, nor was she introduced to the man, who was about the same age as Tuyen. He sat at a desk towering with piles of paper files that threatened to engulf him, and acted as both judge and secretary for the procedure. Tuyen sat at the side of his desk, a position of friendly familiarity with the scales of justice, while Tiep was directed to a chair by the wall which faced the desk adversarily. Once again, I'm the defendant, she thought. She turned to look out the window. The cement courtyard was deserted and lonely; this close to Tet, people hadn't been showing up for work for several days now. There was a decapitated plum tree outside, by the side of the building. No doubt it had been sentenced to death for the mess it created with its blossoms and fruit. Still, its roots were pushing their way up from the earth, ferociously escaping their confinement by ripping wide cracks in the cement.

The judge asked a few perfunctory questions about the parties' testimony. His honeyed voice when he asked Tuyen about his desires for the children told Tiep that he was most certainly an acquaintance, or at least if not an acquaintance, then he desperately wished to become an acquaintance. After all, Tuyen was in line for a promotion to be Hai Kham's Deputy Director, a position that positively towered over the seat of a insignificant municipal judgeship. Without acquaintance and favors, this ambiguous and hasty hearing, held on a deserted afternoon just before Tet, could never have happened. Tiep realized suddenly that this is how men with power operate, and that her husband had thoroughly absorbed the lesson: beat the drums of public opinion as long as you can, but when you act, make it as secretive as this late-afternoon hearing.

So was this it—was it really finished? Tiep stood. The judge called after them, "Remember to pay the fee at the desk outside!"

A girl had appeared from nowhere and was waiting for them beside a desk that had been pulled out into the hallway from one of the rooms. She signaled for both of them to approach, but Tuyen hissed, "Let me pay, I'll take care of it!"

The judge's voice floated after her. "You have fifteen days to file an appeal if you disagree with the decision. If not, you can then come to receive a copy of the decree. One for each of you."

Tiep got her bike and left. She walked for quite a distance. She knew that the image of that afternoon—the truncated plum tree and the forlorn cement courtyard—would stay with her forever.

18

Once the long-haul traders had unloaded the last of their dried coconut at the northern station of Nam Dinh—dried coconut for the people of the colder north to stew with meat, or perhaps to eat in lieu of meat—Tiep found herself starting to fidget. Everything southern seemed far away now, hazy and bleak; now there was only Dinh, palpably close, her passionate, enduring rogue of a man. Her body felt suddenly alive, fresh and overflowing with emotion and memories, light with imaginings and occasionally even shivering with delight. Dinh had told her that, when he came to visit her, he'd felt a sudden surge of vitality as soon as the train passed through the central pass of Hai Van. As though the stronger the sunlight grew and the closer he got to her, the more the years fell away from him. By the time his ferry passed Trung Luong on the Tien River, his desire was almost more than he could bear. He was drenched in sweat anyway, from lugging his bag carrying the pressure cooker and a Soviet-made ironing board for her, so after disembarking he ended up taking a detour to a beach for a quick swim to tame his desire, and only then presented himself to Tiep.

Tiep stood at the window and watched the steam engine laboriously belching steam, as though choking on something. She gazed at the fields, each one as tiny and square as the courtyard of a peasant's house, and the timeless tableau of water buffalo in front and wooden plow behind. When they stopped, she watched the train staff swabbing out the septic containers of the train and selling them to the local vegetable-farmers. When they moved again, she watched and thought, washed in the pungent odor of rotting lotus flowers from the endless ponds that flashed by in the dreary winter morning light.

Hang Co station was still half asleep when they arrived; everything and everyone was sluggish and tardy in the cold of the winter. But Dinh appeared instantly, loping low beside the train, his arms outstretched. He was wearing new jeans, a jean jacket, and a white pullover sweater. With a cowboy hat and a few extra inches, he might have been the leading man in a Hollywood western. Tiep had to laugh: no doubt the jean outfit was a present from his eldest son in Eastern Europe, but it was a little showy for a man over fifty. Still, it was an improvement on paper glued over rips in the knees and two gigantic patches in the rear. Tiep pushed the window screen down and stuck her head out. Dinh grasped her hand, assailing her with a dizzying tornado of rapid-fire questions, ending with, "Pass me your things and then just crawl out the window. I'll catch you. The door is too far and too crowded!"

Tiep laughed and shivered at the same time. If she had been in his arms at that moment, no doubt she would have fainted dead away from sheer emotional exhaustion. It astonished her, the sheer intensity of the misery that washed over her together with love and carnal desire. When she had left her children, she had felt nothing but a deep and enduring maternal instinct in her heart. But once she was near this man, she found that every cell in her body quivered as though finally coming alive. Why did the two have to be in conflict, why this constant seesawing between them? Dinh was like a magnet; from far away she could resist, but no matter her intentions, once they were near each other she had no choice but to throw herself at him along the straightest path possible.

She allowed Dinh to lift her down. She felt as though she were floating, then suffocating. She no longer felt self-conscious about passerbys' stares when she was in his arms. Her mouth ached, numb with pity for herself and for this man who was transformed into a child whenever he had her.

Tiep pulled her hat further down on her head to protect her ears from the cold. She was wearing a dark-red wool coat with black edging—Thu Thi had picked it out for her—that gave her the air of a stylish young woman returning from an overseas job. Carrying her bags, she and her cowboy joined the stream of people straggling out, disheveled and untidy from their three nights battling the road. Dinh disappeared into the parking area and returned pushing a red Babetta motorcycle that was evidently the successor to the Green Fish. He fairly quivered with pride at the chance to prove that he had at least been able to ratchet his life up a step. He invited her to join him for a bowl of pho noodles.

"Well, I know we wouldn't have to wait in line like before, or sit on low benches and eat with holey spoons, but I'd still prefer to start with a cup of coffee," Tiep said.

Dinh licked his lips in regret. "Here near the train station, there's not a proper cup of coffee to be had. If you want real Hanoi coffee, we'd have to go all the way to Cafe Lam!"

They settled on a sidewalk stand near the Palace of Fraternal Soviet–Vietnamese Relations. A cold wind was blowing through the treetops and sending yellow leaves stampeding down the street. Every now and then a boastful '79 Honda motorcycle would zip past, stirring up the still-decrepit streets. An old man wearing a faded ancient overcoat, equally ancient cloth shoes, and a defiantly perky felt beret made his way along the sidewalk, absorbed in his perambulation. The scene was utterly foreign to what one might see in Saigon or Tiep's beloved southwest. Her flesh protested against the winter cold. She could imagine, almost palpably, the coziness that lucky couples feel in this weather, and her eyes welled with tears at the thought of her Dinh facing the elements alone with his meager resources and far-away love.

"Hanoi coffee is good, really authentic," Tiep said as she snuggled up to Dinh and relished the flavor of hot drinks in winter weather.

Dinh hugged her closer, swaying slightly. "It's because we don't cut it with corn. But it's so strong it keeps me awake, and makes me that much more miserable when I'm missing you."

Tiep cupped her hands around the broken-handled mug. Unlike the uncertainty of her previous visit, this time she came to Dinh as naturally as a wife to her husband. She felt more confident now, felt she had the right to love him and care for him. Six years had passed; how many days and how many nights was that? All she knew was that a spool of thread was unrolling before her, and she had no choice but to stoop down and run after it, forever following that tiny thread as it led toward Dinh. She lived for their letters. Two weeks down and two weeks up, she always kept track, and if a letter was a few days late, the desperation would begin to set in.

"When we are sitting together like this, I feel like I want to die now, at your side, just to have it done with!" It was a crazy thing to say, she knew, but she felt the tears coming on again. She was tired of crying by herself in the darkness or in the moonlight on her office balcony; she wanted to cry in front of Dinh. She wanted him to witness her sobbing before he could appease her with his reasons and excuses and then lead her to whichever friend's house he'd lined up for them.

But he didn't launch into his usual equivocations. Instead, he breathed in her ear, "Don't you think I suffer as much as you from your southern days and my northern nights?"

They sat without speaking for a long time. Tiep gazed, glassy-eyed, at the sidewalk of this city that somehow had become inextricably bound to her heart, no less than the longing she felt when she thought of her family's ancestral orchard. Finally, Dinh pulled her to her feet, clucking his tongue.

"Come on, let's find a place where we can lie down a bit!"

This was the way it had to be, Tiep knew. She wanted to hear his voice, even if it was only mouthing the justifications that always softened her resolve. It was better to hear the excuses than nothing at all.

And anyway, if they didn't find someplace soon to be with each other in the complete freedom they both dreamed of nightly, even if that freedom was confined within the walls of a second-rate hotel... well it would be no different than rescuing a victim of starvation and then refusing them that life-giving drink of water.

Dinh drove her back to the train station and stopped in front of a shabby three-story building whose appearance clearly marked it as a hostel for itinerants passing through the train station rather than a hotel as promised by its sign. The lobby was deserted except for a row of thermoses lined up behind the reception desk and the pungent odor of charcoal cooking. A receptionist appeared, wearing an old blue sweater under a blouse stamped with the hostel's logo. Her hands were busy with knitting needles and a snarl of yarn.

"Do you have a marriage license?"

Dinh put on an earnest expression. "What, we have to carry our marriage license with us wherever we go?"

Just like when Dinh visited, Tiep thought. She had requested a booking at the Nha Trang Writers' Retreat, one of her perks as a member of the Central Writers' Union—she was grateful now that she had followed this particular piece of advice from Boss Poet—so that they could all spend a few days at the beach. After that Dinh would hop on the train back to Hanoi and Tiep would arrange for the children to return home alone before checking into the Retreat to write. Cozy with the feeling of family togetherness, they'd arrived in Nha Trang and set off in search of a hotel to house their unconventional group before they each went their separate ways. In the end, even though the children called Dinh "Daddy," they had to rent two rooms for lack of a marriage license. As she handed Tiep the keys, the receptionist winked and said, "Say what you will, it's not a bad idea to have an extra room to hang up the bathing suits to dry!" At the beginning, Tiep and Dinh took one room and put the children in the other; but after Vinh Chuyen started sneaking out at night to swim by himself, they moved the children into their room and the second room did truly become the laundry room...

This time would be different, Tiep decided. She would enter the fray to save Dinh the indignity of having to pay for an extra room just to hang up the laundry.

"We were married in the south back during the war. How can we show you a marriage license that we were never given?"

The girl looked up from her knitting for the first time, her eyes curious. She imitated Tiep's southern accent. "Well Saigon is Saigon, ma'am. Here, if we don't do things according to the book and the police come by to check, I could be thrown in jail."

But in spite of her words, her hands were stuffing the knitting needles into a pocket and then fumbling under the counter, as though she really wanted to find a set of keys but just couldn't quite manage. Tiep stepped around the counter and slipped a few bills—yes, she was actually bribing the little bitch—into the girl's pocket. "We'll return the room in a few hours," she whispered, tacitly admitting their illicit relationship. Once more, a desire for propriety welled up in her and a wave of anger at Dinh flared. She had the sudden urge to bite Dinh's head off. Instead, she followed Dinh and the receptionist, who was cheerfully prancing up the stairs with a thermos in her hand.

In their dreams, they always fell upon each other as soon as they reached the room, to drink deep of that life-giving water. In reality, the water turned out to be a cold deluge in the face, just because of that damned piece of paper. Everyone demanded that piece of paper: the Party demanded it; her children demanded it; her family demanded it; her friends couldn't understand why she had visited the north twice now and still didn't have it. And of course every last hotel and hostel demanded it. Without that piece of paper, it was impossible to present oneself as a respectable person anywhere under the sun of their homeland.

Tiep stretched out miserably on the bed. It was always the same. From afar they agonized under the weight of longing and desire, but when they finally met, their romantic imaginings were inevitably stripped from them, robbed from them by these vexatious and ever-so-practical problems. She listened to Dinh's cajoling.

"It's not easy to leave a woman, Tiep! I moved out four years ago, and I still get the occasional relative from back home stopping by my office, crying and counseling and wondering why we can't each just take a step back, because wouldn't it be better for all concerned if we couldn't just ratchet things down a notch. A man who leaves his wife gets hammered no less than you did, being accused of debauchery by those people from the Standing Committee."

"But why am I the only one who takes action, and you get to sit there and make excuses? Your oldest is back from overseas and your second has finished university. Your daughter got into the university she wanted. What more are you waiting for?"

"Oh, that reminds me, I want you to meet my oldest son this time. My mother too, she's been in Hanoi ever since her eldest grandson got back. She wants you to stay with her at Hoa's apartment for a few days this trip."

Tiep's heart fell bitterly. Dinh was back to playing the "mother" card. She felt like an athlete who's just seen the red card calling a foul.

"You want me to stay in the same house with stiff-necked, oh-so-principled Mr. Su?"

Dinh clucked his tongue lightly. "No worries! With my

mother there he won't dare say a word! I've always dreamed of having you lying beside me in a house where my mother is sitting somewhere very nearby. I could go to the end of my life satisfied, if I could only achieve that dream."

It took her a long time to thaw under his patient and skillful caresses. It was as though he had spent the entire year planning out in his head a step-by-step progression of movements carefully designed to win her over.

Afterwards, they made their way to Dinh's "living mailbox" on Son Tay street. Phuc was a writer and a born Hanoite with two daughters who were always painfully aware that every expectation was higher for them because their mother, Phuc's second wife after a divorce, had left to work overseas as exported labor in a desperate attempt to "save ourselves since heaven isn't going to." They were sickly, hungry little girls, living examples of what happens to families who are spewed out of the iron rice bowl for the crime of opening a second chapter of their love lives. The eldest was old enough to help around the house, but the five-year-old, the child whom Phuc, in his humorous manner, described as the product of a "marital mugging" by his wife, was as pale as a neon tube. She missed her mother with the ferocious longing of a child who is too young to express her feelings or find other pursuits for relief. When Tiep tried to talk to Dinh about their future, he often trotted out these two girls as vivid proof of what might happen to them.

Phuc's family home was as small as a nostril and relied on a shared outhouse-style toilet that didn't even have the basic amenities of ceramic footrests and a water cistern with the occasional lump of shit floating in it. Still, as the oldest son in their family, he did at least have the privilege of being allotted the front part of the house, which was favorably positioned, looking out onto the street. His space consisted of a single unfurnished room and a tiny kitchen that doubled as a shower when a curtain was pulled around it. Phuc showed Tiep and Dinh to the rickety steep stairs that led up to the loft nailed together from shipping crates, warning, "Dinh, remember not to do anything to collapse the loft and crush the girls and me down below, you hear?"

Compared to their stay at Ky's place, their time in the cramped loft was downright heavenly, even if it did involve an outhouse. Their fear of imminent assault or official machinations on the part of Dinh's wife had been relieved by an iron command from Dinh's mother: "Child, if you get jealous and do anything crazy, I myself will take Dinh by the hand and lead him to the courthouse! Do you understand me?" As for Hanoi itself, it was churning with the underground currents of a new age: barriers were being broken, enterprises launched, opinions voiced, chains thrown off, hope emerging... only the public faucets remained as they always had been, indifferent and unruffled amidst the changes. They gave Dinh and Tiep the perfect excuse to stroll around the tiny triangular public park at night—Tiep had to supplement her wardrobe with Phuc's wife's old winter clothes—as they waited for the crowds to thin around the faucets. Finally, at two or three in the morning, when the city was still and deserted, Tiep would scoop water from the yellowing aluminum tub under the faucet into buckets for Dinh to carry back to the house's cistern. It was an inexpressibly sad sound, the echo of water cascading into the cement cistern in the still of night. It took at least ten trips to lay in enough water to satisfy the needs of the denizens of the house, who were still nervously reminding them to take it easy on the loft.

One morning when the radio was predicting yet more storms, Dinh's second son Bao appeared at the house. He was a fair-skinned, bookish, and frail-looking boy. He didn't look at all like Dinh, but he was the child that Dinh talked about most. He was wearing a magnificent leather jacket, no doubt a present from his brother, and looked as elegant and pure as an egg still in the nest. Dinh and his son greeted each other warmly with hugs and kisses; then the boy turned his curious gaze on Tiep. The "inspection" lasted only a moment before he gave her a friendly smile.

"Auntie, will you make me something to eat? Something with noodles? I'm in the mood for something special, not just everyday food, but restaurants here aren't very clean."

So it was that one more of the many knots binding Tiep and Dinh's hands had come unraveled. Tiep felt as though she were emerging from a dark cave into luminous, sweet light.

"Let's make it crab noodles," Phuc chimed in briskly, noticeably relieved. "I'll go to the market!"

Dinh licked his lips. "I guess all you're getting at home with your mother is ready-made food, eh? Roast or boiled meat bought at the market?"

His son pouted. "Unlike you, who used to drive us all crazy with your clanking and clattering in the kitchen!"

Dinh said to Tiep, "Did you know there was a time things got so bad I had to buy a hunting gun and go shoot birds out in the countryside? To give the kids a little protein so they wouldn't end up malnourished."

Bao flopped down and rested his head on his father's knee. He said dreamily, "In the south, there must be birds and fish everywhere just waiting to be caught, right, Aunt Tiep? I've read Son Nam and Doan Gioi and loved their stories!"

Tiep couldn't have imagined she would be received with such utter sweetness. Dinh explained to her later that it was because his children understood him, and that Bao was closest to him. And anyway he was old enough to understand that his father's soulmate was bound to be a likable person, so why waste time stonewalling? Tiep wasn't sure. She believed in bioelectrical connections between people, and the natural affinity that one decent person will feel for another. She also believed that events were being driven by the invisible hand of fate, which she and Dinh had no choice but to accept with all its pain and ecstasy.

Tiep went to the market with Phuc and his daughters. The tiny field crabs they needed for the noodles were sold in braces, each crab painstakingly wedged in a row between two strips of bamboo. The little bunches of greens were similarly clamped. It was a clever ploy; although the little braces of crab looked neat and were easy to carry, they allowed the seller to slip spoiled crabs in with the fresh ones and robbed the customer of the opportunity to select their own product. As always, Tiep was astonished by the close-fisted, calculating, and conservative nature of the Hanoites.

After their shopping was done, Tiep wanted to treat the girls to balut eggs, but Phuc intervened quickly.

"My wife and I have never allowed them to eat street or restaurant food. Haven't you noticed how we even have to boil the water they brush their teeth with? This society is a dump, but at least we are determined to give our daughters a minimum level of protection!"

Indeed, when they returned to the house he insisted on boiling the girls' noodles separately and washing the vegetables himself at the public faucet "to deal with that barbaric fertilizer made with human shit that the vegetable-growers here use." Tiep arranged lunch on an aluminum tray she found in the kitchen and placed it on the mat spread out in the center of the room. Dinh's son sat up and hugged his knees. He looked as though he had come to a decision.

"Dad, I'm thinking of looking for a way to leave!"

Dinh looked as his son, uneasy with the premonition that something of vital importance was about to happen.

"Leave? To where? Why haven't you discussed this with me?"

Tiep sat down next to Bao and asked, "Is it because of your parents' situation that you want to leave?"

The boy made a dismissive gesture. "Nonsense, Auntie—don't you and Dad go senile on me like that!"

"So why do you want to go?" Dinh pressed him. "And where?"

"Where can't I go, you mean!" his son chided him gently.

"But why do you have to go anywhere at all?"

"You know well enough. Why ask?"

Tiep intervened gently, before the situation escalated. "So tell us, son, where do you plan to go?"

"I'll go to Russia! I've got a network all lined up. Security is slack there right now, so it's easy to get in and easy to make money."

"Your brother Hoang is planning to go back too, isn't he?" Dinh asked mournfully.

Bao popped a bean sprout into his mouth, and said with callous cheer, "You bet he's going back! He told me he knows the family wants him to stay, but what for, just to choke on dust for the rest of his life?"

"If others can stand the dust, he can stand it!" Dinh argued, still stunned.

Bao turned to look straight at his father, surprised. "Human shit for fertilizer, public faucets, outhouses—isn't that right there more than enough reason to want to find a way out? I'll bet you and Uncle Phuc here are dying to go too but just don't dare. Every generation has to find its own way, Dad. When I think about getting up at three a.m. to stand in line just to buy a bottle of musty state-produced fish sauce, I can't stop shaking!"

"But why don't you go to Poland with your brother then? Why Russia?" Dinh said weakly, admitting defeat.

Phuc chimed in. "It's chaos over there right now."

But the boy was determined. "The more chaos, the easier it is to make money, Uncle!"

The meal continued, but it was tasteless now. Tiep could see that Dinh was antsy and upset. The realization that he had been left out of his beloved son's calculations was forcing him to confront his tragic impotence in determining his children's future.

The little round clock in the corner of the room chimed. Phuc's younger daughter spoke up.

"It's time, Father!"

"Time for what?" Dinh asked, surprised.

Phuc smiled self-consciously. "It's the time their mother

is eating dinner over there. We have an agreement that we always stop what we're doing at this time to think about each other."

Everyone burst into laughter. Dinh teased, "Sappy and romantic it may be, but I do believe I'm starting to tear up!"

Tiep, however, was choking up for real. "Being gone for such a long time, and the kids so small, she must miss them terribly!"

"Don't you be so sure!" Dinh said mischievously, licking his lips.

Phuc scraped the last bit of crab out of the pot and added it to his daughters' bowls. "Well, we had no choice. After we were audacious enough to make our second-chapter relationship official, no government job dared touch us. In those circumstances, if my wife hadn't gotten this gig as an export laborer, I would've ended up a gigolo to some old widow for sure!"

Dinh gave Tiep a meaningful look. "You see? You keep pestering me for that piece of paper, but if we aren't careful we'll be thrown out on the street and end up export labor in some foreign country! Writing is a dicey profession as it is. If we want to be left alone to do our thing, above all have to be sure the heads that hold our stories are safe!"

Phuc stood and fetched a basin of water with an old towel floating in it from the kitchen and invited his guests to wash their hands.

"I'm not afraid of that stuff. I'm just not sure I have the balls to write!"

"If you want to have the balls, you've got to protect your whole body, right?" Dinh argued. "No body, no balls!"

Phuc paced back and forth, as though he were looking for something but had forgotten what it was. "Let me ask you this. Do you think that an author who ends up in prison because of some slip of the tongue—or the pen—is that badly off?"

"I don't make slips!" Dinh snapped.

"I don't either," replied Phuc. "But I realize that no matter what, people like us have to get in the habit of eating as little as possible, drinking as little as possible, even breathing as little as possible, because we don't want to join in scrambling and snatching and scratching at each other just to get someone else's leftover rice and soup dregs."

Hesitantly, Bao piped up. "Your wife is in Germany, Uncle—that's nothing to be pessimistic about. Who knows, maybe circumstances will change and she'll make you rich, eh?"

And so it went. Like any conversation between discontents, talk rambled through the postwar situation to subsidies and cooperatives and queues and separation and political factions to finally end up on publishing and royalties and character and conscience...

As Tiep was cleaning up, Dinh's daughter Xuyen arrived on a bicycle. She pushed her bike up on the sidewalk but stopped at the door of the house. She was a beautiful girl, just stepping into her most radiant age. She glanced at Tiep with the appraising, curious, and coolly aloof gaze of a stepdaughter with a new stepmother. Then she turned to her father.

"Grandma wants Aunt Tiep to come to Aunt Hoa's place to meet Hoang. She said that Bao should bring her, not you Dad."

"I wonder if she's going to give them a yellow light or a green light?" said Phuc cheerfully. "You mean to tell me you didn't ask her, young lady?"

Tiep stepped out to join the girl on the sidewalk. "Do you remember me? The lady sitting at the tea stand by your apartment back then? You've grown up so fast!"

Xuyen smiled and looked away, beautifully youthful dimples puckering her cheeks. "Dad told me. I wondered, that day. Well, I'm off, okay?" She jumped on her bike and started to pedal away, then turned to shout mischievously. "I've found your little nest, Dad, so there!"

Dinh ran out, shaking his fist at her affectionately. "You're dead if you tell your mother!"

Like a true scion of any sternly traditional clan which preserves itself through its eldest sons, Hoang had been idolized and lionized by both his mother and father. Hoa had once told Tiep, "My daughter's envious of him, you know. I mean, the whole family jumps if her Older Cousin Hoang so much as accidentally gets a piece of gravel in his rice! The day he came home from taking his university entrance exam, I asked him how many points he thought he'd scored. Without a second thought, he told me: for all three subjects, I guarantee you a cumulative twenty-nine. And he was right! It was more than enough for him to get into university. How many kids like that do you know, eh? And yet his parents are splitting up; it's gut-wrenching when you think about it. Eh, Sis?"

Every time Tiep thought about Dinh's children and family she felt her backbone dissolve. She wanted to just fall to her knees and let events run their course. How could she ask these intelligent and kind people to give her the clear-cut, explicit recognition she craved? And what about her own children and her own clan? Why was it that human beings needed the comforting atmosphere of family in order to endure, and why did losing it feel so like a slow death by poison? Tiep remembered Thu Thi's anxiety after her father's remarriage, when she and her brother were still living with a mother who was called "slimy." She remembered the glistening, speechless eyes of Nghia and Little My at their reunion and Truong's sad, abashed gaze after years of separation in obedience to Aunt Rang's directive. She remembered how Hoai had doubled over as though kicked in the stomach when they wheeled her son out of the operating room, his body oddly incomplete with only one and a half legs and the dismembered piece lying primly in an orderly's bucket, and how she had felt that all of her troubles, which she had thought so grievous and overwhelming, were nothing in comparison to her sister's sorrow. She remembered her mother lying ill in the hospital, her eyes empty and soulless after too many nights without sleep. She remembered how, after her mother recovered somewhat, the old lady had stared at Tiep for a very long time as though seeing her for the first time since giving birth to her, and how she had then turned her head away on the white hospital pillow and said, "No matter what you do, child, your life will always be full of suffering!"

There was only one wall left to scale on the road back to her family, and that was Aunt Rang. Tiep was avoiding that wall until she and Dinh had become a respectable couple. Once that happened, she would go there with Dinh, it had to be with Dinh, and if need be she would kneel and she would make him kneel to grovel for Aunt Rang's forgiveness, acceptance, and affection.

Likewise, Tiep knew that her audience with Dinh's eldest son was of the utmost importance to him. Her own confidence in the rightness of their relationship meant nothing if this boy didn't approve. She told Bao, "I'll ride separately on Phuc's bicycle rather than have you take me. I appreciate the offer of a ride, but if your mother found out she might take it out on you."

Bao said nothing but his expression was agreeable. They mounted the bicycles while Dinh hovered nervously.

When they arrived at Hoa's apartment, it was Dinh's mother herself who opened the door at Bao's call. She gave Tiep a quick hug, warm and affectionate, then said briskly, "Hoa and her husband are gone. Bao, let's leave your Aunt Tiep alone to talk to Hoang. You can take me to Thuoc Bac Street to buy some medicinal herbs, eh? Go on inside, Tiep, you can have a nice chat. Hoang, where are you? This is your Aunt Tiep, Hoang!"

Tiep knew that the old woman had arranged for Hoa and her husband to be elsewhere, and that she herself did not want to be a superfluous third party in the two-party duel that was about to take place between her eldest grandson and her son's mistress. Like a general who has finished laying out the battlefield, she now left it up to her underlings to fight things out however they wished.

Tiep eased herself into the living room. Hoang stepped out from the inner room. He was a sturdy young man, more imposing than one would expect for his age, with his mother's round face. There was a softness about him that was in distinct contrast with his father's uniquely Nghe An toughness.

"Was the train ride very tiring, Aunt Tiep?" he opened politely.

Tiep gave him a suitably vague answer and lowered herself carefully onto one of the two settees that faced each other. The young man chose to sit in a chair. His soft, tapered fingers, no doubt very much like his mother's, stroked the wooden arms. The two sides gazed at each other gingerly.

"Who's looking after the children while you are here, Aunt?" he asked finally.

"I live at my office, so there are others around and the security is good. Anyway they know how to take care of themselves. My daughter is fifteen already."

Hoang looked away sadly. No doubt he was thinking about his own brother and sister, who shared the same predicament as those two faraway children.

Tiep took the initiative. "I've heard that you are planning to go back overseas rather than stay and work here?"

Hoang stretched his legs. They were soft and pale, slender and elegant, not in the least like his father's. He thought for a long moment before answering.

Finally: "Don't say anything to my grandmother, okay? She's still on cloud nine because I came home. If she knew I was planning on going overseas again she'd fall down sick!"

"But why are you and your brother so determined to leave?" Tiep asked, doing her best to make her voice intimate yet authoritative.

The young man scowled. "Don't you think it's better to be a patriotic Vietnamese from overseas, Aunt?" he asked.

She thought about that. Then said, "This morning I asked Bao this same question. Are you leaving because you are distressed about the situation with your parents?"

Hoang responded immediately this time. "No! My brother and I are educated people. Our decision to go is based on our situation as citizens of this country; we don't bring our personal problems into it. And even if we are distressed, we can't do anything about it. Naturally it would be better for us if our parents could find some way to get along."

Tiep sensed that she should not ask any more about family issues. She turned the topic of discussion to Eastern Europe and the Polish Pope and religion in general in Poland, and his studies and underground business activities there. The conversation became relaxed, even enjoyable. Then suddenly, when Tiep was expecting it least, Hoang lowered his voice to say, "Will you be staying in Hanoi long? You've never met my mother, right? I've reminded Dad and want to caution you too: my mother is easily excited and quite unpredictable. I'm sure you understand my meaning?"

Having said this, he stood with the decisive motion of a respected and responsible eldest son. "Let me bring your bike down for you. I need to leave before my mother starts wondering where I am."

Tiep was disconcerted. It was as though his every word and gesture carried a hidden message for her. She didn't know if she should be encouraged or worried about such an ambiguous meeting. Later, she told Dinh all about it over tea. As always, he assuaged her concerns.

"All we need is for our kids not to actively condemn us or disrespect us. It's good enough, Tiep."

Phuc joined them by the teapot and chimed in. "If you wait until everyone has given you a complete vote of confidence, you'll be pushing up daisies at the Van Dien cemetery before anything is resolved!"

When the conversation reached the issue of how Dinh's mother would react to the news that her eldest grandson would return to Poland and might request permanent residence there, Phuc added, "No matter what, she's going to leave you two hanging high and dry a while longer. At first her excuse was that Hoang might not come home if he were upset about a divorce. Now that he's leaving again, her extended misery is sure to extend your own!"

After that, Tiep didn't bring up the subject of marriage again. She could see how upset Dinh was by his sons' mutual decision to leave. Reminding him of that court paper suddenly seemed beyond the pale, downright inhumane, like forcing a sick man to do hard labor.

At least Dinh's dream came true. Sometimes, after taking Tiep around to his favorite spots and historical sites to further educate her about his Hanoi, the Hanoi that was buried somewhere under the current veneer of corruption and squalor, Dinh would lead Tiep back to his sister's house for the night. Just as he had promised, his brother-in-law proved himself to be a congenital coward before his mother's towering authority, and his sister Hoa said nothing except "poor sister Cam" this and "poor sister Tiep" that, along with a few "poor Hoang and Bao and Xuyen" or "poor Thu Thi and Vinh Chuyen"—it didn't matter that she'd never met them—they were all to be pitied and loved.

Mealtimes were pleasant enough, although things went more smoothly when Su wasn't present. After that came the evenings Dinh had always dreamed of: under a small mosquito net, Tiep rested her head on Dinh's arm and dozed, half-listening to the murmured conversation between Dinh and his mother as they gossiped about the latest goings-on in his hometown. She felt as though they were soothing her to sleep with a kind of strange two-part lullaby, rising, falling, now lively, now lilting. It was the same atmosphere she had loved back in her childhood, listening to Aunt Rang and Hoai chat with each other like mismatched girlfriends over the familiar murmur of water hyacinth and the rustle of leaves along the riverbank. Only now it was a man lying beside her, and holding her, the man fate had decreed for her, and as each moment passed she felt herself being lulled ever more deeply and bound ever more tightly to this new community, yet one more clan that would demand yet more sacrifice from her: sacrifice to keep his mother happy in case she fell ill when her grandsons ran away again to far-off countries; sacrifice until his children were a little older and a little more understanding; and sacrifice to help his Crazy Bertha come to terms with the situation and gradually accept her retirement...

Tiep's second trip to Hanoi ended with a trip to the hospital when she realized her period was late.

"Why shouldn't we take the opportunity to have a child together?" she asked Dinh that night as they wrestled with the decision.

"We have five children between the two of us already," Dinh opined. "And we have a calling which requires a lot of free time. We need an undivided spirit that we can devote to literature."

"So what is the point of us even living together someday then? To have a house full of literature? It's nothing but a game, a useless game!"

"If we have this child, we will be as tied down as our good friend Phuc. One thing will lead to another and before we know it our whole life is past. And who knows but we won't start fighting about jobs and money and the children?"

"But isn't love without progeny nothing but selfish sexual desire?"

"No! With the few resources we have, we need to be supporting our love, Tiep, our lifestyle and our work. We have those—we don't need the bond of a child."

Tiep despaired at the perversity of her life. She had produced children freely with a man she didn't love, and now the man she loved was telling her to restrain herself and all but forbidding her to bear their child.

But did they need a child as a thread of common blood tying them together? She agreed with him that, for them, such a bond was not necessary.

The hospital in the Hang Bun district was very similar to

the maternity departments she had known at home, with the single difference that each patient who came for an abortion was required to submit a pint jar full of urine for testing. At first Tiep couldn't understand why they should need such a large amount of urine to run a few routine tests; later, after it was over and they had escaped the doctors and nurses, her fellow patients whispered to her "They make us do it because they sell the urine to the vegetable farmers and the jars to the bootleg liquor brewers!"

Indeed, if it hadn't been for that minor detail of the pint jar of urine, Tiep's trip would have not been half bad, even if Hoang's reception of her was more ambivalent than his younger brother's.

19

Tiep gratefully plopped down her luggage and the sack of presents. After the gamut of emotions she had felt in Hanoi—on fire, inside out, in freefall—it felt good to return to the earth's surface and this room with its plum leaves and abundant moonlight. A feeling of serenity enveloped her as the weariness of the long trip dissolved. She was anxious to wrap her arms around her two children. How much of a woman's twenty-four hours every day is devoted to her children? she wondered. Is it possible to determine the proportion? Is there even a proportion, or is it all-encompassing? An idea flared suddenly in her mind: Why keep demanding official recognition, why take that final step? Why not just be lovers who occasionally meet to shake each other up, set each other on fire, and then return to these moments of tranquility made that much more precious? But her heart, that self-important dictator which delivers blood to the whole body and so is prone to considering itself the final authority on all matters, resisted immediately. Lovers never last, it whispered. And you can no more bear the thought of Dinh with another lover than he could bear the thought of you with another man. There is no such thing as a lifelong lover…

Tiep stepped in and glanced around the room. Vinh Chuyen was nowhere to be seen, but Thu Thi was stretched out on the bed. When she saw her mother, she threw off the covers, rushed to her, and collapsed at her feet, sobbing loudly.

"Mom, there was a letter!"

Tiep was taken aback and not a little annoyed. "Why are you crying over a letter?" she asked.

"It was the strangest letter, Mom! It wasn't from Hoang's and Xuyen's mother, it was from some lady named Mao. It said that Daddy Dinh is a dirty two-timer, a womanizer, and... and more!"

"Where is it now?" Tiep asked warily.

"I burned it. I... I was afraid you... you wouldn't be able to stand it!"

She was right; Tiep couldn't stand it. The shock flattened her. It was a brutal blow, like a poisoned arrow that skewered both mother and child with one shot and left them mortally wounded. Enraged, she yelled at her daughter.

"An earth-shattering letter like that—how dare you burn it!"

"I knew you wouldn't be able to bear reading it!"

"Why are you crying? What's it got to do with you?!"

"I don't know myself, Mom! I just feel like everything's falling apart. I feel humiliated. I don't know how I should feel about Daddy Dinh now!"

She was right. It was humiliating, shattering. It reduced everything else to ashes. She realized she was not angry at her daughter. Her rage, towering and stony cold as a mountain, shifted to wrap itself around Dinh, to bury him completely. She set her face in an impassive expression in preparation for the long road ahead. She helped her daughter up to sit on the rattan settee. For herself she twirled the desk chair around and settled herself in for the interrogation.

"Okay, you burned the letter. So now it's your duty to tell me everything it said, so I can figure out what it means!"

As best she could understand from the fifteen-year-old girl's spasmodic, painful, and necessarily abridged retelling, the letter told of a "relationship of several years" between Dinh and the woman named Mao, about "my memories of our nights together," and about a time Mao had stopped by Dinh's room at the Hanoi Writers' Union office and peeked in, only to see him in bed with another woman!

Tiep couldn't listen to any more. Nor did she wish to force the child to repeat verbatim the words which were no doubt etched onto the empty white paper of her mind; it was one thing to read them, but to make her actually speak the words was something different, a kind of torture. She sat motionless for a while, then without a word pulled the presents from the bag and told Thu Thi to go find her brother. She wanted to escape human contact for a while. She felt deaf and dumb and there was a ringing in her head. She felt as though everything had collapsed around her, everything had been crushed and buried, and all that was left was a physical sensation of hatred, emergence, war, and destruction.

"Oh, Mom, while you were gone Vinh Chuyen was bitten by a dog!" Thu Thi suddenly remembered.

Tiep heard her self as though from far away. "How is he?"

"It's just a normal dog. The neighbors have tied it up to keep an eye on it."

"And?"

"I was so scared, I ran to tell Aunt An Khuong and Uncle Ba Bien. They took Vinh Chuyen to get vaccinated for rabies."

"Why did you have to get them involved in it?"

"I was scared. They told him to avoid eating mung bean

candy for a while. That mung bean candy you brought home, we'd better hide it or he might eat it and die!"

"Why haven't you gone to find him yet? You let him lollygag all day out in the street and next thing you know he's going to be bitten again!"

Thu Thi couldn't understand why her mother was being so sharp and cold to her. She ran to leave, bewildered, not sure if she should be angry at her mother, or her brother, or the man she called Daddy Dinh, or at that poisonous letter.

Tiep took a cursory shower and checked the kitchen, which she noticed Thu Thi had cleaned carefully in anticipation of her arrival. Thu Thi returned to report that her brother's bicycle was gone and he had probably gone off to his father's house or maybe a friend's.

Tiep pointed at the agency's telephone in the hallway. "So why are you standing there? Call and see if he's there!"

She stood there, holding her breath until she knew where her son was. It didn't do her anger any good to find out that he was indeed at his father's. For the first time, she allowed her dissatisfaction with their father to slip out in words.

"They don't love him anyway. Why does he grab his bike and ride over there every chance he gets?"

"They" referred to that Aunt Tam of his, a housewife in the truest sense of the word. Tiep had heard that the woman was trying to make out like a grand lady, the wife of a VIP; she ordered Tuyen's driver around and wore western-style skirts and thick makeup even at home. If a guest happened to ask who Vinh Chuyen was, she'd tell them he was a nephew from the countryside, living with them so he could go to school.

Tiep stood in the kitchen, combing her hair and pelting Thu Thi with instructions.

"Cook dinner, then call them again to tell your brother to come home for dinner. You two go ahead and eat, don't wait for me. I have something I need to do!"

In fact Tiep had no idea where she would go. She just knew she had to get out, to find someone, to find satiation, movement, relief.

Mao. She had no doubts but that Mao was real. He was so far away, so amorous, and so self-indulgent, how could there not be a Mao! And she, she had been saving herself, had been faithful for long enough. She had locked the gates and thrown up high walls all these years, and what did it get her? Stubborn and fearless, willing to endure the trip between north and south, and what did it get her? Nothing but a daughter sobbing with humiliation because a letter had dragged her into her mother's sex life. It had to be true. There could be no smoke without a fire, and no letter without a Mao. A Mao who knew everything about her, even the address where she and her children lived.

A name came into her mind. Like a counter to Mao. An anti-Mao. Thuan. The road to where his unit was stationed was windy during this time of day, but so much the better—it would cool the roil of emotions inside her, not to mention give her a sexy, wind-blown look. She had met Thuan on her first trip to Cambodia. She had been invited to take part in an extended education program for soldiers stationed in remote places. A panel discussion was held between a group of artists and authors from the southwest, who sat on a row of chairs, and the crowd of soldiers opposite them, who sat on the sandy earth under the palm trees. That night, Tiep's eyes had been drawn to a strangely fair face that was staring at her. She recognized the look; she had received many such gazes back in her guerrilla days when she went out to youth club nights at the provincial Committee of Propaganda and Training. Now, seeing that gaze again almost twenty years later, she felt a plethora of possible tomorrows awake within her. She was still attractive, she knew; she had an air of natural candor, an authenticity that sparkled, oh yes she knew that. But this young man was impossibly handsome and fresh, he didn't seem to be in any way related to battles and bombs and the barren dry earth of this remote place. When the discussion concluded, she stepped down and deliberately made straight for this strange young man to thank him for the gift of his admiring stare, and for being so fresh and bright. That was how they met; afterwards, they had exchanged letters as friends, peers in talent who were bound by a thread of sentiment that neither knew how to define. Since Thuan had returned to his home base for good, they met only occasionally, when the Writers' Union newspaper held a meeting that involved both military and civilian contributors. Thuan had never been to Tiep's place, and the few times Tiep had made her way to his room with its writing desk shaded by a memorably large jackfruit tree in the Infantry Extended Education officers' quarters, Thuan was always nervous and reserved. No doubt he was holding himself back because he had heard about Dinh, but he never asked Tiep about it.

Tiep flashed her Writers' Union membership card at the guard and was waved easily through the security gate at his base. Thuan had just finished dinner in the mess hall and was sitting with a toothpick in his mouth and a copy of Literature Magazine spread out on the table before him. Tiep clapped him on the shoulder from behind. Surprised, he sprang to his feet. His face registered consternation, flushed, then went numb with pleasure. The toothpick plummeted to the ground, only to be kicked out of sight as though he feared she had caught him red-handed in some shameful activity.

"Why are you always so ill at ease, my friend?" Tiep teased. She placed her hands on her hips, and immediately they both fell into their customary roles: one active, forceful, mischievous; the other self-effacing, reserved, and clumsy. As always there was a pleasant, but decorous, space between them. Tiep continued her attack.

"Why don't you say anything, eh? Your tongue's gone numb because you're wondering why I've come? Don't you want to know?"

Thuan still hadn't regained his equilibrium. "You always just appear and disappear without any warning. What's the point of asking why?" he said shakily.

They shared a pot of tea as they always did, premium Thai Nguyen tea, delicious. They had the same rambling conversation they always did: what are you writing now, what have you published, have you been on any trips lately, how's the newspaper since Boss Poet was let go, have you read the poems of Phung Khac Bac yet, oh they're wonderful why don't I copy some out for you? He insisted that Tiep sit in the best spot, the hammock under the jackfruit tree. When she was close to Thuan, Tiep always was reminded of the rows of good corn, the verdant dike banks, and the dainty rivers and high October skies of his native homeland in the north. His was a friendship that was both pure and self-sacrificing and, she realized, it was a friendship that could not be played with. Tiep stood up, wondering as she always did how such a wholesome person could exist in this world.

She left Thuan's base and pedaled her bike back in the direction of the city. She passed by the bus station near her office, stopping only briefly to be sure Vinh Chuyen wasn't loitering out in the street. The intense rage was still burning inside her. She decided she had to go to Quy's house, to see those pensive eyes and taste that feeling of unfinished desire. Just to sit across from him in the dim light of some coffee shop and share stories fervent with emotion. She'd never yet experienced the murky pleasures of flirting. That Man had taken possession of her body with groping haste, and then there was Dinh...

Dinh, her Dinh, overenthusiastic, intoxicating, controlling, and with absolutely no capacity for moderation. Like the horrifically hot Lao winds that sweep through his home town.

It had been several years since Quy had fulfilled his dream of a tangerine orchard outside of town. He'd built a house there, just off the main road, and it was rumored that he drank a lot when sad. Tiep stopped her bike on the shoulder of the road and peered in. She saw Quy sitting and whittling something, surrounded by neatly trimmed bonsai plants arranged in the courtyard. His body was relaxed and serene, a characteristic he had inherited from his parents, but under the dim light from the street he looked tiny and isolated. Behind him, the woman Uncle Tu Tho had loved was playing with a small child, no doubt her granddaughter. The child was twittering something in her grandmother's ear.

Tiep found she could not approach them. She could not tempt a man such as Quy to a coffee shop to put to the test that which they had never voiced aloud. Uncle Tu Tho would not approve of them leading each other astray in such a thoughtless, impulsive way. If Tiep showed herself, Quy would show a judicious level of surprise, then stretch out that elegant neck to study her, evaluating, reflecting. He would unhurriedly ask if she were just stopping by for a visit or if she needed anything. Then he would smile gently and say, "You know you can tell me anything, Tiep—what is it, why can't you tell me? How odd… well, I'll see you later, go on home now and be careful, you hear..." all in that same resigned, mournful voice she had heard the day he had left her on the bank in Dong Dung.

How awkward that she couldn't think of a single person to seduce.

But then Ba Bien came into her mind. The ex-ARVN officer worked sometimes for the Writers' Union as an English translator. Bien had always been a thoughtful and unconditional friend. Perhaps it was because he was naturally good-natured, or because he respected Tiep's talent, or because he was an educated man; or maybe it was because he wanted to build a friendship that rose above their country's history, its past, its division of hate. Whatever it was, she hoped that it meant that this friendship would be different from her friendship with Thuan and Quy. She trusted that this friendship, this edifice that the two of them had passionately and painstakingly erected, could survive anything, even an affair.

She'd heard that Bien's wife was a consummate fishwife

who had worried away every last ounce of fat on her body with her jealously. Tiep certainly couldn't just show up at his house. Women like that were convinced that every other female wanted their husbands, and with Tiep's notoriety there was little chance she would give her a pass. But Tiep knew a way. She stopped by the post office, the same one where she had waited for Dinh's phone call so long ago. She felt fearless this time; she was an author, an infamous author no less, so a phone call to arrange a liaison with yet another sap wasn't going to change anyone's opinion of her. She punched in the number and waited casually. Bien owned a bookstore and was one of the first people in town to have acquired a private telephone. I'll hang up if his wife answers, Tiep decided, but I hope it's his son. As it turned out, Bien himself answered.

"Well, if it isn't the traveler! Back in town, eh? Since when?" Bien purposefully avoided using any of the problematically familiar pronouns they usually used with each other, no doubt to avoid arousing his wife's curiosity.

"I've just gotten back. I need to see you!"

"When and where, just let me know!"

"Right now! The coffee shop by the post office!"

"OK! Should I bring the motorcycle?"

"No, it's near your house; why bother?"

Just as Tiep had guessed, Bien arrived at the post office posthaste riding the Honda that he still kept from his years as an officer in the enemy regime. Tiep didn't know in what hellhole Boss Poet had discovered him all those years ago, but after introducing them Boss Poet had whispered in her ear, "This fellow's English is excellent, he can work with us translating stories for the newspaper. Be sure to feed and water him well, you hear?"

In both his words and actions, Bien had proved to be hard-working and sociable. He cared little for money and never refused to help a colleague in difficulty. If there was loss, he compensated for it; if joy, he shared in it; if grief, he came to offer sympathy, and if success, he came to offer congratulations. His exemplary behavior and congeniality often left Tiep wondering how this exquisitely scrupulous man could ever have worn the uniform of an enemy soldier or been sent to a re-education camp. It was he who had slipped her books by major authors that she had never had the opportunity to read, having lost her youth to the war. She knew that she occupied a very private, deep corner in his heart, but Bien controlled himself so perfectly that she could only take tiny, fervent sips of this relationship that had so much social significance in a still-divided country.

"Let's go for some pomelo compote!" Bien suggested. "Did you miss pomelos while you were gone?"

It seemed he, too, wanted to go someplace, the farther away the better, to sit together in the garden of some private and quiet café with a properly poetic atmosphere.

"What about my bike?" Tiep frowned.

"Let me find someone to watch it. I know some people who live near here."

"And when we come back to pick it up and your friend finds out you were out with some lady, what then?"

Bien gave a sharp laugh. "God, an iron lady like you worrying about trifles like that?"

Tiep couldn't help but laugh with him. Here she was getting set to entice a man to take the plunge with her, and she was worrying about what people thought! "No, no, I was just worried about you!" she protested.

"Don't be! The old lady swore off jealousy a long time ago!"

On the motorcycle, his back was close and intensely familiar, and not a little seductive. Suppose I put my arms around his waist, Tiep thought. She thought it, but didn't do it. Instead, she let her body fall back so that, in her sidesaddle position, strands of her hair were tickling the back of his neck appealingly.

"If only the city fixed up this road, we'd probably visit the old cafe more often, eh? When I think about the future after you're gone, it's going to be a pretty empty place!"

"Why do you think I'll be gone, Bien?"

"Well, aren't you planning on moving to Hanoi? How are things with the two of you anyway?"

"Too many complications!"

"It's the complications that make it worth it, if you've got the guts to follow it through to the end."

Bien led Tiep to their usual table. They used to hang out with Hieu Trinh here, but nowadays it was usually she and Bien and An Khuong and Boss Poet, a lively and conveniently gender-balanced group. It was December now, and the pomelo trees in the cafe's garden were heavy with fruit in anticipation of the Tet holiday. Nestled among the trees were small stone benches with very low stone tables perfect for leaning across to whisper sweet nothings.

Dinh had told her that despite its festive bustle in preparation for the New Year, December was his least favorite month in the north. "It's the coldest month," he'd said. "The cold goes right through to the bones. It steals away one's confidence and vitality. And the rains!" Their last night together, they had lain fully dressed against the cold in Phuc's loft. Dinh's back was as rough as a python's skin under Tiep's possessive fingers. They made love with hampered, gentle movements. Dinh never let her out of his arms, knowing he was about to lose her, worrying about her long trip back and the even longer days ahead.

Damn, Tiep thought, I'm thinking about him. Worrying about him. Missing him. On the dark, chaotic night he'd taken her to the train station, he'd all but lost the ability to speak. His cheeks seemed to collapse, and his eyes were desperate and bloodshot, rolling with misery. No, no! I don't want to think of him anymore. I have to discard all thoughts of him and concentrate on Bien.

But under the reddish light of the café, Bien looked dried-out, bony, and utterly trustworthy, not in the least bit sensuous or passionate. Tiep spooned the pomelo compote daintily into her mouth. It was delicious. Carefully sifted mung bean mixed with clarified coconut milk and threads of pomelo peel so crisp one could hardly believe they had come from a pungent, bitter pomelo peel. They hadn't been processed so much as transformed through some sort of marvelous evolution. She leaned forward over the low table. That's me, she thought. I'm fragrant and rich and right now going through a marvelous evolution!

What she said was, "So which translation do you think is better, Bien? *A Time To Love, A Time To Die* or *Time To Live, Time To Die*. Which title better captures the spirit of Remarque's novel?"

"Well, you've got to be loose and creative in your translation, while still respecting the original."

"But I can't read the original. That's why I want to know your opinion."

"Hmm. 'A time' is different from 'time'. 'A time' is the looser translation. Translating it as 'time' is more mechanical. It sounds stiff, and the meaning isn't clear. It doesn't accurately reflect the functions of the words and meanings."

"So you think the pre-75 Saigon translation is better and more accurate?"

Bien hesitated, considering. "I suppose you could say that," he admitted finally.

Tiep once again thought of Dinh. He and his friend had debated these two translations, and Dinh had been effusive in his praise of the southern translation, as she had.

But here they were falling into their usual topics of words, literature, and work. Tiep changed the subject.

"Bien, if you didn't have a wife, or you had to be separated from your wife for a long time, how does a man take care of... things during that time?"

Bien hesitated again. Perhaps the subject was too unvarnished for him, too awkward.

"I'm not sure if you are asking about things in terms of emotional needs or biological needs?"

"I'm asking about sex," she said evenly.

While Bien floundered, trying to find an answer for his brazen friend, Tiep remembered Dinh telling her that during periods of abstinence he would have wet dreams on a regular basis. Then he told her about his dreams, and how they were always about her, and how he always felt completely wrung out afterwards...

Bien shook his head circumspectly and gave up. Tiep stood.

"It's a bore talking to you anyway. And why are there so many mosquitoes today?!"

Indeed the mosquitoes were out in hordes that night. It was fortunate for Tiep, who used them as her excuse to have Bien drive her back to her bicycle.

As she pedaled home, Tiep thought of the spells of longing she always felt right after leaving Dinh. Like a meat-lover who has suddenly been forced into a strict vegetarian diet, waves of hunger would sweep over her body, a shameless, urgent, and enduring need in the most sensitive parts of her body as real as the need for food and drink. She could ignore it during the day, make it wither like sleeping-grass when exposed to sunlight, but at night it broke out of its cage in a way that made her want to do anything but sleep. What to do? Women in the countryside had their midnight sessions of grinding rice or pulling duckweed, and women in the city had their cold showers; her mother had a gaggle of children and an entire orchard to keep her busy; Aunt Rang had a "dynasty" to maintain and her homemade cigarettes as big as her finger; Hoai had an amputee child to care for and cry over; even Little My had remarried a wholesome young man and was now producing a continuous stream of children. But as for Tiep, now that her children were all but grown, what did she have? Only her typewriter and her sheafs of paper. The short stories that her readers waited for so anxiously were written on such messy, long nights, when she felt no desire to sleep, when the moisture between her thighs had dried but a dull ache remained that was exhausting yet somehow sweet. Sometimes she tried using her hand and pretending it was Dinh, but afterwards she would feel wrung out, discouraged, and muddled, completely different from the pleasant, fresh, alive feeling that burst over her when she was with Dinh. And so there was no help for it, she had to sit down at her desk, insert a fresh sheet of paper into the typewriter. The cascading clack of the typewriter always roused her mind and reminded her of her commitment to writing as well as earning their daily living.

Thu Thi was glad to see her mother, and greeted her as if she had just been gone on another long trip. She reported that Vinh Chuyen had come for dinner but then had taken off on his bike again. She pressed close to Tiep and stared tensely into her face, then blurted out, "You're mad at Daddy Dinh, aren't you? That's why you took off?"

Tiep didn't answer. Thu Thi tiptoed along behind her.

"What would you do if I hadn't burned the letter, Mom?"

Tiep turned on the child, annoyed. Why did her daughter persecute her so? "I would photocopy the letter to send to him, let him study it but good, and then after he memorized it I would burn it and make him drink the ashes so he'd never forget!"

"I knew you'd do something like that, that's why I burned it!"

"What are you talking about? And anyway, it was my letter, how dare you open it and then just decide on your own to burn it?"

"But the letter was addressed to me, Mom."

"What? How could the letter be addressed to you?"

"Exactly, that's what I thought! But Mom, I've figured it out. That Mao lady was jealous of you, so she was trying to get at you through me. It's very wicked of her, to take her jealousy out on your kid!"

"Don't make up excuses for burning that letter!"

"I'm telling the truth! The letter was addressed to me, with my name and everything. It proves that this lady is real and that she is a close friend of Daddy Dinh's, else how would she know every last detail about us? She wants me to hate Daddy, to tear us apart, to break up the whole family!"

"Swear to me, was the letter really addressed to you?" Tiep couldn't imagine what sort of woman would do such a thing.

"I swear, Mom!"

Suddenly Tiep felt ashamed. Enough, she'd been too heavy-handed with the child. Naturally an attractive and semisingle man like Dinh would not lack for women willing to come to him and spend the night. Tiep did not know the true nature of the woman's relationship with Dinh, but it was clear that she had competed with Tiep and lost. Her letter was nothing more than a poisoned arrow to skewer both mother and child before withdrawing in defeat. Her own reaction to it had been exaggerated by the pain and insecurity of her situation.

"My poor child," Tiep murmured, and drew the girl into her arms. They stayed that way for a long time, gradually relaxing into each other's embrace as though they had just come through an accident and couldn't believe they were still in one piece.

Tiep never did write a letter to Dinh to beat him over the head with the incident as she had planned. Instead she spent sleepless nights thinking, trying to understand, if only imperfectly, exactly how many stages of a woman's life she had completed, and how many more she had yet to struggle through. She remembered how frightened she used to be of being labeled "promiscuous," that word she often overheard when the young men of the Sub-Committee held their summer self-examination meetings at the guerrilla base, sitting under a banana tree and swatting at mosquitoes while denouncing each other. Then how she had believed that Tuyen was a classic henpecked man who would never victimize anyone, yet he had managed to martyr several women before finally ending up with his Ms. Tam. Then there was the lily-livered journalist; while Tiep believed in her pure and unconditional love for him, he was helping himself to several plump female colleagues who made no demands on him for propriety or sacrifice the way she did. Finally there was Dinh; although she knew he carried condoms in his wallet and often spoke of men's "affliction," she had always believed in him with her whole heart. Indeed, without such blind and heedless trust, she could never have managed to stay faithful to him for so many years. But was her love for him true, or just acquiescence to fate and the inertia of pride and her concept of propriety?

The bitterness buffeted her at night, but it subsided and gradually disappeared into whispers of selfless forgiveness and memory. There were so many memories! Her mind brimmed with images of Dinh's attempts to compensate: trips on the cranky Green Fish with his box of tools always at hand for repairs on the fly; the poems he copied out longhand for her because he knew the war had robbed her youth of school and books; the friends he had dragged her to, or dragged to her, so that she could grasp and appreciate the reserves of the Hanoi spirit that had not yet been buried; the special noodle dishes and delicacies that he prepared for her himself; or the way he sat in front of the gate to the Temple of Literature and gingerly removed each strip of dried-out banana leaf from a banh gai cake so that she could have her first taste of what he called the distilled essence of Vietnamese origins... He had loved her truly. He had never allowed her to waver, or sulk, or even breathe when he had her in his arms. "Don't think just because I'm a talker that I'm an easy catch!" he had often told her in a voice that was jaunty yet mournful at the same time. "It takes a lot to make me fall in love, my dear. And anyway everyone knows about us. All right, so I'm a flirt, but ask yourself: if I managed to catch the whopper, a real live Ms. Tiep on my hook, how can there be any room on the hook for another fish to bite?"

Dinh was a gift, given to her by his Crazy Bertha who had not known how to trust and love him, and so had lost him. Suppose he were not in her life? Tiep would sometimes close her eyes to endure that question, but the immediate feeling of suffocation it brought on was more than she could bear. And so she would force herself to rise and walk over to sit at her desk. A sense of peace about Dinh would envelope her, and she would throw herself into mobilizing the words and sentences that would lead her on.

Like a faithful accomplice, Thu Thi never said a word to her Aunt Hoa or Aunt Nghia about Ms. Mao and her damnable letter. And Tiep gradually learned to quench the resentment that still smoldered in her.

20
1990

In the end it came, the day Dinh feared most. His mother passed away, still anguishing over her grandsons and what would become of them in those far-off lands. His sons' absence also meant that the responsibility of maintaining her altar would fall that much more heavily on his shoulders. Tiep tried to imagine how he would cope with this horrifying event, and whether the pain of being orphaned was lessened or magnified when one was almost sixty years old. No doubt it was never easy to overcome the grief of losing one's mother, no matter what one's age.

And now that there was no reason for further delay, how would he handle the intricacies of a divorce, given his natural abhorrence of paperwork, courts, and conflict, and his wife's expertise in the same?

Almost two years had passed since Tiep's meeting with

Dinh's sons. During that time, Dinh had continued to urge her to wait for his mother's sake—consider her your mother too, he said—because eventually, once she had come to terms with her grandsons' desertion to the West, she would surely give him the green light to submit a petition for divorce to the courts. "Don't think I am hiding behind my mother's skirt to leave you hanging, Tiep!" he told her. "It's just that I believe in filial piety, in virtue. Mother is almost eighty and Hoa and I are planning a celebration in honor of her longevity. You must come up to join us, and I believe that one way or another Mother will arrange for you to participate in peace."

Tiep found she no longer knew what she wanted when they had this conversation. Their relationship over the past few years had become a comfortable rhythm of visits back and forth. Love and longing, careers and children... the distance seemed necessary for them all to flourish in safety. Even if she were able to pressure him into a divorce, would she be able to leave her teenage children? After all they had been making it work for over ten years now. She and Dinh had been surviving like two fish stranded on the riverbank, kept alive by the occasional sprinkle of water from their north-south visits and all the complications and honeymoon excitement that came with them.

After the news of his mother's funeral, Dinh sent further news that he had managed to purchase a little "bee's nest" for them in an area where insects and birdsong could be heard during quiet evenings. Tiep imagined a lonely altar in need of a practiced hand to care for it, and a man curled in on himself through the winter nights... She sensed a change coming, silent but insistent, and that the separation of herself and her children was unavoidable.

But if Tiep was uneasy, Thu Thi was no less so when she realized that, once that small piece of paper arrived from Daddy Dinh, her mother would inevitably leave to join him in Hanoi. "Mom, how can you possibly leave with a clear conscience when we are still stuck here, living in an office where we can be kicked out at any time?" she asked.

There was only one way. Tiep would have to go begging.

The first night, clutching a neatly wrapped copy of her newly published novel, Tiep waited by the massive iron gate of the provincial governor's personal residence, squatting like a stubborn toad under the light of the streetlamps. At least the bulbs had been upgraded to high-wattage lamps that could cut through the fog.

The second night the mother toad brought her daughter toad with her, for company and cheer while passing the hours.

The third night, she took the wrapping off her novel so that her pen name, printed in bold, imposing letters across the cover, was easily visible. In place of a visiting card, which seemed overly formal, she stuck a handwritten note between the pages. Then she and Thu Thi waited, sitting on their sandals to save their legs from squatting. Tiep comforted her daughter.

"I'm determined I'll get in to see him tonight. If he doesn't invite me in, I'll break the door down!"

At last, a guard with the earnest demeanor of a member of the security police cracked open the gate and took the book to deliver it inside. A while later he returned and opened the gate slightly wider, just enough to allow Tiep and her daughter to slip through. It appeared that the provincial governor had an alternative route into the house—either that or he was capable of kung-fu movie tricks like flying through the air or burrowing through the ground—because Tiep had not once seen the Mercedes that everyone knew belonged to him pass by during the three nights she had kept watch and yet there he was, comfortably ensconced inside the house. She realized it had been naïve of her to think she could ambush him at his front gate. Officials as important as Uncle Ba here would certainly have several entrances to their private homes; there would have to be a side gate and back gate as well.

Uncle Ba was waiting for them on a heavily upholstered

divan in the living room, as casual as a cat in thin shorts and an undershirt. His wife appeared briefly, no doubt to inspect this unusually determined supplicant, then disappeared into one of the numerous rooms inside. Conventional wisdom in the province held that Uncle Ba was a dedicated leader who, whenever he saw a peasant waving a petition, would stop his car to receive it and review it immediately when he got home. But it was also whispered that Aunt Ba had taken to smuggling diamonds after Liberation in '75, and was currently engaged in smuggling cigarettes. Her operations were big enough that they had come to the attention of the police, but they'd classified her as someone they had no choice but to tolerate. Trying to keep her in jail would be like trying to convince a live frog to stay on your plate.

Well, it was no business of hers right now; Tiep was there to submit a petition to a position of power, not to a pair of shorts and a t-shirt with a smuggler for a wife. Tiep signaled for Thu Thi to sit properly beside her on the divan. She had prepared a short but sincere spiel, complete with bulleted points in her mind.

Sir, your niece here joined the guerrillas at fourteen and my father was martyred in Con Dao, and I come before you with no black mark either on my record or on my conscience and (breathe).

I am one of the premier authors of our area—see, here is my membership card for the Central Writers' Union (show card).

I have two children, and while my ex-husband has remarried, been promoted, and assigned a new house of the highest rank, I have had to raise our children all these years in a room in my office that has no running water and (breathe)

Although I haven't received a raise for these past seven years, I have continued my work without complaint. I consider it my sacrifice and contribution, and I would like to present you with a copy of my third published book...

She finished, feeling like a person who has just run through a desert, and produced a neatly typed petition filled with solemn entreaties. Over the past few years, she had learned only too well that nobody pays attention to one unless one squeaks a little bit.

Uncle Ba skimmed through the petition, then picked up the supplicant's gift, which was still fragrant with the smell of printer's ink.

"Whatever happened to that poet who used to run your agency?"

"Sir, he requested leave to retire to his orchard with his new wife to take care of their children."

"His mistress, you mean. She's not his wife! You literary types just keep shooting yourselves in the foot with that same offense. How can you expect the Party to be lenient?"

Offense it may be, but not as big an offense as smuggling diamonds and cigarettes! Tiep wanted to retort. But forget it, what was the point of backtalk? She was here to beg, not to argue a case before a court.

"Have you had any collections published recently, Uncle Ba?" she asked sweetly. Like Hai Kham, this man was a scene in Boss Poet's tragic drama, an author by virtue of the fact that people wanted to gain his favor.

Uncle Ba spread his fingers and ran them through the thick hair on his calves that betrayed his peasant origins. "Ever since your poet was dismissed, the poetry movement has certainly suffered," he said. "What a great loss for our province!" Then he bent over the coffee table to scrawl a few lines in the corner of her petition. "Tomorrow morning go to the Committee office and ask for my deputy. He'll take care of you."

A real apartment! It turned out that an apartment could be handed out as easily as a bundle of spinach when a man with power wants to grant a favor. Tiep received her "bundle of spinach" the very next morning at the Committee offices. Overjoyed and overwhelmed, she bustled about preparing for their move, delighted in the knowledge that as Vinh Chuyen started high school he would no longer have to bounce back and forth between his parents and would no longer be able to complain "you live in an office with no running water and a public faucet that's barely a dribble. Get a house and then you can expect me to stay with you!" He might not know that he was entering the age of rebellion, but Tiep knew it and had to take measures. If she hadn't waited with her petition and exploited her reputation as an author and full member of the Central Writers' Union to arrange a place of their own, he would have stayed with his father more and more and eventually the indignity of being treated as a stepchild would have pushed him out into the streets in a blind rage, maybe on his father's bright red DD Empress motorcycle, and then...

The apartment block had been built on a large reclaimed graveyard, a land of reeds, will-o'-the-wisp, and sewer rats. Tiep's family was one of the few that arrived early, anxious to get settled. On the day they moved in, there were still coffin-planks strewn about the banks of the sewer ditch. That evening at dusk, Tiep and Thu Thi had to plant incense sticks here and there about the area to mollify the spirits.

The apartments were designed as a row of connected railroad flats, and were grievously cramped and cheap. The construction company had knocked five inches off the width of each unit so that a small lot would be left over at the end of each row, which they gleefully sold off, dividing the profits. The floor was raw concrete, naturally also watered down to maximize profits, and it cracked like a fried rice cake under Vinh Chuyen's stomping feet.

"You call this a house?" he sneered. "At Father's everything is nice and roomy and there's a tile floor. If the roof leaks, he has someone fix it. The only good thing about this house is that you don't have to stay up counting every drip of the faucet like at your office. Makes life easier for Sis I guess... but as for me, I'm going back to my father's house!"

He was right about the water, at least. The day they had picked up the keys and opened the door for the first time,

Thu Thi had run straight into the kitchen and turned on the faucet to stand there in ecstasy as the water cascaded out over her cupped hands. It was the end of taking turns, she and her brother, watching the water dribbling into the tub set out below by the public faucet, the end of dashing down when it was nearly full to scoop the water into a bucket and lug it up the stairs. It was the end of the mournful, agonizing sound of water dripping into an aluminum tub in the night, and the insecurity of having no place to call one's own, no place to be free, no place to avoid being "slimy" if their Daddy Dinh came for a visit.

Several days later, Tiep and her children received another happy surprise: in one of those unimaginable coincidences that life sometimes serves up, the old lady with short hair, their old Auntie who had been so helpful that night in Diep Vang, showed up as their neighbor on the left. Ten years had passed since they had last seen her. Several of her incisor teeth had rotted away, her hair had turned pure silver, and her back was bent like a shrimp, but her spirit was as spry and sharp as ever.

"The day my son took me to the Housing place to pick a unit from the map, I saw your name and asked what Tiep it was, was it Tiep the author, and when they said yes I told 'em just put me next to her, I don't need a corner apartment or anything. See, I knew what had become of you because I see your picture in the paper all the time. Well! Here we are, Auntie with all my nieces and nephews, isn't this a blessing? No, my son is going back to Saigon, his wife and kids are all there. I was given this apartment as part of the government assistance program for survivors of martyrs of the '30-'45 war. His father, you know!"

One day, Tiep was standing at her desk, which was now pulled up by the apartment's painfully hot westward-facing window, and noticed Uncle Ba passing by on inspection rounds. She ran out, intending to say a few words of thanks. But he showed only surprise when he saw her.

"You're the author, aren't you? And you live here?"

Well, why should he remember, she thought, when all he gave me was a bundle of spinach?

"And what's this sign advertising ice for sale?" he continued. "You mean to tell me authors are in the business of selling ice these days?"

"I sell ice so that I don't have to sell my conscience, Uncle Ba!" she responded cheerfully.

From that day on, time flowed on as coolly and inevitably as ever with everyone else. But it seemed to stop and stagnate for Tiep and Dinh.

Several more years passed, until a day that Tiep would never forget. It was near lunchtime when Vinh Chuyen appeared on his bike from the direction of Tuyen's house. He let himself in through the gate and then, even before it had latched behind him, threw his bike clattering into a corner of the courtyard and ran straight into the kitchen to stand and sob silently. He was seventeen, yet still hadn't managed to grow past the height of the clothesline in the kitchen, and his chest was sunken painfully. Tiep blamed herself, blamed the subsidized sweetened condensed milk she had fed him as a baby that was barely usable and always past its expiration date, and the moldy rice and stewed barley he ate a child. Now as a teen, he often said "It's true that I feel loved when I'm with Mom, but that profession of hers… all year round I don't see her get a single gift, not even a banana!"

Tiep was the first to notice him and follow him into the kitchen to watch the tears pour down onto his broad, easy mouth. He turned to sob into his mother's towel on the clothesline, soundless, strained, and utterly miserable. No doubt he had told himself he would not wail as loudly as his sister did, that he would be different, he was a man! But to his mother, he was her seventeen-year-old boy who rarely cried, and so if he was crying now it could be nothing other than the misery of playing stepson to his stepmother. Which meant, as always, that it was their fault, hers and Tuyen's, for separating and creating the situation in the first place.

She recalled all the times he had come home to mutter to her, "Dad and Aunt Tam are afraid I'm going to go out and forget to lock the house, so they've put the TV and cassette player in their bedroom and lock it every time they leave. So much for watching TV!" or "Dad and Aunt Tam have brought her niece up from the countryside to study here and they've given her my room. Now I have to study out on the street under the streetlamp!" Whatever had happened this time, it must be even worse.

"What's wrong? Tell me straight, what's going on?"

Tiep plunked down in the corner of the kitchen, waiting, soul-searching, agonizing, and impotent. She lifted the hem of her pants to wipe her tears, just as her mother used to do when a storm of tears was about to overcome her.

"Dad and Aunt Tam have been at a memorial service in the countryside for two days now, and the house is all out of rice! And I don't have any money!"

The tears didn't come. Instead Tiep blazed with anger, dry and horrible, as if a hurricane had blown through her heart and added oxygen to the flame of resentment she always carried within her. She cursed Tuyen and the position of power he had finagled with his false front of righteousness and now occupied with such smugness.

"So, why don't you just lock up the house and come here to eat?" she asked grimly.

"I shouldn't have to run over here for every little thing. And anyway, you always go flying off the handle when I tell you these things!"

"What about the neighbors, then? Couldn't you have just run next door to borrow some rice?"

"Go borrow rice? You think if I let the neighbors know my father's house has run out of rice Aunt Tam won't find out?"

Tiep made a helpless gesture. A grand lady like that, with

cars and drivers and a wardrobe overflowing with fashionable clothes, didn't realize that she was almost out of rice? Or had they purposefully let the boy go hungry so he would flee back to his mother's and they would be relieved of this thorn in their side? It seemed the more likely scenario; there was no way that a family of Tuyen's power and position could run out of rice. Just the rice he received in "donations" from the farming communes and counties would be enough to last them a lifetime.

Hearing the commotion, Thu Thi ran into the kitchen. She was carrying a small piece of paper in her hand.

"So have you seen the light yet, Pet? You're not going to stay over there any longer, are you?

The boy reacted as though under attack. "I don't like living with you! You always make such a big deal out of everything!"

"So why come running back here to cry to us then?"

"I was crying to Mom, not to you!"

Thu Thi plunked down on the floor next to her mother and began to wail, "Look how he talks to me, Mom, and after all I've done to take care of him! His own blood sister and he can't live with me, but he can go live with strangers? Just you wait, Pet, and see who listens when you go crying to them!"

Still sniffling, Thu Thi passed the piece of paper to her mother. Tiep recognized it immediately as a telegram. Only Dinh sent her telegrams; the long, rectangular pieces of paper had become familiar to her and the children over the past few years. But this time she couldn't believe her eyes: it was a priority telegram bringing the news that Dinh's divorce had been finalized after an appeal to the superior court. It had been nine years since his separation and three years since the death of his mother. Yet even though the traditional three-year mourning period was over, his powerful Bertha had prevailed at their court hearing, thanks to her numerous official and not-so-official contacts in the court system. He had appealed to the superior court and then, like Tiep when she had lain in wait for the provincial governor to obtain this little graveyard apartment, Dinh had "risked it all" at the personal residence of the presiding municipal magistrate in what was probably the one and only act of begging he had ever committed in his life. Still, ask and you shall receive; or, more to the point, beg and it shall be granted; squeak, and you shall be heard. The lower court decision was overturned and the divorce was granted.

Yet... why did the news of Dinh's newfound freedom not fill Tiep and her children with joy, as she had always imagined it would? Ever emotional, Thu Thi suddenly hurled her body across to hug Tiep and sob silently in her arms. They clung to each other without speaking. Tiep felt happiness yet sorrow, gain yet loss, those same mixed feelings she could never resolve. As though her emotions had gotten tangled up into a huge ball that now rolled after her and the children everywhere they went, always leaving its deep tracks in their lives.

"I'm happy for you, Mom," Thu Thi sniffled, her voice sincere but forced. "I'm happy that we are finally going to escape public condemnation. You've arrived now. But..."

She didn't finish. Vinh Chuyen walked over to them and took the telegram to read. His self-pity of just a few moments before had disappeared, replaced by an expression of deep sadness and apprehension.

"Well, think about it, little brother," Thu Thi told him, somewhat drier now that her tears had been flushed out. "Are you going to come back to live here with me, or are you going to live with Dad?"

Silence.

"If you live with me it'll be better for you and better for me too. Mom has a savings account; she's promised to leave her salary in there for me to use while she's looking for work up in Hanoi. Together with the monthly allowance Dad gives you, it's enough for us to get by. So what'll it be? Sister and brother taking care of each other, or taking charity from people while they cluck their tongues and give you dirty looks?"

Vinh Chuyen paced back and forth, a habit he had acquired while studying under the streetlamps. He still held the telegram in his hand, and looked almost dignified.

"I'm going to go live at the dormitory at Dad's office. There's a lot of empty rooms there, and a mess hall where I can eat. It's more convenient."

Tiep's head was spinning. She was happy at her little Writers' Union under its current "morally upright" boss. And her close friends and relatives never tired of reminding her that "birds nest where the land is good," that countless northerners would happily cut off their right hands if it meant they could have the opportunity to move south. So why should she be contrary and move in the opposite direction? But the fact was that both she and Dinh worried about the provincialism of her home, where people who went an entire year without once cracking a book that could properly be called literature were given the power of life and death over writers whom they considered unruly, unacceptable, and simply taking advantage of their skill with words to cause trouble. One of them had to move, and it had to be her. She would gain Dinh and all of Hanoi as well—but what about the children?

"Vinh Chuyen, why don't you stay here with your sister?" she spoke as though begging him. "Of course your personalities are different, but saying you can't get along with her just isn't a good reason."

Vinh Chuyen sat down in front of his mother and sister. He looked very grown up.

"Thu Thi has a boyfriend, in case you didn't know. Anyway, if I don't live here she can invite a girl from her class to come and live with her. She'd have a roommate and be doing a good deed to boot."

His determined attitude was like a splash of cold water to Thu Thi. "Don't think I don't know you, Pet. You're going to pretend you've got no home so that Dad will feel sorry for you and ask you to come back and live with them, right?"

Vinh Chuyen had hauled himself to his feet and started to leave, but now he looked back. His voice was curt.

"This coming Party Congress Dad is going to be elected to the Standing Committee. When he makes Chairman, you think he's not going to build himself a villa? He's been given land grants all over the place, you know. I know the location of each and every one. Naturally the apartment he's living in now is eventually going to be mine. The other day Grandpa was up for a visit, and I overheard him say to Dad, 'Don't forget you have two children. Do what you want, but if Vinh Chuyen isn't taken care of I won't be happy!' See, I'm not like you, Sis. I know how to swallow a few indignities so I can get the big prize!"

Tiep sat, miserably digesting the fact that her son had quickly and efficiently removed her completely from his calculations for the future. She had known this would happen, ever since she first held him in her arms and saw him smile with Tuyen's smile. She had known when he silently withdrew from her to run back to his father's house and the misery of his stepmother's resentment. He and Tuyen shared a connection created by bioelectricity, by silent devotion to one's blood, and by an intensely practical choice on his part: he would be a citizen of this little province, would live or die in this province, and his father's position on the standing committee was a rich, gold-encrusted backdrop on the stage where he would build his name.

After that Tiep felt time start flowing again, silently and dispassionately carrying her along with it. Dinh sent another message, this one reporting that he had just "emptied my wallet going in with the downstairs neighbors to build an addition—they get a room and you get a balcony where you can get some air. Make arrangements to come on your own, I won't be able to come get you as we'd planned." Thu Thi was stern. "Anyway I've got Auntie next door, and Aunt Nghia too. Daddy Dinh is almost sixty and he's been alone for a long time. You're going to go eventually, so you might as well buy the ticket!"

The next evening Thu Thi brought a young man home. Standing by her desk by the window and looking out, and even more when he opened the gate and stepped inside, Tiep couldn't help but gape: he was tall, well-built, and fair-skinned, and fairly glistened in a fashionable black jacket. He looked like a movie star. Thu Thi had just turned twenty; he was about the same age. She was a linguistics major at the university; he, an economics major. Together they made a brilliant couple, fresh, youthful, and romantic, yet somehow Tiep could not feel at ease. As though she were seeing the same uncertainty, hesitation, and immaturity that dogged her own decisions way back when.

They held a small party so Tiep could make the house-offerings for the last time. A portion of the offering-meal was sent over to Auntie as a thank-you gift for watching over the children. What was left was arranged on a tray for the few guests. Boss Poet came, with the same old khaki bag that was no longer his "mobile office," dazzling white hair, a gap on the other side of his mouth where another tooth had rotted away to restore balance to his smile, and still that half-choked laugh and those sentimental eyes always on the verge of tears. Quy, as gentle as always but more experienced with the bottle now; after a few drinks he asked Tiep, "How would you like to hear some of the old songs from our guerrilla years? I may be old, but my voice is still good." Ba Bien, with his inimitable thoughtfulness and restraint, said nothing except to promise, "Let Uncle Bien take care of the children's English lessons, eh? I guarantee that if they listen to me, they'll have an easier time of it later on." An Khuong who, although she still wore her hair straight with a severe middle part and still spoke in the same sad, melodious tones, had finally blossomed into womanly curves after an affair with a man in her department. She told Tiep, "We take comfort every time we think about you and Dinh. My hope is that when I get back after finishing my Ph.D. in the U.S., my lover will have finished his divorce."

Thu Thi was there of course, strikingly dark, intense, and seductive in a way Tiep had never seen as she sat next to her dashing boyfriend. Vinh Chuyen sat with that stunted, orphaned air of his. He demanded his own bottle of beer, but was refused by his mother's friends who reminded him that his voice hadn't even fully changed yet.

The going-away party was missing fully half of its rightful participants. Tiep hadn't dared to invite her family. Her mother had been to visit their cracked rice-cake apartment several times, but Tiep knew she would not be able to bear the scene of her daughter leaving while her two grandchildren stayed behind. Even less did she dare invite Hoai, for fear of her crying jags and her tendency to nag at Thu Thi every time Tiep's back was turned with "This is your fault, it's because you didn't hold your mother back and keep her for your father; you're such a stupid girl—if only your parents were still together you'd be riding everywhere in a chauffeured car by now..." Her brother Truong hadn't spoken to her in ages, resigned to the fact that his little sister had achieved fame and infamy in equal measure and that any input from him would probably just lead to an argument. Nghia was busy with a long-overdue love affair with an old friend whose wife had died, and his gaggle of unruly kids. And finally there was Little My, who together with her husband had just engineered an escape from the ancestral orchard, partly for their children's education and partly to avoid being left behind like every other farmer in every other remote area at the time.

As for Aunt Rang, that formidable woman who occupied such a special place in her heart, Tiep had had the opportunity to present Dinh to her only once before his mother died and he became trapped in Hanoi by the unwritten but potent northern custom of staying in mourning for three full years. The momentous occasion happened when Dinh was visiting. An unexpected missive arrived from Nghia: "Aunt Rang just came up from the orchard. Truong is bringing her over here tonight and she'll be having breakfast with me tomorrow.

This is your chance to bring that northern boyfriend of yours over to take his lumps. Might as well make the relationship public!" The words blossomed before her like an open heart. She knew that behind Nghia's caustic tone lay a solution, a quiet ordering of events that had been gradually laid in place by this sister who carried not a bit of Hoai's hypercritical tendencies.

That Sunday morning the air was dry and cool. Tiep woke Dinh early, then tiptoed down the steps and gently pushed open the door to step outside. Vinh Chuyen, who had come from his father's house the day before for a visit, was still sleeping soundly, curled up next to his sister under the mosquito netting. The children were oblivious of the fact that their mother and Daddy Dinh were sneaking out, hand in hand, as nervous as a teenage couple presenting themselves for the first time to their superiors' judgment.

The streets were still drowsy and quiet. A clean, cool breeze was blowing, which Tiep decided was a sign that good luck awaited them on these last few steps on their journey to official recognition. When they swung into the Cai Ban market to buy some betel leaves and areca nut for Aunt Rang, Tiep noticed that Dinh Bao seemed to have fewer prying eyes now. She supposed they'd gotten bored; after all, no matter how much they pried, it was always the same man they saw with her, this man who appeared and disappeared like a ghost. Tiep leaned against his back as he silently pedaled the old bike. Even without wrapping her arm around his waist, she could sense his solemn anxiety.

"Do you think I'll get the firing squad?" Dinh asked suddenly. He shrugged and stuck out his tongue in a kind of smile. Tiep responded with an equally forced smile. "I don't believe she can find a gun, but you may very well get a lime-jar smashed over your head!"

Dinh himself picked out a few betel leaves from a large basket of betel and areca tended by an old lady about his mother's age at the head of the market. "The betel leaves here have such large stems, and are so shiny and green," he gushed. "The soil here is amazing!" Tiep reminded him that Aunt Rang liked her betel leaves to be on the yellowish side, and her areca nuts had to have a white center. Dinh crushed the tip of a betel leaf between his fingertips and held it under Tiep's nose, telling her that the fragrance reminded him of his mother. "It won't be long now till my Mom and Aunt Rang will be sitting down together, just as we've always dreamed!" he said.

Nghia's apartment block was deserted as they rode in, a silent testament to the early hour. Dinh locked the bike under the staircase and docilely followed Tiep up to the second floor. They ran into Nghia, who was just coming out of her apartment with toothbrush in hand on her way to the public faucet. She started when she saw them, no doubt surprised by their early appearance, but then smiled at Dinh.

"Well, Younger Brother Dinh, are you terrified?"

She signaled for Dinh and Tiep to wait outside while she returned inside alone. Tiep could hear the unmistakable sound of Aunt Rang clearing her throat, then sounds of Nghia tidying up. A moment later the door was thrown open and Nghia's face, appropriately tense, moved to one side. Dinh stepped boldly inside. Tiep remained behind, but she could see Aunt Rang hurrying across Nghia's cramped apartment. Seeing Dinh, the old woman did an abrupt about-face, her foot describing a tight circle on the floor, and sat down on the bed. She said nothing, only pulled her basket of betel towards her and opened the lid to prepare a quid. Nghia winked at Dinh in an attempt at moral support.

Dinh stepped forward, then sat down on the floor near the bed. He almost looked as though he were kneeling before the old woman. His words came out in a rush: "Auntie, I'm that bastard Dinh who was bold enough to fall in love with your beloved niece. Why are you chewing betel so early in the day? You know that betel knife is too small, right, Auntie? If you want to cut my throat you'd better find something that will do the job a little more easily!"

Tiep entered now, and approached her aunt from behind. She threw her arms around the old woman, buried her face in her back, and breathed deep that familiar and beloved fragrance of betel leaf. The thick atmosphere of tension began to soften. Tiep and Nghia sobbed softly. With the exquisite sensitivities of a commander who is always aware of the lay of the battlefield, Tiep's formidable aunt finally spoke.

"Well, Madame, you've obviously prevailed, so what are you crying about? And as for this fellow, what are you doing down there? Sit up here properly and tell me, how is your mother?"

Dinh could barely contain himself. He grinned madly, like a defendant in a capital case who suddenly hears the judge declare a suspended sentence. He sprang up immediately to perch on the edge of the bed. With two hands, he politely offered her the package of betel and areca they'd bought.

"I picked out the betel leaf myself, Auntie; it wasn't your Tiep."

Aunt Rang face relaxed, and for the first time she looked directly into his face, studying it. "Your mother chews too, does she? You must be younger than I thought."

Dinh laughed and continued his banter. "So you must have imagined I was some snowy-haired old man who just liked to prey on young girls, eh?"

Aunt Rang smiled now. She poked her small betel knife under his nose threateningly. "Don't you be getting ideas! I never forget an offense! But that said, go ahead and make your arrangements. My niece is worth more than gold or pearls to us, and she's been through enough misery. Don't add to that by forcing on her the shame of being a mistress, something less than. You hear, child!?"

The final knot has been untied. Tiep gave a sigh of relief. Whatever else Aunt Rang said, she knew that from now on events would unfold, one after the other, just as after a typhoon the cleanup begins and a new life is built...

The guests trickled home. A rainstorm blew up. Auntie poked her head out of her apartment next door and worriedly asked Thu Thi if her mother really planned on leaving in this weather. But Thu Thi was firm. "She's already bought the ticket, how can she not?"

As they packed, mother and daughter took turns in the bathroom. They each knew that the other was going in there to cry in private, then wash her face and return to the work at hand.

In this modern decade of the nineties, the train trip to Hanoi had been reduced to an almost-civilized forty-eight hours. Tiep bought a sleeper car ticket this time so that she could bring along her possessions. Clothes, including castoff winter clothes from overseas that were sold out of big shipping cartons at the market; her indispensable and trusty typewriter; several boxes of notebooks full of reference material; and a few books she couldn't bear to part with.

While still at home with Thu Thi and Vinh Chuyen, the torment of parting had been mixed with a longing to be with Dinh; but now, the farther the train carried her away from them, the more Tiep became obsessed with thoughts of her children. She stewed over plans to bring Thu Thi to Hanoi as soon as her core courses were finished. She had to have her daughter with her, there was no other way. She would see to it that her daughter's life was different from her own ill-starred journey: the girl would have a university degree and not get married until later in life, and when she did it definitely would not be to that boy with the movie-star looks. Her daughter needed someone better, someone who could match her and command her respect.

Dinh had rented a Railway Company automobile—the entire car just for them—and had the driver bring it right up to the train tracks to meet her. He was the thinnest she'd ever seen him, consumed by the stress of money and housing, and obviously at the limit of his endurance of the limbo of being neither bachelor nor husband. In the car, he held her tightly as though afraid she might disappear, or rise into the heavens, and betray him to escape back to her family.

Hanoi was comfortably familiar to her now, with its cool autumn weather and all the romantic memories that Dinh had created for her. In the south, this time of year, there was nothing but rain and flooding. Still... Hanoi had Dinh and his family but Hanoi did not have her children. She was bereft of family here, except for Dinh. She felt breathless as she sat beside him, but it was not the giddy breathlessness of a new bride or the proper pride of an official wife—it was the sheer panic of a mother who was abandoning her children to take a husband a thousand miles away. She couldn't get that thought out of her mind. It loomed between them like a wound.

The "bee's nest" that Dinh had prepared for her was indeed cool and airy. It faced out over an area of fields and orchards so that Tiep could sit and gaze out and miss her mother and aunt and sister to her heart's content. There was a single room for both living and sleeping, and the small, square patio that Dinh had managed to add on by pooling his money with the downstairs neighbor but hadn't yet managed to scrape up the money to pour a proper cement floor so it looked pockmarked and wretched. There was a writing desk pulled up next to a double bed. On the wall, an altar had been hung with jury-rigged hooks so that Tiep could officially participate in Dinh's responsibilities to his mother, who now gazed down at them with a grave expression from the photo on the altar. No doubt the old woman was pleased that her Dinh had followed her deathbed instructions to go ahead with the divorce, and that he now had a woman who would take care of him as his mother had.

Dinh followed her gaze to the altar. "I had always dreamed that my mother would live with us," he said fretfully. "But I couldn't make it happen."

Tiep stood as though frozen in the middle of the room as Dinh bustled around her, neatly arranging her boxes in a corner. Then he turned to her and spread out his arms, charming, overflowing. Tiep didn't move for a moment, then suddenly clutched her stomach and toppled over. She crashed to the floor, distressed and contorted, like a tree in a storm. She wanted to scream, to cry, to dig into the floor and disappear. She wanted to part the earth and rip the skies, anything, just so that she might catch a glimpse of her children. If only she could run back home, if only she could see them one more time, just one more time!

"What's wrong?" Dinh tried to lift her up and sit her down in the chair, but she struggled free.

"I can't forgive myself! How could I have left my children like that?"

Dinh looked nonplussed. His face twisted, no less flustered and tragic than hers.

"But... but this is what we always dreamed of. Every day and every night, all we wanted was to live together like this...

Silence.

"The children are grown. You'll get over this, and they'll get used to it eventually."

"Oh really? You've lost your mother, have you gotten over that yet?"

Dinh drew her into his arms comfortingly.

"But you're alive, my dear. You have me, we're a happy family now. I'll help you take care of anything the children need. Granted they're far away but I know how to take care of things. They'll be fine."

"But why couldn't we live in Saigon? Why can we only be a happy family in Hanoi?"

"We've got no house in Saigon, no family registration that would allow us to buy a house, no acquaintances to fix things for us. If we tried to live there, we'd end up spending all our time worrying about food and money and clothes and rice and there'd be no time left for writing. Do you understand? We've promised ourselves to each other for eternity, we're starting over from the beginning, with nothing but our two hearts and our four hands!"

Tiep tried to push him away.

"But a thousand miles! I can't possibly bear such an immense distance. Do you understand that? The longer this goes on the less I'll be able to bear it!"

She thought of that chilly morning several days before. She thought of Vinh Chuyen turning away to go back to the house, so small and bony, the image of loneliness and deprivation. She thought of Thu Thi standing stubbornly outside under the strawberry tree, even though her polka-dot cotton dress was too thin for the cold, until the car that was carrying Tiep had disappeared. She had Dinh now, but for the first time she no longer wished she could split herself in two to divide herself between them. She just wanted to run back home to her children.

"Well, we've talked about the possibility of bringing Thu Thi up here..." he said weakly.

Tiep moaned, "But what about Vinh Chuyen? Without Thu Thi he'd be completely alone!"

Still, she let him lead her to the bed. He lay down beside her and gently wiped her eyes and nose. So this was it then? To live with the man she loved, she would have to forever suffer the mournful condemnation of her maternal conscience? Had she really understood the cost, and how long it would take to pay? In order to be truly happy, someone had once said, one must have three things: a job to do, a person to love, and something to hope for. Well, she had the job of her dreams and the man who was fated for her, but what did she hope for? That her children would one day forgive her?

Like so many times before, when she traveled to Hanoi and missed the southwest and then returned to the southwest and missed Hanoi, she wrestled with the sensation of see-sawing, of rootlessness. She felt like a deathly ill patient who was listening to her body as it fought the disease, miserably waiting to see who would win.

She cried in Dinh's arms for a very long time that night.

And once again she wondered, as she had wondered so many times over the years, if she were offered a choice in the next life, which would she choose, romantic love or maternal love? She knew the answer now. She knew she could never choose one or the other. If there was such a thing as another life, she would choose both kinds of love, one contained in the other, intertwined and inseparable.

21
Spring 2002

A briefcase hooked securely over the plastic basket in front, a duffle bag of clothes and other miscellany knotted tightly to the seat in back, and she was ready to go on the little Chaly moped they had bought from a dealer in Japanese castoffs. Dinh was insisting that she wear a helmet that was "made in" somewhere, although exactly where they didn't know. He tended to be overcautious with his loved ones, perhaps to compensate for his complete inability to exercise caution with his mouth.

"No, you have to listen to me. I don't care if it's just a 50 cc bike. I don't care that you don't even need a driver's license to drive it. You still have to wear this helmet!"

Despite her doubts of the helmet's quality, Tiep sat still and allowed her husband to fit it on her head, delighting in the tickle of his large, coarse fingers under her chin as he fumbled with the little red buckle on the chin strap. Before they had registered their marriage, Tiep had estimated his ring size to have a wedding band made for him as a surprise. She still remembered how the gold-seller had laughed when she had tried the ring on her big toe and found it fit perfectly.

Now he was tinkering around the bike, reluctant to let

her leave. His image was distorted through the blurry visor of the helmet and he avoided her gaze, but she knew he was wearing the same anxious, glum expression that he used to get when they still lived at opposite ends of the country. Twenty years had passed since Dong Dung, and nine since they had become husband and wife; why couldn't they shake this feeling of melancholy every time they parted? As though they were afraid that, in the absence of the other, everything would become empty and meaningless.

But she was leaving him behind anyway, with his meals of brown rice flavored with black sesame seed, an empty bed, and their apartment which, although they'd expanded it and made it quite comfortable by now, he couldn't stand when she wasn't in it.

She putted out of their dusty housing block, cutting through clouds of grit kicked up by construction, then crossed the To Lich River, which was also under construction, the victim of an endless project to line its banks with stone that involved interminable digging, fixing, and building but somehow never got finished. Only the waters were quiet, as black and odorous as they had been twenty years ago.

Tiep wove her bike across the chaotic traffic of Nguyen Trai street, then turned onto the wide concrete road that led to Cau Giay and Thang Long. This was the first road trip she'd taken without Dinh sitting right in front of her with his thick, solid hands and his odor of sweat mixed with tobacco. A feeling of loneliness swept over her. Why did she always feel this way whenever she left him, and why could she never get used to it? Even when, as now, she was on her way to seek out that very loneliness, to create an environment where it could thrive and be her fellow-traveler, to help her with the work she intended to do.

She loved her humble little Chaly moped. It was gutless to the point of pathos, but she had no need to go fast in a city with such abysmal streets and a driving population that competed with each other for every last inch of pavement.

She had bought it herself with money saved from countless all-nighters spent writing—"pulling the plow" as Dinh called it. But it had made her the target of no little unwelcome curiosity: "Two accomplished writers in one house, you must have plenty of money, why not improve your image a little?" As though people had nothing better to do than sit around and gossip when they saw someone fail to "upgrade" to a motorcycle at least as nice as the neighbors'! Dinh and Tiep would only smile blandly when confronted with such questions. It was enough that they understood why they loved the little Babetta they had stored neatly in the corner of their apartment like a museum piece, and this loyal Chaly. Let the neighbors wonder why they didn't trade in their bikes, why they didn't have a child together, and why they still loved each other against all odds. And why they had to find a way to separate whenever they wanted to write...

The road that the authorities liked to call a "speedway" was pitted and bumpy but at least it was familiar. For years now, ever since she had moved to this city that fate had decreed for her, she had managed to make enough money to gradually distance herself from the state-run Vietnam Railway with its green-and-red cars, its stink, and its stingy reserves of water and even stingier portions of toilet paper. Nowadays, when she returned south for a visit to her children, it was by airplane. She would take a taxi along this road to the Noi Bai airport during the light of day, and in spite of Dinh's presence behind her like a heavy stone weighing her down, she always left, taking to the skies with elation at the thought of once again holding her children in her arms. The trip back was different, it always happened at night and was filled with feelings of coming down, coming home, the rolling road and a warm, glowing Dinh right in front of her while her children receded into the distance, indistinct, out of sight. Even though she made several trips a year, the feeling of seesawing between two homes never went away. There was always an edge of anxiety and confusion that she could not resolve.

The afternoon shadows were lengthening. She should have set off first thing that morning, after their morning coffee filled with stories that they never tired of telling and never tired of listening to. But Dinh had pulled her down to lie with him again in that way he had, sometimes burning with passion, sometimes selfish, and sometimes clearly as vulnerable as a child. His clinginess made her vacillate: perhaps she should just stay home and forget about the tiring work of writing and literature. She could be like everyone else, work a day job, maybe write a newspaper column on the side at night, take it easy, enjoy herself, and enjoy the money they'd earned, like others who had reached the age of knowing that nothing really mattered.

Then Dinh suddenly smacked his lips and said, "Oh well, I've got to get some writing done here too," and Tiep knew that she had to go, she had to create something for herself as well. When she had first moved to Hanoi, they had gone through a stage of compensating for all the joy and outings and lovemaking they had missed, until they were full to the brim; then after that there was a stage of slaving away every night, each chained to their desk as though chained to a millstone, gazing wistfully at the other person's back as they sat laboring in damnable silence just to make ends meet with a little left over to fix up the apartment and better their lives. They had passed through both profligate joy and niggardly hardship, and now that their lives had finally settled into a smooth, uneventful routine, it was Tiep who came up with the suggestion that they should part for a while, so that the loneliness might return, and in that loneliness they might be able to work as it suited them, in complete, focused silence. More precisely, although Tiep did not tell him this, Dinh's constant love and restlessness, his sheer profusion had swallowed up that fragile sheath of space that Tiep had maintained for herself for so many years. In their little apartment, always so full of guests, and their shared meals and shared bed and shared stories and shared fears and shared compromises, the days passed in the blink of an eye with no hope of eking out a minute or two for herself. She had been occupied long enough with her womanly passions; now, like a salmon, she felt it was time to return upstream, to be sacrificed and offered up in that supremely natural act of giving birth.

Perhaps because it was Tiep's first time to travel outside of the city by herself, or perhaps because of her late start, or perhaps it was the chill northeastern wind, but she couldn't shake the longing to turn back to Dinh. Why does it have to be this way, she thought, why should a woman with a pleasant, breezy apartment and a fine husband in every sense of the word, in short an ideal life, leave it all to go sink herself into a worthless pursuit like literature? Is isolation really all that important? She knew she was riding toward her own misery, but still she continued on. She was a disciple and literature was her religion; she had to follow it, even though few people in this world could comprehend why.

As she putted up the incline of the Thang Long bridge, she realized for the first time that her little Chaly might not be up to the exertion of a long road trip. She thought of Thu Thi, and the day Dinh had taken her to see the Thang Long bridge on his red Babetta. The motorbike had broken down just as they were starting up this same incline. Thu Thi had tactfully kept her silence, but afterwards she adamantly refused to join her mother in Hanoi as Tiep and Dinh had planned. Tiep didn't know whether to blame it on the height of the Thang Long bridge, or on the reek of cooking-charcoal in their apartment which was irrefutable proof of the difficulty of their daily lives. Or perhaps it was because the world or her mother and the world of her Daddy Tuyen were too much in conflict, the girl was being squeezed in the middle, and so had no choice but to opt for a familiar place that did not in any way appear to be taking sides.

After that, it was inevitable that her handsome, slender-waisted consort should move into the apartment that Tiep had left, and that a wedding should follow. It was a monumental affair, complete with policemen to guard the cars which carried the highest provincial and district officials thither at her father's invitation. Tiep felt that she and her daughter had lost each other somehow. She hoped that it was temporary but feared that it was permanent...

These days, the speedway was littered with billboards to entertain the eyes of passersby. Tiep had had enough; she turned her little bike into the Phuc Yen district. Several years before, Dinh had brought her here on his red Babetta to show her where the Party had once exterminated a "den of Kuomintang," and no doubt also to relive some old memories that he would have stored meticulously away in that elephant's memory of his. During the war, he had volunteered to stay at home with their sons while his wife left to take a university class here, and it was here that his daughter was conceived. Tiep had heard it said that men treasure memories of emotions forever, whereas women, while they pour themselves heart and soul into any given period of their lives, can more easily move on. It was true that when they talked about the past, Tiep told copious stories about Tuyen but Dinh generally kept silent; thinking about it, Tiep realized that she could dismiss her memories of Tuyen but Dinh could not do the same for his first wife. After all, the woman was still the mother of his children and had birthed to his clan a boy who was a first son of a first son. She was still the woman whom he had abandoned, regardless of the righteousness of his reasons. Tiep recalled the first time she and the woman had met, through the machinations of Dinh's sister Hoa. "Elder Sister Cam and Elder Sister Tiep simply must meet!" she would say, "They've got to overcome the anger, reconcile for the sake of the family, patch up this cold war!" and so on. In fact Tiep did want to put the past behind them, so that Dinh's sons could be at peace with their lives in the west and his daughter could move normally between her parents' houses. And anyway, Tiep was used to taking impossible steps, one more wouldn't kill her.

It happened in Hoa's living room, a place that had become very familiar to Tiep. Hoa stood at the door to the inside room, officiously playing the part of the mediator, turning this way and that to talk to the two women inside and out. Dinh's daughter was there too, tense and dubious. The woman inside refused to step out to meet Tiep. Tiep heard Hoa say, "Sister Cam, if you don't come out here I swear I won't consider you my sister any longer!" Finally, Cam emerged, a curled lock of hair gracing her forehead, her still-beautiful eyes gone dull as they focused on her inner struggle, and her flower-petal lips pulled slackly into a mechanical, forced smile. Tiep stepped forward and grasped the hand that Dinh had once loved, then protected with his excuses, then abandoned when it pounded out the letters that set the power of the Party on her. It was now the hand of a person who had given it all up, her position, her office, and her ambitions. It rested cold and limp in Tiep's fingers, as though it had lost all its energy and was powered only by residual animosity.

Their meeting was brief and awkward, but at least no fights broke out. The wall between them had been dismantled. Her love for Dinh drove Tiep to seek out the woman again, and then again. There were many more such meetings after that at the house where Xuyen lived with her mother. Without Dinh present, things seemed to go more smoothly, but it also revealed starkly the terrible void at the core of the house: the absence of the man they had always thought would be their roof and protector.

The more Tiep visited, the more she realized that when a man remarries he gains a second family, whereas when a woman remarries she leaves behind only failure and ruin. Her mother and sister had visited her in Hanoi once, to see for themselves "how you are getting by all by yourself up there." Hoai told her that Aunt Rang's only comment on her marriage was "Well, the ancestors must have blessed them, at least the basket has been mended!" Her mother, naturally enough, cried the entire trip from the north back to the south, stopping only to say, "No matter what, her life will be filled with suffering." Even much later, after Tiep had somewhat adapted to a life split between the two ends of the country, her sister Nghia still sobbed every time she saw her off at the airport as though they would never meet again...

The autumn sun was golden, the same cool, honey-colored rays carried on breezes that sang of music and poetry that in the south heralded the coming of Tet. There was that thought again: such wonderful weather as this, why should they tear themselves away from each other to bury themselves in a task that was as endless as the ocean? Tiep saw a field by the road, stubby with the remains of the rice harvest and surrounded by a bank of golden beardgrass. She recalled that it was this same kind of grass that had once led a famous poetess astray:

I should have been more careful
My blouse was covered with prickly grass
Professions of love are as fragile as smoke
Who knows if your heart might change?

Tiep stopped the bike and removed her helmet to stand gazing aimlessly out at the landscape. The isolation was tangible, she could hear it, touch it. When she was young, she had loved the rice fields best when they were ripe with grain. Her family did not farm rice, so she had never had to "sacrifice her back to the sky and her face to the earth" in that backbreaking labor. But just before the harvest she always wished she could slip through the rows of rice of their neighbor's field, the one in between their orchard on the near side and the stand of trees on the far side that hid her maternal grandparents' house. Later on, when she grew into a dreamy young woman, she preferred the fields right after harvest when they were filled with bright golden straw that she loved to walk on, to feel it yield with a rough ticklish sensation under her bare feet. Now that she was middle-aged, she found she best liked fields filled with old straw, like the one she was looking at now: afternoon sunlight, brittle stubble, perfect for walking over in a long, loose skirt that would drag and catch. She couldn't resist the urge to lie down at the edge of the field on a cushion of beardgrass and chew on a blade of grass.

White clouds on the horizon, a few scattered golden leaves
Have the leaves all gone home to the forest?
Autumn follows the leaves
Autumn blows out to the sea
Following that infinite current, Autumn fills the chrysanthemums...

Why did you write Autumn fills the chrysanthemums rather than Autumn is filled with chrysanthemums? Tiep asked herself, as though asking the beardgrass-covered poetess who had long ago passed away together with her eternal lover. It moved her somehow. This was why the world needed poets and writers, to stand a simple word like *fill* on its head. This was why those poets and writers had to suffer the complicated tangle of their talent and their fate.

Our love is like a column of trees, standing firm against the storms
Our love is like a quiet river, leaving the rapids and floods behind
All that is left is you and I and our love
All that is left is you and I and our love

Lying in the field now, Tiep imagined the pleasant space of the Dai Lai Writers' Retreat, where she had called ahead to reserve a private room. There was a gentle sloping path leading up a hill and another path that circled the lake with a little island in the middle. Dinh had once sailed her out to the island in a cast-off skiff powered by a nylon sail he had improvised with that ever-active mind of his. Tiep smiled. She would sit by a window and look out at the graveled patio that always made her feel that she was in a private villa; then she would set her pad of paper on the desk and commune once more with that sensation of solitude she used to know when she sat by that window with the plum blossoms back in the town where her children were. She was sure now the feeling would taste sweet in her mouth; everything was as it should be, as it was destined to be, and she had all the time in the world. That rolling ball of seemingly endless thread had finally come to an end; she had found the quiet waters and gentle beaches at the end of the rapids.

It felt good to just lie here, unthinking, putting off her writing just a little longer. Then she heard the sound of someone's motorcycle stopping too close to her, followed by the crunch of hurried male footsteps, and suddenly Dinh was looming in front of her. He looked down at her, swaying, as if in a dream except it was better than a dream because he was there in the flesh, as always a mother lode of wide-open charm. He was panting slightly, as though he had just caught up to her after an exhausting chase.

"God above, draping yourself across the grass like that with everything hanging out, you could lose your bike, your virginity, and your life before you know it!"

Tiep pulled him into her arms, her lover of twenty years. "You figured you'd follow me to Dai Lai and make it impossible for me to write, did you?"

He settled himself next to her, but his face was serious. He said abruptly, "Something's just happened, you need to stay calm. Shortly after you'd left, this express letter arrived from Thu Thi. Here."

Ever since the state-run post had started offering an express mail service, Tiep and her daughter had managed to narrow the gap between them somewhat. It was a short letter, only a few curt lines: "Mom, I need you, I'm miserable. My husband has found someone else, and the woman even called me and demanded that I give him up. If only I'd listened to you, if only I'd followed you to Hanoi. But now I need you. I've always needed you, Mom!"

It was just like every other time something happened to her faraway children. She and Dinh would be enjoying clear skies and suddenly news would arrive that a storm had descended. Storms always came on when the skies were at their most peaceful. Tiep sat up, her back bent double under the burden of her exile.

"It was bound to happen," Dinh added. "He is just a kid, still immature. He didn't get his degree either, so he's had to make a living by the seat of his pants. To me, this isn't as bad as when they found out neither of them would graduate. That's what pushed them off the right path, sent them into freefall. After that, I knew they were at high risk for problems like this!"

Tiep thought of the day she and Dinh had received that horrible news: Thu Thi was short one credit. Military practice, the subject she had always considered "moronic." Her handsome husband prided himself on being a fixer and figured buying off one credit would be child's play. And so things ran their course, well-greased with equal amounts of pride and pouting, and concluded with both of them blaming the curriculum and their bad luck at having the only incorruptible professor in the country. Dinh and Tiep were as bitter as if it had happened to them and considered it their greatest failure as a couple, even though previously they had never considered university degrees to be worth the paper they were printed on.

Afraid that Tiep was dangerously close to fainting, Dinh gently eased her to her feet.

"You'll have to make arrangements to fly down immediately—literature and novels can wait. But you need to have courage. Remember that everything is up to fate!"

In fact he was being overly worried. Tiep had suffered through much worse in the past, and she knew she could handle anything life threw at her. Nonetheless, once Dinh had delivered her back home and she had flung herself onto their bed, the relentless mental questioning began: Was life really such a zero-sum game that when Tiep gained something her daughter must suffer loss? The law of compensation, yes...but how could heaven be so callous to her? Was this yet another price she had to pay for her "unseemly ambition," as Hoai called it? Or was it because of the sheer degradation of the Vietnamese educational system, through which Thu Thi had been forced to wade alone and finally escaped only to be felled by this new tragedy? Was it Tiep's fault for abandoning the children, or Tuyen's fault for introducing them to a materialistic world which had sucked them in and made them self-indulgent and resentful, dazzled and infected them, and now it was their turn to pay the price?

Well, there was nothing else she could do. As she dragged herself to her feet to prepare for the next morning's flight to the south, she recalled how relieved she and Dinh had been after Thu Thi's wedding. The young couple were on the verge of graduation from university, they had thought; they had a house and a kid and each other and in the future would most certainly have it all. For a mother like me, how much longer will it be until I have come to the end of the road of my maternal responsibilities, she wondered, as she had wondered before and would wonder again, as she always wondered when the umbilical cord that tied her to her distant children stirred and tugged. Apparently the road ahead still stretched long, leading down rapids, across rivers, through oceans, and ending only in that grim mound of earth that is the end of all human journeys; and even then, no matter how utterly exhausted that little mound of earth might be, there was no guarantee it would be the end of her story. More likely, her maternal instinct would survive and carry on in Thu Thi and then in her daughter and so on and so forth forever: weariness and joy, glory and bitterness, motherhood and life.

A broken marriage, incomplete education, and small,

innocent children: the circle of Tiep's life had not yet closed and already the circle of her daughter's life was overlapping and imitating hers. This was her shadow, her tragedy, her inadequacy. This was her guilt, which she always and ever carried, as long as the path of motherhood still stretched out before her.

Author's Biography

Da Ngan is the pen name of Le Hong Nga, born on February 6, 1952, to a peasant family living in a small orchard on the Hau River in what is now Hau Giang Province. She spent nine years with the Viet Cong resistance movement, then later became a member of the Vietnamese Writers' Union. She is currently the Chief Editor of Prose at the Hanoi Writers' Union weekly newspaper, *Van Nghe* (Literature).

In her own words: My father was a Viet Minh cadre during the resistance against the French. Being the only boy in his family, he did not regroup to North Vietnam after the signing of the Geneva Conventions in 1954 but rather stayed in the south as an undercover operative. He became a political prisoner under President Ngo Dinh Diem and died in Con Dao prison when I was ten years old. In accordance with the Vietnamese concept of filial piety, five of his children, including myself, followed in his footsteps to join the resistance. I left to live at the guerrilla base when I was fourteen years old and had just finished middle school. The fighting was particularly fierce around my family's orchard, which lay squarely in the corridor that connected the guerrilla bases of the upriver provinces with the Area Nine base in U Minh. Because of this, most local youths chose to join the resistance.

I worked as an intern reporter for the provincial resistance newspaper. However, it was decided I was too young and physically small for the job, and so was returned to my family for a time. Just before Tet Mau Than (1968, the infamous "Tet Offensive"), I was called back into service and sent for professional training in journalism at the Area Nine base in U Minh, which was the command center for the entire southwestern region. It was there that I had the opportunity to read the literary greats—Sholokhov, Tolstoy, Dostoyevski,

Chekhov, and even Hemingway—thanks to the Propaganda Department's remarkable library which consisted of piles of books stored in crates fashioned from corrugated metal sheets and hidden in a secret concrete bunker or carried by small boats into the jungle whenever the enemy staged a raid. I was a good student, winning praise for my writing style and the attention to detail in my articles. Many people predicted I would eventually become a writer. The Area Nine base wanted to retain me another year for further training, but the Province demanded my return. I set foot back on the provincial base on the same day Ho Chi Minh passed away: September 2, 1969.

My new boss was a former teacher under the French. He "adopted" me and, through daily conversations, gave me a good grounding in literary knowledge. But the war grew ever fiercer, and he was killed in the rainy season of 1970. I was sent to live with the local people and follow the guerrilla army units everywhere except into actual battle, to write articles for the newspaper. Later, I was sent to live in the city of Can Tho as an undercover correspondent, writing articles and sending them back to the guerrilla base from the very heart of enemy territory.

I married in 1972, but it was a match formed by the exigencies of war. After giving birth to our first child, I left active duty and returned to my extended family, who were living as evacuees in an enemy-controlled area in conditions of great privation and in constant fear that my connections to the resistance would be discovered. After the Paris accords were signed in 1973, I and my extended family returned to our orchard, only to find it had been leveled by bombs and poisoned by defoliant chemicals in the back-and-forth fighting that preceded the signing of the Accords. Leaving my daughter in the care of my mother, I started classes for the local children, both as a way to help the country and to maintain my status as a cadre in the resistance forces.

The war ended in 1975. I returned to my old department and continued to work as a war correspondent. During the 1978-1979 war with Cambodia, I made 4 trips to that country embedded in Vietnamese army units and had many experiences which I have yet to write about. I spent a large amount of time at the library, preparing for the literary career I had been dreaming about for so long. My second child was born in 1976, and in 1978 my first short story was published in the local literary journal. From 1980 on, my essays and short stories were published regularly in Hanoi.

In 1982, I met the author Nguyen Quang Than at a Writer's Workshop organized by the National Writers' Union, and in 1993, when we were married, I left Hau Giang to join him and study at a university in Hanoi. I have been living with my husband in the capital ever since.

Published works and awards:

Five collections of short stories: *A Cozy Life*, *The Dog and the Divorce*, *At Home*, *A View from the Other Side*, and *Da Ngan - Selected Short Stories*. Awarded second prize by the *Army Literature Magazine*, her first literary prize.

Two novellas for children, one of which, *Home is Far Away*, was awarded the Vietnam Writers' Union award in 2004.

Two novels: *A Day in the Life* (published in 1989) and *The Insignificant Family* (published in 2005), which won the Hanoi Writers' Union award in 2005.

In addition, Da Ngan has published three collections

of essays, written two scripts which have been made into films, and is preparing to publish *The Headwaters Flow On*, a collection of 20 short stories written in Hanoi. She is also currently working on her third novel.